Praise for Adam Nevill

'This is riveting, and Nevill is fast becoming Britain's answer to Stephen King' *Guardian*

'A wonderfully creepy and disturbing novel'
Independent on Sunday

'This emotionally intense, intellectually challenging supernatural novel explores secret geographies of conscience while raising hackles, and is addictively readable'
Publishers Weekly

'Adam Nevill has forged his reputation as one of the UK's best horror writers by writing elegantly stripped down, deceptively simple novels' *SFX*

'Frighteningly relevant and all the more compelling for it'
Starburst Magazine

'A fiercely original imagination . . . a book that never looks down upon its readers and continuously delights with its unique approach to the classic haunted house trope. And it's scary as hell' *Upcoming4me*

'An ambitious, scary and remarkable step forward in the career of one of Britain's finest horror writers'
ThisisHorror

'Nevill is proving to be a strong creative force . . . It won't be long before Hollywood comes knocking to adapt his books' *SFCrowsNest*

Lost Girl

Adam Nevill was born in Birmingham, England, in 1969 and grew up in England and New Zealand. He is the author of the supernatural horror novels *Banquet for the Damned*, *Apartment 16*, *The Ritual*, *Last Days*, *House of Small Shadows*, *No One Gets Out Alive* and *Lost Girl*. In 2012 *The Ritual* was the winner of The August Derleth Award for Best Horror Novel, and in 2013 *Last Days* won the same award. *The Ritual* and *Last Days* each won the RUSA for Best in Category: Horror. Adam lives in Devon, England, and can be contacted through www.adamlgnevill.com.

By Adam Nevill

Banquet for the Damned

Apartment 16

The Ritual

Last Days

House of Small Shadows

No One Gets Out Alive

Lost Girl

ADAM NEVILL

Lost Girl

PAN BOOKS

First published 2015 by Pan Books
an imprint of Pan Macmillan
20 New Wharf Road, London N1 9RR
Associated companies throughout the world
www.panmacmillan.com

ISBN 978-1-4472-4091-4

3 5 7 9 8 6 4 2

A CIP catalogue record for this book is available from the British Library.

Typeset by Ellipsis Digital Limited, Glasgow
Printed and bound by CPI Group (UK) Ltd, Croydon, CR0 4YY

For Gill, Bernard and Liz.
And in memory of Graham Joyce and Michel Parry.

Men must endure
Their going hence, even as their coming hither

William Shakespeare,
King Lear

ONE

The last time he had seen his daughter, she'd been in the front garden. Two years ago.

In his mind the father had replayed the scenes of that hot afternoon more times than it was possible to remember. One thousand times, in the first six months following the abduction, might not have been an exaggeration. The father suspected that his wife, Miranda, had relived that afternoon even more than he had, with each replay incrementally confirming her absence from the world. To this day, he believed much of his wife was still standing in the front garden, outside their old house, bloodless with shock.

He'd rescreened his memory's shaky footage – at first sun-blinded, then too dark, all recorded during the worst kind of day that anyone could dream up – for clues, then reshot it to imagine different outcomes, then repeated it on loops to punish himself. But in his clutching at the brighter sections of his recall of that day, and in his clawing at the vaguer opaque patches of those crucial, booming minutes, he'd always recognize, almost immediately, that he'd begun adding details. The more he forced his mind to remember, the greater the temptation to insert himself acting quickly and decisively; in ways that he had not done at the time.

But the original script had remained a final draft, and could not be rewritten no matter how hard he tried.

The front garden was tiered. The first time he saw the place, when he and his wife were house-hunting, he'd been reminded of a jungle step-pyramid, or a hillside divided into layers by ancient farmers. And during the two years they had lived there, with him often working away from home, his wife had steadily and neatly cultivated the slope, level by level. Corn and potatoes, courgettes, pumpkins, marrows and kale had grown upon their street-facing garden. Behind the house, on the long, level garden, tepees of bamboo poles had created a thicket for beans, and glittering polythene cloches, flashing like pools of water seen from the air, had stretched to the rear fence. The back garden had yielded all the fruit they could possibly want.

The father had moved his family from Birmingham to the coast when the Thames flooded one too many times, the new tidal barrier still unfinished. This meant that tens of thousands, then hundreds of thousands, and finally millions, had left London for the second city, a landlocked place of Jurassic limestone, not prone to floods and high enough to poke above the waves that might one day rise ninety feet, or more, the world over. And with some terrible irony, the exodus from the south-east headed to the place that had started the Industrial Revolution, with its heavy reliance on coal-burning. Accompanying the masses were the banks and businesses, and most of central government, and all of its affiliates, forlorn but adapting: a steady stream of colonizers retreating from the rising waters and street strife too plentiful to police. The evacuation had pushed up the house prices along the length of the retreat, but as London had most of the country's money, it was forced to give some of it back.

During the great migration, the father's house in the south of Birmingham, close to its last good school, had sold for more than he and his wife had known was possible when they'd first bought the property. They were one of the few early winners as the world's food markets collapsed and food exports slowed to a trickle, before finally running dry for all but the devious and those of means. Once all the arable land between the cities had been consumed by the growing of genetically modified, drought-resistant crops, few new homes were built. Every field where sheep and cattle had grazed, every city park, football field, grass verge, motorway embankment – every inch of green space – was given over to the new crops, as meat and fish vanished from the shelves of stores.

The father, his wife and their baby had moved to the coast, but not to a place that was going under the waves. They found a place where hardly any had wanted to live for a long time because there were so few jobs, and there was some time remaining before the latter surges of refugees would arrive. The father had moved his family into a house on one of the hills of Torquay. It had a view and a big garden to grow food. Everyone had been growing food in Devon and going vegetarian by necessity for a decade.

The house on the hill had felt like a safe place to be in times changing from bad to worse, with no relief in sight: a house protected by trees, but airy and light, swept by sea breezes, and so far removed from the lines of angry, glittering traffic and the mean instability of the city they'd left behind, they had thought this the best place to raise their only child and to cherish that solitary soul with all of themselves.

On *that day*, their daughter had been in the front garden of their house on the big hill.

The father had been in his room upstairs, the home office, writing messages to a woman that weren't work-related and should never have come from a married man. Through his open windows came the swish of distant traffic: mostly local, with the frequent grind of freight lorries carrying grain from the breadbasket of East Devon and vast, cultivated Dartmoor.

The sounds of his daughter rose and fell from below the window, as she gave her mother a commentary on her activities, something that always made him smile. He briefly watched her as she hefted a small plastic bucket filled with new potatoes from place to place, moving swiftly and with purpose. Then he sat down again at his desk.

In the front garden, his daughter had been on the third tier of four, her mother on the fourth, closer to the house. His daughter had been halfway between the house and the street.

The father had heard his wife walk into the house below. She had entered through the patio windows that opened onto the front garden from the living room. They ate most of their meals on the patio outside from late spring to the beginning of autumn, and the paved area had become an outside dining room.

As his wife had come into the house, she had called up to the father: 'She's down in root crop. Taking potatoes in a spaceship to Nanny's.' The father had laughed, but could not deny that although slightly touched by the description, his mind had been on other things that afternoon, and the potential of another woman's body at a food management conference the following month. He'd known his wife was instructing him to keep an eye on their daughter from his window. And he'd intended to do so once he'd completed the business he was engaged in; once he'd finished the message in just the right way, in a tantalizing but non-committal fashion.

His wife had carried two buckets filled with shallots and cucumbers in through the living room, along the hall, and into the kitchen. She had placed the buckets on the floor before the sink unit. Then she had emptied the cucumbers into a colander and slipped it into the sink. The father thought he remembered hearing the water come on hard before the flow weakened. There was a water shortage, as usual, that summer. Much of what had been held in reservoirs from the floods the previous winter was now needed to irrigate crops, though most of the water was required to cool the new power stations, and always would be.

As the tap ran, the father had heard his daughter say, 'Mummy'. There was no alarm in her voice.

The father had been close to the end of the final sentence he was typing and began to rush the message so he could look out and see what his daughter wanted. His daughter had repeated her call from the front garden, in a slightly higher voice. Downstairs, the kitchen tap was still running. His wife had not heard their daughter.

Outside, his daughter had spoken again. The father had heard her say, 'What's that?' He had thought she was addressing her toys. She didn't speak again. But the father had heard the rattle of plastic. That was his daughter's bucket dropping onto the dry topsoil.

A few more moments had passed.

His wife had turned off the tap in the kitchen. In the near distance, the father had heard the clinking sound of the metal gate at the end of their property. The gate stood at the end of the cement path that ran along the side of the house and down the slope to the road.

At the sound of the clink the father had hurriedly pushed his chair back from his desk, abandoning the email exchange, stood up, and gone to the window.

Though he'd always been paranoid about the traffic so far below, his daughter had never once ventured to the end of the front garden unaccompanied. Even if she had explored that far, she would not have been able to unlock the gate latch.

He'd thought the metallic clink had signified an attempt to open the gate by a visitor to the house, probably a hawker or an evangelist. But he had not heard the telltale scrape of the heavy, lopsided metal frame across the first paving slab of the front path. Only those familiar with the gate knew to lift it first, then push or pull it open or closed.

The father had looked out of the window at the front garden. He could not see his daughter on the third tier, or the fourth tier closer to the house, or the second tier further down on what had once been a lawn. The first tier was crowded with trees they'd left in place for privacy so that the front of the property was screened from the street.

His wife had come into sight and walked across the patio, nonchalant and relaxed. She had been wearing green rubber gloves, denim shorts, one of his t-shirts and running shoes. The father could see the top of her head and was about to say, *I can't see her*, but didn't.

His wife had looked about quickly, then behind herself and into the house. Her voice steady, she'd called out their daughter's name, and calmly went back inside.

The father had thought of the trees at the bottom of the garden and wondered if his daughter was hiding. He played hide and seek with her most days he was home, and there were two places in the copse where she would lean against a trunk with her hands over her eyes and believe herself invisible. But the father could not see her pink shorts or red shirt amongst the darker greens of the trees, which were thick enough to hide the garage roof. As he searched the trees with his eyes, he had become aware of the faint sound of a car engine idling far below. A door had whumped shut, and had been followed by exactly the same sound.

His wife had come out of the house more quickly than she had entered it, and stood still. Her posture had transmitted an instant trill of alarm into the father that pinpricked along the bottom of his stomach. She'd started walking briskly across the patio towards the vegetable patches and onto the second tier, where she'd glanced at the bucket. Here, she had turned to the house again and noticed the father's face at the window. Momentarily, Miranda had appeared relieved; clearly she'd thought that the father had been watching their little girl the whole time she had been inside the house with the vegetables, and he knew where their daughter was.

She must have seen something in the father's eyes

though, because her face had adopted the expression it assumed at the precise moments when their daughter lost her footing beyond an arm's reach. His wife had returned her attention to the garden and called their daughter's name again. A short but awful silence had followed. She had looked up at the window of the father's room and said, 'Where is she?'

As if in a spiteful riposte, a car engine had revved and they'd both heard tyres ripple away from the kerb below their house. The father had felt as if he was standing in a lift that had suddenly dropped through space.

No, no, no, no, he'd chanted in a faux-cheery tone of voice, not out loud but inside his head, as he ran from the room and down the staircase and through the hall, the living room and onto the patio. By then his wife was amongst the trees on the first tier, repeatedly calling their daughter's name in a tense, hurried voice.

The father had run down the path, leapt down the steps to the bottom level and had seen the gate ajar. All of the air inside his chest had seemed to cling to the top of his lungs. Somehow, within less than a second, his mind had replayed every single bright yellow road safety poster he had ever seen in his life. But he'd heard no traffic, so if his daughter was in the road there was no danger from approaching cars.

He'd thought of his daughter's last words: *What's that?*

And that was the first moment he had suspected that she might have been taken by a stranger. When the idea entered his thoughts, his mind had reeled horribly, as if he'd just climbed off one of the small roundabouts in the local play area. He had lost his balance and gripped the gate with all the strength of a dead man's hand.

Holding his breath the father had stepped into the road. His legs were quivering and he'd felt concussed. The street had suddenly seemed brighter, but the air was cooler than it had been as he raced through the garden.

His wife had called his name from the trees. Her voice on the verge of tears, she'd added three words: 'She's not here.'

At the top of the road, a long one that ran from the hospital to the main road that he used to get to the motorway for work, he could see three vehicles, about three hundred feet distant: a white car turning into their road at the top, a red car waiting at the stop line to turn left, which it did as soon as he looked up the street; and behind the red car was a black one, a full electric SUV model. Brake lights on the rear of the black vehicle had glinted, two cherries in the sunlight.

The top of the road had shimmered dusty. There were no pedestrians.

The father had begun walking towards the end of the road. He hadn't run, because part of him was desperately trying to refute the notion that she had been taken from their garden. He'd suffered a constant morbid anxiety about her safety since her birth, but what he felt right then amplified the instinctive dread to such a level that his ears had popped, and the stiffening of his gut had stifled his breath.

'She's not in the garden.' His wife had come down the steps and into the street. He hadn't been aware of her descent. Still unbelieving, the father had glanced at the neighbouring properties, across the road and behind him, trying to make his daughter reappear with the power of his mind alone.

At the T-junction the black car was still waiting for its turn to enter the traffic. The father had found his voice and called out his daughter's name.

Behind him, above him, he had heard his wife again. She had returned to the garden. Her voice grew shriller as she'd called their daughter's name into the still, humid air.

The black car at the end of the road had not appeared to be in any hurry. From a distance of two hundred feet, the father couldn't read the number plate. His legs had felt old and insufficient, but his jog had soon become a sprint and he'd begun crying with a similar intensity to the way the child he'd just lost cried when she was frightened.

The black car had turned left, onto the main road, and had vanished from sight.

TWO

Pink slippers no longer than his index finger, the uppers designed into mouse faces; she'd pulled out the whiskers a long time ago.

The father wiped the sweat from his hands on the bed sheet and placed the slippers on the mattress. Removed another item from the pink rucksack: a shirt so tiny that the dimensions, more than the memory of *her* wearing it, momentarily seized the workings of his heart. Sometimes, he would take out the shirt, hold it to his face and believe he could still catch a trace of the fragrance unique to his child – malt mixed with soap.

The shirt was yellow and the bear printed on the front held an ice cream. His daughter was wearing it in his favourite photograph that always rested upon the bedside tables in the series of small rooms he rented, like this one.

Preserved in that image at three years old, she was standing in their garden, amidst umbrellas of pumpkin leaves that hid her legs in a vegetable plot so bright the print appeared blanched. Smiling, she revealed small, square teeth, as the sunlight caught her raven hair, creating a sheen on the crown of her head. Shielded from the glare, the dark gemstones of her lowered blue eyes glittered with joy.

Cloth Cat came out of the pink rucksack next. The soft

toy was a present from the father's brother, who lived in New Zealand. If Cloth Cat ever strayed far from their daughter's hand, the father and his wife had panicked. He'd once climbed over a fence at night to search a park for Cloth Cat, convinced that his little girl had dropped the toy over the side of the pushchair without him noticing, earlier in the day. Retracing the afternoon's walk, he'd moved between rows of millet covering two square miles of a former West Midlands green space, the crop arranged like phalanxes of a great army of old, every soldier carrying a spear. Torch in hand, the father had searched a mile of ground for the toy cat, along each of the sun-baked tarmac paths, his eyes so alert they'd ached. The toy was irreplaceable; his wife had already looked through the online trading sites to discover that numerous kinds of cats had been available, but no Cloth Cats. His daughter would never have been fooled by a usurper.

The father did not find Cloth Cat because the soft toy was still in the place his daughter had forgotten she'd 'posted' it. While her father had searched through the darkness of a blackout, Cloth Cat was safe inside a kitchen cupboard at home, and had been the whole time the little girl had cried for the toy's loss.

Some time later, the girl stopped reaching for Cloth Cat. A giraffe and a frog with long legs became new and constant companions. Yet when the father believed it safe to store Cloth Cat in the garage, the toy returned to the girl's favour and became the centre of her court all over again. The father often tried to imagine his daughter's face if she and Cloth Cat were ever reunited.

He cared more for his memory of her than he cared for

himself, and he kept her things safe and close so that no more of her would go. But when his mind turned to the numbers of people who were now crammed into this island, he could understand why his family had never been a priority to the police. When he considered the refugees, the millions, with more and more coming in every day in great noisy leviathans of motion and colour and tired faces, he realized the authorities had never had the time to look for one four-year-old girl. And whenever he watched the news, he understood why so few of the missing were ever found – because very few were even looking for them.

The emergency government claimed the population still stood at ninety million. Others claimed the population of the British Isles was now closer to one hundred and twenty million. Either way, he and his wife were simply lost amongst the millions. When he'd accepted this after the first year of his daughter's abduction, he had simply sat down in silence. His wife had lain down and never really risen again.

In the first year, he and his wife had made hundreds of phone calls together, and sent thousands of emails to all kinds of individuals and departments. Sometimes they met harried people who listened to them for a while. Pictures of the girl were shown on television and appeared on websites too. This continued for days on television and months online. And the father had also walked and walked for the best part of that first year and shown her photograph to as many of the millions as he could reach, which wasn't many. And while he implored the troubled faces to understand, he came across many other people showing photographs amongst the crowds, along the streets, in the towns and villages, and as he walked he knew that he had truly gone mad from the loss of his little girl.

He would never be able to adequately describe to anyone how stricken he'd been nor express the tormenting repetition of his thoughts. No combination of words would ever suffice. And he came to believe that when minds were forced to function in such a way, they simply broke.

For two years their lives had been solely concerned with grief. Not only had their child gone, their capacity for happiness was taken with her. Maybe this was something the abductors never considered: the insidious consequences of their actions, the deadening longevity of effect. Or perhaps they were euphorically aware of this, and the far-reaching ripples empowered them through the curious mental alchemy of the narcissist. If this was so, then he had the right to destroy them.

The father rose from his knees and lay on the bed, curled himself around the slippers, Cloth Cat and the shirt. And only then did he begin to shake.

Four hours later, the call he'd been waiting for arrived, so the father wiped his face with a towel and cleared his throat of the clot his grief had laid there.

The communication was voice only, without visuals. As if he had willed her to call, it was Scarlett Johansson, and she gave him the details of the next man he was to visit. The sex offender's name was Robert East.

THREE

Robert East's bungalow stood at the far end of the close, behind a low front wall of Cotswold stone. Before the pink stucco house front and the white stone drive, a neat brown lawn had died between opposing rows of ornamental shrubs. Wooden blinds blacked out the sun in every window. There was no gate. Nice when times were better, better than most now they were not so good.

During reconnaissance, straight after Scarlett's call, the father had peeked at Robert East's bungalow for the first time. Nothing had changed in the street in the three subsequent days when he'd driven past, or watched from a distance. All of the same cars were in the same places. And again, in the dry foliage of the front gardens, not a single twig or leaf stirred as if the heat had preserved the place as an arid still-life.

There were only six properties in the cul-de-sac, owned by people keeping their heads down in the best bit of Cockington. Three bungalows in good shape on the right-hand side, every curtain shut and all the blinds down. Out front: two Mercedes, one Jaguar. The discreet glassy bubble of a small spherical camera lens could be seen on the front of two of those places, watching the cars and front windows.

Two concrete town houses reared on the left-hand side of the street, clutched by the brittle arms of overhanging skeletal trees. Two storeys with lots of glass faced the sea, cut into the side of the hill seventy years gone. Balconies were empty and windows were closed, but someone was still up early to watch the sun rise in the building neighbouring his target, because the living-room blinds were open on the first floor. The glass was black and reflected the wide dome of sea in the bay.

Two street lamps had cameras. He would also be seen by the cameras on the properties as he walked the length of the short road. Not reason enough to abandon ship. The father didn't want to waste any more time because time changed the memories of people he needed to speak with. Time moved faster now, and the lives it drove forward were ever filling with gathered debris of the mind and senses. Too much catastrophe in the world needed to be comprehended, with more and more happening all the time. It was the age of incident. Merely at a local level in Devon, there was the hot terror of summer, the fear of another flood-routing winter, cliff erosion, soil erosion, soil degradation, blackouts, and the seemingly endless influxes of refugees.

Up above, the sky began to bleach white-blue from blue-black. When it became silver-blue with sharp light in an hour, the heat would boil brains. It was already twenty degrees when he parked one street down and covered the car's plates, before moving on foot through the trees opposite Victory Close. Nerves as much as exertion made him sweat harder.

It was a quarter past five and after driving up the hill to

get here, the father hadn't seen a single moving vehicle. Not much work in the town now and never much work traffic in this part of the town anyway. These were the homes of the over-sixties who didn't need to slave until they dropped cold in a warehouse aisle or a field. Senior management, retired executives and some gang lieutenants up here, but no real high rollers. These residents had never made the top two per cent, though they'd tried, and had mostly checked out of the labour market to slide through the grim and steady collapse in as much comfort as they could hope for. They endured power cuts and a diet of synthetic meat with seasonal vegetables, but still enjoyed lifestyles far beyond the reach of most. They'd done all right. Even then, spot-check security patrols would be all that most budgets covered here. Maybe one would roll through every hour; that was all the local Torbay groups offered. But in the heat? *All services are experiencing difficulties . . .*

The near-impossibility of a citizen enlisting help in a crisis was also in his favour. Community spirit was thin on the ground, even in the better parts of town. People heard shots popping and they locked down, grateful it wasn't their turn. In many parts of the country, who even knew who lived next door? The national characteristic was mistrust.

That summer, the elderly poor had lain dead in their beds from heatstroke all over this town, often discovered by smell alone. The acknowledgement made the father uncomfortable, but the way of things had a big upside on a 'move'. This hour of the day was also the low tide of crime. Hard cases were up all night and slept late. Not the father. He was no pro but he was getting better at this.

The father checked his kit: rucksack on his chest, immobilizer, mask and stun spray in the front pockets of his shorts: easy access left and right. He hoped to be in and out by six. He checked his watch. Sipped tap water from the bottle he kept in a rear pocket of his combat shorts. Pulled the bush hat low and slipped on sunglasses to make a visor across the top of his face; indoors he would mask up in cool cotton.

But, for a while, he couldn't move his feet towards the bungalow, and pissed against a tree instead. His guts slopped and reared and his underwear clung wet with sweat around the waistband and between his buttocks. His breath was loud around his head as if a man with asthma was standing at his shoulder.

Shivering with nerves, he forced himself to visualize his approach: brisk and confident on a straight line down the left side of the close, face lowered. And then he was off, almost before he'd made the decision to move, going through the trees, onto the road.

Buildings and trees jumped in his vision, and his legs didn't feel too good over the first ten feet of tarmac. All he wanted was to sink to his knees.

He cleared his mind of everything but the hardwood door at the end of the street. Number 3: unlucky for some.

FOUR

As the father moved through the refrigerated gloom of Robert East's bungalow, the newsreader's solemn voice seemed to boom in each empty room like the intonation of a curse.

Following Spain, Italy, Turkey, the Benelux and Central European countries' decision last month to reclose their borders, the newly formed French government is now considering the reclosure of its own borders, claiming its territory has again been 'overrun by refugees'. President Lemaire has declared the current situation an 'uncontainable and unsustainable humanitarian crisis'. The move has drawn fierce criticism from the Scandinavian bloc and Great Britain, the latter describing the policy as 'destined to cause an incalculable loss of life amongst the most vulnerable people on the planet'. The British nationalist leader, Benny Prince, applauded the news and urged the British emergency government to follow the French example.

The airwaves had long surrendered themselves to a relentless round-the-clock litany, sound bites from the biblical stories of a species' epochal demise. Many people thought it was best to not know, to take one day at a time. He'd never been like that. For the father the news was gripping, then monotonous, and finally meaningless. He took long breaks from the media but then its catalogue of despair became compulsive again. Reset, start over.

This was the end of the international summary, less pressing stuff that most could cope with thinking about. The alarm of the forest fires in Europe had obscured Britain's thoughts in black smoke for an entire summer. At least the volume of the broadcast must have smothered the crack of glass and the bang of his knees on a wooden surface in the utility room, when the father had upset a tub of clothes pegs and sent three plastic bottles of detergent bouncing across the lino. No intruder alarm had been set either, which meant he would be able to work onsite this morning. A confident man lived here.

The father masked and gloved up in the kitchen: a horror-show face of white cotton complemented by rubbery octopus hands.

He noted the single plate and coffee mug in the draining rack, then entered the hall on swift feet, and paused, listening for signs of movement beneath the broadcast.

Nothing.

He entered a dining room, his torch beam scouting the walls, and saw immediately that it had been a long time since a meal was eaten there. Everything was filmed in dust. The Easts had once kept dogs too: two spaniels. Photographs of the dogs covered the wall dominating a long-disused dining table with leather chairs for six diners. And when *she* had been around, Robert East's wife, Dorothy, had been fond of glazed ceramic figurines: little girls with lanterns and puppy dogs, small boys with shepherd crooks, ballet dancers and saucer-eyed kittens. Their shiny faces had an innocence and frivolity unsuited both to the times and the sole remaining resident's history.

Dorothy had been gone six years. Her cancer had been cured twice without much fuss, but flu had cut like a scythe through the over-sixties in 2047. But her little people, and their pets, still crowded the shelves of a cabinet between the china plates and bric-a-brac in two corner display cabinets, either in homage to the woman, or because of the widower's laziness. The little shiny people all looked past the masked intruder in beatific wonderment. We all have our mementos, the father acknowledged, but how long should we keep them, when memory is just one more thing to break us?

The father moved out of the room and further down the hallway, looking at the pictures on the walls: Robert and Dorothy sitting at the captain's table on a cruise ship, tanned faces and bottles of wine, real chicken.

No children in the marriage but Robert made up for that in other ways. A shame the dogs hadn't been enough, or the father wouldn't have been here at five thirty with a can of stun gas in his hand.

Evidence of a solitary widower depressed the once-elegant living room too, all underwater shady now behind the closed blinds. A settee, unruffled by use, huddled next to an easy chair equipped with a clip-on dinner tray. A white plastic trolley on wheels stood beside the chair with bottles and packets of medication, arranged around the TV control. Robert's chair was close to the big wall-mounted media service. A melancholy home for sure, but the guy had cruised into his seventh decade, even after what he'd done.

According to the father's handler, Scarlett Johansson, Robert East was a man driven by his appetites, and the father thought it a rare mercy that most people did not share such hungers. But Robert had invested a great deal of time and effort into satisfying his urges. When the police finally found time to investigate Mr East, they had learned of his expertise in lying and charming and manipulating and tricking his way to children. Robert's whereabouts were right too for *that day*.

Scarlett said Robert was never a suspect for his daughter's abduction because there was no evidence against him, or anyone else for that matter, and because he'd had an alibi the man had been ruled out during the brief investigation of 2051. Robert had always been good at alibis. But sometimes, his ambition had exceeded his ability to remain unnoticed.

Scarlett was unsatisfied with what had been done two years before: a solitary police interview with Robert East concerning his daughter's abduction. Time, manpower and resources were in short supply during the Torbay riots of '51. Time, manpower and resources were in even shorter supply in 2053. *Critical*, the father had been told, and so many times. The situation was always *critical*. But nothing was more critical to him than his little girl, and all the father had to do this morning was make certain that Robert East was not *the one*, by any means necessary.

Inside the hall the father paused again and listened hard.

In other news, tensions have increased between Beijing and Moscow on the Sino-Russian border as the Chinese refugee crisis intensifies, extending into the fifteenth consecutive year.

Time to engage. The father moved along the passage to the three bedrooms. Two closed doors, the third ajar: the master bedroom.

Successive droughts in the 'north Chinese plains' have devastated agriculture for two decades. The recent wheat harvest in the north plains was a near-total failure, following the third monsoon failure in five years, and in combination with the depletion of the Yellow River and the region's deep aquifers; the fresh-water shortage was far more critical than was estimated by the Chinese Government in 2047. The water shortage has been classed as irreversible by the UN.

The father found Robert sitting up in bed, watching the news intently, taking bad tidings from near and far, and maybe wondering what it all meant for him.

. . . a potential relocation of one hundred million Chinese citizens into Siberia, within two decades, will be, the minister quoted: 'absolutely necessary'.

The father reached into the bedroom, flicked the lights on, and stepped inside.

'Who are you?' Robert said, with too little surprise, as if uninvited masked visitors in his home, during the early morning, were not unusual. Maybe they weren't. These werc strange times.

The Russian government has declared that all possible options will be considered to reverse the 'increasing and unmanageable' flow of migrants from the east.

Anything could happen.

'Don't get up. Stay still.'

'What do you want?' Robert's dentures were not in his mouth. His gummy voice was now girded with outrage at the intrusion, and sharp with contempt for the stranger at his bedside. If the man had been frightened or infirm the father might have struggled with the morning's work, because what he most feared in these situations was his own sympathy. Gnarly men and obstinate men, who had wrought trauma on small children, helped him slip into the red room of the mind, and in such a hot place he was someone else, another man. He had been such a man, a man that boiled, on his three previous moves.

The father swung the torch beam into Robert East's face. 'Information.'

'Who are you?' Robert rose up from white bed sheets: a scrawny upper body in the bundling of pyjamas, the turkey neck thrusting, salt-whiskered chin jutting, his eyes slit mean. Long fingers immediately spidered about the bedside table, clawing for the phone, maybe a panic button.

The father looked absurd too, and a fright, in the face-clinging Balaclava and bush hat, but he didn't read fear in Robert. This man was an old friend of confrontation, crossed boundaries, invaded privacy, awkward conversations. And regardless of whether Mr East knew anything about his daughter, he hadn't paid any kind of price for what he'd done to other children. He'd remained cosy up on this hill, nested in reasonable air-conditioned comfort with no winter flood risk. The father clenched his fist around the stun spray, took a step forward and punched down hard, knocking the man's head into the wall.

Spit leapt silvery from Robert's lipless mouth. The hair at the side of his head swayed like a bleached sea anemone, waving its fronds in shock. His mouth formed an 'O' and his eyes widened, before *he* – before the fiend that Robert East really was – returned into the small black eyes like a devil's spirit repossessing what it had been jolted from. All white and wattled with rage, Robert turned his face to the father and roared like an old silverback gorilla slapped by a chimp.

The father hesitated, stunned, cement-footed by this dragon belch from a frail, birdy ribcage, horned with cadaverous collar bones. He hadn't expected Robert to have such leathery bellows. A pterodactyl, he thought unkindly, erupting from its cotton nest. And soon, Robert was all veined pate, fringed with wisps, big bony hands clenching, and clawed feet kicking at the sheets in his petulant haste to get up, get out, and to get at the trespasser.

This how you kept your pervy peers in line, Robert?

The father wished he'd hit the man harder. Half measures and indecision would sink him, so he readied the stun spray canister, no bigger than a lipstick, and puffed the aerosol over the man's skull. With his own face turned to the side, his hand shielding blowback, he made sure to vapour Robert thoroughly.

Scarlett had once called the gas 'evil shit'. Not long after they'd become acquainted, she'd supplied the father with a pick-up location, where he'd found the police-issue nerve agent, amongst other equipment, zipped inside an old vinyl school bag. She'd once said that a face full of the gas was like a combination of inhaling black pepper and dipping your head into lightless arctic waters, forty below. Eyes would feel wind-whipped sands and weep sulphuric tears as the frontal lobes crackled to ice. Evil shit indeed.

The 'final shit', the handgun, the father had procured for himself.

Robert steam-whistled and clutched his face. His torso toppled, skull-thumping the carpet between the father's ankles. By the waistband, the father hauled the rest of Robert out of bed and set him down, face first in his tears. On the ground, Robert started to shiver inside his pyjamas and vest like a scared child. For a few minutes he'd be insensible, incapable, with all of his inner alarms screaming about the pepper and the ice, the pain and the lightning storm that his thoughts now staggered through.

The father put away the evil shit and unzipped the rucksack strung round his front. Dipped his chin inside, with the small torch clamped between his teeth, and took out the 'kinky shit': a rubber ball on a leather strap.

Pulling Robert's head up by the straggly white trim on the eggshell skull, the father cupped the gasping mouth with his rubbery hand, the ball gag sitting in his palm. Without the impediment of dentures, the gag went into Robert's maw like an unripe plum. The father then buckled the ball gag tight at the back of the old man's head, strapping the tanned furrows of skin good and tight. He finished by cuffing the man's wrists, and that was easy as the hands were clamped over a pair of streaming eyes. He was getting better at this.

Rolling Robert onto his back with his foot, the father surveyed the long fellow more closely. Rangy shanks and old bones. He hadn't bathed in a while either and smelled of sour cream and vinegar.

The father unholstered his bottle of chemically treated saline from his rucksack and doused Robert's face, shaking the container empty. Robert moved his hands to let the tepid liquid relief swill and rinse out his eye sockets. He spluttered, coughed like a bull, then fell to groaning and clawing at the kinky shit between his gums, now stuffing up his head with old Wellington boot fumes.

'Nasty, evil shit. Can's full too. And I'm not shy with it, Robert. I'll discharge it all day in this room until it rattles dry. I've seen eyes bulge like beef tomatoes after two doses.' The father tapped Robert's hip with the toe of his hiking boot. 'On your feet, or your knees if you can't see shit. And take me to your stash.'

Sat in the recliner, Robert was scared, chilli-eyed, shuddery, and locked in by a dinner tray like a baby in a high chair. Cuffed hands lay limp in his lap. His media devices were lined up, side by side, on the coffee table. 'That's all in the past. I've never reoffended.' And that was all Robert seemed inclined to say.

'When you were barred from the care homes, how did you get your fix? Who was in your last crew? Names, Robert. Names and addresses.'

'I told you, I never reoffended. My wife . . .' He swallowed. 'My wife was seriously ill, and I—'

'You ever really cared about her, you wouldn't have put her through seven kinds of hell.'

The father felt his advantage slipping away. A recurring problem with the spray was the escalation of fear in the victim of a second dose, or something else just as bad. The discomfort of the gas was intolerable, and the afflicted even began to believe they'd done nothing wrong, that they'd hung up their boots and never been near a single mother with a drug addiction again. That was no good, and nor was a false confession to stop the agony: a timeless problem with torture.

The father put the can on the coffee table so that Robert could see the little yellow pillar from hell, filled with compressed fire and brain-freezing skull-fuckery. 'Robert, we both know your predilection is something you'll never recover from, and it's not something you will ever resist when it calls. You may not even be in control of your legs when you see a set of swings and a seesaw. Until your sex drive starts to resemble the dead lawn out back, it's a white-knuckle ride. I've done my homework and I understand, so denial is just no good to me.' The father checked his watch. 'I'm on a clock.'

'Someone is coming . . . friends, they—'

'Sure, sure they are. And you'll have plenty of time to freshen up once we're done.'

Something that might have been hope flickered across Robert's face, before the emotion's strength failed and could not pick up the miserable, suspicious, downcast mouth that would be set in stone long after the father left the premises. And now the two of them were in the living room and the tussle was behind them, the father was beginning to self-hate. A distant version of himself wanted to beg forgiveness for what he had just done to an old man in his bedroom. But the father wheeled that self away and shut it inside a back room of his head, and then he swallowed the key.

He went rummaging in the rucksack again, fetched out the photograph in the plastic bag, moved closer to the easy chair. Robert's eyes followed him, wary, but no longer beseeching because the contempt was seeping back. In what little of the father's face that he could see, the eyes and nothing more, Robert had just glimpsed a trait that he believed he could work on: a weakness. The father had seen this near-hidden but eager expression in men like Robert before; they wanted a lowering eyelid, a flicker, a dilation, something like that, something near-imperceptible. Robert wanted to know what people cared about, as if the information was a toehold on a sheer rock face to work on, widen, expand into a handhold, then a ledge, eventually a cave they could settle down inside to begin whispering. Get a trickle of sand moving, some loose ground. Keep it up until there was a rockslide of trust and familiarity. Then he was holding the rope and someone else was dangling at the end of it. The father had used blunt instruments on Robert, but suspected the man had finer tools to work with on him. *If you let him.* But this wasn't a game of chess, not any kind of negotiation either, because such things had done the world no good; there was never agreement when it was required, there was nothing left but self-interest and the necessary force to achieve it.

The father skipped to closing statements and sentencing. He hardened his tone, but kept his voice low. 'There will be no explanations, no excuses. No chatter. The jury on you came in a long time ago. We'll never bond, Robert. If you say one more word that I feel is moving us away from the very specific information I came here to gather, then I will spray you like a greenfly and put the rubber ball back inside your mouth. At your age, two, maybe three doses will give you a cardiac arrest. So, how about no more doses and you just find it in yourself to tell the truth.

Now, this is what I know. You were the owner of an agency that supplied staff to care homes for children. You supplied three homes with carers. But you also employed your mates, with whom you shared similar interests.'

'Ancient history,' Robert said, in an aristocratic drawl. His face had faded grey, and gone all pinched around the mouth. Welling eyes were lidded and even looking down a long nose at the father, who was out of his seat like a jack-in-the box to swipe up the spray can.

Robert flinched. 'Sorry,' he barely said.

The father slowly returned to his seat and settled himself. 'You were always the ringleader. You oversaw everything. Anything your group did, you knew about. Two of your associates vanished into Thailand a few years before 2051, a year that is very pertinent to today's meeting. The third, Billy Furrow, was killed in prison in 2050. So none of your inner circle was available to me, and could not have been involved in the abduction that I'm here to investigate. But you may have had associates in the area who knew something about this snatch in '51. I don't entirely fancy you for the crime, Robert, but you are just the sort of bird that would flock with those that did take . . .' The father cleared his throat.

'Social workers blew the whistle on you in 2046. Under Section 47 of the Children Act 1989, the local authority had a duty to investigate any child in danger, or suffering abuse. A social worker in Plymouth demanded an investigation into all three care homes that you were intimately familiar with. In fact, one social worker believed you, in effect, ran these homes with your mates.

'You pleaded not guilty to seventy-two counts of taking

indecent photographs of children between the ages of three and six. Seventeen counts of indecency with a child were also added to the charges. So you might understand why your protestations about your sick wife and never re-offending hold no water. You were sentenced to seven years in prison. The sentence was reduced to two years due to chronic overcrowding after the Bristol riots and you were freed the following year. You came home and I can only assume that it was business as usual.

'Most of your known victims were children in care, but you were a regular stroller around whatever seaside attractions were still operational, as was revealed by your photographic archive. You were getting on, but you were probably still active at the time of any abductions in 2051. Statistics suggest that you would still be, at the very least, in the loop.

'After 2048, the police lost sight of you. This means they were no longer looking at you, Robert, in 2051. A few years had drifted by since you went down, and things changed here, didn't they? The Greeks, the Spanish, and many more of the Africans who'd made it as far as Europe, all hit the beaches and stormed the ports and tunnels. Three million people were directed into the south-west, because it was still the least populated part of England. So by 2051, no one had the time to look for one little girl any more. And you must have been rubbing your fucking hands, Robert.

'But in 2051, a year that I will never forget, the local police's Child Protection Team consisted of two people. One of them killed himself last year. Depression suicide. The other one doesn't work any more. They did what they could, but working knowledge of the case, and of the many sex offenders in this county, is now thin on the ground. The team only has one full-time member of staff now. Did you know that? And the social workers are drowning in a tide of sick, malnourished and traumatized children, in temporary accommodation and refugee settlements, down the coast. I bet you can see where this is leading and you are beginning to understand why I am here. There are other ways to look for missing children, Robert, and I am one of them.'

Robert's nostrils flared, either from suppressed rage or humiliation. 'Home Guard, eh?'

'Now, not only do you have a classic profile for a repeat sex offender, but your preferred victim's gender is female. Your preferred age range is three to six years old, and that's another reason why I am here today. There is no wiggle room. So I want you to take a good, long look at this picture and then I want you to help me with my inquiries. OK?'

'Vigilante. Thought they'd cleared you out.'

'Clear your mind, Robert. Concentrate.' And then the father turned the picture around and held it a few inches from Robert's face.

In anti-climactic fashion Robert asked for his reading glasses and the father was uncomfortably reminded of an expert preparing to inspect a sample within his field of expertise.

The father trussed Robert's ankles with the second set of cuffs, scanned the area around his chair, placed the stun spray back in the rucksack, then went and collected the glasses from a table in the master bedroom. He was not convinced Robert needed the spectacles; when he returned to the living room, the man was eyeballing the picture on the coffee table, and wasn't squinting. Even after all they'd been through, he still took the father for a prick.

'I recognize her,' Robert said, looking up directly into the eyes of the father, who adjusted his own feet to remain steady. His blood had bloomed after shock, hope, terror and euphoria had left him dizzy and erased all the colour from the room. But Robert waited and was in no hurry to blurt. He let the tantalizing detail hang, and the father no longer wanted to hit Robert; he wanted to beg and plead with him for another sentence, a name, a date, or place. And Robert knew this. 'I remember the news story. Was she taken from a garden?'

The father only nodded because he didn't know what to say. This was a clever move. Robert was already creating distance by suggesting, quite convincingly, that he couldn't remember the details of the abduction. But an abduction of a child in Robert's town was the kind of thing the man would remember with exacting clarity.

Or was Robert telling the damned truth? The father never knew, not really. Neither did psychiatrists, or police detectives, parole boards, or any explorers of the mind. He'd long come to believe that all actions were symptoms of selves that came and went like smoke rings, in and out of scarlet doorways, thickening then dispersing. The autocrat in the deep was never glimpsed. He lay in the primordial black and fired signals from unreachable fathoms. No one saw his face. The ruler of us was unique and ineffable.

Sullen and flattened by the realization that there would probably be no great revelation that morning, the father regrouped his wits by an act of will. 'I'm on the brink of crop-dusting your bloody chair, Robert. You gotta do better than this.'

Robert swallowed. 'There was talk . . .'

The father leaned into him, his vision flickering around the edges. 'Where? Online?'

Robert nodded. 'Around that time. And I don't know anything else about it, I really don't—'

'Get on with it.'

'There was talk about it, about who could' – Robert paused to choose his words carefully – 'have involved themselves. No one local was the consensus. Or, at least, no one ever mentioned anything that convinced me.'

'But some of them claimed to know something?'

'No more than jests and things like that. About, you know, what might . . . People pretended they knew.' Robert swallowed.

At the mention of 'jests', Robert must have seen the blood bulge the very skin of the father's eyeballs. Robert may also have seen a screaming mouth in each of the pupils facing him, while the father sensed the house rise a few inches and then drop without rattling a single porcelain knick-knack on the mantel. His anger was white-hot coals followed by the cold of deep space. One of his hands fidgeted at something else he kept inside the rucksack: the final shit.

'Perhaps it was someone you knew.' Robert offered this in a conciliatory tone of voice, as if he were talking to a dangerous simpleton.

'I don't know anyone that awful.'

'Addicts, they'll take anything to sell.'

'Enough of these straws your claws are clutching at. Let us return to the jests, Robert. What precisely did you and your peers find so funny about this abduction?'

'Not *me*. Never. I was just saying that some pretended, the more garrulous elements, that they knew . . . where she was, who she was with . . . That sort of thing.' He cleared his throat. 'But I think the prevailing opinion was that a visitor to the area, an opportunist, may have been responsible.'

'And?'

'Moved her elsewhere. Abroad. Possibly. Or . . . did something unspeakable and then covered their tracks.'

Unspeakable. The terrible three hours after a child's abduction when the abominable, the unthinkable, could occur, but was something to laugh about online for Robert and his *mates*. Shaky as a scarecrow released from its pole, the father moved his feet.

Robert's turmeric-puffy eyes pleaded with him; even in a burning squint they could read the change in the intruder. 'I'm afraid I cannot help you. If I knew anything I would hardly keep it to myself. Abduction was never . . . I'd never taken anyone's . . . I would never . . . What are you doing?' Robert turned his head this way and that way to see why the father had gone behind the easy chair. He even attempted to rise.

The father said, 'Sit,' in a voice belonging to some other man.

Robert stayed seated. 'Nothing, there is nothing more I can tell you. Names. I have names of others who may be able to assist you. Who were around at the time. Who were intrigued by . . .'

The father came round from behind the easy chair and leaned over the coffee table. He took Robert's equipment from the table top and placed everything on the TV dinner tray. Stuck memory pins into the back of anything with a memory. 'All of them. Every one of them,' he said. 'Numbers and email addresses. Your passwords, user names, the sites, encryptions, links, the places. Download them from everywhere you store your filth. If the names don't check out, then God help you, Robert.'

Robert started typing with cuffed wrists, his hands moving like featherless ghost birds, bony herons descending and alighting from the screen. Occasionally he glanced nervously at where the father stood, just behind his right ear, watching his progress and making sure that he didn't send a message. Sweat rolled from the tip of Robert's nose.

But Robert did as he was bid, and his paprika-rimmed eyes, wetter than a beagle hound's, peered at the glowing screens as if cross-referencing, annotating, listing, footnoting: a rat scholar. He stopped typing after ten minutes. 'That's everything,' he said, a show of contrived penitence deepening his tone.

The father collected the items and removed the pins, slipped them all inside his rucksack. Robert would never give the father everything, not even on pain of death. He'd given him something, probably details of those men incapable of reprisals. There would be some sites loaded with visuals too, which the father would never have the stomach to trawl through. Scarlett Johansson would want it all. Her 'associates' would then sift through the materials on behalf of all of the other agents in the field.

The father refilled his bottle of water in the kitchen and

returned to the living room, sipping. It was really warming up inside, the heat now pushing its great bloat through the utility-room window that he'd left open down the hall. He thought about his car and knew it was time to go.

Robert now looked as miserable as the faces seen at the windows of municipal care homes. 'She was your daughter,' he said, with what sounded like deep resignation and genuine woe.

The father cleared his throat. 'Your home is filled with memories, Robert. I can see that. But let me introduce one of mine. There was a little girl who was loved so hard . . .' His voice started to break.

'Don't, please,' Robert said, as if the father was being rude.

'She was taken. Two years ago. Her family want her back . . . so much.' The father's eyes smarted and his throat began to swell enough to prevent much more talk. He rummaged inside the rucksack and moved further behind the easy chair, out of sight.

Robert's voice rose. 'I can't help you. You think I would keep information back from the authorities about this?'

'I do, yes.'

'I know what I have done was wrong. But it was in the past. Well before 2051.'

The father bagged Robert's head and pulled the drawstring tight.

'Oh God, no,' Robert said as if from down a well. He tried to get to his feet again.

The father took a few steps back and killed the overhead lights. 'Someone, somewhere, will be glad I'm doing this. Here's one for the kids.' The father shot the dart into the man's wrinkled neck.

Robert's ankles were tethered but the rest of him shot forward and snapped off the plastic dinner tray and landed on the coffee table, hard, his elbows barely breaking his fall. His entire body convulsed.

Eventually, after the first shocks abated, he turned his hooded head to reveal the outline of a nose and an open mouth, gasping. There was a muffled sob from inside the cloth bag.

The father took out the final shit and pressed the handgun against the side of the man's skull. And it seemed so simple, such a simple act to perform: just a short squeeze on the trigger and every memory of those small, pale bodies, the frightened faces, reddened and stained with tears, or mute with shock and confusion, would be gone from this man's head forever. One more death, and the end of a man more deserving of death than most leaving the stage these days. This very man, with his head in a bag, could simply be shot dead one hot morning in his own home. The father believed he could actually do it now. Not before, with the others; murder had seemed too much for him. But we change, he thought, we change as we are aged by the heartbreaker called life.

A murder, an execution, would bring scrutiny, eventually. And no, he would not kill Robert East, and he had to remind himself that he was a father with a broken heart and a broken head, but he was no killer.

Nor did the father believe that this man had taken his daughter, though knowing he had put his hands upon other men's daughters made it hard to ease the gun away from the skull below him. 'If you warn your friends, if you breathe one word of my visit to anyone, I will come back. And, with God as my witness, I swear I will use this.' The father dug the handgun into Robert's temple hard enough to make him cry out.

FIVE

'Did you move?'

'Yes. This morning.'

'Where are you now?'

'Back in my room.'

'Good. Stay there.'

'For how long?'

'Until I know if Robert East reports you.'

Since the morning's move he'd come to the conclusion that some detached part of his mind had overseen his seemingly effortless extraction – the removal of cuffs from Robert East's pale wrists and ankles, the final threat of reprisals, the unhooding of the twitching man, the walk to the car through warm, dusty, yellow air, the slow drive through a sun's brightness that carried false hopes of happiness, to transport him away from Cockington and to his dim temporary lodgings further down the coast in Paignton. Keeping him on the road, regulating the twitches, ticks and sighs that threatened to well up in waves and crash to panic or remorse, while adrenaline drained like sewage and made his hands shake: all such reactions and activities of body and mind were managed and governed by an unfeeling administrator of his functions. Perhaps part of his jittery inner parliament now relegated more compassionate impulses to the back benches of his mind. There they could only whistle and jeer, as the *mover* and *shaker* was driven home and put to bed without judgement.

He was also getting fitter over the terrain and distance too. Not sluggish with aches, or anxious to the point of nausea, like he'd been on the first three moves; he was not so delicate now, or so skittish in the head, not quite an athlete, but a keener amateur.

'What did you get?'

'All of his gear. The usual stuff, passwords, names . . .'

'Good. Leave it with the hotel reception. Someone will collect it today. Was he hurt?'

'I used the immobilizer, gas too. I don't think . . .'

'Go on.'

'I don't think it was him.'

'No, but there might be something, a connection, a trace, some small detail amongst what you have taken. We will be thorough. You did a good thing today, but you have to stay strong. We're doing as much as we can.'

'I know.'

'And I have someone else.'

'Who? Let me get—'

'I have to go. But I'll call you soon with all the details.'

'Name? What's his name?'

'Bowles. Murray Bowles.' She finished the call.

The father called his contact Scarlett Johansson because he'd never met her and had become familiar only with her voice. The first time they had spoken her faint American accent had struck him as immediately distinctive and reminded him of an old film star in her younger roles. And because his handler only ever referred to herself as a 'friend of the family', in the early days of their association he told the woman who her voice reminded him of. She had laughed and told the father that he should call her that. His contact had remained Scarlett Johansson ever since.

Over the last year few people had contacted the father; not even the colleagues he'd worked so closely with for fifteen years, nor his old friends from university. Whenever he saw an unrecognized caller on a screen, he picked up in case it was Scarlett. She contacted him at accounts that she provided; these, and her own idents, constantly changed.

Who was she? He didn't really know, but guessed that Scarlett was a police officer and a member of an overwhelmed Child Protection Team, somewhere in the counties of the south-west. He knew one protection team was still attached to every police force in the country, but the teams were rarely made up of more than two people. Sometimes, one man or woman now worked alone.

Maybe Scarlett Johansson had handlers herself and had been chosen to contact some of the parents who had lost their little ones. Perhaps she had been told that he was the right kind of person for collaboration because he'd once been arrested for assaulting a convicted sex offender, a man who'd shrugged off his approach and his request for information about his daughter. The man had not even been in the right part of the country when his daughter was snatched. But the father had needed to do something and the man's indifference had been inappropriate. It had taken four men to pull him away and to hold him shaking against a wall until an auxiliary police officer arrived on a bicycle.

Charges were pressed, but circumstances were taken

into account and he'd been released with a caution. Scarlett Johansson had known about this incident and of the father's need to *do* something. Somewhere, off the record, discussions must then have taken place about his suitability for making moves. If deliberations had happened between factions in authority, in times of so little restraint, he had been told nothing of them, nor of any assessment passed through the secretive processes that involved Scarlett Johansson.

Handlers were probably politically motivated and working in collusion with the nationalists, long the most popular political movement. His wife thought so, and Miranda believed he was being used to harass criminal elements in certain areas of the country. She feared he would be asked to eradicate them too. Such clandestine strategies were not unknown. But it was also possible that these officers of the law were good men and women, helping a father find a stolen daughter because *they* could not make things right any more. Maybe there were a great many Scarlett Johanssons who offered parents a respite from the torments of waiting for news, the harrowing silence that inexorably moved parents further, and still further, and yet further away from the exact moment their worlds were rent by events that had nothing to do with heatwaves or storms. The father hoped so, though he didn't really care where the information came from. He didn't know how it all worked, he just wanted help.

During one of those days deprived of his daughter, inside that sleepless blur of exhaustion and grief and terror, Scarlett Johansson had called him, and on the day his child had been missing for twenty months, one week and two days.

Scarlett Johansson had called him many times since. Even though she had a tendency to speak quickly, as if afraid of talking to him, the father would ask her to repeat herself. He made sure he never made mistakes when he recorded information, because so much had already been overlooked or completely ignored. And he would record every fragment about these men who did not care about other people, or could not care, not really. This awareness had made his four moves easier. And he was still not convinced by the apparent remorse he had witnessed amongst those he'd interviewed. Nor did he believe that the people he hunted could change for the better. That assurance also made his dealings with them easier.

SIX

One week after his visit to Robert East, his lip-licking desire for strong drink enticed the father out of the hotel room and he ventured into Paignton town centre to buy a bottle of Welsh rum. He'd been locked away, living off bread, imitation cheese and real fruit, while waiting for Scarlett Johansson to call and give him an *all clear*.

Even though the range of food dwindled, alcohol never failed to appear in stores and markets. No one in any kind of authority would dare take the alcohol away. Wine drinkers were sometimes bereft, but their privations were the least of anyone's worries.

In the twenty-four-hour supermarket, the rum was pricey, and stacked on the higher shelves, protected by cages. His funds were not being replenished, and nor was this a special occasion, but he needed to drink. And he was no longer drinking to forget but to remember, to access revelations arising from his outlaw deeds.

The supermarket had once functioned as a hotel for tourists, three decades gone. The place once boasted a small pool and a ballroom. A sign for satellite television and the Jacuzzi was still attached to the car park wall, like graffiti made in bad taste.

The upper two storeys of the building had been

partitioned like most properties in what used to be a functioning town centre, appropriated by local government and now a seething ghetto of dysfunction, bordering a redoubt of beleaguered families, who maintained their own neighbourhoods' security arrangements in the surrounding areas of Preston, Goodrington, Churston and Galmpton. This former hotel suggested it was now a ground-floor pharmacy for alcoholics and elderly residents unable to migrate like rare butterflies; those with no option but to flutter about their bleached, toxic habitat in the town centre, behind the vast concrete seawall of the esplanade.

Every south-facing window upstairs blotted out the sun with blinds, curtains, blankets, duvets, faded sleeping bags and plastic sheets, suggesting a familiar hot, dark, unbreathable atmosphere, reeking of sanitation issues, bleach, tobacco, fried oil and sweat.

Bottle in hand, the father returned to the car and unlocked it, instinctively moving his head in feigned nonchalance to watch for faces at windows. But as he made to duck inside the vehicle, he saw a large and strange figure, painted upon one wall of the parking court. On the way towards the store he'd mostly looked at nothing but his feet, and had somehow missed this mural. But it demanded his attention now.

Striding, as if gripped by a purposeful haste, the long figure was depicted as if it were heading swiftly across the rendered cement wall towards the dented bins. Above the tacky rind of dried piss at knee level, an erect posture suggested the thing swept, wraithlike, on thin legs, through the variety of scrawlings, logos, statements, mad gibberish and gang taggings. Curiosity made the father pause and look more closely.

The portraiture had been artful. The father could not fathom the true motives behind such a creation, though maybe the mural had been created in irony, amongst so much apelike vandalism.

There might even have been a fire here once, a vehicle booming and fiercely roaring up the wall of the car park, during some sudden explosion of local frustration, and from out of the oily scorch marks, this rangy thing had subsequently been etched and extended across the grimy cement, as if it had appeared from soot and belching smoke, some grim abyss or coke-choked oven that fumed beneath the tarmac.

The gown or cloak was tattered, frayed away from sticklike limbs, so loose and spare, that spiked the folds and billows. Like trailing rags of cloth around a disintegrating kite frame, a vessel flung aloft and battered in strong wind, a fluidity was also evident in the entirety of the picture: an effortless prance, or a leap in a ballet for the graceful dead preoccupied this figure, and the length of the stride was unpalatably feline.

Ashy fragments fell away from the garment's hem and great round sleeves, becoming a slipstream of finer dusts, or a black aerosol of dross. Pebbles or seeds drifted from the bone hands too, sifting through a metacarpal sieve to the littered ground.

The father moved around the car for a better view, but soon recoiled at the sight of the impression of fleshless feet, vaguely sandalled.

But there was something close to beauty as well as

terror in this graffiti. A sense of a diminishing of the begrimed and overcrowded town around the blackened wall, as if the crooked world was mocked by this figure, or utterly absolved of . . . *significance*.

There was no street lighting at night in the area, so it was doubtful the figure had been drawn then. By day it seemed unlikely that an artist would have remained unbothered for long enough to paint such a work. No council would have sanctioned it either. The father wanted to know why it was there and what it meant, because it really meant something to someone. His desire to understand became strangely urgent.

No one had tried to embellish the figure with a cock, tits or a toothy smile either. It simply cut a swathe unopposed. And who would deface the figure once they'd glimpsed the partial head inside the cowl? The whites of the eyes revealed misery, even ecstasy, or maybe a combination of each. Within sharp sockets, the eyes seemed to stare upwards or inwards, an expression morbidly religious, or tragic. The father had not thought in these terms for a long while, nor been affected by anything artistic since the afternoon his little girl was taken. He was reminded of other times and experienced the slight disorientation that came with the sudden sense of better days.

Now that he looked more closely at what there was of a face, it seemed tightly papered in flesh, or perhaps it was a mask, the long features drawn and weary as if from the sight of epic suffering. One face for all. No strength remained to keep the jaw shut, and the mouth gaped beyond beseeching for mercy, a morsel of food, or a drop of water. The figure seemed beyond all of that and was still rushing further into . . . the father didn't know.

Around its unsightly feet a skilled hand had written: *Usque ad mortem*. Latin. Something from a dead language, and he didn't understand what it meant, though the mural did remind him of the very little he knew of medieval art that celebrated death in old churches. And he briefly imagined that this was a sign, or metaphor, that *it* all had to end: *this*, *us*, the world. He imagined this was the figure's true message. Let us all sit down exhausted and die in our unlit homes.

The father climbed inside his car, shaken, though not sure by what precisely, and now wished that he had not looked upon the wall.

That was the first time, his first sighting of the figure, but it would not be his last.

SEVEN

Heavy head, soft bones. He didn't have a shirt on and was still slick all over. He dripped. Thoughts of the coming move against Murray Bowles punctured the father. His strength seeped out of a hole in his body that he couldn't find. He had to repeatedly visit his ensuite bathroom to drink water.

Moving to and fro made him feel weaker. It had been thirty-seven degrees that day and was not much cooler at night. Kent had had the highest temperature: forty-one, even hotter than predicted. The next day it was going to hit forty in Devon. For three months the lowest recorded temperature had been thirty-four degrees. You moved, you stayed hot.

The room was too cheap to have air conditioning. Powering A/C was too costly for the near-defunct hotel chain, so he conserved his strength like the area conserved water and electricity. Until the three new nuclear power stations were finished, the whole of the south-west would sweat and spend more time in the dark. They got everything late except for refugees, that's what the locals said. People should have been used to delays and power cuts, but they still watched keenly for progress, as if reactor readiness could be achieved by force of desire alone. People had learned that the power could not stay off for long. It wasn't only darkness they feared; it was what the darkness did to *other* people and to them too.

Through the evening the father obsessively checked the water meter in the bathroom, filling jugs from the cold tap. At midnight he ran another *cold* shower with the timer fixed at one minute. When he stepped out he didn't dry himself. He lay on the bed with most of his body upon a towel. The room's only window was open and the street below was quiet. No breeze. He'd kept the lights off to trick his mind into thinking the room was cooler. He could smell the sea.

To distract himself from his nerves and the heat, the father looked for local news. He got national. All available channels had switched from the Gabon River Fever aboard the refugee ships drifting off the coast of Italy, and moved away from the new bug in Hong Kong, to continue the summer's top story: the forest fires. Flashing into the darkness of his room came the onscreen pictures of the blaze in Spain, Portugal, and France, filmed from as close as safety would allow, and from space, where the smoke was visible as a black cloud over the Mediterranean. Subtitles ran across the bottom of the screen to tell viewers that more firemen were missing, fifty this time in Spain.

He tried another channel, then another, but similar pictures continued to flicker across the dark walls and ceiling. There were long lines of black rubber sacks in a vast warehouse with grey walls. People wearing masks walking between the rows of dark lumps, like scientists waiting for pupae to hatch. The caption said Paris.

That summer an expert called the heatstroke a 'climate

holocaust'. Like all bad things the phrase caught on quickly. As the father drove back to Devon two weeks before, he'd passed refrigerated supermarket trucks, taking their cargo out of Torbay Hospital and up the M5 at night, on their way to the makeshift mortuaries near Taunton. Airport buildings were now being used. So many had come to the coast to retire, but were retiring from life sooner than they'd anticipated. The care homes were emptier after three months of such heat, or at least the cash-strapped bedlams were. The refugee camps were not air-conditioned either, and the heat had cut a swathe through their elderly too.

Every second summer now.

There was not much worse than being old, the father had decided long ago. But he still wanted to be old, and when his time came he wanted his daughter to be there and to hold him in her arms like he was her baby.

The father took the mute off.

Reports cited a death toll of three hundred thousand across Europe, and climbing with the mercury. Old people, refugees, the homeless: the usual suspects. The summer records of '29 and '33 had been broken; '47's body count was now in sight. The European summer had been set a new challenge of how long it could smother, and of how many it could take away.

Crop losses too of thirty-two billion euros across three months of heat and drought. Atmospheric carbon emissions had leapt again. Another positive feedback: plant stress. Plants and trees were throwing out what they were supposed to be sucking down. Another loop getting tighter, closer than the air, every second summer. At times, when the father struggled to breathe, he thought he could sense all of the dry, exhausted trees releasing their last gases like dying breaths.

Pictures of river beds came next. They made him feel worse than the sight of flames shrieking through the tops of trees. Brown trickles in cracked mud: the Rhine, the Po, the Loire. Rainfall down ten per cent with poisonous algae blooming in depleted lakes. He tried to imagine what the algae looked like but didn't have the strength. People were being told not to drink the water or bathe in it to escape the heat.

White smoke above a forest in Germany. *Them too now.* Red coals smouldered beneath the plumes. The trees reminded the father of tall, thin people, all panicking and unable to move their feet. These pictures made breathing seem more difficult and he thought he could smell smoke again.

An area as big as Denmark was already ash and black bones in southern Europe. People thanked God there wasn't much wind. A small mercy. A land mass as big as Luxemburg had gone up in northern Spain a few years back and choked Barcelona. The father only briefly considered what the scorch mark would be like in ten years' time, by 2063: a black smudge the size of France? No one could bear to think that way. Guesses and estimates were unwelcome in most company.

Pictures of a rockslide, filmed from the air, followed. Mountains in Switzerland were falling apart. Glacial melt rates had also reached new records.

When the news moved to North Africa he switched channels. No one could look at Africa and not believe that they were next in line. He flicked down two channels and waited for the local service to come on after the international links.

The British nationalists' shaky unity, The Movement, had endured a big rally earlier that day, followed by a sluggish, heat-battered march through Torquay. He'd heard them in the distance that afternoon: drums, muffled chants, the odd tinny blurt through a microphone.

The Movement planned to walk through Paignton the following day. Progress would be slow because even The Movement's determination would stumble in such heat, but there'd be more people than usual in the area, and the available police would gather further along the coast around the refugee camps, filling their boots with sweat they could ill afford to lose.

Heat kept people indoors. A good thing because the recipient of the father's coming move would probably be home, just like Robert East had been. He'd go in real early, when it was a bit cooler.

The father turned the screen off and looked at the open window: a black square of hot night. He dropped the blinds as a precaution. An intruder would disturb them and the noise would wake him.

His thoughts swam. The bottle of rum was empty. He hadn't intended to finish it in one sitting. It used to take him three nights to go through a bottle. Half-asleep, drunk, feverish, then strangely chilly, always more dreaming than thinking, the father waited and waited for Scarlett to call.

At eight in the morning, she finally made contact. The father believed he'd dropped off only for a few minutes in the night, but could now see the intense bars of light at the side of the blinds.

'I have the address,' she said. 'You ready?'

EIGHT

The father peered through the windscreen at the sky. Glimmers of dawn's thin light seemed more evident. Soon there would be a merciless clarity for early-morning eyes to squint into.

If the heat was to last forever, he knew that everyone would go mad. Or maybe everyone had already gone mad without being aware of the disintegration, and not only the mutterers or head-slappers, the screamers or the too silent, who were plentiful. But perhaps those still shuffling through domestic routines, or frantic with some purpose, in what was called the war against the climate, were incapable of fully remembering what life was like before. Back when? When was it not like *this*. When was that exactly? He often wondered if the lucky ones were those who had known nothing more than this.

When it had gone five, he was still sat in the car, slowly sweating and sipping at his water bottle. Public information about heatstroke stayed on repeat in the local media he had playing. He knew the health advice by heart like an old song: symptoms to watch for were quick, shallow breaths and a rapid pulse followed by dry skin, nausea, dizziness, irritability. Stay indoors, do not move during the hottest part of day, use cold compresses, stay in the shade, sip water. *Stay, sit, sip.*

There had been no room in intensive care since June so good luck with an ambulance. With heatstroke, a coma might be only a stumble away. And a move could be a boisterous business, as was the retreat or extraction. If there were delays or tussles, he would need to periodically check his skin and make sure the sweat never stopped leaking.

He returned his attention the house across the road.

The last time the father saw his target, Murray Bowles, the man had been returning to this address, carrying two fabric bags packed square with cartons of food. And the man had managed to remain overweight, so he wasn't eating only soya products, fruit and vegetables. He was probably supplementing his fare with sugary black-market victuals, and they weren't cheap.

Bowles didn't work, but lived alone in a three-bedroomed terraced house that looked close to being condemned. In the frenzy of resettlements from flooded Liverpool and East London to a county already swollen by the surge from southern Europe and Africa, the father wondered how a rehoused sex offender had become the sole occupier of a three-bedroomed property, even one so poorly maintained. Benefits would never stretch so far. Bowles had *friends*.

The bay windows of the street-facing rooms on each floor were permanently curtained, the window sills revealing a permanent litter of objects just inside the glass: plastic bottles, crockery, bunched-up clothing, the back of a circular mirror. The attic had been converted into another floor; its bays were also concealed by blinds.

No one else had entered or left the house with Bowles during the three days the father had watched the property, parked outside, on the other side of the road. And each time the father had seen Bowles that week, the man hadn't changed his shirt. He looked like an ogre from a fairy tale; he looked like the cliché of a child molester. The father had discovered that *they* often did. Longish, unwashed hair mopped his wide skull, the black locks forming greasy fronds across the broad forehead, and dangling over a rubbery-looking collar, unless they had been scraped tight behind his ears. The man's round-shouldered posture was a result of a perpetual lowering of the head, chin dipped to sternum, as if he were a big, harmless, shy man: meek and self-conscious in collared shirts stretched out by a ponderous belly and slabs over his hips. Where they stumped from his shorts, his pale legs were thickly haired trunks.

It was easy to imagine the creature's outer flesh as soft and slippery, but the father detected a tough core in a large body; the doughy shoulders and arms suggested an unappealing strength. This was a man who might hold on tightly. A physical sense of the man grew the longer the father watched him, and as they inexorably drew closer to each other. Imagined textures, the weight and density of the body, taunted the father until the man's dimensions began to seem entirely unassailable, the damp fleshiness unmanageable.

Bowles would always close his front door without looking over his shoulder, seemingly oblivious to his surroundings. Just in and out he went, short journeys, the small eyes shielded, half-closed.

No lights had come on in the hallway during the evenings. The father had wanted lights. Perhaps it was the idea of being in a close, dark space with Bowles that appalled him more than the sight of the burly figure. And the longer he had waited, the more his imagination effortlessly refashioned the big man into an opponent light on his feet with the eyesight of a rat, aware of the father outside and simply waiting for him in a familiar darkness. Something about this move just did not *feel* right. A nervy suspicion endured, not helped when Scarlett gave the father notes and warned him 'not to underestimate the suspect'. When in role as a sadist, apparently Bowles was fond of blood and a veritable master of the universe.

Going in early Friday morning would have been ideal, but the father was still outside, watching, on Sunday morning. Plans had been made and remade. He had carried out more reconnaissance than normal. Lengthy preparations hadn't reaffirmed his purpose, but only made it vaguer. More than heat was holding him back here.

The sky faded to a treacherous Atlantic blue, with a promise of cool air that would never come. A dilution to a milky blue would follow, before a canopy of polished steel would burn unprotected eyes. He could not be here in daylight. There was barely the best part of an hour of semi-darkness remaining. He wiped the sweat off his face with a forearm, started the car and drove to the place where he'd decided to park in an adjoining street. He would enter through the rear garden.

*

Fir trees covered the rear of the property, but he would break cover the moment he pushed between two leaning fence panels, rotted away from a concrete post. There was nowhere to hide in the garden. Even without ambient light, if anyone was to look from the rear windows at the back of the three terraced houses confronting him, they would see him.

He'd need to move slowly because the back yard was an obstacle course designed by those who cared nothing for a rear outlook. The smell of desiccated grass by the broken fence clouded his thoughts and hampered a strategy that became even less clear in his mind, less convincing, until his plan entirely fell away. He was tired, had slept badly for months, was thinking too much but resolving nothing. His head was not right for today's work. But would it ever be right again?

Elderly private owners occupied the house on the right. Their garden featured an orderly array of crops around bleached stone paths. Two families shared the house on the left. He'd counted five children earlier that week and wondered if the parents knew who was living next door. He thought of the children playing outside their neighbour's shabby house, and the father shivered with a sudden, mad desire to do the move fast, and at gunpoint, eschewing nerve gas or the police immobilizer.

According to Scarlett, Murray Bowles had already served a three-year sentence in the early forties for the physical and sexual abuse of children, before appearing in court in 2046 on twelve new charges of indecent assault and the rape of minors. The latter abuse was sadistic in nature, though he served no more than three years. He was out in 2049 and housed at the seaside in Margate. In 2050 he moved west, to Torbay.

In the late thirties Murray Bowles was a suspected affiliate of Ken 'Santa' Barret, a reviled paedophile and one of the last child killers to get the nation bristling for the death penalty, before such things were swept away by record rainfalls, European hurricanes, floods and rising sea levels. In Nottingham 'Santa' Barret's group had killed two brothers in care during a sadomasochistic ritual. Rumours suggested more children had been killed by the ring. Five of the twenty boys and girls that Santa's secretive group had abused were never found.

'Santa' Barret was killed by other inmates in prison in 2043. Besides Murray Bowles, none of Barret's associates had ever been traced, and Bowles's connection to the 'Santa' murders never stuck due to lack of evidence.

The father knew why Scarlett Johansson had made Murray Bowles available to him: he'd mainly groomed from care homes in the East Midlands, like his master, and they'd often moved the victims into rented flats. Two children were imprisoned for over a year, and Murray Bowles had arrived in Torquay the year before his daughter was taken.

Bowles couldn't drive, but may have been part of a group. Parole officers had kept an eye on the man once a month for thirty minutes since his release from prison, but he hadn't been a suspect for anything since 2049. According to statistics and case histories, that didn't mean much during the quiet periods of predators like Bowles, and all of the offenders were mostly off radar now; there were far greater priorities to occupy the police and social services.

He should have been told about Bowles before. That bugged him. A notion that the four men he had made moves upon thus far had been mere practice, and that he had been surreptitiously tested and trained in advance of this hot morning at another stranger's house, nagged him. As his wife suspected, maybe tendrils of the Home Guard scandal, created by factions in authority and their associations with paramilitaries, were now coiled about his neck. God knew he had reason to be here, but he didn't want to be used for general organized harassment, or another paedophile cull. He did not want to engage in anything not directly connected to finding *only* those who took his little girl.

On his way into the rear yard, the father passed a plastic water barrel, a bulging shed, soaked and dried out too many times. A trellis had sprung free from a painted cement wall. Weeds and tree roots extending for water made the patio uneven like the deck of a ship coming apart on black rocks. He stepped over a sink, its pipes plumbed into nothingness, and skirted greening sacks of sun-bleached refuse. At the kitchen door a taint of sewage wafted about his face. Only one first-storey window was uncovered.

The father found the right tool in his rucksack and began working at the door, in the gap between the frame and the lock. A secondary glazed door, but cheap, the glass all tapioca bubbles and mist.

He entered the kitchen soon after, stun spray and torch in either hand, and stood in a room long and narrow like a galley on a canal boat. A scrap merchant's mound of mismatching pots and crockery and plastic formed a small mountain over the draining board, the sink and small kitchen table. Packets of soya meals for one were stacked in a precarious tower. The father could smell gas mingling with damp-softened wood. A silent, lightless house lay beyond an open door at the far end.

What carpet there had once been in the hall was worn through to flattened threads, spider-webbing wooden floorboards. There were no decorations on the walls peppered with ancient Rawlplugs protruding like grubs; the interior had not seen paint or new wallpaper for decades.

A front room was choked with boxes and cases and shadowy humpbacks of junk piled over dim furniture. A dining room facing the garden had mustard-coloured curtains, red lino peeling off the floor, pale but dirty walls. Someone had broken the brick fireplace apart with a hammer but left the rubble on the floor, as if work had been abandoned as strength failed and futility numbed good intentions.

Moving up the narrow staircase, he felt the newel post and bannisters moving under his hand, and a sebaceous odour clung to the dark and warm space of the stairwell. The first-floor landing was the same, the smell even stronger, as if a hot animal had been driven indoors by the heat of the day and settled to its heavy respirations in the gloom.

Four doors on the first storey: all closed and painted a sickly vanilla colour. He thought they must open onto three bedrooms and a bathroom. Frosted-glass panes above each door suggested distorted views upon horrors selected and refined by what sparked inside Murray Bowles's vast and shaggy skull. The father imagined the ghosts of former tenants: an elderly working-class couple, retired from council jobs in Walsall, now shivering and aghast at time's remorseless disintegration, and its rehousing of villains inside their old home.

There was a solitary picture on the wall of the first floor, between two of the doors; a curious place to hang a frame, almost as if it was a warning of what inhabited the nearest rooms. He lit it up.

And recoiled.

A flat black, but somehow receding, background pushed out a figure in the centre of the canvas: a painted corpse. Naked and grinning, its ribs were exposed through the sickly green wash of its skin and the belly was hollowed out. It held up two thin arms and upon each hand was balanced what could have been a rose-coloured fruit.

The father squinted, moving closer. At the grey paps of the skeletal figure, lifeless babes swung, suckling. Three others seemed to squirm like larvae between the dead figure's legs. Ghastly cherubim, pallid and puffy, the infants looked up with tired white eyes. Below the babes were words within a small scroll: *Nihil. Nemo*. They meant nothing to him. Latin again, and an uncomfortable reminder of the graffiti in Paignton; here was another emaciated figure suggesting decline, perhaps even death with a hint of depravity. In the darkness, the father found the connection deeply disconcerting.

Sickened and disoriented, the father continued to frown at the picture with an appalled incomprehension, until a door was yanked open and banged against a wall beyond his torchlight.

He flinched.

Heavy feet bumped loose floorboards. Frantic breaths of animal excitement filled the unlit cave.

Behind you.

The father's torchlight raked the ceiling as he turned.

The blue lightning of smashed nerves erupted through one shoulder, and he fell forward, his arm dead. Pins and needles sparked in the pads of his fingers, at the end of his distant hand, swinging below the agony of his shoulder. The torch dropped, bounced, rolled, and shone sideways across dirty canvas shoes and a grubby ankle bandage: Bowles. The encroaching scuffles of the big feet filled his vision, until the father staggered away, across the dirty carpet.

Air whisked past his ear, ending in a plaster-gouging thud as a second blow narrowly missed his head. The air was then carved in two again, as a long weapon was pulled back high, eager to achieve its pulverizing designs upon his skull. A light fitting exploded on the backswing. This and the entanglement of the weapon with a light cord bought the father time.

He could see little, but with what remained clear in a mind traumatized by pain, he interpreted the location of his opponent's exertions and motions within the smelly passage, and shambled towards the end of the corridor and to the window as if to pitch himself through.

Big feet thumped after him, carrying the phantom whose rage seemed fuelled by the laboured breaths of this wounded stranger on invaded terrain. Another swipe of air, accompanied by a grunt, brought an object whisking close to the father's spine. Whatever was swung clipped his buttock then smashed into the heel of his booted foot.

After dragging himself the last two steps to the window, crazy and sick from the fire inside his shoulder, and now his heel, the father fell against the curtains. And knew at once that he was trapped. His skin iced all over at the idea of being smashed apart like kindling.

Foul fabrics issued a tomb's trapped fragrance. Distant light from his discarded torch glimmered about a bulk silhouetted a few feet before him. The figure appeared gigantic, grazing the ceiling and struggling to forge its vastness through the cramped passage. Again the ogre's club fell.

The father dropped until his buttocks rested upon his ankles.

Out smashed and tinkled the glass of the window above his head, the violence swaddled to a muffle by the wretched drapes.

The father rose from the gritty floor as the club was yanked free of the dusty impediments, whooshing backwards to prepare for another blow. His useful hand stretched itself towards the great shadow. And he sprayed, aiming for the boulder of a tatty head. A shoal of small droplets, an invisible rain, pattered over the colossus.

Down came the club as the ogre roared at the first sting of venom. The father launched his body under the falling club and struck a thick paunch with the shoulder not ablaze with pain. The ogre clutched at him. Fingernails grazed the father's nape like tines across pastry. And the two of them huddled, briefly, like worn-out wrestlers, held up on sweat-glossy shins, before the father slipped away, under a wet armpit redolent with farmyard scents, and hurled himself back towards the staircase.

Behind his noisy rout, the nerve agent's caustic sizzle

found fine tissues in the giant's yawning head. Puffy sinuses and fleshy tear ducts now blazed with chemical fire. There was a scream, a chaos of a living intruder alarm.

Enfeebled by the gouging pain inside his shoulder, the father stumbled down the first few stairs, then fell down a few more. In the torch glow, and through the bannisters, he glimpsed the bear-like shadow above, banging its great feet and swiping the air in rage, spitting out what burned its sinuses like inhaled cumin.

Inside the rucksack, the father's weak hand pawed about, an injured crab inside a disrupted rock pool. Finger-tips brushed steel cuffs, the ball gag, became tangled in a chain then freed themselves. His eyes implored the stinking darkness for help, but the torch was kicked even further away by the ogre's dance.

Towards the top of the bag, his fingers located the cold metal of the handgun, and spidered over the shape to find the handle, trigger guard, safety catch. Then he backed himself up the wall, dipping his face to shake it free of the tickling lines of sweat that slathered his cold, ashen cheeks inside his Balaclava.

Bowles stopped his rampage, bent double on the landing, and the father could see him clutching his wet face, as if the man were attempting to peel away the incendiary vines that smouldered so deep. The ogre spat, gargled and swore. Above these sounds of distress, the father listened for any signs that the neighbours had been roused by the breaking glass, the bullock bellows and wall thumps.

At the top of the stairs, the father found a light switch and clicked it down. Only one bulb had been smashed, but no light came from the second fitting. The power must have been cut, which explained the ogre's practised shuntings through the dark. 'I've a gun,' he called out. 'I'll shoot you through the mouth if you don't shut it.' The father's voice was weak and trembled from the pain in his shoulder. He pictured his torso was now rent asunder, with a scapula smashed like pottery, a collar bone leaking marrow.

'I ain't got nuffing,' the ogre cried out, before it took to dry heaving.

Another voice rose from beyond a closed door. 'Bowwy? Bowwy? You get him?'

There was another man inside the house, but the father did not know how this could be; he'd seen no one but Bowles enter or leave the building for days. He didn't know if he should bolt from the house or go for the torch.

The ogre ignored the other man and continued to cuss at its flooding eyes.

'Bowwy, Bowwy.' Again the voice, muffled in one of the first-floor rooms. 'I'm coming out. You get the bastard? Who was it? That junkie cunt?'

Slapping one hand against the walls and doors, the ogre slobbered and thumped away. Spitting, it finally fell at the bathroom sink and clawed the taps.

The father moved across the landing, shaking at the agony that was his shoulder, until he reached the torch. Some feeling was seeping back inside the dead arm. He pocketed the handgun and picked up the torch.

A second door in the passage clicked open. The father turned and shone the torchlight into a pale face that instantly recoiled like a sea creature, back into its stale darkness. The door closed.

Standing outside the room, he heard a scattering of objects beyond the door and guessed that the second man was going for a weapon. He glanced at the ogre on its knees in the bathroom, dousing its face and grunting. If these two men chased him, there would be noise and shouting outside.

'You want it? Eh? You fucking want it?' the second man cried out from inside the room.

The father slipped the torch under the armpit of his injured shoulder, whimpering at the merest movement of that joint, drew his gun and booted open the door. The torch shone through, but too low. He leaned his weight backwards, onto his burning heels, to raise the beam. Torchlight whipped across disordered blankets about a camp bed, a floor strewn with clothes, empty bottles, a screen on a table, an old wardrobe, and finally onto a bony face belonging to a small man with thinning grey hair, who wore a t-shirt with a stretched neck and underpants that sagged off his waist. The man held a glass bottle. 'Weren't me,' he said. 'Ain't got fuck all to do with me. Bowles brought them here.' The man then frowned, stupefied, as he took in more of the father's bush hat and Balaclava. Bending even further backwards, the father raised the torch into the man's eyes.

'You ain't the filth,' the man said, almost joyously, as if he'd bested the father at some ruse, before raising his arm to hurl the bottle. Without a thought the father shot through the torch's yellow glare.

The snarling face jerked. There was a brief hint of a small black hole, punched above an eye, before the back of the grey head scattered wetly across the messy room, like a handful of pebbles flung hard through a leafy bush.

The father lowered the gun and moved away.

Bowles now sat with his back to the toilet, a dirty towel pressed into his face.

Dear God. He'd just murdered a man while swept along in a rush of anger, adrenaline, joyous endorphins bathing his shoulder from the inside, and a reckless desire to destroy anyone who opposed his presence. The car was a long and terrible run away. Shots fired would sometimes bring a patrol car. The address wasn't in the town centre, where violence was habitual, but would righteous neighbours, sharing these hideous walls, know the sound of a handgun? He wondered all of this while aware of the wasted seconds. The weapon had made a short, dull, slapping sound and was hardly fearsome on the ear.

The father looked to the next set of stairs, which led to the loft conversion. A closed white door was visible. Feet retreated from behind it and lowered voices rumbled. But whoever was there soon fell quiet as if they knew he was listening to them. The father recalled a loft conversion seen from outside. 'Who is that?' he said to Bowles. 'Up there?'

Bowles stayed quiet.

Beside his foot, the father saw what he had been struck with: the polished handle of a snooker cue, unscrewed for demolishings in confined spaces.

Bowles peered at the father around the side of the towel, with one sphincter eye. 'What you want?'

The father had to swallow to speak. Still so deeply puzzled by his actions, he also needed to force himself to remember why he had come to this place where he had become so unwound, so quickly. 'Information.' His good hand opened the rucksack. Two of his shaky fingers found the photograph of his daughter. He went and placed it on the bathroom floor, stepped back, then retrained the handgun on the big man.

The father glanced again, over his shoulder, at the loft door when a bed strained its springs as someone above climbed onto a mattress. Curious, the father moved the torch onto the door and saw the padlock, then returned his sweat-stinging eyes to the figure on the bathroom floor. 'What am I going to find up there?'

'Nuffing.'

'That so?' The father wanted to fire the gun again before the police arrived, so that Bowles would never get away with what he had done in this house and in other places. 'The picture. Look at it.' The father shone the torch on the photograph. 'Lean forward and take a look.'

Bowles obeyed, then leaned back. 'I didn't take her.'

'Who did?'

He shook his head.

'Give me a clue or this might go off again.' The father shook the gun in the air.

'I tell you anyfing, youse will kill me.'

'Your friend's dead. I don't want to kill again, but I will. The photo.'

Bowles shifted about where he sat. 'You have to ask Rory about her.'

'Who's Rory?'

'He lives down the front. Says to me, he knew who done that one.'

Bowles's one available eye closed, issued fresh tears.

The father scrutinized the man's face. 'Second name? Address?'

'Forrester. Lives in one of them old hotels. The Commodore. You won't get near him though, cus he's mobbed up wiv the Kings.' Bowles smirked as if proud of even a minor association with this group: *Kings*. He was referring to an organized criminal gang, who would be running something in and out of the area: drugs, wealthy refugees, prostitutes, meat, medicine, like all of the other gangs; mostly stuff that was no longer manufactured in the country any more, or exported from others, which was nearly anything people wanted badly. Kings: they sounded familiar. Yes, they'd murdered a lot of people in Bristol.

'The Kings? More stupid pricks? How many stupid pricks live in this town? If I had known there were this many stupid pricks here, I would never have come in the first place.'

'You don't wanna know.' The figure's anal eye moved to the painting on the wall. Something approximating pride appeared in his plump face.

The father took out a pair of cuffs. 'Put these on. You can take me to Rory now.'

'No chance.'

'Better there than here.'

Upstairs someone had started to move again. Bowles glanced up, unable to conceal his concern. He then peered at the father and opened his mouth as if to explain something. The father shook his head. 'Cuffs.'

Obediently, Bowles cuffed his own hands, though as loosely as he could manage on his doughy wrists.

'Tighter.'

The father listened to the clicks as Bowles ratcheted the metal tighter. When the steel indented the man's flesh, the father lowered the gun. 'That door to the loft, where are the keys to the padlock?'

Bowles's swallow was audible. 'It was Nige who brought them . . . Anyways they like it here. Council says we gotta take in refugees, if we's got spare rooms, like.' The man's voice was almost a whisper by the time he completed the final sentence. Whatever he'd told himself about why he kept the attic door padlocked was losing veracity and validity the more he saw of the father's eyes within the Balaclava.

The father listened for sirens. Heard none. 'Keys.'

On the verge of tears, Bowles said, 'Please don't, mister.'

NINE

I am an imposter. A tired, so tired, father. An idiot with a spray can and a gun. A fool in a land of monsters, who took up arms and became a clown.

Lying on the bed, the spent muscles in the father's legs thumped with aftershocks. Furnace heat swelled from the baked and dusty ground outside the hotel and beat against its steel, glass and oven bricks.

The gun rested on the bed beside his knee, taunting him with estimations of his future: the years that must now be spent in a stifling prison. Unable to stand the sight of it, he used what little of his strength remained to zip the handgun inside the rucksack. Using a foot, he pushed the bag to the bottom of the mattress.

As soon as he'd returned to his room, he'd surrendered to his body's desire for stillness and for fuller assessments of damage sustained. Morning's searing light had already revealed torn trousers and bloodied knees, collected in the rout, and his forearms were blotted by cuts and striped with scratches. The pain in his shoulder continued to pulse through his left arm and across his back.

At least this strange passivity supplanted the riot of thoughts that had driven him through the early hours. Partial recollections of those intense, furious seconds in the darkness had lessened, then dispersed like a tired but once frantic crowd, to leave a curious calm about the wreckage in his memory. His body was loose-limbed but heavy now, flat, exhausted, and he was no longer the man who had done *that*. Whatever electricity had crackled along his nerves and roared through his blood had earthed itself. The hate-filled ape inside him had slipped away, in shame or astonishment, and gone back to the dark to leave a frail, shaken soul in its place. How many times would that creature have to come out shrieking before it cindered him, or refused to leave?

Pulling hard on the neck of a bottle of Welsh rum, he closed his eyes and prayed for this all to end, and for him to find, or bid farewell, to his daughter. Her picture lay on the pillow beside his head. Her father, he knew, had gone too far.

The father had now waited a long time for the throwing wide of the door. Even though he had shot and killed two men that morning, the police had not come for him. He'd expected their swift arrival, preceded by distant but encroaching sirens: the ancient song that trilled the blood's memory and alarmed ne'er-do-wells into fights and flights. But who knew what would even be investigated any more? And in the slow, hot hours behind drawn curtains, the father discovered ample time to consider his retreat.

After the killing was done, a man in the house neighbouring Bowles's unlit hive had come out of his back door, naked save for a pair of jeans. He'd turned his torch on the father: a bush-hatted felon in a scrapyard. The neighbour had confronted the father's wet, white face, and illumined a man aghast at his sudden commitment to terrible, irreversible actions. Right after he'd shot Bowles, the father had yanked off his Balaclava and been sick in the kitchen. A reluctant executioner with no stomach for what the world asked of him, he'd then dripped half-digested tofu Bolognese and DNA all through the crime scene. It had been the second killing that had rendered him witless and harrowed him ashen in a stranger's yard. He had been reborn a man permanently removed from the safe ground of a decency that he'd always taken for granted.

Just after the neighbour appeared, the father had launched himself at the rear fence, and careered over the crooked paving slabs on rickety, half-numb legs, his knees reduced to creaking hinges, his mind jumping with subliminal flashes: blooded flesh, white faces, loud voices, gun shots.

Bowles's neighbour, a father too, who had dared to brave all odds by bringing children into an old world down on its knees in the heat, and adrift upon its back in the floods, had quickly retreated through the back door of his home, struck dumb with fear and disgust at what he'd seen over the garden fence: the bush-hatted puker, the stumble-wreck killer, tripping his way to bustle through the fence's rotted planks like an animal affrighted in a pen.

To have made another father even more afraid of what lapped at the shores of every home in treacherous nocturnal tides now smote the father's heart as he lay alone in his hotel room. At this he felt a terrible shame creep through him, more than at the red deeds he'd performed in that dim nest of molesters that were never to be undone. For his own sake, the father had already assumed that the darkness of the ogre's grim halls would eventually settle into a persistent though manageable trauma, but that the family next door would have to linger in perpetual anticipation of another killer's arrival in the night.

Hours passed and the heat in the room broiled the father out of brief sleeps, basting him in an animal lard of remorse and misery, outlining his scarecrow bones with sweat, as a corpse leaves tracings in a winding sheet. He periodically gulped warm water from a plastic bottle, wincing. Even swallowing hurt his shoulder. Had he not been so lean, muscle meats and fats would have borne the impact of the ogre's club. As things were, the snooker cue had ricocheted off actual bone. Left him splintered and tattered: a messenger of judgement and death, but one ungraceful and ramshackle in the grim businesses he now conducted at the houses of men who ended childhoods.

He watched the foul flower of the shoulder bruise open in the noon light that spiked silvery-yellow through the solitary window. An indigo stamen grew upon his back: seeded, black-and-green-veined like a new tattoo, Japanese vivid. A pistil and petals, scarlet as roses, bloomed over his collar bone. The arm below was near-unusable, the skin curiously nerveless from the elbow to fingertips. A deeper magma of molten pain glowed from the wrist bones to his neck and threatened to erupt if he moved. The father imagined the X-ray that he could not risk having taken of the ghost bone in its darkness: a split humerus, the acromion reduced to debris, a skin-balloon of hot water fattened with pink jellies. But at least it was the left arm.

Accident and Emergency was a white glaring precinct inside his imagination, filled with husks, barely fluttering human moths on drips seeking hydration. He'd seen the footage. Even if he were seen by a nurse, amongst the kidney failures and bodies floppy with heatstroke, months of rehabilitation without the possibility of physiotherapy might yet be required for his shoulder.

He imagined his remaining funds squandered on private physicians, or the endless waiting at healthcare centres run by the NGOs. He suffered a clear premonition of indifferent medical professionals, the nurses, orderlies, porters, all twitching on amphetamines to stay awake, and beyond insensitivity to the death and misery the heat had wrought on a people already disrupted by riots, assorted head-smashings, clannish murders, poverty, shortages, rage, humiliation and mistrust: a maelstrom that had gathered momentum with every storm that lashed across the sea to Great Britain. There was no medical option, not for his work. If he fell in this business he stayed down.

The father swallowed two of the last eight painkillers: strong for headaches, irrelevant in the matter of smashed bones. He rinsed them down with the half-pint bottle of rum. Returned the bottle to the bedside cabinet, found his phone and called the last number Scarlett Johansson had used, and waited. And waited some more.

'What happened?' When her voice appeared in his ear it was so clear he would not have been surprised if she had been standing beside his bed.

The sound of the only voice in which he'd recognized understanding, sympathy and cooperation aboard his solitary voyage, made the breath catch in his throat. A woman who sent him to torture sex offenders was his only companion now; a person who pitched her words like a businesswoman with no patience for small talk. The closeness of her brought a great sob, like a gassy bubble, up through his chest.

'Are you all right?'

The father burned with shame at the sound of the grief that had bassooned from him. He swallowed hard to still the tremors of his vocal chords. 'I'm sorry.'

'Where are you?'

'Back at the room.'

'Are you hurt?'

'My shoulder.'

'What happened?'

'It went wrong. Things . . .' He blew air out, tried to empty himself of emotions so pickled and sour and yet still racing. 'The police will be looking for me.'

She did not speak for a while. In the pristine air of the connection he listened to the silence of her thinking. Finally, she ventured, 'Do you need a doctor?'

'Not sure. A broken bone, maybe. My shoulder. I'll wait till tonight, see if I can move my arm again.'

'Lot of nerves in the shoulder. One of the worst places to get hurt. Let's start from the beginning.'

He did and was forced to remember and recount what he had discovered in the attic: two unwashed faces above thin bodies, huddled beneath limp coverings, their tousled hair silhouetted by the torch and then lit up. Suspicious eyes had blinked, wide and smarting in electric light, in those young faces long-banished beneath that roof. Boys, who had been locked away in a space reeking of perpetual damp and subjected to monumental solar heat. The attic had been a triangular roofed cage, stunk out with sour flesh, piss in pots, kidney and ammonia, pungent underarms, assorted trash fumes beneath hot bin lids.

'It's OK now,' the father had said to the boys.

The small faces had merely watched him in an uncomprehending suspense. Neither looked English with their black eyes and sallow skin. They never moved, but Bowles did. Half-blind, and still cuffed, the ogre had risen from its bathroom refuge and hurtled its bulk down the first-floor passage.

Anyway, they like it here.

The father's horror became a billowing of hot blood within his skull. When the heat dispersed, it left him white and cold and jangly. But on newly swift legs, he'd run down the ogre.

He'd fished out the gun from his pocket, still eschewing the less lethal immobilizer option, and fired from the top of the steps as the moving bulk below turned the bottom corner of the stairwell, Bowles's big hand bringing a sound of splintering wood from the newel post. Halfway down part of a wall erupted like wet chalk.

The father bounded down the stairs, three at a time, the torch handle between his teeth, his eyes not moving from the white disc of light that guided his booted feet.

He caught Bowles in the back with the next shot as the big man bustled through the kitchen. Bowles flinched but barely slowed. The father didn't think the handgun was up to such a task, and re-aimed for the black streak ahead of him, moist and sticking to the shirt, taut across the broad back, and he pulled the trigger twice more.

The ogre at the far end of the kitchen lost his air after

those two shots, as if winded by a blow to the gut, and grunted liquescent, before stumbling against the refrigerator. But Bowles's big legs were not to be stopped and they kept on going, though with less decisive steps upon the patio, where he needed to rediscover his centre of gravity as if he'd just risen on old feet from a chair.

Despite merely walking through the hall and kitchen, the father found himself gaining on his quarry. His gun slapped again, a crack echoing against mould-speckled walls, the tinny sink and laminate-cupboard hollows, and a fresh small hole punched itself into the beast's flanks. Slap of a rivet. That bullet really punctured the leviathan, kidney or liver shot through that bled black and fast. The ogre had tried to move his bound, pudgy, tentative hands behind his body as if to touch the newest wound.

The father fired again and caught the side of the man's neck. A smoking hole dimpled the fatty ham, wet-slapping like a hand against a bug inserting a tube to drink. Bowles finally lost his balance and fell heavily, without a word, sideways into something metallic that clanged and scraped across the patio.

When the father came out of the back door, Bowles was already on one knee and about to push upwards like a weightlifter tugging a load onto his shoulders. The father aimed for the base of the big head, fired twice, maybe three times, he couldn't remember. But there were visible holes, big grunts, and Bowles lurched to hit the fence. His fists punched a plank out. Beneath his chest the cement pooled dark-oily. He made no further attempts to rise and only shivered in the warm morning air, while his cheeks and lips moved as if he was talking in his sleep.

The father returned to the kitchen so he would not have to look at what he had done outside. That morning was the first time in his life that he had fired a handgun: a device that no citizen should even hold, but that was something he realized too cruelly in retrospect. He had not been able to stop once he'd started; that was how it had felt, like he was an excitable baboon amusing itself with a deadly advantage happened across in a hunter's tent.

In trauma, his mind had become a red-black carousel, emitting rusty iron music, played backwards. The father had pulled up his mask. Nape and scalp pinpricking icy, his stomach had splashed all of its matter onto the lino. Bow-legged with nausea and punch-drunk from shock, he'd then gone outside and swayed about the filthy yard, aiming his body for the rear fence. Surprised by the neighbour when only halfway there, the father had tried to turn away when he realized his mask was gone, but had lost his balance and fallen.

The father had risen from his stinging knees and moved more quickly, to force himself through the split fence panels. By then his breath was a wind all around his head, and his eyes were flitting to the sky, the houses, the trees, the tarmac, his spattered boots, and would not be still. All of his clothes were wet through with sweat.

He still had the gun in his hand when he reached the car. The hand loosely cradling the torch swung limp under the planet of pain that bumped the side of his neck.

He hit at least two cars on the way back. Didn't have the wherewithal to activate the navigation and tried to drive manually, having to steer with one hand while going too fast, and crashed his way out of Upton, the car reduced to a tin can filled with mania.

The father swallowed. 'He saw me,' he said to Scarlett. 'The neighbour. There's sick in the kitchen.'

'You have a firearm. You never told me. Why? You have the evil shit, the immobilizer. What were you bloody thinking?'

'I got scared after Andrews.' On his first move, Malcolm Andrews had beaten him badly before he could get the spray into play. Afterwards, he'd wanted to command a greater range and more decisiveness, just in case. The immobilizer was an antique and only had one charge, was too all or nothing. Both items he'd been supplied with forced him to get close to his targets. Too close. He hadn't liked extracting the dart from Robert East's convulsing body either.

When he bought the handgun from a black marketer's armoury, stored in a mobile home in Stourbridge, he'd shuddered with genuine terror, but also shivered with a schoolboy's glee. From the point of sale, he'd suspected that, one day, the gun would go off in public. Guns really shouldn't exist, he now thought, hopelessly. But they were so plentiful; it was far easier to buy a gun than a pound of meat.

'Two? You shot two of them? Christ alive!' A momentary loss of nerve from Scarlett fanned the father's panic.

What had he been thinking? He'd been injured in a darkness only lit up by blooms of agony and panic, those curious undersea creatures of the head, greenish arachnids with tracery legs, flashing and vanishing. He'd been bushwhacked by the ogre. Another ghoul had then opened a door and asked for progress on his battering. Small footsteps had creaked in an attic. How did he explain the nightmare of the lair to his handler, all of those movements in the darkness? Because that was what it had been: a cavern, unlit and stinky, with caged victims who'd faced terrible futures inside a black humidity, and rubbings of unclean flesh that could arrive at any time out of a hot, eternal night.

'There were two of them. Bowles was waiting for me. He must have heard me get in. When the other one came at me . . .' He thought himself a boy, split from a cat brawl on a playground, buoyant and near-dreamy with adrenaline, trying to allocate blame for the presence of blood under a nose.

'The other one?'

'Bowles called him Nigel.'

'I'll check the name. And the boys, where are they now?'

The father swallowed. He tried again to remember what happened before he shot Bowles, to find a sequence amidst the abattoir jumble in his head. 'I found them, and . . .'

'What?'

'Then I chased Bowles. He ran. I shot him. I had to clear out. The neighbour saw me. The boys were still upstairs.'

'What about your mask? Tell me you wore the mask?'

'I took it off to be sick.' The father's voice lost its strength. He felt himself regressing as he sifted through the wreckage of the move, this burden of disaster he now shared with a friend who had given him a chance to find his little girl.

'Did he see you?'

'Yes.'

'Were they dead? Can you be sure?'

Dead. The word's weight had curiously evaded his full comprehension. Shock and revulsion had left little room for a consideration of the real consequences of squeezing a trigger. But the word fell through him like a crash of a great cymbal now. Reverberations harrowed his teeth and his very hair became erect with static, lifting upon a cold scalp at the presence of that word in his ear. *Dead.*

He'd put out two lives. Those little lights were doused prematurely the world over, every day, and in their tens of millions for some years. But he'd never expected to contribute to the great blackout, even in such dirty water as he forded now. Seeing the world, feeling its temperatures upon the skin, dreaming, thinking, all of that was now gone from two men. Even if they had chosen to revel in things that would sicken any decent heart, they would no longer breathe again.

'I think so.'

'You think?'

'Pretty sure. I hit . . . the first one in the face. Bowles a few times.' *At close range.* And it had been a determined and intimate execution with a pistol, as if he were some half-uniformed rebel in Central Africa, a place that surpassed even biblical depictions of hell. His gorge rose again as he thought of the blood from Bowles's pallid neck running dark on the greening patio. 'Oh, Christ.'

'I'll second that. But the first thing we do is stay calm.

Stay put. Don't go out for a while. Or at all, unless your shoulder is broken. If they have food and water downstairs, then buy that. I'll reach out and see what is being done. We can't even assume that the neighbour called the police, and someone needs to recover those children.'

He heard the descending note of disappointment in her voice. He'd said enough to ruin anyone's day, but still not enough. *Out with it all.* 'And . . . cars. I hit cars on my way out.'

Scarlett Johansson didn't say anything, but her silence was worse than any words. He could almost hear the ropes he dangled from being severed. She'd not work with him now, not again, and he didn't want to be himself any more. 'There's something else.'

A sigh. 'Go on.'

'Bowles. I questioned him, before . . . and he said a man called Rory, who lived at The Commodore, near the front, knew something. Rory Forrester.'

'Good work.'

He wanted to weep from the shred of quiet approval. 'The man, this Rory, he's mobbed up. With a gang, *Kings*. That's what Bowles said.'

'Bloody hell.' She said this under her breath, which made it worse. '*Them* . . . OK. I'll look into it. You get any hardware?'

'No. I was in and out in . . . minutes, I think. It seemed much longer, but they attacked as soon as I moved upstairs. There wasn't time for anything but a few questions. I sprayed Bowles. But if he hadn't run, if there had been no . . . no one in the attic, it wouldn't have happened. Any of it.'

'We didn't know he had company, but suspected he was active again. He must have been forming a new group. How is your head?'

'Head?'

'How do you feel?'

'I don't know. What you'd expect, I think.'

'You think you can manage to lie low?'

'Yes.'

'I'll call you when I know more about the situation.'

'This Rory, I need to move on him—'

'God, no. Don't even think about it. Bowles was a liar. A sadistic predator and a liar. It could be misinformation. I'll need to check this thoroughly before we do anything. And if this Rory is down at the front, it'll be problematic. Not even the local force will go down there any more, unless it's really serious. You're not an army and you are upset, you are hurt. You have to stay where you are.'

'I'm concerned about the time. We've never had a lead. And we have a name.'

'She's been gone two years. A few days or weeks will make no difference. Not now. I'm sorry.'

TEN

For six days he stayed in his room. Night and day he cradled his shoulder, and sometimes he wept; the joint and corresponding arm became a sick child, pale and huddled close to the parent's warmth and heartbeat. Tepid showers were the only highlights of each day, taken for one minute of bliss. But in the close heat of the room the sweat would immediately gather anew in his runnels, cracks, valleys and pits.

Most of the water apportioned to his room he drank from the bathroom tap. Each afternoon, he allowed himself one sink full of cold water so he could push his face to the bottom of the porcelain basin, with the wrist of his right hand held under the running tap to cool the molten blood that pumped close to the skin.

He shuffled between his room and the vending machine in the unmanned reception two floors down when he needed to eat. Every step made him gasp. The cartons of food were manufactured by his last employer, cultured micro-proteins he'd helped distribute years before, with a sense of urgency as world food prices rose and exports thinned. The dinners were flavoured and shaped to resemble foods once eaten in better days. Few improvements had been made to the product since he stopped working in logistics, a time he barely thought about now.

When his company began distributing the product fifteen years before, the father had wondered if, one day, he'd find himself eating the food originally intended for the starving: a heavily processed nutritional substance designed to supplement overseas food aid when the grain reserves dropped, then all but vanished. Producing bulk over variety had quickly become essential. But every synthetic foodstuff, produced by the country's untiring chemical plants, was now eaten domestically to replace meat and dairy products. Nothing reached the listless brown skulls of Africa, or the terrible encampments erected in southern Europe.

The meals in the machine were three times more expensive than those sold in shops, but he bought them and ritually heated his dinners in one of two microwave ovens in the kitchen area, then made a careful return to his room. By the time he sat at the little table, the food was cool enough to eat with a plastic spoon, though even the bovine movements of his jaw sent little shudders of pain into his shoulder. Shifting to sit or lie sideways, and constantly rearranging the spare pillow upon the bed that his body dampened, he made attempts to ease the relentless aches. Movement in the fingers of his left hand was the only good sign, and on the strength of that weak fist alone, he delayed any attempt to reach the hospital in Shiphay. The hospital was close to where he and his family had once lived, and he could not bear to look upon that hill again, or to see the silhouettes of the old houses march back into his memory.

When he managed to sleep, it was at odd times: noon,

from six in the morning until nine in the morning, for half-hour stretches during boiling afternoons to awake sweat-drenched. Or he took naps during humid evenings in which his own animal smell polluted the small room. On the third night he fell away into a void so deep, he awoke in the middle of the following day as the sun pushed its fiery red surface against the side of the building. Only to fall asleep again, or maybe he just fainted, to wake after midnight.

Whether patchy and broken, or long and seemingly comatose, his sleep came alive with things he feared were signs of a brain broken like crockery on a hard floor, then put back together in new sequences that barely resembled the original.

Awake, he filled the hours by watching nothing but news on the stations the room's media service offered. Old films and dramas, documentaries and comedies were available, spread across too many other channels as always, but for the last two years he'd allowed himself no entertainment, long ago deciding that he'd lost the right to leisure or pleasure. Anything composed of levity or trivia would somehow unbearably remind him of times he'd permanently lost.

Day and night, coated in sweat and periodically groaning at the metronomic pulse of pain in his shoulder, the father simply lay as still as he could manage and watched the stricken world.

Broadcasts told him that close to half a million people were thought to have now expired in the heat from the Mediterranean to northern Germany. The great fires had ebbed, then started again, then ebbed. The heat on the ground had made them impossible to fight from anywhere but the air, so they had continued to burn for a long time.

Broadcasts told him that the Egyptians had bombarded the Ethiopians again, and that the Ethiopians had shelled the Egyptians. The vast foreign farms in Sudan, Mozambique, Ethiopia, the Congos and Algeria had been ransacked again by the starving and the Islamic militia groups. Saudi Arabian grain convoys leaving Sudan had been attacked and looted. Mercenaries had responded. In the broadcasts a lot of dead people were lying in the various reddish soils of the African continent. A loose and volatile confederacy of rebel leaders had accused South Africa of hoarding food.

But what worried the father more than anything, what actually made him close his eyes, was the news that the sixty million hectares of arable land leased to foreign powers in Africa were now producing crop yields of grain that were down by sixty per cent.

The number made the father feel sick. Even the abandonment of most foreign-owned livestock and biofuel farming interests, two decades before, in order to grow drought-resistant grains, had come too late for Africa. The quick and irreversible slide into starvation, collapse and evacuation, across the entire continent and beyond, seemed as contagious as the two new pandemics.

A strain of SARS coronavirus was thriving in teeming Asia. They were calling the new bug SARS CoV11. Broadcasts switched between this and the Gabon River Fever in West, North and Central Africa, where cameras peeked through the side of shanty houses and viewed what looked like colourful sleeping bundles at rest on the earth. Towns of driftwood and corrugated iron were eerily still. Clumps of thin people lay against each other at the side of unsurfaced roads, unmoving. Men holding guns had rags tied around their noses and mouths. A child lay still against the depleted breasts of its mother. Bulldozers made great rents in red soil. Bodies inside plastic sacks were rolled into the pits. Black smoke fumed from pyres that men tended with long sticks like shepherds of old. An airport in yellow smog in Korea. Armed police and men in white suits gathered around grounded planes. Technicians squeezed liquid into trays from pipettes. Freight trucks idled at roadblocks. More face masks. China, the Philippines, Thailand, Nepal, Bangladesh, the east of India: they were all coming down hard and fast with the bug.

In other news, Russia and China expelled more of each other's diplomats and imposed new sanctions upon one another over Siberia. Not too far away, there had been another coup in Pakistan, on account of the long-term fresh-water crisis, where men continued to stamp on Indian flags with sandalled feet, strike their heads with their own hands, and kick up the white dust from the ground of their arid country, while a large group of Indian generals crowded behind a podium to face the press.

Eventually, by the fourth day of his confinement, the father preferred to sit in silence with the media switched off.

ELEVEN

Scarlett Johansson called the father at seven p.m. on the sixth day.

Naked, he was standing at the foot of the bed and slowly raising his left arm away from his body, sideways first, then to the front, as if he was performing some slow semaphore for landing aircraft. From what he could gather from the myriad online sites that he'd visited, his shoulder was probably not broken but deeply bruised; at worst the bone was chipped. If there was no fracture his left arm would still need to rediscover mobility before it seized. Around his arm and back, the red and black flower was turning green and yellow. Progress.

'The man you shot was called Nigel Bannerman. He and Bowles were tight in prison . . .' Scarlett listed the man's crimes and the father closed his eyes as they were recited. 'We reached out to sympathetic individuals in your area to check on developments. There is some good news: the case will remain open, but it will be absorbed into a variety of unsolved murders going cold.'

'Thank God.'

'You better had. The murder squad's caseload down there is unmanageable, so this will not be a priority. Possible causes of the double murder are currently revolving around politically motivated vigilante activity. Big nationalist support in the area. Organized crime hasn't been ruled out either, but no one fancies a loner for this, and no one on the job is demanding your immediate capture for clipping Bannerman and Bowles. They've known for a long time that sex offenders and paedophiles began clustering around the refugee situation, so my gut tells me the police won't be gnashing their teeth over a slight reduction in those numbers. Though I don't think killing is something you will ever be comfortable with. This cannot happen again. You do understand that?'

'It was never something I intended to do. What about Robert East?'

'He never reported your intrusion so we needn't fear a connection there. As for the others, Tony Crab now has dementia and no one is connecting this to Malcolm Andrews or Bindy Burridge, who still haven't reported you. Above-national-average rates of the usual are massively in your favour here, public disorder, domestic violence, rape, alcohol-related violence, gang violence, drug running, you name it, so the local force has more than enough to keep itself occupied right now.'

The father swallowed. 'The two boys in the attic?'

'Greek. No record of them entering the UK. Social services are going through the records of Greek nationals with refugee status, to see if they can trace any relatives. They may have been trafficked.' Scarlett Johansson didn't say any more. If his daughter had been trafficked abroad by a paedophile ring, his search was futile.

Millions had been displaced from southern Europe alone, augmented by further scores of millions from the

Middle East and Africa, and all pushing north into Europe. It had changed the continent. Every man, woman and child south of France was steadily fleeing drought, heat, starvation, the wars and innumerable diseases that accompanied each dilemma. The biggest migration of a single species ever known on the planet was underway, and it had never been easier for someone to go missing. One third of all the refugees were children.

The father knew how criminal gangs had found people willing to do anything to escape their own countries, and then escape the refugee settlements they found themselves herded inside. Gangs had found an infinite supply of defenceless, weakened, frightened and confused people upon whom they could force their will. He also knew from his own exhaustive research that the UN and Interpol's estimate of children being used in prostitution, in Europe, at the time his daughter was taken, was close to one million. It was anyone's guess how many more children had since become subjected to sexual slavery.

The father wiped the sweat off his face with a forearm. 'This Rory Forrester, what do you have?'

'He'd done hard time for rape and indecent assault as a youth. Got in with a gang in the south-east. And his last known occupation was trafficking. He was arrested and imprisoned for running Asian girls in London. Came out and drifted to Portsmouth according to his parole records. He's been off radar for two years. The local force had no idea he was even in the area.'

'But they'll go and pick him up?'

'Not likely if he's with the King Death gang. As I said, the police have a full plate with this lot already. The county is crawling with King Death gang activity. Illegal tobacco and drug farms on Dartmoor. Illegal pork and poultry operations. Bootleg cider outfits and people trafficking because of the camps, which are the most sought-after refugee destinations in Europe. The Kings are into everything now, everywhere, and taking it all over. Construction of the camps, land sharking to take over property for redevelopment, false IDs, any kind of contraband, gun running to the jihadists and the nationalists, car theft on a massive scale, black-market meat. It just goes on and on and on. Some in government think the problems they're causing should be a greater priority than the climate. And after the riots, the police and army abandoned the snatch policy in Torquay.'

'So he just gets to carry on? Like they all do. No one goes looking for them. The precedents have already been set. Jesus.'

'Not quite. He'll be investigated for sure. Eventually. When the resources and timings are right, they'll look for him. But you don't set the pace here. And neither do I.'

'But how long? When will this Rory be investigated? Are we talking weeks, months . . . or longer?'

'I don't know. King Death is a very nasty organization. Probably the worst gang now, in most parts of the country. They go back decades, as long ago as the fall of communism in Russia. Trans-national crooks to start with, smuggling imports with high rates of tax. They evolved into kidnap and ransom specialists years ago. You might even remember the kidnapped children of the solar field industry executives in 2036. That was them. There's rumours of dozens of other high-profile targets kept out of the news, who paid significant ransoms to get their executives back, and their executives' children back. That's how they made their biggest paydays until drugs, arms, food and medicine expanded the franchise. But trafficking has been the most lucrative business for them yet, in combo with where it bleeds into the sex trade.

'They've forged links with all the local elements that came in with the refugees, the Kurds, Serbs, North Africans. You name it. There is no single ethnic bias any more. When cross-border intelligence folded, it's anyone's guess how many of the hard core came here from eastern Europe. But Interpol believe they've upwards of eighty thousand foot soldiers in the UK alone now. These outfits are one of the few success stories from the last twenty years.'

The father, like everyone else, had seen gang members around the coastal places where he'd drifted, and watched them strutting about the better harbours, often outside the large homes he had driven past, beyond the towns; buildings they took possession of with huge sums of cash combined with intimidation. Lots of fat men, foreign and home-grown, taking ownership of the lifeboat island of Europe, shouting communications at screens, or admiring their own clothes and cars. Standing on long driveways, opening and shutting boots, or playing with dogs, seemingly laconic men, lazy in expensive clothes, drinking wine in the better hotels sealed behind high fences, their feet spread too far apart in arrogant contentment; men on loungers beside swimming pools. Swine dressed in whatever the French and Italian mills could still produce and sell at grotesque prices. The wealthiest and most important were never even seen; they had private grounds, penthouses, subterranean mansions and compounds with walls the father would never scale.

'I don't get it. Why would they kidnap my girl? We didn't have any money. Not real money. We didn't count. I was a regional manager. This doesn't make sense. For them to target us, we'd have to have something they wanted.'

'You're right, it doesn't make sense. And your guess is as good as mine. But look, let's not get carried away with hearsay from Murray Bowles. He probably only told you so he could intimidate you with his affiliations. If she was taken by a gang then she was taken for . . .'

'What?'

'Something we probably don't want to talk about. But that seems unlikely. It would be near-unprecedented for a gang to snatch a middle-class child from a middle-class area, with no prospect of a significant ransom. Your family does not fit the profile to lose a child to sex traffickers. It's not impossible, but it is unlikely with far easier catches in the refugee and substance-addicted populations around the fronts.'

Trafficked. She'd mentioned sex traffickers again. The father felt his soul slump to its knees at the merest suggestion of an international connection, of an impossible widening of the geographical area beyond that which he could hope to search.

'It's difficult to believe,' Scarlett added, 'but the police have almost no intelligence coming from inside the King Death organization, and they can't verify what testimony they do get either. But if there's a King connection, reprisals for snitching are very harsh. I want you to go and refresh your memory on the Bristol drug wars in 2047, so you can see what we'd be up against.'

The father clenched his one good hand into a fist. 'There are methods that are sometimes used to extract information. I have read about this. I know it happens.'

'Torture? Sure. For suspects of political killings, high-profile assassinations, terrorist links. But nothing will be pulled out of the bottom drawer on a rumour about a sex trafficker and one missing child. Yours is a very old case now.'

The father momentarily forgot the pain in his shoulder and ground his teeth. 'I'll do it.'

'You won't. You've done enough. This mess is containable, but anything else could see you caught, or worse. You cannot risk putting yourself anywhere near this group, because what happens then? You'd be risking everything, yourself, me, our work, and our assistance for others in your situation. This has gone far enough. I'm sorry.'

'We're close.'

'No, we are not. We have nothing concrete.'

'Bowles wasn't lying. I know it. I know he wasn't . . . He had this picture. It was horrible, strange. Not something a man like that would . . . I don't know . . . have in his house. A picture of death, I think. But it seemed to suggest something else, a connection. To King Death? Maybe. And this Rory Forrester is in with them. There must be something in what Bowles said.'

'How do you know? From pictures and some lowlife bragging about his mob affiliations? We'll need a lot more than that.'

I don't agree.

TWELVE

For the following three days, the father stared at a screen in his little room, searching, filtering, speed-reading, occasionally pausing to sit back, light-headed and nauseous from both the heat and the impact of the pictures and films he'd found. It had not taken him long to realize that if there was a King Death connection to his daughter's abduction, the odds had changed and the dangers had increased incalculably, perhaps enough to make him want to never leave the room again.

Distant incidents in Bristol, London, Glasgow, Cardiff, Leeds and Plymouth were refreshed in his memory: lists of casualties, and passport photographs of scarred, tattooed and emotionless faces of men who had done things to people that would not have been out of place in medieval battles. Deeds gradually accepted by the public with a numb resignation. Another unanticipated consequence of economic inequality, the refugee crisis, the repeated disruption from heatwaves, storms and floods; all opportunities for the gangs to fast-track their interests through extortion, bribery, kidnap, blackmail, intimidation and violence.

A relentless spate of face-saving revenge killings and turf wars had raged during the forties: throttlings, burnings, head shots, and beheadings. Each method of murder becoming a gang signature in a grim competition to heap even greater horrors onto a world already weeping with horror. But above all others, the Kings truly were the reigning monarchs of ruin, vice, corruption and murder.

He'd turned his face away from the screen at the sight of what they'd done in Bristol in '47. Members of the public had found the bodies before the police, then taken pictures and posted them: images of eighteen headless shapes with their hands tied, photographed on the carpeted floor of a terraced house. The victims had been people traffickers reluctant to submit themselves to a more ruthless tribe that favoured decapitation to make its mark in a terrible decade: a never-ending carousel of flame, black smoke, glass-strewn streets, bodies under tarpaulins, riot shields glittering in sunlight, placards, aerial footage of felled buildings in other countries, churning brown water moving too fast through places where people had once lived, trees bent in half, tents and tents and tents stretching into forever . . . And King Death flourishing in chaos.

A grinning bone figure fluttering in rags was a more aesthetic trapping the group boasted. And so insolent was their self-assurance, the foot soldiers even tattooed the figure upon their throats, or covered their entire backs with it, entwined with mortuary rolls, with deeds they'd performed cryptically scripted in Latin. On the street, or in prison, the ink was a better form of protection than body armour.

Independent journalists had long claimed that the group had never been properly investigated. If they murdered their own and members of rival factions, but not the general public, the neutral but overwhelmed police had apparently maintained a policy of 'containment and observation'.

The climate, civil unrest and terrorism were being cited by the Home Office as the priorities of the times; every other year there were evacuations of civilian populations from parts of the country newly, or more severely, ravaged by the weather. The standing army had guard duties and relentless patrols around power stations, crops, solar farms, factories of the synthetic food industry, and the gated communities, whose own private security operations constantly lured police officers and soldiers away for more lucrative work. There was the processing and management of the vast influx of refugees to be taken into account, the roads to be kept clear during evacuations from flooded areas. All of these things preoccupied the protectors of law, order and security. A person only had to watch the news for ten minutes to be convinced by the official explanations for why the country had been engulfed by crime, both opportunist and organized. Not even the wealthy were immune.

There was no escaping *them* now. *They* had been accepted, normalized, like too many other terrible things. And they were into *everything*, that's what Scarlett had said, particularly private industry and politics.

Always a folly, as well the father knew, to presume that people would forget the old world and make do with its salvageable, serviceable relics. Gangs supplied when others could not, or they hoarded the assets for themselves. To believe that ordinary people would go without meat and embrace grains and synthetics was a mistake; they'd known that in food logistics twenty years ago. Black markets were inevitable. People knew that what they wanted was available somewhere. People knew where they would rather be. People would pay anything for medicine if they had a sick child.

After the father had returned his daughter's things to the rucksack and the rucksack to the wardrobe, his hands were shaking. Closing his eyes and staring at a single point in the distance, he'd tried to wipe his mind clear of the images he had absorbed of King Death's victims, and of his own: the two were uncomfortably similar, like symbols on converging routes of a critical path funnelling towards a distant rendezvous.

When he felt better able to face an inspection of his equipment, he laid all of it out on the bed and reloaded the handgun. Then sorted out his last set of fresh underwear. After he'd dressed, he looked online at the satellite pictures of The Commodore, and the home of Rory Forrester, an affiliate of King Death.

Before he left his room, he left a voice message for Scarlett Johansson. 'I'm sorry . . . I am going . . . I need to speak to Rory Forrester, today. Whatever happens, no one will ever know that you helped me. I swear to you.'

THIRTEEN

As he walked to The Commodore, the father recalled the distant sight of the town and harbour, many years before, when he and his wife had first viewed Torbay from the sea while holidaying. They had boarded a ferry from Torquay to Brixham, and from the deck they had watched a vista of white buildings cover the cliffs and hills like a child's blocks: an imagined city, startling in the glare, masquerading as an El Dorado, a Tangier, or Pegeia, the moored pleasure boats and yachts heraldic, their masts the lances of knights assembled in the bay.

Distant crowds about the harbour might even now startle awake dim memories of old Cannes and Saint-Tropez, at least in those who once knew such things, from when this place had called itself a Riviera and had promised cold drinks to sip on shaded patios, bristling seafood platters, and the wearing of cool summer cottons upon salt-bleached decks. Even now, the many pillars of the former retirement and holiday apartments, all given over to the exodus from the flooded low-lying coasts, the swamped cities, and the first and most fortunate refugees, might still look grand from a distance, though from nowhere other than the air, or from far out upon the sparkling sea.

With every footstep through the outskirts of what

remained of Livermead's little peninsula, nearly all washed away now to the kerb of the road from Preston, the father clung to the shadow behind the vast seawall and moved east.

People milled and turned away, nudged the father, their faces challenging or unaware, constantly changing. One side of the long road, leading to the harbour, was black with shadow, and within such precious shade many figures huddled. They were mostly foreign and unwilling to spend more time than was necessary inside the camps, the crowded chalets further east, or in their noisy housing blocks inside the town. Old wheezy buses, and a few cars, passed slowly on the single carriageway.

The crowds. Whenever he encountered them, the crowds added a sense of futility to his quest that was near-unbearable, and he would swallow his despair like a lonely seabird with trash in its gullet. Because no scene remained static, none was ever replicated in any exactitude. Streets and roads, towns, villages, cities, were endlessly repopulated, with more and more faces filling smaller spaces all of the time. People learned to look above so many heads, and inside themselves, to escape the burden of such numbers, this cognitive tonnage of multitudes. So where, inside such numbers, was one little girl with startled blue eyes, jet-black hair that she'd inherited from her mother, a skipping walk, and who was always so quick to cry when frightened? *She was only four and so small when her feet left the soil of her home.*

How would one tiny face be remembered now? Hundreds of thousands wandered these paths every day, came and went, vanished. A mind could not store so many faces in an incalculable array of moments, left behind within so many days, weeks, months, and years.

Two years.

There had been no eye witnesses the afternoon she was abducted. Not one.

No one else is looking for you now. Only Daddy.

Someone had to speak up, either someone who had been present and helped sweep the small figure aloft, or someone with secret information. They needed to whisper soon, or spit the story from a reddish, tooth-splintered mouth, to lead him nearer to *the one*.

Did you cover her little mouth, or drug her? Did her eyes ever open again? Did they open and see a monster? Did a heart no bigger than an egg break open, as the gulf widened between that garden gate and her dark eyes?

For every tear she shed, I will pluck my retribution from your living flesh. Her terror and her anguish will be yours.

The father walked deeper into the harbour and forced himself to put away those thoughts that still came most days, and which turned his head bloodless and wooden, like a carving that grimaced through the pain of old regrets. Everlasting was the agony of such remembrance.

No coastal paradise here either now. The father might have become a wanderer in ancient times, put ashore in a sweltering hive of pirates, slaves, cut-throats, urchins and pickpockets, the dusty and desperate, wide-eyed beseechers and apostles of mutating faiths, increasingly confirmed by the signs of the end of times; all driven here from places baked to clay and burned to dust, arriving at a town besieged and battered by a remorseless yet increasingly lifeless sea.

Few but the young offered smiles to each other around the high-walled harbour, as they slipped and side-wound about the thoroughfare, beneath sun-desiccated buildings that the Victorians had erected and never envisaged so begrimed and peeling as they were now, two centuries after the coal furnaces and fires of the Industrial Revolution belched.

Above the harbour he saw the long wounds of cliff erosion, interspersed with the white rubble of the tower blocks that came down years before, when the rains moved the topsoil in red gouts and gushes of clay rushing to the sea. Abandoned clifftop buildings, standing like potential suicides with toes aligned at the edge, gaped eyeless at the treacherous bay that had thrashed them with storm winds and tidal surges, so many times over so many years. The town had not been abandoned, not yet. Scarred and fragmenting, it still teemed, because there were fewer and fewer other places left to go. But when would all of this be finally washed away, he wondered, and its foundations bleached like beak-broken shells?

Men watched the father from where they leaned against walls and beside doorways about the marina, surly sentries beneath holed signage that once offered discos, swimming pools, fish and chips. Above the signs reared the relics of neo-classical arches, cupolas, grimacing stone balconies and other bourgeois pretensions. When he met the eyes of the men, they turned their heads but left the father with the impression that they were not uninterested in his presence.

Smells of fried soya, oil, home-grown sugars, beery carpets sun-warmed and aromatic, and sounds of vintage electronic music drifted about the crowds, the stifling air additionally thickened by sweat, sea salt, and sewage. Great gulls with horrid beaks and expressions reduced to simple, functional cruelties, seemed keen for those below to stumble and fall. Their guano created a messy stucco down the drainpipes and pebbledash.

All around the inner harbour, and the vast concrete seawall that blotted out the murderous horizon of water, the father sidled and ducked through the drug sellers, the palms of his hands raised like closing doors. Offers of cocaine, amphetamines, ecstasy, heroin, mostly home-grown and cooked now, were whispered like forbidden, mystical words from a motley of teeth-flashing diviners and soothsayers: Arabs, Africans, Greeks, Spaniards, Turks, Algerians, Egyptians, the red-faced, heat-blasted English, all muscling and sweating about the sea front, before the pubs and ice-cream concessions, the cannabis cafes, and those restaurants still open and selling imitation meat and fish concoctions.

Everyone was a farmer now. How much you could grow and how large the marrows, fruits and root crops were the new obsessions, and the new competitions now that designer baubles and flashy interiors were not an option for any but the *two per cent*. About the fringes of the legitimate market – offering fruit and vegetables, grown on front lawns, roofs and excavated patios, all local produce the wooden boards claimed, and a surplus from the country's new breadbasket as the east coast slowly sank beneath the waves – bootleg booze, exotic prostitutes and drugs waited inside yet darker rooms.

Clothes were recycled and sold here too. Remade, homemade, washed and heaped upon trestle tables, as were stolen and bartered electrical goods, and the agricultural tools made in the new industries of the Midlands. Stores had been commandeered, or leased through favourable terms by the belligerent, militant councillors, and now sold and resold the junk-shop fare of things no longer produced or imported. He'd seen the same in Totnes, Plymouth, Exeter, Brixham, Bristol and Bath: open-air markets encroached upon and infiltrated by black markets. Farm workers, itinerants, the resettled, foreign and domestic refugees, drug addicts, more alcoholics than he believed possible in any single place, had all now gathered where holidaymakers and retirees once flocked.

The father wasn't hungry but bought a sandwich, the filling burning with local mustard, and a bottle of orange juice squeezed fresh by Portuguese refugees in a distant grove on Welsh land where sheep had once grazed. And then he moved up the road into grimy Torre to find The Commodore.

He'd tried to visit the place two nights before, but the streets were too busy with unpleasant antics. Earlier that morning, he'd driven through quickly too, as the sun's fire licked the horizon, and he'd glimpsed the closed doors to the old hotel as he passed by, while trying not to look at the building. Up here, there was nowhere safe to leave the car, so he'd attempt an infiltration on foot, and he'd be unmasked until he was inside.

In two hours the heat would make this climb up

through the town near-impossible for all but the fittest, and would drive the irritable hustling crowds of the town and harbour back indoors, like wasps into the holes of a brick wall.

When he arrived at the warm buffets of lingering waste, one mile above the town and sea front, someone with TB coughed as if in warning like the bell above the door of a shop. The sound gruffed from the innards of a boarded-up building with no front door, which had once sold gifts to families on holiday. Damage from the winter riots had not been repaired this deep into the town, or even been cordoned off. Charred bones of timbers protruded through the red-brick musculature of once-white hotels and local businesses. The sickly, chemical taint of an old blaze hung over the sun-dappled ruins. By the day's relentless light, the father could see how the anger of the displaced and jobless, this purposeless mass, had punched itself drunk against the masonry and timber that tried to corral it here, before pissing up the ruins.

From shadow to shadow, with his chin dipped, the father sluggishly nudged himself upwards, engulfed by fresher and fouler exhalations from the very buildings, alleyways and cramped pavements: a dying town's breath that he could taste, emitted with an air of bitterness that could only become hate, sublimation, or the shame of a poverty that grew to madness. Under a peculiar gravity the father's spine succumbed to a curve, as if in holy reverence of the wretchedness heaped about him. How could spirits ever raise themselves here? They all clung to life but gave it little value.

The colony of addicts founded in Hele had long ago

reached this far south and then swelled into every available room and beneath any vestige of shelter. To think he had crept down to the coast too, with a wife and baby, to start again, and to flee the human ruins deposited and multiplying in the cities as the economy collapsed. But the incapable, unemployable, transient, feral, vulnerable and hapless, the dispossessed and broken, the abandoned, had been barely contained by other regional authorities and they had already been taking up residence in much of South Devon before he arrived. *They* waited on the other side of every town now, just over the hill. They were everywhere, the wretched, and their numbers would only grow. And yet here he was, a tired man of no funded or legitimate occupation, sifting through human and structural debris, looking for a stolen child. He wanted to laugh loudly and freely and madly like the ragged pockets of intoxicated sots about him, who even now, in such appalling heat, burned themselves towards a new day's sprawling confrontations.

About the former hotels, restaurants and luxury apartments, all transformed into a grubby sprawl of hostels, the eyes that regarded the father seemed bereft of anything but cunning or resentment. Distinctions between men and women were not always clear. Faces had been carbuncled into unique formations of bone and scar tissue from falls, sun-blistering and fights. Baseball caps trammelled down unwashed hair above the rusticated, sunken faces of the drink-embalmed and weather-mummified, who were yet still living. Soiled clothes in the wrong sizes, caped by old jackets given out by the Red Cross, formed the uniform. A species successfully crossing with the rodent; perhaps a farsighted evolutionary leap towards becoming envoys for the future, when the planet's aridity seeped further north.

From either side of a front path leading to a former bed and breakfast, two desperate prostitutes who no longer made much effort offered pained smiles made grotesque by missing teeth. But the father made sure not to meet any of the eyes that peered at him. Any twist of distaste around his mouth could ignite a rampage of dirty shoes, scuffling into the curious dances of mayhem. But nor could he appear intimidated. Indifference and preoccupation with other matters were the arts and wiles the less desperate had learned in order to avoid interaction in places such as this.

As he neared a crossroads, a termite hill of cheap concrete high rises reared on his right: the Beach Haven Estate, thrown up ten years ago for London's East Enders and the impoverished Spanish, but just as quickly maligned into one of the ten worst places to live in the country. The flats were his landmark and one he'd noted as an approach to The Commodore, now partially concealed upon a hill on his left side, amidst other former hotels, and the dusty, motionless palms.

At the back of what had once been a Chinese restaurant, now trying its hand as a surgery run by a charity, he showed a collection of dirty children a carton of chocolate, while not at all insensitive to the irony of his tactic. If Bowles's testimony had been correct, the local young may well be familiar with Forrester as a dispenser of praise and favours. And as the children brushed against the father's pockets and his rucksack, offering cheek and challenges and lots of spit to plop near his shoes, he wondered out loud about his old mate, Rory, at The Commodore. Was he on the second floor or the third?

'He's first floor,' one of them said, unthinking, as the father peered at The Commodore, a 1930s town house converted into a hotel, and in turn into a flophouse for parolees, then refugees, and finally used for new purposes the council and police had lost track of. And there it was again, upon a wall: King Death, rising in black rags, grinning, spray-can-etched between two ground-floor windows. Its long arms were flung wide, daring the foolhardy to come closer.

The eyes of the other children now moved subtly to watch the two teenagers on vintage bicycles who had appeared and were circling the small gathering, their two-wheeled mounts artfully remade by oily-fingered tinkerings with scrap. The faces of the teenagers were near-permanent sneers, browned rictuses beneath the peaks of baseball caps: a default setting. The bicycles creaked closer in tighter circles but never stopped, and the riders never addressed him. The father moved away from the crowd, but it followed him.

He kept his hands deep inside his pockets, wrapped around the nerve gas and the stun gun, ignoring the first tugs on his shorts and rucksack, before he shrugged off another set of more insistent fingers that flicked the end of his watch strap in an exploratory fashion. He increased his stride away from the medical centre and climbed concrete stairs to a car park filled with rubbish that curled around two sides of The Commodore.

The children waited in the car park, amused at his entrance into the warm darkness of the building, as if he were an imbecile about to attempt some feat that had already defeated a multitude. There were no cameras here and the father wondered if he could risk showing his face to the kind of men who would never report him to the police.

And around they went, stamping their feet like a pair of heat-enraged apes. Palms slid over slick flesh, clothing was gripped and yanked uselessly in a dance of two drunkards, prison lovers enraptured. The father was the younger and fitter of the pair; Rory's senses were dulled by the alcohol he reeked of. But neither was a natural street fighter. There was little evidence of coordination or balance, scant progress made in the scratching, or from the dull thumps of fists pulled free and swung, or much control amidst the cussings and grunts of these rough-trading beasts.

In the melee, Rory's teeth had twice closed on the father's face and he knew the man was straining for his nose, or a lip, with those Neolithic teeth, browned at the root and yellowed like corn at the tip, as if from chewing an Iron Age diet of nettles and seeds. Rory's head itself seemed newly resurrected from the dawn of human settlements in the area, a crude skull found in a clay pit amidst shards of broken pottery, but now tight with ruddy, sun-spotted skin, suggesting a new regression – from ape to reptile.

Together, they eventually fell towards the bed as Rory turned within the father's arms and slid to his knees as if to cover his head, before curling into a ball.

From where the nasty little blade was then so swiftly procured the father had no idea, but Rory brought it up fast and into the curtain-shrouded room. The father put out a hand, as if to stop a thrown ball, and his hand pricked painfully, and then something slipped deeper through the meat of his palm and pushed apart the finger bones. Punctured and airless, he yanked himself off the skewer, and fell away.

Rory came up to his full height. His eyes, spider-webbed with blood vessels, flared with excitement, with delight. He stepped to the father, swiped the blade through the air at the level of his throat. Then paused, grinning, only to feint and jab at the father's ribs. The father caught the older man's scrawny forearm in mid-air with his blood-slippery hand, and gripped the loose, chilly skin, felt it move over muscle like a fish plucked from shallow water. Tugging Rory closer, he kicked out and his instep struck his opponent's knee.

On impact, Rory's face drained grey. He swore, pulled free, and after a laboured hop, reassigned his weight to the other foot.

The father tucked his sliced hand, dripping warm and dark red to the elbow, under his other arm, and moved back to the door of the room. Outside, he heard footsteps on the stairs, and not only one pair. A crowd was gathering.

Thick heat swaddled his brain. He could have been mistaken in believing that Rory had been waiting for him in the hot gloom of the first floor. Perhaps a call had been made from the street, because Rory had been sat on an old sofa in the communal area of the landing, his hair still mussed from a long, hung-over sleep. A mad king on a red velvet throne, waiting to give an audience to a messenger from beyond his fiefdom, he'd even smiled at the father as he climbed the last few stairs to the first-floor landing, as if they were old friends, and asked, 'Who is you looking for?'

'Rory Forrester,' the father had said.

'What you want him for?' Rory had asked, and the father had known who he was speaking with.

'It's private.'

'Who is you?'

The father mumbled something about being a friend of a friend from the prison he knew Rory had served time in, and that he wanted some business with Rory, because he knew Rory was a man who might be able to hook him up with *something* that he had buyers for. During the brief, tense exchange, the father had looked about the landing and at the fire door, the three closed white doors, and the window facing the new sun that partially blinded him and concealed Rory. Below him in the stairwell, he'd heard footsteps enter the building, possibly those of the curious children.

'Where you from?'

As he stepped closer to the sofa, the father told him he was from Brighton. 'You're Rory?'

'So what you after exact?'

'A couple of kids. White.'

They'd gone into one of the rooms, and one so chilled by air conditioning the father had felt momentarily unwell. And in that moment of disorientation, Rory had turned quickly and tried to headbutt the father, who'd blocked the impact of the big red face with his forearm. The force of the fierce, scruffy head had still knocked him back against the door, which slammed shut.

The father had yanked out the stun gun and fired wide, the dart crackling off into the half-light, and Rory had closed with him before he could free the spray canister from his other pocket. And around they had gone, slapping for purchase, for eyes, ears, throats, testicles, desperate to keep their feet and find advantages or weapons.

Now, Rory could only spit and curse at the pain in his knee. In a bark more than a voice, he said things to the father of such ugliness that the father felt his deepest disgust for the man yet, and he unzipped his rucksack with his uninjured hand. Delving inside, he found the handgun quickly, then introduced the final shit into Rory's immediate future. 'Yeah?' he said and walked at the man.

Abruptly, Rory shut his prehistoric mouth, but the father still wrestled with a hot and bulging urge to shoot the hoary face at point-blank range.

Rory threw the knife onto the bed and held one arm out, while the other hand remained clutched at the injured knee. The proffered hand wavered, was stained yellow, rough-palmed. 'Bowles,' Rory said, in a fuller comprehension of the situation. 'He grassed me up. For what? I ain't done nothing. Not wiv kids. That's why you is here, from them Nazis? I knew it was them that done Bowles, but you is barking up the wrong tree here, mate. You got the wrong man. I ain't no nonce.'

Slipping two fingers inside the man's nostrils, the father pigged Rory's nose. Pulled his gnarly head back and shoved a knee in the nape of his neck. Made him slobber like a sow in soils dung-plastered. Rory's face, held to the chink of daylight, was synthetic corned beef, purpled and reddened with rashes and broken blood vessels. He smelled as winey and ethanol-soaked as newly varnished wood. His neck was tattooed with a spidery black King Death draped in rags.

The father managed to speak through ragged breaths. 'You know who took a little four-year-old girl, in 2051.' The father said her name, but with difficulty, as if the stench and squalor of the room could stain her precious memory. 'You were part of it.'

'Nah-ah. Not me.'

'Your name's coming up.'

'Weren't nuffing to do with me. Let go.'

'Liar.'

'I know who you want, but s'not me. Not Bowles. You got the wrong people.'

'Tell me what you know or I'll fuck you through the ear with this.' The father burrowed the end of the handgun into the man's earlobe. His left shoulder screamed for relief, the hand below was now a purple dirigible, dripping burgundy syrup from four fingers.

Rory's eyes rolled, his skin going sallow. 'No. Mate. You's got the wrong man. On me mother's life. Let me up. I can't breathe. My neck . . .'

'Tell me what I ask or I'll disable you. I'll start with your ankles, work my way up. I'll fuck you up, then shoot you through the eyes, prick. And in hell you can ask Nige and Bowwsy where bullshit got them.'

''K, 'K, just let me up.'

The father took his fingertips out of Rory's enlarged nostrils, which the man immediately seized and tried to claw back into shape. Tears spilled down the seared cheeks and blood returned to the mottled forehead. 'I just heard fings, like.'

The father watched him, kept him covered with the gun. He'd developed a good eye for contrived bids for sympathy and remorse.

'It was in a pub, like. Dolphin. Ages ago, like. In Exmuff. Ain't even there no more. But people was saying she was took to order, like.'

The father nearly swooned, and almost smelled again the fragrance of shampoo and the warm perspiration in his daughter's hair, where he burrowed his face after she woke and curled upon his lap and watched cartoons in the living room, before he buttered her toast and poured milk onto crackling cereal. 'Which people? Names.'

'Was a fella called Alexis. Big fella, like. Him and this guy I didn't know. His mate. Was called Boris, I fink. Ruskies. I was helping them with a fing. Booze and pork that was coming in froo Plymouth that the navy didn't know about. And they was all pissed up. We all was, like. And they watched this fing on the news and they looked at each other. I caught it, like, this look they give out. And I was saying something about what a shame it was, cus she was such a nice-looking girl, and all that. Then Alexis says she was took. Kids get took all the time, they said so. Ransom money. Someone else told them it was done that way. Stole to order, like.'

'Who told them?'

Rory shrugged. 'They didn't say no names. You don't ask questions to people like that. They was full kings. It don't go down well. They's fink you is a grass.'

'There was no ransom demand. The parents were not wealthy.'

The shrug again, twinned with a show of fear belied by the loquaciousness that was now coming too easy. *Acting out*. 'I never seen nuffing but that picture on the news. Sweet girl, I thought. Lovely girl. Kind of face you remember. I ain't fenced or trafficked for years, like. Totally gone off all that. We's all make mistakes. Don't mean you can't change. Kids was never my fing anyway. You's making a mistake right now, finking I took her. On my mother's life, I swear to you I had nuffing to do with this.'

'What do the people in your *community* think? Men in your trade, who also made your *mistakes*? Men who kidnap children? Men who'd sell anything to the nonces?'

'Nah, nah, nah, you's got me all wrong, like. And the kiddie groups that was still down here then, the rings, like, didn't have nuffing to do with it. Wouldn't need to buy no one like her neither. Too risky. Why'd you take someone like her when there's thousands down the coast in them camps? No one's watching them. They's could take their pick, like. Why go into someone's house and pinch a kid? Fink of the risk of somefing like that. I'm not saying there's not some who might do it, ones that is a bit cracked, like. And if it was one of them, then she had no chance, and you is wasting your time. But that was a snatch to order, Alexis said, so he must have heard somefing, like. Alexis was into all kinds of fings. He was running them brothels they busted in Bristol. Bringing in the girls an' everyfing. He knew if they was snatches, or if they was just pervs taking kids. He would have heard somefing, like. You go up a drive and snatch someone's kid out the garden, like, when her mum and dad's back is turned, then you is fearless or you is desperate. Stands to reason. You ain't in control, or you got the stones to take what you want anytime, anywhere.'

The father found Rory horribly convincing, despite the lack of specifics. In the first lightless era of his own grief and despair, when he'd considered the whys and hows, his instincts had suspected a loner, a predator, an opportunist, deranged by its urges, who had seen them out and about as a family and followed them home after biding its time. Scarlett Johansson had always thought the same. 'These Russians. Where are they?'

'Who, Alexis? Don't know what happened to him. He ain't around no more. But they's all over, Kings. They's running most of the coast now. Dover froo to Plymouth. Police won't take them on. Too much grief. But you needs to ask them, the King hard core. I can hook you up with some. I got *friends*, like.'

'Then you're coming with me, out this door, right—'

And then the father realized Rory had only been so forthcoming, and so emphatic and loud of voice, because the corridor outside had fallen ominously silent, until the moment the door opened quickly. And before the father could turn about, the very air behind his head exploded white and his ears whistled like the whales that once drifted in the cold darkness beneath ice flows long vanished. His final thought, before his hearing whined beneath clods of muffling, was that he had been so close. That at last he had names. Two names: Alexis, Boris. He'd had something, but now he was going to die.

A sense of his daughter bloomed bright then diminished like a spark.

The father turned so sprightly, his finger squeezing the trigger as his heels swivelled, and as his hand pointed in outrage at the thin-headed youth, who had kicked in the door and blazed near the father's ear, but somehow missed in its excitement and nerves, with the gun held out sideways as if the youth was some hip-hoppity gangsta of old.

The father fired through the eye-stinging smoke that wreathed the doorway and made the figure shake as if electrocuted. The bony head clicked back and threw matter noisily up a wall, mercifully unseen in such poor light, and from its thin and angular silhouette the father knew he'd put out the mind of one of the teenagers on the bicycles.

The smaller shadows about the dead boy's legs that had gathered to gleefully watch death, though not this one, scattered and bump-slap-bumped down the stairs like the frightened children they actually were.

A shuffle of motion sensed more than heard in the room behind brought the father back around and into a crouch with his gun held out and his second hand gingerly supporting the trigger hand, like he had learned on how to steady a weapon. Rory was up and coming, with the recovered, and now flashing, knife, but already taking a lurch into the gun's ultimate purpose at a very favourable range. The father said, 'Stop.'

But Rory was not for stopping, and probably knew he had no choice after what was fetched out of Bowles's place on stretchers, all skull-shot and liver-punctured. And if it hadn't been for his kicked-in knee, Rory might even have reached the father and slashed about his face with his mean blade. So the man just came on, gibboning like some old, half-lame troglodyte enraged in a cave mouth. The gun coughed and Rory stumbled, a hand immediately at his throat that gargled like nothing human.

The father had aimed for his chest and momentarily wondered how far astray the first shot had gone. And in an urgent desire to not hear the wet wheezes from the devastated throat one moment longer, the father went and stood behind the figure, now stooped over and dripping into the sink, and he shot a black smoky hole behind its big red ear. In the mirror on the wall, Rory's cheek flowered black rags.

The father turned away and wiped his face.

Outside the room, doors were opening, slamming shut. Out of the hot, coppery darkness of The Commodore came rough voices rising. Feet boomed on the stairwells.

A gun barked twice. Plaster cracked and spumed dust ahead of where the father stumbled. He'd ducked late, after the shots had already found the wall, and fell at the bottom of the stairwell. Putting a hand down to break his fall, red lightning struck through his eyes at the movement of the fine bones in his bulbous paw, stabbed deep by a rapist and slaver.

So wet was his injured hand now, and dripping with his own outpourings, it might have been immersed in a bucket of oil to the elbow. The father could not make a fist and whimpered with pain as he rose to his feet, and started for the front doors. They were open and a white glare illumined the tatty woodchip walls, torn linoleum, yellowed safety instructions that he staggered past to get outside, and into the afternoon inferno. His breath steam-trained in and out of his chest, his knees clashed together and his feet were scuffling.

Above him in the building a voice shouted, 'Pack it in,' in response to the shots fired. The father had not heard the phrase in years, but familiarity brought no comfort. 'You's'll bring the filth in!' followed the first order. 'Finish him outside. Round the back.'

'He's done Rory,' someone else shouted, outraged in a distance muffled by the walls.

The father fell from the front door and waved his gun in the sudden volume and brightness of the air that engulfed him. He wanted the crowd at the perimeter of the car park to see what he was holding and ready to use.

Small figures scattered like cats into the scrub of dry flower beds around the edge of the tarmac, puffs of sand heralding their retreat. Three boys slid over a low concrete wall. Taller figures reared back, tensed, or crouched, but didn't run. A sharp-nosed, ferrety face under a baseball cap spoke quickly into a device, one finger plugged into the other ear, like a soldier calling in reinforcements or the coordinates of the enemy's position. Behind him, men bellowed and thumped their way down the stairs and into the reception of The Commodore. Shoes slid as they slowed near the doors.

He trotted backwards, away from the old hotel building, his gun sights wavering all around the door of the front entrance for the first man to come through. *Shoot eight times, count them. Last one in your mouth.*

The father turned in the car park, his feet dragging

across loose stones, and the world wheeled through his jittery vision. He couldn't run back into town, or push up into Upton, Barton or Hele on foot; those places were too crowded, and he imagined doors and windows being flung open as he stumbled in the street, and long queues of people behind him, keeping pace, running him to ground until the bullets were gone.

The sun got inside his thoughts and scattered them like the ruminations of the sun-blinded and heat-stroked. Images from news footage of the riots, all of the ones he'd seen over decades, came into his head: stripped bodies like inert seals on the sand, grubby and leaking black, face down in the streets; charred bones raising thin forearms from the skeletal interiors of cars, still asking for help in grinning death.

The father looked to the hill above The Commodore's roof, tiered with grubby white or red-brick buildings. Steep ground offered a variety of walls and gates that would have to be scaled with yards to run through, but at least there were trees up there to crouch behind, winded. The town was made of hills, so uphill then, and all the way in this heat, maybe under fire from below? To get where? The father caught sight of the sky, blue-white and silvery, reflecting the heat back at his face like a vast sheet of polished tin. His hat band was sopping. This was it.

He had names . . . *Alexis, Boris* . . . was closer to *her* than he had ever been. Or was he? The information could all be bullshit from some old slags in their dung heap.

But if Russians had snatched her up, then why? No ransom demand. To be trafficked? *Child prostitution. Gone away forever across the sea. A chain, a tiny bed, and her little head too broken for tears.* 'God, no,' he roared, and his voice seemed to frighten the youths more than the handgun that he waved in the air. You couldn't mimic that kind of pain, the total mindlessness of it. The father started running.

The men of The Commodore followed him out and across the car park to the rear wall, and then over the wall; in glimpses, the father saw the figures behind him, through tree branches, and through the burning sweat that ran from his hair and blurred his eyesight. A bald man, scalp nut-brown and shiny, wearing a white shirt open at the neck, pointed left and right, to direct the others after the father. There was another wearing combat trousers, another in shorts and a dirty vest. He could hear them kicking themselves up the second garden wall he'd just thrown himself over.

Up and up and up he went on legs of cement, his hand enormous and thumping with damage, and his left shoulder now feeling like a repaired ornament come unglued from careless usage. Red handprints stained the walls he'd clambered over, whorls and wipes of scarlet glittered on the leaves he clutched at. *Follow me. Just follow the trail. We'll do the final bit up here amongst the broken fences and uneven patios, beneath the grey faces of alcoholics at windows, sweating behind thin, orange curtains.*

Hat down his back, the drawstring around his throat, the knees of his trousers torn through, he floundered through a third garden and cut his stomach on rose thorns as he came down to the patio of what might have been a private house. A back door slammed.

In the next yard he fell into, he entered atop a trellis

fence that splintered under his weight, and the father just sat to get his breath on the stone patio in the wreckage of dry timber, wiping his eyes with the back of a forearm. The air was too thick to get into his mouth and seemed to waft under his nose, but never come inside. His underwear was sodden with sweat, the front of his trousers were dark.

A man called out, 'Cunt's 'ere!'

A gun shot cracked off all the glass at the rear of the dirty white building. The father never heard the end of the bullet's journey.

Too exhausted to be frightened, the father looked about the boundary of the yard to find the shooter, and happened across the keen blue eyes of a pale face. On the far side of the yard, the man must have been standing on his tiptoes to hook an arm over the panels of the fence still upright. At the end of the arm was a hand, greened by faded tattoos, which gripped a handgun pointed directly at his stomach.

The father rolled just before the gun barked. A bullet varoomed off the patio and smashed a hole in a cement-block wall in the neighbouring garden. Lying on his side, the father pointed at the wooden fence beneath the grimacing face and pulled off two shots. The fence splintered, the face vanished.

The father got back to his feet like a sweat-sheathed prize fighter knocked delirious after fifteen rounds under sun lamps. Black spots speckled his vision.

On the other side of the fence he'd fired through, he heard something like a hot and tired dog panting in the shade, followed by a whimper.

The father lurched out of the yard, down a paved alley

between the building and the fence. He came into a street and immediately saw a crowd about ninety feet away. They saw him at the same time he came gasping into the sunlight. Both sides paused and stared at each other.

One of the figures broke from the crowd and came forward, the others formed an arrowhead behind the leader, who held some kind of rifle. The father fell to his knees, and with two hands he aimed his gun at the crowd. They scattered, all save their leader.

The leader cringed, then let the shotgun roar from waist-level. A sapling ten feet in front of the father was stripped of its papery leaves. Parked cars dinted and pinged and spider-webbed on the left side of the road. The father ducked his head and felt something impact the rucksack on his chest, sting his belly and one ear like a piercing with no anaesthetic. He fired at the man with the shotgun and missed, as the shooter loped to the side of the road, doubled over, cussing himself for firing too quickly.

The father looked about himself in a brief reprieve from the flailing of his limbs, this dragging of a heavy body, this skirmishing with sweat-filmed eyes. He might run further up the road to find cover behind a low wall, but if the others who had followed him up through the gardens were close, he'd be amongst them at any moment if he tried to get any higher. These buildings were terraced on each side of the road and that man with the shotgun could not be allowed to fire again in this cement gully, which now resembled a funnel for the exhausted to die inside.

The father stood, tucked his purple hand under his armpit, teetered sideways to get onto the narrow pavement, then jogged downhill past the parked cars to where the crowd was peeking from behind wings and bumpers. Two faces were open-mouthed at the audacity of the father's bandy-legged approach, right at their position. Others ducked or fled. Yet more came down the sides of houses behind him, from the garden he'd just fled, panting like old farm beasts put to the plough.

Sirens wailed in the distance, or maybe down by The Commodore, or maybe further out, called to some other fuckup.

Upon hollow feet, the father covered the last of the ground to where he had seen the man with the shotgun crouch. And the man stood up quickly, between a brown car and a yellow rubbish skip left to rust at the kerb. He came up from the dust spitting his 'Fuck's and 'Cunt's and 'Shite's in anger; a freckled red beast with meaty shoulders wearing an old tracksuit top; a sergeant of stoats with hands like red tubers. His florid face dripped milky sweat from his own nerves and exertions in pursuit of his quarry. This man knew all would be decided now, in mere moments, and he jerked the double barrels about.

The father shot him through the mouth from a yard distant. He didn't think, just let the frightened and wounded animal inside his head point and pull from an unmissable range, and the big man swung away from the waist, dropping the gun. Metal clattered on tarmac like an alarm trying to call time on such barbarism. The man dropped to his knees, then onto his face, his hands wavering about his head briefly, before falling limp.

The father stepped over the broad, trembling back and tried to pick up the shotgun, but his grotesque and swollen hand could not have raised a spoon. The shotgun was old, the wooden stock broken. Something from a farmer maybe, or a clay pigeon shooter, but fallen into the wrong pair of hands, like all things that do harm. The father kicked the shotgun under the parked car and staggered away, down the middle of the road. If he could not make it into a side road he'd be trapped.

He was cut off from behind, from higher ground, where so many men had now come into the street, out of an alley. Shots were being fired wild: one whined close, another thudded into a car door behind the father's fatigue-drunken heels.

The father turned right as soon as he could, but onto another narrow, steep slope. He believed he had another fifty yards in him before his heart gave out. Not even adrenaline would get him much further, or stem the agony in his punctured hand. Cars revved up the hill from below, roaring in his direction. This is why the police stayed away. You tried to stop *them* down here, you interfered with their dealings and affairs, and out smashing went the windows, and whoosh went the cars on fire, and pop-pop-pop went the guns from amongst the crowds.

This is it.

The father fell inside a small concreted front garden, another hostel with piebald walls. There he whinnied and shuddered; a workhorse who'd dragged steel artillery through a muck-filled trench, his flanks lathered with sweat. Kneeling down, he tried to control his breathing, and to still the thought fragments that showed again and again the last expressions and the wounds of the heads he had shot through that morning. It was never supposed to be like this, or end like this, but a perverse spirit inside himself looked upon him with admiration.

What a place to die.

There was a lot of shouting in the street he had run from, angry voices, barking, organizing, as if people were marshalling a rout. Nothing drove or ran into the side street where he crouched, but faces peered round the corner and eyed his position behind the low wall, on his knees, cornered, winded, wet through.

He heard a car in the narrow lanes below, joining the fray. Its horn blared. There followed some banging of angry hands on a roof or bonnet, followed by kicks of feet against a door. A straining whir of acceleration seemed to arise in response and a black car turned into the side street where he hid. The father didn't know what any of this meant, but assumed there was some disagreement over who got to kill him. But he wouldn't be taken alive, and he acknowledged this with a clarity that both surprised and relieved him.

The father stretched up, to shoot at the car, to shoot over the low wall, to shoot out the windows, and to shoot into the passengers. He had enough gas in his tank to fulfil the desire. They would know him here. In these final moments, on his knees, in this place that he despised, he'd share his burden with them today; a weight that had taken away everything he'd ever cared about. All here would know the black misery and rage, and the dousing of the warmth of the heart that was far greater than any shortages, poverty and disputes within this murderous heat. They would know that a man could lose his entire self in one afternoon and never recover it.

The father said his daughter's name and felt grief expand inside his chest, then surge up his throat, becoming near euphoric when it flooded his mind. He would fire empty then walk into their response. And he suddenly wanted the quick stabs of hot agony. He wanted their reprisals. He wanted to be free of wanting.

The driver called the father's name from the slowing car, then shouted, 'Put it away.' A hand reached from a side window, the palm outwards. 'Get in!'

The father hesitated. His gun hand lost tension, his focus blurred. Someone knew his name?

'Get the fuck in!' the man in the car yelled, decisively, but barely containing his own panic.

FOURTEEN

The car was driven at furious speeds. The father closed his eyes and waited for the reforming of metal, a snowstorm of glass blown into the car's interior.

There was no collision, not even a scrape.

His getaway made a permanent cut in its speed only once they were several miles clear of the town and moving along a single-lane road, shielded on both sides by hedgerows. Beyond the road, drought-resistant wheat spread its golden blanket over the gentle hills and continued out of sight. The father guessed he had been driven north of Torquay.

Whenever the man behind the wheel leaned forward in his seat, a cloud of sweat, darkening the entire rear of his shirt, became visible. A handgun was tucked between his legs.

After the father stumbled out from behind the wall and fell into the rear of the car, it had sped away with the door still open and one of his feet hanging in thin air. As if stone chippings from the road had been flung up, three dinks sounded from the rear of vehicle in quick succession. Only when the car slowed to turn at the summit of the hill had the father been able to slam the rear door shut. More shots had been fired up the road from the junction without finding their mark. Someone had recovered the shotgun too. That went off in a dim, ineffective boom, but the weapon did not fulfil its potential that day.

No one followed them. No helicopters arrived to buzz overhead.

The father had collapsed across the rear seats and remained still and silent, mostly staring at the beige ceiling of the car, occasionally using his uninjured hand to wipe the sheets of sweat from his face. He drank a pint of water in one draught but could not look at the wound in his hand for long.

'Your handler, the woman you call Scarlett Johansson, reached out. She said you were about to fuck everything up, for everyone, at The Commodore.' It was all the driver had said by way of greeting once the father was inside the vehicle. The man said nothing more until they were free of the old housing stock on the fringes of town, and beyond the temporary settlements that formed a corral reaching off to Exeter.

When the police officer stopped the car, he said a lot more. 'I'd be a liar if I said there was no silent rejoicing amongst our lot when the likes of Murray Bowles, Nigel Bannerman and Rory Forrester get moved on, but there are too many of them for you to get through. I can't let you run round the county executing the shite. You can't play this kind of lottery for much longer before you buy it. By all accounts that's nearly happened twice.

'We've close to twelve hundred sex offenders we know of in the county. We've more people traffickers down here than doctors. We're rife with indentured slavery. We're the major producers of domestic heroin now. We've gun runners, amphetamine labs, meat smugglers, war criminals from Africa and the Middle East keeping their heads down in old holiday chalets right up to Ilfracombe. The nationalists have made us their home from home. We've forcible evictions by mobs, property scams and land grabs, and more unsolved murders than we've got men on the ground. We've over twenty homicides per officer. And you've just given us another handful.'

The driver paused and swore under his breath, wiped the wet sheen off his face. 'They've smashed the cameras out all over the town. You ask any of them kids back there to reel off the ever-changing plates of our unmarked cars and they'll do it. We had the Royal Marines on the streets all last summer for the riots. Things have been very cagey since. And here's you walking into the bloody Commodore, wearing a sun hat, and going mad with a shooter in some King Death clubhouse. You thought all this heat would keep our hands full and hide one man on a mission, eh?'

'I'm sorry. It was never meant to happen.'

'Heard that before.'

The police officer was breathing rapidly, coming down from his own near-death experience and talking quickly. The father suspected he took crystal. 'We can only hope that disorder, mayhem and chaos do you a large favour. There are more than enough home-grown head-bangers to keep us occupied. But with all the new arrivals, it's bedlam. And we don't anticipate it getting any better. Criminals like it here. We've the navy chasing their boats all through the channel and into the Atlantic off Cornwall. They're having to commandeer anything with an outboard on it. The navy get called away to another hot spot and it's a free-for-all down here. The shitheads know it. Think of it. Think of the numbers coming in and running through here now. What can you do? What can we do? The Dutch are running into Belgium, France and Norway with the sea lapping at their heels. The French don't want any more Africans, so where do they go? Two guesses. The rest of the Greeks and Spanish got to go somewhere now too. They ever have elections here and I don't need to tell you who will get in. The whole world is moving north, mate. The rules are changing and the tone is changing. Every country for itself. What comes next? Every man for himself? You think I jest? You've seen the news.

'We've had to make a truce with half the gangs round here, but it's not really us you need to hide from. Not after this morning's high jinks. We ain't really got time for you, mate. Others have a longer reach though, and more eyes and ears than we can dream of. So, I'm sorry to have to tell you, but this is no way to look for your kid down here. Things are too complicated. You can't come back here. Not now. Not after this morning. Not for a long time. You know that? You gotta stop.'

The father had let the police officer sound off. Like him, he could tell the speed of his blood was gradually slowing too. Their urgent, spiky thoughts were wilting inside the hard shell of the boiling car. Judgement was returning from exile, disbelief raising its head. They were sodden, haggard from adrenaline, from fight and flight, fight and flight again, until it was the same leaden sensation. They'd soon grown sluggish in the heat as if tired and sleepy after a large meal with wine.

After he'd finished speaking the detective fell quiet for a long time and stared through the windshield. When he next spoke, he said, 'I could use a drink,' and removed a metal flask from the glove compartment. 'Fuck, it's hot. Forty-fucking-five. You haven't got much to say for yourself either, eh?'

The father knew all about the futility the man had spoken of. He knew all about odds too, and statistics, and remote chances, because 2051 had been a good year to steal a child. Back then, the father had learned to resent all that was going wrong in the world for his own reasons. He'd only possessed the capacity to go mad from the loss of his child. He'd no time for Bangladesh, even when eighty per cent of it was underwater. Greece, Spain and their fires, same thing. Africa, yet another bad year. China and its droughts, he had no head space left for imagining the numbers forced to migrate. Australia on fire, again. The Central Americans who died against the fence in the United States after the Mormons came into office. None of it had mattered to him but as a cruel diversion that took people's minds away from one missing four-year-old girl in Devon. His solipsism had been planetary in size. He'd defy any mother or father of a small child to think differently.

The father finally gave his response. 'In 2051 there were three hundred and eighty thousand cases of missing children recorded in this country.'

The officer turned his head to the side and looked over his shoulder, his expression unreadable, save for a default wariness blended with irritability.

'Seven out of ten came home in twenty-four hours. Lot of kids without parents in the camps were hard to keep track of, but most came home. Of those still missing, five thousand of the children were abducted. Half of these were also recovered in seventy-two hours. They were mostly taken by family members. Lot of pissed-off divorced fathers and mothers out there. My little girl didn't come home. Many of the others who were abducted were found later, alive and well with extended family, relatives. My girl wasn't found.

'But one in ten of the five thousand abducted children were taken by strangers. Five hundred children in one year. Mostly snatched from the care homes and refugee camps. Three in ten were killed, and they were murdered within hours of their abductions. The rest were taken and kept alive for other reasons. There were three hundred and fifty children in this category, taken by strangers. Nearly half were eventually found alive, but in places they should never have been. And they had endured things that no child should have to even imagine.

'I can only go on probability, and the probability that the majority of the outstanding one hundred and sixty-two missing children still being alive is good. Statistically, sex offenders would have killed forty-nine of them and hidden their remains. That leaves one hundred and thirteen children abducted, still missing, but maybe still living as captives. One hundred and thirteen children. My only hope is that she is one of them. It's not much of a hope, is it? But it's why I do this.'

Once, in the early hours of another terrible morning when a special kind of clarity engulfed the father and his fidgeting and muttering ceased, he had sat up in his disorderly bedclothes and written a letter to his little girl as she smiled at him from a photograph at his bedside. To this day, he kept the letter in his wallet. He knew it by heart.

Even though you were stolen from me and your mother, and even though our hearts are broken and we love you more than ourselves, you are not a priority to the authorities. The people who go missing, the people who are robbed, and even many of the ordinary people just like us who are murdered, are not priorities. Not now. Not any more.

You will always be my priority.

You will never be forgotten and I will never stop looking for you.

I promise.

The father cleared his throat. 'We thought there would be reconstructions. A media campaign. Wealthy benefactors. Nationwide DNA screening. Exhaustive interviews with sex offenders to shake free a lead. These had been our hopes that year.

'Don't misunderstand me, a child stolen from the garden where she was playing still mattered to people. Maybe even to most people. For a while. It mattered to some for even longer. But for most, such a thing never mattered for long. These things don't. They can't. Not any more. Who has the thoughts . . . the space in their heart for a missing child in these times?' The father closed his eyes, swallowed and composed himself. 'Thank you . . . for helping me. But if you wanted me to stop, then you should have let them kill me, because the only thing that will stop me is my own death. I've come too far now. I've gone too far. And she's still too far away from me.'

The detective looked at his lap as if considering the use of his handgun, pulling the trigger out here amongst the silent fields as the father knelt like a penitent in the wheat.

The father rose from the seat and opened the rear door, watched by the officer's hard eyes in the rear-view mirror. Cradling his punctured hand beneath an armpit black with sweat, the father unlatched a gate and entered the wheat field. He knelt down at the edge of the crop and sobbed. He wept with pity at his broken body, the pulse and sting of his hand, the ache in every bone inside that arm, the dead weight of his depleted legs. He wept for himself because he had killed a teenager. Shot and killed someone not much older than a boy without being able to identify a shred of remorse inside himself. He felt even less for the others he'd left for dead: three men, he thought, but what had happened was too vivid, perhaps too vivid to be trusted, but then soon unclear too. Besides Rory, did any of them speak to him before he shot them? He couldn't remember their last words, and had little sense of them but for quick flashes of their faces, their animate eyes. He wasn't alarmed by his callousness, or maybe he was in shock. He hoped he was because he hated himself for the recognition of a trait that explained why so few cared about his daughter. *This is how we are now.* This is what the world was trying to tell him. The great dieback from drought, famine and disease was making inroads into the herd; the other animals were running wild-eyed with foam-lathered flesh. Their teeth were showing inside red mouths that cried out uselessly. There was panic. Clubs and rocks were being seized and hoisted aloft to defend what little was left, fences were being erected. Grieving mammals were thinning to extinction; their little ones went first. And it wouldn't stop.

The sun burned his neck red and made his thoughts swim. The magnitude of the loss all around him was sickening. He'd sooner take death than a permanent realization of how things were.

The police officer touched his shoulder. Passed down the silver flask. The father nodded his head, took the flask and let the rum burn his throat. The officer knelt beside the father as if they were pious men and about to praise some capricious goddess of the fields for the bounty provided. 'Bloody long wait ahead of you in A&E for your hand, but I'll take you somewhere to get it looked at.'

'Why?'

The officer's eyes became distant and he turned his head to partially conceal his face. 'Cus I know what it's like.' He took something from his pocket. Held the screen out to the father, who looked down at an image of a laughing boy, no older than two, wearing blue pyjamas and surrounded by toys on a carpeted floor.

'Yours?'

The detective nodded, face stricken, his mouth hopelessly trying to smile as if at some fond but spoiling memory.

'Taken?' the father asked.

'Flu.'

'I'm sorry.'

The officer slipped the device back inside his jacket. 'Your wife know about this?'

The father shook his head. 'She isn't doing so well. Not since we lost the little one.'

The officer looked away and nodded as if this was what he had expected to hear. 'Money?'

'Not much left.' The father sighed. 'We sold the house. Spent the savings we put aside for our daughter's future. My wife's parents helped a bit too, as much as they could. There was a small fund once, some donations. That's gone now. I haven't worked in two years.' He'd often wondered if he would find work again. There was no more money coming in. Welfare would amount to a miserable, static existence somewhere near his wife and her parents. If he made it back into logistics, and the work involved food provision and distribution, he would be classed as a key worker. The emergency coalition government only had to class something as *key* and a worker wasn't left with much of a home life.

He feared his time on the road and inside the houses of strangers was coming to an end. The idea of stopping should have brought guilty relief, but he could not identify a shred of it. To stop when he finally had a lead was an unbearable prospect. To have come so far and altered himself into . . . he didn't really know beyond still being *her* father, but he'd lost sight of land in most other respects. He was committed. And he knew now that he would die as simply that, *her* father.

The officer exhaled noisily, then drank from the flask. Passed it back to the father. 'What you got?'

'Not much. Until today.'

The man stared at him hard, as if to bore out the information, and the father told him what Rory had said. After hearing the story, his saviour resumed staring into the distance, but at least he seemed to be taking the testimony seriously. 'It's thin. But that doesn't mean it's worthless. Bowles grassed up Rory after you shot Nigel Bannerman?'

The father nodded.

'And if Rory said it wasn't a sex offender who snatched your girl, you'd better hope he wasn't bullshitting, because he's no longer available for cross-examination. And you drew a blank on the others? Your handler told me about the first three nonces you visited, Malcolm Andrews, Bindy Burridge and Tony Crab. Were there others?'

'A man called Robert East.'

'He dead?'

'No. He never reported me.'

'A slow process of elimination through the most likely leads that your handler pitched out. You do realize that this whole area could be underwater by the time you've door-stepped the last of them?'

'The names. The Russians. They mean anything?'

'Nothing. But believe me, I'm very familiar with the outfit he's talking about. King Death.' The officer screwed up his face with distaste. 'They're like nothing we've ever seen before.'

'That bad.'

'Worse. With them, it's . . . even a religion, you know? Some kind of religion mixed with the worst kind of human behaviour. Like the jihadists, but without an ultimate goal that we can see, besides filling their pockets.' The officer scratched through his thoughts to find the right expression. 'Bristol. Remember Bristol years back? Chantilly Road. All those people beheaded in a turf war.'

The father nodded.

'We've had it down here too. Decapitations, and the rival shite have been vanishing all over. These guys move in and local gangs move on, or are moved out of the land of the living. All the bodies of their enemies that we've found, or *they* have left for us to find, don't have heads.

'The symbol of King Death is part of some mumbo-jumbo mystery about where they draw their power from. But they mostly prefer to remain enigmatic.'

'This symbol. A thing dead, but in rags. I've seen it. On walls.'

'It's in plenty of places. All over the coast now. Foot soldiers put it on their bodies to signpost membership too. They don't worry about us. But that sign is a fuck-right-off in prison, and on the streets. Some of them completely cover themselves in ink. They've got a kind of philosophy going on too, or so we were told by serious crimes. It dribbled down to the street criminals from somewhere else, abroad maybe, the cartels in South America, with some old medieval stuff from here in Europe. It's a mash-up, but they embrace chaos. That's their bag. They claim to draw their power from chaos and death itself. And they like these bold gestures, these ritualistic killings. Sprinkling bits of Latin here and there as if their cause is holy, foretold, that kind of BS. Everyone's at it, Temple of the Last Days, Church of the End of Days, same thing. All the traditional churches have had a field day too, a right old comeback. But some of these Kings are really big on superstition, omens, stuff like that. There's this reverence they like to cultivate around themselves, especially in prison. They brought in an expert to help us understand them and he said it was all about the romanticism of death. Marks them out down here, makes them even more sinister.

'They've mixed in Santeria, Buddhism, Catholicism, Satanism, witchcraft, all of it and more, even physics. And they reckon we're destined for chaos, everything is, and they're preparing to survive in it. They might have a point, eh? And they reckon that all of this, the world and us in it, right now, is the *fin du monde*, the end of time.

'Most of these guys are thugs, but there are a few, the more dangerous ones, who are really into this philosophy, and they don't fear death at all. They just think it's some kind of passage. You know what the shaman nuts, their spiritual guides, want? They want to ascend to become the "special dead", that's what we were told, so that they have some insight after a "transcendence into the long night". They want to still be around, in the everlasting "after-death". But that's already close, all around us apparently, and getting bigger by the day. Only some of them can tap into it. These seers. But afterdeath is going to swallow us all soon enough, while they'll command some kind of privileged position in it. That's the gist of it, I think. The murders are part-ritual. Signs, they say, that light up in another place, so their patrons, or something nasty over there in afterdeath, can bless them, or something like that. There's no judgement, no heaven or God, not for them. Death itself is the entity and also the place that they're connecting with. Something like a force, but cold, totally indifferent and as chaotic as deep space. But they'll be all right over there. It's all nuts. Can you believe what some chumps will kill for these days?'

'You can't do anything about them?'

The police officer shrugged. 'Not much. They're like an army now. They'll take the worst head cases from every nationality and there's no shortage of volunteers. They've been giving the jihadists in the north-east guns and explosives, as well as the nationalists in the south. They've all the trafficking and the vice here, all franchised through affiliates. Men like Rory. It's the disruption, the chaos, they like. Tactical, see. That's what I reckon. Like politicians and terrorists, they create diversions, spread resources thin, then capitalize, exploit the weaknesses. And I don't think they've ever had it so good as over the last decade.' The officer looked at the sun as if to curse it.

The father nodded. He'd read many of the same things online, but much of the information about their culture had seemed too fantastical for him to readily believe, so he'd skimmed it. 'They really killed all those judges?'

The officer laughed, but not pleasantly. 'That's not all they've done. They're suspected of a shitload of high-profile disappearances. They're getting into everything legit too. Politics, councils, the emergency government, law, refugee groups, food, transport, us. Lot of *respectable* people are watching their backs for them and are in their debt now, or so we assume. But you never heard that from me.'

'Could they—'

'Have taken your girl? They'd have no qualms if it paid well, or if it served their interests.'

'We had no money.'

The officer pursed his lips, rolled his head. 'You got any enemies?'

'Not that bad. Would . . . what about child prostitution?' The father became faint, imagined Rory's grinning face, Bowles's attic, the thin silhouettes sitting up in bed, the lock on the door. All of the blood in his body seemed to run into the soil and leave him feeling cold on a day when the sun was hot enough for its surface to be nudging the earth's troposphere.

'They are certainly not above that, but she doesn't fit the profile. They've snatched a few from the camps and care homes to top up the specialist brothels. But your case isn't a fit for that profile. Too risky unless it was bespoke, so it's doubtful. If they were involved, I'd say they were paid very well to do it for someone else. A contract.'

'That doesn't make sense.'

The officer shrugged, but not with indifference. 'I . . .' He stopped himself.

'Tell me.'

'When it happened. Your girl, when she was taken, I was drug squad. My gut told me it was a paedophile. Loner. Cased you and your family and then just couldn't help himself. In and out. Biggest day of his life. Whether she's . . . still with *him* or not is anyone's guess. We don't bloody know. But whoever took her would have to slip up, or get copped trying it on again, or suffer a breach in his security, to give you any chance at all of finding her. And his secrecy must be pretty bloody airtight if he's kept her hidden for two years. That's the angle your handler's been working on too. Not saying I'm right, but that's what my gut told me was probable. Child protection is the worst bloody job there is and they have no choice but to outsource.'

'I thought the same, until I met Murray Bowles.'

The officer nodded. 'Stands to reason. But in the

unlikely event this outfit are involved, the Kings . . .' He held his hands up.

'Where do I go? Who do I speak to?'

'You don't. You'd need to re-mortgage the house you don't own any more, just for one of them to consider giving you information. And that was before you whacked Rory.'

'Informers? Don't you have them?'

'Of course, but do they inform on this lot? Never. Where would they hide after they'd told us something we could use? In prison they blind snitches with toothbrush handles. If what Rory said was even half true, you and he would have got it in the neck, literally. Out here, they seal the leaks with machetes. Trademark.'

'Someone would talk. They always talk. They always say something to someone . . . They can't keep it inside their criminal skulls.'

'Rats do squeak.'

'It's all I have.'

'It ain't much. And it's a death sentence the moment you stick your beak in, or a very severe beating. Trust me, you'd never walk again. They'll smash your vertebrae with a hammer. Seen it a few too many times. You'll wish they'd cut your head off. Rory probably only gave that much up because he thought you weren't leaving The Commodore alive. Did he go for you?'

'Twice.'

'Knife?'

The father nodded.

'He's got form. He's been fingered for two murders. We didn't even know he was living in there.'

'It's why he had to kill me. Bowles had put him in the frame for my daughter, which put his gang connections in the frame for her abduction.'

'Long shot. Real long shot. And let me be the detective, OK? How many others bought it down there today?'

'A younger one, a teenager. About eighteen, nineteen. He was on a bike outside and had a gun. He nearly killed me. I don't know how he missed. He . . . was standing right behind me. And there was a man . . . a man behind a fence in one of the yards on the hill. Who fired at me. I think I hit him. And then another one with a shotgun in the street near where you found me.'

The officer whistled. 'I'm counting six on your account in two weeks. A spree, my friend. They saw your face too, dozens of them.'

The father took a deep breath.

'You're done in this town. You can never risk setting foot anywhere south of Gloucestershire again. Even that's no guarantee of your safety. Or your family's. And there'll be an investigation and that will eventually lead to Bowles and Nige, known offenders, both done with the same shooter as Rory and his mates. They'll get DNA out of the blood you splashed everywhere. But I'm going to assume your daughter was also at the heart of the earlier *discussions*. So if those other nonces you visited pipe up, when your mug shot gets circulated, you'll be charged for them too.'

The father nodded.

'Grief-stricken father starts knocking over sex offenders. The whole country will be cheering again. Nonetheless, you can see how this shit works. How deep you can get so quickly, and now you're probably wondering if you need to go back and cover your tracks by whacking the first nonces you visited. And they'll be thinking the same thing. Is he coming back, the man in the mask? I know your methods. I've been briefed by your handler, and you're in the game now and the game never ends. This isn't for you. This isn't your game. But there's little point in me confiscating your weapon because you'll get another, won't you? Maybe you got a taste for it too. Execution.'

'I never . . . it wasn't execution. Nigel Bannerman tried to kill me. That was self-defence.'

'Bowles?'

'He ran. I wasn't thinking. I saw the kids in his loft and I lost it. Lost control. Rory I only wanted to speak to.'

'How did you think that was going to work out? I don't know whether you're a good liar or a bloody amateur who's been very lucky, though your hand may be telling you different right now. There might be nothing in Rory's information at all. He was thinking on his feet, giving you something so he could add value to himself. And what was it, some hearsay from a pub that no longer exists, from two men whose second names we don't even know? You've got to listen to your old movie star, Scarlett Johansson, because what you have is thin. Very thin, but four men died for it today. How many more d'you plan to rub out on a rumour?'

'It's something. More than I've ever had.'

'Slightly more than fuck all, if I am going to be honest with you.'

The father ground his teeth. 'Why are we here?'

The officer considered his answer for a long time.

'Because if I was you I'd be sitting right where you are now. I wouldn't take a break from shovelling the shite into hell, if I had the slightest chance of bringing my boy back.' He looked away from the father. 'I'm sure you've done your homework and I'm sure it's made everything worse for you. The way you feel. You might have lost your mind because you know what can happen to a child. But I know more about what happens to these kids than you ever will. So let's just say that I have sympathies at a time when it's hard to see the lines that separate the good from the bad.' The officer looked at the father again. 'What's the end game? Ask yourself.' The officer swept his hand to indicate the field, the sky, the terrible sun. 'It's more of this, getting worse and worse every bleeding year. If we don't blow each other up, the climate will see most of us off. Food and water, that's what it's all about now. That's not going to change, is it? There's the potential of another pandemic now too. Something very nasty. Difficult to treat. Inoculations are a long way off too, or so they say. As a public official, I have been told not to cause alarm, so I'm giving you that lead on the QT, but it's already here. And it could be big.'

'Jesus Christ.'

'That's who we need right around now. His face wouldn't be unwelcome.'

'How far has it spread?'

'Springing up in Central Europe. The Continent. Maybe the south-east now too. First cases. Mostly just rumours, but something's building. I think we all know that, and if this bug is a dead end, there'll be another soon after, something big, far bigger than what's already been doing the rounds the last twenty years, like the bug that took my boy. So I often have to wonder will anything matter for much longer, these bits and pieces that some of us still hang on to, like the law, rights. Maybe it's all simpler than we think. Maybe it's already happened, that final change inside us. The gloves are off. They are in Africa, South America, Asia, southern Europe, if we're going to be honest. We've seen it on the news. And it doesn't look so unusual now, does it, no matter how bad it gets? People in those places are not thinking like we are any more, because in those places people have it far, far worse than us. I do wonder how long we can give each other assurances.'

'Me too.'

They sat in silence for a long time and finished the rum.

The police officer eventually stood up. 'Let's get your hand sorted. I don't need to tell you that our conversation is totally off the record.'

'Of course. What about your car? They saw it.'

'Stolen.'

'Your face?'

'I was in Exmouth all day. I'm still there right now.'

'But back there, what will be said?'

The officer pursed his lips. 'Initially, another head case with a shooter, business as usual. You picked the right place to do it in, unless you've started a riot we don't know about while we're sitting here chewing the fat. A dead teenager can still kick it off. Depends on the parents, if there are any. Then there'll be harder questions asked, autopsy, ballistics, descriptions. Something worse is bound to crop up meantime and cause delays to our lot. Fingers crossed, eh? But Rory was a King, so they'll pursue their own inquiries. They'll be after you now.'

They walked back to the car. The officer paused before he climbed in. 'You know she won't look the same. Not like you remembered. If you ever become one of the luckiest men on this planet, just remember, she'll be six.'

'I'd know her.'

FIFTEEN

After the hospital, his sedation and exhaustion were embraced by the unrelieved heat of the hotel room. Morphine pills for his stitched and bloated hand, antibiotics, rum, fatigue, sleep deprivation, and a fever quickly provided a surreal medium for his notions to swim through.

Slippery with sweat, and falling in and out of sleep for two days and nights that became indistinguishable, the father talked to the figures of the air. Maybe his mind finally found the maelstrom it had been crawling towards for years: a blur of nonsensical visions, infuriating repetitions of memory, and the cruel torments that his dreams inevitably turned into, bedfellows of a madness he'd foreseen the very day his daughter vanished.

The subjects of his second and third moves, Bindy Burridge and Tony Crab, appeared in opposing corners of his hotel room and whispered to each other. And in this delirium, Bindy was all bone from the waist down. *Look at what they've done to me.* Tony Crab had no eyes.

Neither of the men fought back when the father had appeared in their tiny rooms, in what had once been a library and a clothes shop, respectively. Bindy, the mole creature, with the small, white, plump hands, had wept and pleaded for mercy when the father took away his glasses to spray his face. Tony had just started to shake, pale with terror, and wept. They had told him nothing of use and swore they knew nothing about his daughter. The devices they owned they handed over without resistance, along with their codes. Both men had suffered terribly in prison. Bindy had only partial use of one arm and wore a scarf to hide the scars around his throat. Once they were released their records were leaked by the local police forces and entire streets had turned upon each of them. They'd been relocated hundreds of miles from home when the father had caught up with them. Sex offenders in the slums were often doused with petrol and burned alive, and for doing far less than interfering with children.

His own bitterness, his fear and rage, populated the room, appearing in different forms in the distance, before reappearing close to his eyes when he was no longer sure if they were open or shut. At one point, in one of the many wet hours of gibbering and writhing, or sitting up to speak to those faces beside his bed, the father came awake only to find himself as a doll in a tiny, cold bed. The walls of the room had reared up like cliffs. He'd closed his eyes and gulped water from a bottle. The liquid was warm and tasted of plastic.

When he fell asleep again, fragments of his conversation with Malcolm Andrews, the first offender he'd ever visited, played on a loop accompanied by the distant cacophony of children in a playground. And then he dreamed of bones. Mountains of bones in rags, withered shanks, parchment-skin faces yawning silently, dusty and still, one piled upon the other, tier after tier, rising into the dying light.

His wife was in the bathroom too, crying, always crying.

Rory's throat was shot out again and again, his ruptured cheek flapping like rubber. Nige Bannerman's punctured skull littered the darkness wetly. Bowles was a whale harpooned on a patio, leaking black.

A vast crowd of thin, naked people, their flesh dark, were then running through his room in fright. They kept coming and coming, kicking up vast clouds of salty dust. Something the size of a hill rose in the near distance and stared down. A fire in the surrounding trees changed direction again, and the father climbed out of his bed and ran amongst the thin people.

His daughter had been knocked to the ground up ahead. She wailed, but he couldn't reach her, was shoved to the side, pushed about before he could regain his balance and turn towards the sound of her cries. When she fell silent, he woke up.

Eventually, the father lay face down on the bed to stem the sight of the people that came and went, came and went, through the room. The past, the present, and nonsense, all coming together in the same space. But sleep would only return him to their old home in Shiphay, where he was running through the front garden, leaping from one tiered level to another, before finding himself back near the patio doors. He couldn't see his daughter but could hear her saying, 'What's that?'

The black car pulled away, over and over again, and the father ran up the road through air as thick as treacle. The sunlight was blinding, the street made from white stone, its glare forcing him to squint. In the distance the car turned out of the street, and the father's feet slid down the hill, back to the front gate of their house. Down there the world was grey and damp. His wife was on the lawn, sobbing, screened from him by the trees. The father saw that the street had become a cemetery filled with small headstones, tiny angels and sprays of brightly coloured flowers. His daughter spoke to him from out of the ground and said she was with friends and couldn't come back, and he sat up with an anguished cry that must have been heard in the neighbouring rooms of the hotel.

Finally, when sleep's insistent torments released him, he could taste the sea's brine in his throat. His eyes were swollen and the bed was sodden.

Once the fever had broken, and he was able to stand easily, the father took a shower and spent a day propped up in bed watching the news, or just staring at the curtains.

His ribs and hip bones were visible through the skin of his body. It had been a long time since he'd taken a hard look at himself in the mirror, but his weight loss still came as a surprise. All of his clothes in the room were soiled.

He continued with the antibiotics, but stopped taking the morphine pills to avoid dreaming, and ate small meals from the hotel vending machine. The two days he'd waited in A&E to see a nurse, and picked up an infection, felt like a lifetime ago. The police officer had driven him to a hospital in Dartmouth where the queues were smaller, but the heat was everywhere and so were its pallid victims. But while he was recuperating, at least the temperature outside dropped to thirty-three degrees.

In Spain, France and Portugal the fires were being

contained in smaller areas too, but the new pandemics in Asia and North Africa were both being linked to the European ports and some UK hospitals. Like the ongoing famines in Africa and China, it was unusual for pandemics to supplant the relentless coverage of the fires, or the hurricanes and floods, wherever they were occurring, unless the bugs were getting out of control. The father's thoughts turned to what the police officer had told him beside the wheat field.

There had been at least a dozen pandemics the father could vaguely remember now, and all in the last three decades. Plague, legionnaires' disease, E. coli of the blood, hantaviruses and various strains of influenza had killed millions, but labs somewhere had always investigated recognizable DNA and RNA and eventually detected the antibodies and antigens necessary for vaccines.

Viruses flourished repeatedly, but briefly; many inexplicably died away, evolutionary dead ends, or they hit a volley of the latest antibiotics in the northern hemisphere. They always became footnotes to the bigger deals when continents were on fire, water filled city streets, mudslides took townships down slopes, or cities were blurred by hurricanes. But the news stations were claiming the new pathogen from Asia was SARS CoV, and that alone was enough to make Centre for Disease Control sweat buckets, and the story was persisting. Never good signs.

The new Asian SARS bug had been listed as a worldwide health threat a few weeks before. He hadn't known that. He did remember a report about a plane in China, sometime in the spring, before the onset of the hottest summer that Europe had ever endured. But that plane was now being cited as key in the latest pandemic. And China Airlines Flight 211 had carried three hundred people, from Zhejiang to Beijing, fifteen of whom were already running high temperatures and barking chestily at take-off. By the time the plane touched down, hours later, two hundred and ten other passengers had been infected. Within weeks, three thousand healthcare workers, their patients, and the patients' visitors had been infected and died from the same virus across eighty of Beijing's hospitals. By that time, the WHO in Geneva became aware that the severe, acute respiratory syndrome had already spread to Hong Kong and nine other Chinese provinces. Familiar statements of alarm had been issued, but he'd lost sight of it in other news because of the fires and what India and Pakistan were lumbering towards over water, again. But here were the latest reports of thousands of new cases of SARS in Vietnam, the Philippines, Thailand, Nepal, Bangladesh, the east of India, and South Korea. Decades of pollution, fresh-water shortages, chronic overpopulation and a food crisis in half of its territories, civil strife, the gradual but certain economic collapse, the continuing desertification of one half of its land, with one tenth of its entire population estimated as still being homeless after the floods of 2038: there was always tragedy in China. But amidst the usual flux and chaos, there were claims that the new bug's infectiousness, in combination with its lethality, had rarely been seen before. It was like an extreme form of pneumonia, with flu-like symptoms: blinding headaches, high temperatures and chills, crippling muscular aches, a persistent coughing of bloody phlegm leading to the degradation of the lungs.

The Canadians were now reporting its appearance too, as were the Americans, the Japanese, and the Russians after weeks of denial, and nearly every refugee camp in and around China and India had it too. In Europe, however, it had not seemed to pass beyond a few thousand people, and mostly in the central countries.

The Guangzhou Institute was now calling it the eleventh SARS coronavirus, but the first that boasted pre-symptomatic infection: by the time the affected felt unwell they had been highly infectious for days – they had gone to school and work, had shopped in crowded markets, helped fill public transport to capacity, breathed on international flights, queued for clean water, and slept in crowded refugee camps. Just scanning the reports made the father feel even weaker than the heat, the infection in his hand, and the drugs already had.

The crisis is ongoing.

He stayed in Devon for another week, but neither Scarlett nor the police detective called him.

His hand became an ugly blue and purple colour but was healing and no longer so swollen. His shoulder ached and remained stiff, but the worst of that injury had passed. More than anything, he was lucky to be alive.

When he tried to contact all of the recent accounts that Scarlett Johansson had used, he found them disconnected, and the father suspected he would never hear from her again. Against her advice, even her orders, he had gone to The Commodore and he had killed four men. Nothing about that morning's carnage had appeared on the local news service.

If Rory was a King they'll prefer to pursue their own inquiries . . .

They blind snitches with toothbrush handles . . .

Out here, they seal the leaks with machetes . . .

They'll smash your vertebrae with a hammer. You'll wish they'd cut your head off . . .

The hotel was costing him too much money and he knew he'd be incapable of making a move for a few weeks. When he did move again, he would probably need to take food or valuables from his victim. The downward spiral: you could always fall further, and there were no limits now.

He would go back to Birmingham to see his wife, and he could not help feeling that he was going back to say goodbye.

SIXTEEN

'You're hurt,' his wife said.

'Nearly better now.' The father tried to conceal the stiffness in his movements caused by the shoulder, its pain revived by sitting for so long during the drive up to the Midlands.

He took a seat in the garden chair beside Miranda, on the small cement patio. It was the only place to sit, because the entire lawn had been transformed into a market garden. The father nodded at the plots. 'Your dad's done well this year.'

'Yes,' his wife said, a faint smile playing in her eyes, and she turned her attention away from his bandaged hand, now supported by a sling that he'd bought to restrict the movement of the entire arm. 'We've a surplus in the garden this year,' she went on. 'Even with the water shortage, I've read that the country has a surplus too. Three months' grain, they're saying. When was the last time anyone had that?'

'About 2023, I think.' The surplus would be consumed by the coming influx of refugees. It would have to be. And anyway, the more you grew the more people ate. Having more didn't make it last longer, but he didn't tell his wife that.

'Would you like something to eat?'

'No. No, thank you.'

'You've lost so much weight.'

'So have you.' And she had since the last time they'd met, over two months ago. She'd always been thin for a tall woman, but had steadily diminished in the last two years. What had been slim was now haggard. She never used to wear her hair so long, but it now flowed unkempt, threaded with silver. Her knees and ankles seemed too big, her hips too wide and sharp. She'd stopped painting her nails, and not a trace of make-up had graced her face since the day they had made the last of their recorded pleas.

'I brought her things back,' the father said, to revive the conversation after a long and uncomfortable silence. 'I'd like to take a few more items, if that's OK?' He would have done so anyway, from out of the boxes in the garage, where they had remained in storage like some forgotten exhibition at the Museum of Childhood, awaiting revival.

His wife nodded. 'Will you be going back?'

'Eventually. Need to build my strength up first. I'm waiting on a few calls.' He'd still heard nothing from the police detective.

His wife swallowed noisily and looked out at the flowers bordering the turned earth, the rubbery chard and reptile-skinned marrows. Her dad had even managed to grow grapes along one side of the garden. The two greenhouses were thick with tomatoes. 'How was your trip?'

'Do you really want to know?'

'If . . . if there is anything . . .'

Anything he said would consume her with anxiety and with dread. He'd been shocked by the ways his own mind and heart had so quickly turned after the abduction, but his wife had been born partially stricken by so many solvents of the heart, which would readily burst into flame and char those imagined future times when all could be normal, or manageable. It hadn't taken an abduction to make her a pessimist.

'All vague, I'm afraid. Anyone been in touch with you?'

She shook her head.

The father reached across the divide between their chairs and touched her wrist. She started at the contact before looking at his hand. She took it and squeezed his fingers. Her eyes were glazed with tears. 'She would be so proud of you . . .' Her voice disintegrated.

'Shush. It's all right.'

'. . . her daddy. He never stopped . . .' She couldn't finish and her voice rose up through the octaves until her words wobbled and then collapsed.

'And neither did her mummy.'

His wife swallowed. 'Lots of people have been kind. In the forums. The groups. Mum and Dad have paid for a new photo-fit. I'll give you one.'

The father remembered what the police officer had told him about how his daughter would have changed. 'Any good?'

'She looks like a stranger. I . . . I was very upset when I saw it. It made everything worse, to seem even more hopeless. I don't know who that girl is, in the picture. In the others, I could still see her. I could see myself.'

The father smiled. 'That's because she looks like you.'

'They used photos of me again, of how I looked at her age. But I still couldn't see us, either of us.'

'Please . . . please,' he whispered. She was getting upset again, agitated, the first tremors of a franticness that were once followed by a bloodless shivering that the father found terrifying and unbearable to watch.

His wife's reactions to his visits were invariably the same and he had learned not to come rushing in, twitching with unproven ideas, with untested possibilities, with wild leaps of the imagination. His demeanour was quieter these days and he'd felt himself settling, slowing down, unconcerned by anything but his purpose. He wondered again if this should worry him. He also wondered when, or even if, he would feel any remorse for killing six men within two weeks. 'I shouldn't have come.'

'No. I wanted to see you. I missed you.' She'd not said that in a while.

'God, I miss us. All of us. It's why I do this.'

His wife nodded, sniffed and wiped her eyes. 'I'm sorry. I've not been very supportive since you left the last few times.'

'That's OK.'

'I couldn't agree. Not with their methods—'

'The information is not coming from the nationalists,' he said.

His wife sniffed, touched the side of her eyes. 'You don't know that. But it's all right. I don't think I can care about any of that any more.'

The father nodded. 'If the information came from the devil himself, I wouldn't give a damn.'

His wife turned to him, her eyes wet but suddenly smiling. 'I want you to know that I am better . . . than I was.'

'You take your time. We're dealing with this in different

ways, that's all.' And it was why they could not be together much; her despair and his rage had made a formidable blend. When they'd needed each other most, they had often been apart, even if they were in the same house.

'I've started going through her things.'

The father nodded. Two years ago, her parents had sorted out all of the clothes and toys, and he knew it had not been easy for them. His wife's mother had even collapsed the first time she went into their daughter's bedroom; one of those days, so long ago, that he wouldn't let himself revisit any more. One of many days of blame and madness, of fists through walls and shouting into phones, of walking in streets and tugging elbows. Time had healed nothing of their broken hearts, but at least it had allowed them to function.

The father looked out at the plots and remembered his daughter helping them as they sowed seeds and uprooted spuds in their own garden; her little patrols for snails, woodlice and ants, the endless hospitals for the poorly insects, crushed by her own little fingers as she transported them inside second-hand plastic beach toys. His throat thickened.

Miranda cleared her own throat. 'Her pictures . . . her pictures, more than anything, have helped.' Their daughter had been a fastidious artist, a painter in a homemade smock, busy about the table her grandfather had made for her out of a garden gate. The father smiled.

'It's how she saw the world,' his wife said, her voice suddenly stronger. 'How she depicted what mattered to her. It tells me more than her toys and clothes, and what I can remember of the games we played, those endless games.

Naughty toys, poorly toys, good-girl toys. The films I still can't watch, but her pictures. They've . . . helped me. We're in every one. Her mummy, her daddy, our house . . .'

The sight of the garden dissolved in front of the father's eyes. 'Don't,' he whispered, but his throat felt so blocked, he didn't know if his wife had heard him.

'In every single picture, we're there. And all of us are smiling.' Her voice lightened and filled with a tone he'd not heard in years. He'd forgotten she had such a voice. 'She was happy. I can see it in the pictures. Even with our big shoes and crazy hands, we're all happy. We made her happy. If nothing else, she was a happy little girl. She always was. With us. We had that. At least we had that.'

The father was awake when the call came through. Beside him, his wife lay quietly, facing the curtains through which the hated sun bloomed a late summer dawn. Part of her back was uncovered, but he no longer looked in shock upon the pronounced vertebrae of this woman whose loss he doubted he could fully imagine. Miranda never stirred.

The father picked up the call, leaving the bed as silently as he could. 'Hang on,' he said to whoever was on the end of the line, and made his way to the bathroom and locked himself inside. The house stayed quiet as if trying to overhear his conversation.

'OK.'

The voice of the police officer from Torquay filled his ear, and into his mind flooded a warm, fond sense of the man who had saved him a few weeks before, and then sat beside him at the border of the wheat field on the day he had shot and killed four strangers. 'How's the hand?'

Sat on the bath, the father clenched and then opened his hand and extended his fingers repeatedly, until his muscles became supple and the stiffness vanished. 'I can make a fist.'

'Good man. You in Birmingham?'

'Yes. Three weeks and counting. I thought I might see out the summer.'

'Good riddance to it. I wish I could say we'll never see another one like that again, but . . . you know. Hold on to your hat though, because the rains are coming.'

'It's going to be wet for sure.'

'So if you're ever coming back, you'll want to move sharpish before the roads get closed all over the southwest.'

The father's spine straightened. 'You have something for me?'

'I've never been one for small talk, so I'll get to it. You're off your handler's radar now, so forget about Scarlett Johansson. No hard feelings, eh? But I don't need to remind you that this out-of-hours work isn't about our career development or reputations. Our lives are at risk now, hers and mine, by having had anything to do with you, because of the King Death angle. You understand this?'

As he suspected, he had been cut loose by Scarlett, abandoned and judged a dangerous liability after his performance at The Commodore. He assumed the detective had taken pity on him, and as soon as he'd heard the man's voice, he'd realized how much he needed to maintain his belief that there were some on the side of those who had lost their children; officers who had lost faith in the public departments they served.

'Of course. If it wasn't for her . . . I wouldn't . . . I'd still be out there, wandering. And you saved my life. Thank you.'

'There'll be plenty thanking you if you do what will be necessary.' The detective left that hanging in the air between them. 'There's a guy down here you need to speak with. But the stakes in this game, and the rules, are going to get adjusted if you move on him. Big time. The odds are bleak. The outcome almost certainly a cluster-fuck that you won't walk away from. You still there?'

The father swallowed. 'Rory, Bowles, where are you on that?'

'That's the only good news I have for you this morning. The death of Rory Forrester has not been fully investigated, or we'd have your identity on file through the blood you left all over Torquay. Ballistics and eye witnesses were canvassed around The Commodore and over at Murray Bowles's house, and then thrown onto the when-we-get-a-moment pile. You cannot, nor will you, ever use that shooter again. Throw it in the bloody sea. I will supply an alternative. Now, as far as I can ascertain, you have been dealt a major break here, because Bowles and Forrester were minor, minor affiliates, and only on the outer periphery of the south-western Kings. Small fry. Cunts. Not the real deal. But all that is now changing. If you fancy another move down here, you'll be paying a visit to King Death in person. You make a move against a full member of an organized criminal outfit like the Kings, you will not be able to leave anyone you *interview* alive. You will have to remain incognito, and you must never question anyone at all, in this legion of pricks, that you are not prepared to kill. Otherwise, there will be swift reprisals against you. And your wife, once *they* know who came a-calling on one of their own. If you want to terminate this call, do it now and you'll never hear from me, or any other distant friends of the family, ever again.'

The father cleared his throat. 'I'm going nowhere. Tell me.'

'Then you're bloody insane, but here goes. The only chap within your reach, and ours for that matter, is a real cocksucker. He's no general, no captain, but a lieutenant in King Death Incorporated, who never gets his own hands dirty. He's a playboy, a pussy hound, a pimp, and a trader in flesh who's done very well for himself in our manor. Yonah Abergil, a sex trafficker of Chechen–Israeli descent, who fled to Britain from Marseille and his businesses have since flourished like bacteria in a Petri dish. I'm sending his address and a few details to the last ident that Scarlett gave you. Now, we believe Yonah was running Rory on probation, to increase his market share in the young flesh on offer in the bits of Somerset sheltered by the levees. Lucrative turf for old Yonah. We can only guess that Rory, in turn, reached out to a fiddler like Bowles to get the ball rolling round the refugee settlements. And you cut that tentacle off before it coiled around a few more Greek kids. But Yonah's fat appendages are still poking around everywhere, so he won't have sweated over the death of a few loss leaders like Rory and Murray Bowles.

'But if the Kings played any part in the worst afternoon of your life, two years cold, then there is a very good chance that Yonah Abergil would know something. No guarantees, but he's the only name I can give you that's not sipping Hennessey in a compound, surrounded by special forces. You go any higher up their food chain and no one will even know your girl's name anyway. I'm afraid the Kings deal with very significant numbers of the *missing*. But Yonah is ideal, and he's all you've got. His security is light. Couple of arseholes in Gucci loafers hang around when he's out and about, but they don't sleep over at his villa. He's a merchant, not muscle, but thinks he's hard. Though he's still of their blood, so his unfortunate demise will be followed up by his mates, and they'll come for you mob-handed if they know who you are.

'There will be cameras onsite at Yonah's place, so wear your Halloween outfit, but not that bloody bush hat. And shave your hair and your pubes off. Don't leave a trace. Glove up, do the works. The shooter will be new, and you will be the only thing that walks out of his villa alive, with one exception. He looks after his dad, who's nine parts gone with dementia, so in the unlikely event that he remembers anything, it won't be taken seriously. And go in at night when the nurse ain't there. You do understand what I am saying? I cannot add any more emphasis to that most essential component of the biggest move of your career. But if anyone is in that villa, with the exception of the old boy, you have to clip them. If you're fingered for this, you're done, and so is your wife.'

The father could barely breathe, let alone speak.

'Can't hear you?'

He coughed. 'I understand.'

'I suggest you turn your conscience off, because you

will be dealing with a man who put his own in the bin decades ago. Think of your girl and do what you need to, yeah? That guy with the crazy big stones who strolled into The Commodore, *that guy*, he's the one you need to be. Then get the fuck out and lock yourself away until I can assess the fallout, as well as any intel you pick up on the job.'

'OK.'

'Oh, and before I go, I have one more request.'

'Go on.'

'As we are now working together, I'm going to need a name. And as you're a fan of the movies, I always liked that guy Gene Hackman, you know, in the old flicks.'

His wife was awake when the father returned to the bedroom. By the way she looked at him, he knew she'd been awake when the call came in. Her expression was a mixture of fear and desperate hope.

'I have to go back.' The father began emptying the chest of drawers and dropping the clothes, which his wife had just washed, onto the bed.

Miranda reached out and held his wrist. He sat down and pulled her to his chest, whispered in her ear. 'I can't say much.' He swallowed at the grim sensation of leaving his wife's warmth again. 'But it's the best lead I've ever had.' Miranda's body tensed within his arms. 'Only, there's . . .' His voice failed him. 'There's risk. So . . .'

She pulled back from his embrace and stared at him in a way that made him recoil. 'I can't lose you too,' she said quickly.

He tried to smile, but felt his face stiffen, his mouth

ache. 'I'll be careful. But I have to do this. I am going to do this.'

'Are you saying goodbye?'

'No.' He spoke before his anxiety gave him pause to think. 'But, in what I am doing, there will always be a risk.'

His wife put her face in her hands. He reached out and touched her shoulder. 'It's going to be fine. But you, and your parents, you will have to go somewhere else.'

She looked at him, her eyes red. 'Go? Where? Where can we go?'

'Some place safer.'

'This place is entirely safe.'

'A place where no one knows you're married to me.'

'My God.'

'Like that place where we took *her* for her first holiday. That place in Wales. When she was eighteen months old. And of all things, that place is still open. They still have the four cottages they rent out.'

'Stop. We can't just leave.'

'You can, and you have to. I checked on the cottages a while back, in case I ever had to, you know, go somewhere for a while.'

His wife looked at his scarred hand. 'After you'd done something terrible.'

The father nodded. 'And you can't tell anyone, anyone at all where you are going. No one.'

'Do you think that I could even bear to see that place again, where we were, with her?'

'Then choose somewhere else. But wherever you go, tell no one.'

'My parents won't leave here.'

'Please.'

'You'd put us all in so much danger? I'm not sure I even know who you are.'

The father felt himself shrivel, inside and outside. His skin cooled, prickled, and a little tremor made him shake. 'I want to be who I used to be. Without her, I never will be.'

'It's too much. This, what you ask, is too much . . . for us, here, in this life. You've gone too far.'

'Then think of this: there is no vaccine for that bug. Look at the hospitals. It'll be the elderly who'll be going out like—'

'Stop!'

'Do it for that reason. Leave here and go to a better place, with your mum and dad.'

'There's always a bug. This one will be like the others. They come, they go—'

'Not this one. I've heard things. Been told things. We can't assume it's like the others. Please leave. No later than tomorrow. You have to tell me that you will go.'

'I can't. How can I tell you something like that?'

The father closed his eyes. 'If I could . . . If there was a strong chance that I could find out what happened, or even find her, would you go then? Just for a while, until I called you?'

His wife stayed quiet for a while, then sniffed and wiped her eyes. 'I would go to hell and back just to know.'

He held her hand tight. 'And I get that. But I'll go to hell for both of us. For all of us. For even the slightest chance of knowing, I will go anywhere. Places that you cannot imagine that I will never let you see. Because she is worth it. Because we are worth it, our family.' He stood up and continued with his packing.

'Can you at least tell me where you are going?'

'Somerset.'

'Somerset!'

'There is someone I need to speak to down there, who might know something. I can't say any more. Get new idents, all of you, and let me have yours before I leave. And I will be in touch when it's safe for you to come back here.'

'Jesus Christ.'

'If your parents won't leave, then you have to go alone. I mean it.' The father buckled his rucksack closed and walked to the door. 'Gotta go now.'

Miranda climbed out of the bed and followed him to the door. When she touched his hand he turned and held her tightly. 'Go,' she whispered. 'I'll deal with my parents. What about your brother?'

'I'm counting on George being safer in New Zealand.'

SEVENTEEN

'On the bed.' The father pointed the handgun at the biggest bed he had seen in his life. From the mirror that formed the entire rear wall of the master bedroom, back at him leapt his reflection: a caped horror show, his face defining itself pinkly through the sodden mask. Black with rain, the new hat drooped around his ears. About his bones, the army surplus poncho was seaweed-slick.

I am nothing but a thing soaked to its skin, in clothes two years ragged, holding a gun. I am shorn, bespattered, psychopathic, bestially liberated. And I am here for you.

Fear in the beautiful green eyes of the woman who should not have been here, transformed into something else that promised hysteria. Panic jittered along her arms like St Vitus's Dance and made her hands flutter before she clutched them to her cheeks.

Minutes before, as the couple alighted from the Ferrari, the father's dripping presence had appeared in the garage. The moment the soles of Yonah Abergil's hand-stitched loafers found the cement floor, an aerosol of the evil shit had pattered over his jowly head. So noxious were the chemicals in the enclosed space, they had all barked like dogs to clear their airways.

Inside the expansive hall, where the father had first ushered them, the girlfriend's confusion had turned to anger. 'Do you know who we are? Do you fucking know who we are?' she had screamed at the man she had found waiting at Yonah's lavish home, wet to his underwear and socks and shivering with more than cold, but pointing a handgun at her face.

'I know what you are,' the father had said to the woman, as the gold and white opulence of the house seemed to vault like a Catholic shrine about them. And her threats helped him overcome the horror of seeing her alight from the car, and not long before he had realized there was a nurse on the premises too. He had not expected to find two women here. There *should not* have been two women here. There should not have been *any* women here.

If anyone is in that villa, with the exception of the old boy, you have to clip them . . . Think of your girl and do what you need to, yeah?

The couple had not seen him emerge from the ornamental trees growing inside the garden wall, or run so quickly across the rain-thrashed drive after the security gates opened. Nor had they seen him duck into the garage behind the slowing vehicle, where he had then hidden, crouching, behind their car; a creature from murky waters, its pincers gloved in surgical rubber and ready to bite. They had not seen him on account of the dark, or the rain that flogged the house; they had not even seen him when the security lights exploded yellow across the front of the property, because they were drunk. Through the wet gusts that gambolled and flapped in from the estuary, growing in power by the hour, Yonah Abergil had driven his rare and expensive car home intoxicated. Why so reckless, the father had wondered, when you have so much?

As the couple had swayed and wobbled out of the blood-red vehicle with flushed faces, their imported clothes had issued aromas from the best things remaining in this life. They had seemed to be of the past, abruptly alien to the father's current existence and how it had been partitioned amongst bedsits, anodyne hotel rooms, and an old family car's hot interior.

In all the hours of waiting, of being dissolved from the inside by the acids of anxiety and the agony of recollection which had filled the last two years of his life, where were these people? They had evaded all that. Fortunes stowed and unshared, they lived deep inside glittering palaces, glass and steel monoliths, or were caged within humming perimeters of electrified fence. And inside that swept garage and living room befitting a tyrant, the father found nothing but resentment inside his deeps. Evidence of a lifestyle he could only imagine had made his lava boil, gut low. *All of this for stealing children . . .* for putting women to work in brothels, the dispossessed into labour gangs. Legitimized barons and sanctioned exploiters, that's what they were. They were the tax-loopholed, dirty-cash-laundered elite, replete and meateater-sheened. They made it too easy for him to think of them with such simplicity. And it was vital that he did hate them, or how else would he kill them all this night?

He ran back over the current situation: *crying woman, man choking on the living-room floor, old man watching his screen, his nurse shackled in the kitchen . . . phones, panic buttons, cameras . . . what to do?* Then forced his mind to return to this bedchamber fit for a spider king, where he had pushed the woman ahead of him.

Once the advantage of surprise was taken, then whatever followed was dependent upon his decisiveness. He was on his own, and more so than ever before. And now they were all inside and individual roles were being established by swift, brutal methods, and as every second ticked by, he was starting to hate himself. He loathed female grief because of how low it made him feel. Next to the woes of young children, he found the distress of women the hardest to endure, and as a man accustomed to disappointing women, familiarity was no defence before their tears. 'No. I didn't mean *that*,' the father said, when he perceived that the woman thought she was going to be raped. 'Get on the bed. I need to tie you . . . I need to restrain you . . . I mean . . .' He was only making it worse. She began to shudder.

'I'm not going to hurt you. Please.' This assurance in his trembling voice didn't do any good. She'd already stumbled backwards, away from him, in her high-heeled shoes, towards the wall beside the vast bed. And there might be a weapon in the cabinet drawers. This woman had already told him about the existence of two handguns in the kitchen. There would be others, concealed, ready to blaze away at trespassers and thieves come to partake of what had already been stolen from others, or purchased with blood money. But how could a woman so beautiful, who looked so frightened, be one of *them*?

Yonah Abergil was lying on the floor of the living room, blowing his nose tanks out and down a suit that seemed to have been tailored with magic. His fat hands and skinny ankles were bound with the steel cuffs, his greasy mouth was hampered by the kinky shit, his face swollen and wet with tears.

Abergil senior was inside a day room that resembled a North African warlord's rumpus room; he was untethered but wheelchair-bound. The father knew that the elderly man had dementia but didn't rule out his attracting attention in some other way. A hidden phone, something like that. Panic button. *You were going to check for them.* The father's chest tightened as the situation began to unravel. Who would come here? More of them, the Kings, or a private security patrol with shoot-to-kill permits, or maybe their friends in the police?

One thing at a time. *Be systematic.*

He would have to check on the old man again once this woman, the mistress, was secure. In the palatial distance, the nurse was still sobbing, her face reddened from the nerve agent he had sprayed her with after he'd stumble-marched Yonah Abergil and his woman into the house from the garage.

The nurse had already run for a phone, or she had been trying to reach one of the guns in the kitchen: the father didn't know because the nurse didn't speak English. She had been hard to communicate with, though his handgun had proven more effective than any muffled verbal efforts, grunted through the cotton clinging to his wet face. But there were too many people, too many rooms, too many phones, too many guns.

Cameras?

The nurse was secured with the cord from an apron in the type of kitchen the father would have expected to find in a restaurant frequented by the super-rich. The stainless steel, coppers, glass and dark flagstones had unsettled him with diffidence. And then the room's opulence had made him angrier. *This is what they have for being how they are.*

A metal pole supporting a breakfast bar now stood between the nurse's secured arms. It had looked sturdy when he tied her wrists. She'd thought the father was going to kill her. They all did. They all expected to be killed; clearly a rule in the world they inhabited, one that swarmed with the vengeful. A world they had refashioned to suit themselves. A world they never expected to turn against them. But they must have entertained doubts that their lives could just go on and on and on like this, while so many suffered . . . with ninety million people out there, fidgeting and restless with chronic stress about blackouts, food, flood water and the terrible sun.

'Away from there!' he bellowed at the girlfriend in the master bedroom. She stopped moving and started swallowing whatever was clogging her throat. 'Forget the fucking bed!' Anger was good. He needed more anger, but not too much until they were all secure. 'Just kneel on the floor, now!'

Kneeling suggested execution in their world; he read this in her eyes. 'I'm not going to hurt you. I am here for information only. From your . . . your boyfriend, or whatever the fuck he is. Yes?'

The woman teetered a few feet away from the bedside cabinets, clearly uncertain whether she believed him. Reaching one hand down to the bed she eased herself to her knees.

'Away from the bed. Here, on the rug. Move!'

She did so, on her hands and knees, and crawled towards him in a way he thought accidentally obscene. 'Stop. There. Put your hands out.'

The father unthreaded the cord that was looped around a dressing gown hanging on the door, and bound her wrists, then strapped and tied her arms against her body with a leather belt. Her fingernails were immaculately painted red, something you rarely saw any more. One of her fingers glittered with diamonds, her wrists rattled with gold.

'Good. Good,' he whispered to her in encouragement. 'This won't take long. You won't be hurt. I promise. Now stretch your legs out.'

'No. Please, God.'

'Just so I can tie them. I will not harm a hair on your head . . . if you do what I say.' The ease with which the words were beginning to come to him made the father feel a combination of relief and disgust.

The woman stretched her long legs out and the father moved to her ankles. Looked about the room, frantic to find another bond with which to tie her legs as both sets of cuffs were already in use on Yonah Abergil. He didn't want her moving to a concealed weapon, a phone, a button. *Maybe one has already been pressed.*

The father ran to the walk-in wardrobe, tore open the doors and chose one of at least a hundred handmade ties. He returned to the woman and knelt by her ankles, removed her shoes. The heels were long, patent black daggers. They brought to his mind quick, hot thoughts of other floors upon which other pairs of high-heeled shoes had once been discarded; memories from deep within his days in the logistics hierarchy when the ambitious looking to move upwards would use any tactic for elevation. Ambition he had taken advantage of, taken his share of. They had been irresistible to him, those girls in tailored suits and silky blouses, whose softness whispered beneath their clothes, whose perfume had intoxicated him as much as the alcohol he'd poured down his neck as he courted them at conventions, at functions, and in the offices where so many games were still played, as the climate raged and the world disintegrated.

He caught again a stronger, sudden sense of himself in the past, a near-forgotten man now. Was consumed by a sense of the tingling, tantalizing, heady excitement that came with a new face, pair of legs, uncovered breasts, a strange voice saying his name, encouraging him, flirting with him, a refreshingly alien mouth on his lips in some half-lit room, far away from home.

He'd often wondered if the state of emergency had added fuel to human desire. People said so. The opportunities for intense reminders of what it was to experience pleasure, to lose one's mind in another's body, were precious. The sense that the chances for such activities, like everything else, were falling into short supply for all but a very few people, may have been one of his motivations and his excuses in hindsight.

The legs of the girl on the floor shimmered under the spotlights in the ceiling. Her legs were coated in a fine second skin of sheer nylon. Stockings. Black to match her transparent panties. He'd seen nothing like it in years. He could see how her underwear clung to her pale buttocks like a dark smoke because her dress was hiked up. There had been so many times when he had not resisted his urges, and when he'd made promises and assurances to ransack the bodies of desirable women. He had been despicable. But this girl had dressed to please that *thing* out there – that people trafficker face down in the living room. With her beautiful legs she rewarded the sexual slavery that he engineered.

The father's arousal was a neglected, confused beast, which tried to awaken its old heat and become an unruly engorgement. And yet he waved a loaded handgun through the exclusive air of the stranger's house, with his face masked. People about him slobbered from the effects of a nerve agent.

Monstrous.

He shut his heat off. The sense that the top of his skull was lifting, his spirits rising, he closed, sickened at himself for feeling desire at a time like this, when he had frightened a woman half to death in her own home.

Lust had always distracted him. Two years ago, he had been asked to watch over his little girl and he had written a flirtatious mail to a woman instead while a stranger had lifted his daughter's small feet from the soil of their garden, and taken her away. He'd once believed losing his little girl was a natural consequence of his behaviour, even a punishment. But there was no reckoning, there were no judgements other than the ones that were made by men like the one he was about to execute. On this, the theology of King Death was right.

He stood up. Collected a pair of clean socks from a drawer, pulled one taut, slipped it between the woman's glossy lips, and knotted it behind her head.

She closed her eyes and wept.

*

With the woman's lover he could not be so tolerant. The man was cuffed at wrist and ankle with penitentiary steel, and positioned in the middle of the vast living room, his knees strapped together with his own leather belt, his head engulfed by a pillow case, like a ready-made crime scene photograph.

As the father trotted down the three marble stairs and entered the vast lounge area, he tried to disassociate the figure from the evening's inevitable conclusion. But when he stood beside the body on the floor, unbagged its head and removed the gag, the gravity of the impending execution became disorienting again.

'You know you die for this,' the man said quickly. 'Your family, your friends. Children. All of them. They die. Bastard. You are bastard.'

'But not before you, unless you use that swine mouth for something other than making threats.' The father kicked the man's shoulder hard.

The blow only succeeded in making Yonah Abergil angrier. 'Bastard! Everyone you know, they cease to exist. In one week, they all in hell. I assure—'

The father's second kick met the man's red face.

While Yonah blinked and coughed in shock and a momentary senselessness, the father regagged him and sprayed the nerve agent over the man's entire head.

The father left the lounge and entered a large adjoining room with a full-size snooker table, a bar, walls covered in original paintings, and a sunken floor leading to what looked like a cinema. Beyond the large glass patio doors, the black surface of a swimming pool was riddled with rainfall.

All this from slavery and murder.

The father uncapped a bottle of whisky from behind the bar and began to gulp. He was wet through but burning alive. His legs were numb. He wiped tears from his eyes and noticed the painting above a fireplace that a fully grown man could walk inside.

The father checked on the old man again. He was still smiling at the large images that flickered around his chair. It was a holographic film, a Chinese action thriller about evil American imperialists with a plan to control the world's fresh water. It had once been very popular. Perhaps the still-functioning fragments of the old gangster's brain liked to be reminded of former glories, schemes in collaboration with corrupt authorities, gunfire, body counts, piles of cash, girls and rare wines on tap.

The dresser was full of blister packs and pharmaceutical boxes. No shortages here, but did the old man need medication now? *The nurse . . .*

Whisky bottle in one hand, gun in the other, the father walked across the house of plenty to where he had secured the nurse in the kitchen. The tea towel stuffed inside her mouth muffled her shrieks at the sight of him. The father held up his hands, palms outwards, to show he meant no harm. Then filled a jug with cold water at the sink. Returned to the lounge and doused the head of Yonah Abergil, who eagerly raised his swollen face into the stream and moved his head from side to side to direct the liquid onto his burning eyes.

The father placed the whisky bottle on the coffee table, sat down, cross-legged, before the blinking, sputtering upturned face and removed the gag. 'This can all stop. Very soon. Your dad gets his medicine, your girlfriend gets untied. Everything goes back to how it was, if you help me. I am going to ask you some questions.'

'Nothing!' The man raised his head and spat onto the father's legs.

The father stood up calmly, collected the whisky bottle from the coffee table, positioned himself behind Yonah and smashed it across the back of his head, making sure the heavier base did not connect with his skull. Yonah's hair was threaded wet and red.

'Or we go on like this. We go on and on and on, all night.' The father reintroduced the nerve agent to his hand and prepared to use it.

Yonah grimaced and rolled away, his neck rearing like a serpent, his head twisting away from another incineration of his eyes and sinuses.

The father followed him and rolled him back to the middle of the floor. Yonah was a big man, carrying at least thirty extra kilos in such lean times, and his gut hadn't been built by cultured micro-proteins. The man's breathing was now under severe strain too, twines were snapping from his cables; the bullock was sagging, poisoned and leashed.

'You think I am a rat, you waste your time coming here, to my home, you fuckin' bastard!' But even after two doses of the agent that had entirely closed one of his eyes, Yonah Abergil's spirits hadn't dimmed entirely. This was no sex offender who'd be shaken apart merely by the shadow of a vigilante.

The father let the man's wet, swollen head fall back to

the floor, where he messily ejected mucus from his nose and emptied his mouth of toxic saliva blended with blood. 'This isn't what you think. I don't want to know about your money, your business. Or whatever else you do so you can live like this, like a python king in its palace.' The father waved the handgun at the room. 'I want you to tell me about one job. One job only. A job when someone was taken. A child. A child stolen from her home, from her parents. A snatch that was performed on your watch. Your turf. You know about it. You would have signed off *the work*. My sources are very good. They ratted you out because you are reptile shit in human form. And thank God there can still be consequences for someone like you.

'So, back to this little girl who I'm here for. Information about one little girl is what you will provide. I want to know where you and your organization sent her. And then everything can be as it was. You understand me, you fat fuck?'

The one red eye that regarded the father struck him as satanic. He saw calculation within it, some mystification, complete contempt, outrage at the situation, and an innate hatred for all but its own. He wondered if the man saw the same thing in his eyes.

Yonah Abergil spat again. 'You come here . . . you end your life for one kid? You come into Yonah's home, you tie up his woman and lock away his father, and you expect me to help you? You think I am afraid of death? I love death.'

The father recalled the thing in the painting that hung above the fireplace in the games room, and its bones and rags seemed to dance and jerk through his mind now. 'I can see that you do. And I can help you with that. And your father too. That old bastard has done his fair share, has he not? King Death? Big men. You think? No. I know what you are. Reptiles.'

The whisky made the father's head spin through fragments of an education long over, and practically meaningless. 'Amniotes. Tetrapods. Cold blooded. Squamata, the worm lizards. You've been around for three hundred and fifty million years, you know that? You began as Protosauria, the first lizards. You grew and survived, and survive you will again. You swim backwards in time because you are Sauropsida, the true reptiles. You have Therapsida, the beast face. I can see it now. You are unredeemable. There is no rehabilitation. You are the face of our times. You flourish because you lay so many eggs. You are oviparous. That means you are an egg layer. We are now in the Mesozoic age all over again because of you and your kind. The great age of the reptile. *You.*'

Yonah Abergil's visible eye changed its expression. He looked at the father as Malcolm Andrews had; at that moment a realization dawned that here was a man unstitched at some fundamental level. Threats and negotiations would not be effective before such madness, such determination.

The father showed the red devil eye on the floor the picture of his little girl. 'Take a good look. She was this age when she was taken from the garden of her home in Shiphay, Torquay. A place she felt safe, where she lived with her mother and her father. You ruined more than one life that day.' The father recited the address, the exact time, the date, the year.

There was no remorse, no softening in the scarlet eye. 'I know of this girl.'

The father's heart stuttered then resumed banging, but too heavily.

'*Oui. Oui.* I remember. I remember,' the man added almost fondly and smiled.

The air of the room seemed to still, but cool with a special tension that paused time. In the distance, from the old man's day room that could have housed thirty people in a municipal care home, gunfire exploded in the film.

The father stayed quiet. He did not know what to say. Secretly, he had never expected to hear the right response. Some vestige of what might have been a redundant decency inside his heart was still reluctant to extract information in this way, because he did not want his behaviour rewarded. But it was the only way, and in time, he was sure, his methods would become standard. This was one of the conclusions he had drawn during so many hours staring at walls, floors and ceilings that needed painting.

'I tell you of this time and you must kill me. *Oui, oui.* Because if I live, then I warn who paid me so well to find men to take her, yes? And then those who have her will soon know you are coming too. I live and I also have to do some bad things to your bitch wife. Your bitch daughter also. I am right, am I not? You must know of us, of how we work. And you are the father, yes? But in this house we are all fathers. Me too. Yes, you did not know that? We are all bad fathers here.'

And as the father crouched, stunned before a glimpse of an inhumanity he thought himself immune to, he detected the tiniest squeak of rubber on marble at the end of his hearing, and he rolled sideways.

The leather settee, a few feet behind him, was punctured and let out a wheeze of air at the same time he heard a handgun bark.

Glass smashed, wood splintered, plaster puffed.

The father saw the white bulk of the nurse, her hand flashing as she fired again, again and again to tear up the room around him.

Yonah Abergil rolled back and forth on the floor, crimson-faced, bellowing orders. 'Kill him! Kill him! You bitch, kill him!'

The father expected to be shot, but the woman continued to fire too wide, too low, or too high. Her bloodless face jumped with shock, her head twitched. She was an amateur, like him, miscast and thrust into the warping, slowing seconds of a murder scene.

The father rolled, then scampered behind the sofa. Noticed two incoming shots had passed through the settee to impact hardwood cabinets set against the wall. That had been the sound of splintering he'd heard. But he was behind no real cover, and fearing the woman's sudden composure and a truer aim, the father came up onto his knees and rested his wrists upon the back of the suite. And fired.

A bleached tunic blossomed red. Became Rorschach-patterned as he hit her twice more. She lost her balance after the first bullet found its mark, teetering backwards on her plump heels, mouth open in horror at the idea of being shot. The father guessed she died sometime while sliding down the wall to thump the floor. Her head remained still, positioned on one shoulder, eyes wide with surprise.

Dead. He'd killed a woman, *a woman.*

He tried to figure out how she had got herself free. She still wore the apron cord, so she must have silently pulled the metal pole from the floor, or from out of the breakfast bar? *Worked it loose, slipped her hands under* . . . How did he not hear?

The voice of Yonah Abergil, the voice of rage, brought him out of his shock. 'Stupid bitch! You stupid bitch!' he screamed at the reddening lump at rest against the wall of his expansive living room.

From the old man's adjoining room the sound of gunfire continued and prolonged the atmosphere of carnage with firearms, the darkness flashing like a dance floor. The old man asked twice for someone called 'Marie', then fell silent.

The father came out from behind the settee and checked in the adjacent master bedroom. 'For Christ's sake!' The girlfriend was sitting up now, and had shuffled to a drawer that she was trying to open with her bound mouth.

The father went to her, seized her slippery ankles and dragged her across the room and through to the living room so he could watch her. The woman's dress wrinkled further up and over her buttocks to reveal all of her to the waist, like a torture porn film with an arty aesthetic. He had initially separated everyone in the house because whoever heard the interrogation would have to die, and he'd contracted inside, like an anemone on a rock, at the thought of executing the mistress and the nurse. Maybe if they hadn't heard the interrogation they could have been spared? But now?

'Turn your face away,' he said to the woman.

She didn't seem to understand. The father rolled her over with his booted foot.

'Bastard!' Yonah Abergil cried out.

The father swallowed the caustic reflux in his throat. Stood astride Yonah. Aimed the handgun at the back of one knee and fired.

The man's screams expanded and echoed throughout the entire house.

The father dragged the woman back to the bedroom. The noise erupting from Yonah was further confirmation that he would not be able to shoot this woman.

Back inside the master bedroom, he knelt beside her. Her fragrance and her fear swamped his face. 'I have to hurt him. We both know it. He's a devil and you sleep with a devil that buys you baubles. He thinks he has inherited the world through slavery . . . and murder . . . corruption. Kidnap. He allowed people to take a child. You all climb into the lifeboats before the children. You are an intimate affiliate of the reptiles. You present yourself to the best of your ability and then willingly writhe in their discarded scales. But I will not hurt you if you stay here and remain quiet. If you try and escape, or hear what he says to me, I will have to kill you. I am closing this door, but I may come back, into this room, at any time. If you have moved, I will start shooting without delay. I promise you that.'

The father retrieved another handful of silk ties from the wardrobe. Strapped her glossy thighs together. Bound another tie behind her hot knees.

He retreated to the games room and uncapped another bottle of good whisky on the bar. Through the door arch, he watched the figure on the living-room floor as he drank. Yonah Abergil squirmed in his own blood, lit up by the beautiful lights.

A phone began to chirp in the distance. The father checked his watch. He'd been at the house for twenty minutes. He returned to the living room, squatted. Through the wall the father could hear the girlfriend sobbing through the wet sock in her pretty mouth. He again held the picture of his daughter before Yonah's face.

'Bitch!' The man spat on the picture without hesitation.

The father carefully wiped the bloodied saliva off the plastic covering, using Yonah's shirt. 'I don't want this to continue. I'm feeling sick. I never feel entirely comfortable . . . But it takes you over, doesn't it, when you get going? And why do you all make it so easy for me? But I'm genuinely thinking that I should end this soon. I'll shoot every fucking one of you to death unless you tell me who took her.'

'Bastard!'

'You want to walk with a limp? Or do you want to sit beside your dad in a wheelchair?'

'You fuck yourself!'

The father stood astride Yonah Abergil and shot through the back of his second knee.

After a tense moment of complete silence, the man withered. His mouth fell open, his one unclosed brown eye bulged, his breathing stuttered and he started coughing. The pain must have been an agony beyond space and time. This was war, the father thought. *I am in war. I am at war.*

A strange peace settled over him as he sat on the sofa. The big nurse had managed to hit the seat three times. The stuffing was smouldering. He could see smoke drifting from one bullet hole. His inappropriate sense of calm was twinned with an anaesthetizing exhaustion, and he wondered if he were now finally comfortable with brutality, or if his mind was shutting down and sliding into a protective shock.

'So this is your last chance, Yonah,' he said tiredly, 'before I really ruin the film your father is watching. I swear to you now, he will not live to see the end credits. The girl. The little girl that was taken—'

Yonah rolled onto his back, gasped, then started to pant, his face white as if all the blood in his body was leaking from his knees.

The father took his eyes away from the legs; he found the immobility of the man's lower portion an unbearable sight. And he suffered more than a begrudging admiration for this man's refusal to talk. What kind of code would prevent a confession at such a time? The father recalled the thing in the painting, the loping thing in rags. *What are you to them?*

Yonah started talking in French, then Spanish, Russian, then what sounded like Hebrew, before his voice disintegrated into the tight gasps of the agonized.

The father stood up and walked to the open door of the old man's day room. The old man turned his head and smiled at the father. The father raised the pistol, half-heartedly, knowing he could not kill the old man he now aimed at.

'*Non*. No. Not Papa!' Yonah screamed from the floor. 'I tell you. You fucking prick!'

The father turned his head in the doorway but did not lower his arm. Yonah Abergil moved his head so he could stare at the father with that one red eye. 'They are dead. Those who take the girl. Semyon Sabinovic is dead. He is the one that took your girl. He was a smack head. Oleg Chorny was the driver. Georgian witch fucks. Semyon started to shoot himself up too high with smack, yeah? Got sloppy. So we arranged to kill him after the job. But his faggot toy, Oleg Chorny, he lived for a while. Another junkie. He goes into hiding but there he also died. Drugs. Another junkie fuck.'

The father frowned inside his mask. He didn't understand.

Yonah spat his mouth clear. 'Oleg and Semyon took her. Drove her . . .'

'Where?'

'To the man that pay for the snatch.'

'What man? Give me his name.'

'We only speak with some fucking lawyer. He paid us two hundred grand to take the girl. This lawyer we done work for before. We don't know who paid him to set up the job. Just the representative we see, the lawyer. But Semyon and Oleg follow this lawyer's car, from the swap. They track the girl's clothes, yeah . . . with a tiny bug, so Semyon will know . . . who he do this snatch for. I know they do it, Georgian faggot pricks. They wanted to see who buys the kid. Semyon's thinking of blackmail, maybe, later. Maybe this is a rich pervert they can shake down. Who knows? But they go and *they* see who buy the girl.'

The father leaned against the door so he could stay on his feet. *Alive?* She could be alive. *Alive. Alive. Alive.*

Pervert.

Maybe not.

'My girl,' the father whispered. 'Who . . . who did they take her to?' He stood over Yonah, pointed the muzzle at the side of his head. 'Tell me!'

'That's it, you fuck. All I know. The man who buy her was cautious, maybe he suspected the car would be followed, so he already paid me to kill Oleg and Semyon, but all through this lawyer. So I already done your work. Semyon got clipped, but Oleg killed himself with drugs when his faggot lover was wiped. They were lovers, queers. The name of who paid for this little girl died with them, the junkie fucks. They tell no one. They only worked with each other, no one else. Maybe if they had shared more, I didn't have to ice them. Now get me a doctor. I'm fucking dying.' Yonah gasped for breath, though whether this was exasperation on account of ratting, or the pain, the father did not know.

The girlfriend whimpered from beyond the bedroom door.

The father shook himself back into an awareness of the room, the carnage, the massacre. He fought through his memory as if it was full of jungle vines to find the name. 'This lawyer, this go-between, what was his name?'

'Oscar. Oscar Hollow. I have the number. In my study. We go there. Call him.'

But he would still have to look for the abductors, in case Yonah was lying. For the abductors now to be dead was too easy. 'These men that took her. Where did they live? Where!'

'They lived in . . . above Brixham. Somewhere by the camps. Devon. But they are dead, I tell you . . .'

'Who else knows they did this job?'

'Only me.'

'Convenient, and the kidnappers are dead?' Even Rory Forester knew something. 'You're lying.'

'OK, maybe a few associates know it was Oleg and Semyon who took that girl. I trust them so I tell them. But I swear that Oleg and Semyon are dead. Only they and the lawyer knew who paid for the girl and where she goes.'

'Tell me more and you can have your doctor. Tell me more about them. Tell me about these pigs that stole a child for money.'

The red eye regarded him, wanting to believe the assurance. 'Oleg was *enlumineur*. He do the tattoos, yes? He was our best. Oleg's tattoos were beautiful.' The man spat his mouth clear. 'Witches. They were . . . you know . . . He and Semyon, they go too far with the old ways from the old countries. Semyon think he know things. Thinks he is special. Some kinda priest. Shaman. Yeah? Invincible? Too many people listen to him, yeah, like Oleg did. They have too much influence. So they are given this job because they are the best at snatches. But this is to be their final job . . . I make sure of that, but we only get one, Semyon, in Totnes, where he had a place. On my father's life, this is the truth.

'Oleg, like I say, he die of a broken heart. I pay the Moroccans to go and see Oleg and snuff him, but they find his body, under the old church that him and Semyon used for their witchy bullshit. They showed me photos. There was no mistake. Oleg was dead. No pulse.'

Yonah closed his eyes and gasped. A curious shudder passed through his entire body. His one open eye looked terribly bleary now. 'Strange men, Oleg and Semyon. They see too much. Both of them. The queers. Two of them together, they were looking in other places for a long time to try and see something. They look in afterdeath, to see if *it* have a face. A face no one should see. But they both see things that send them crazy, or they take too many drugs, who knows? So they take more and more drugs . . . One could not live without the other. The junkie bastards who followed them, down there, they think Oleg and Semyon were prophets. Down there in the old church, the junkies put Oleg under it when he dies. In a . . . in a . . . crypt . . .' Yonah's testimony was becoming garbled, confused.

The father thought of the painting in the other room, the picture on Bowles's wall, the stretched arms of bone outside Rory's hovel. The connections were unsettling. 'What did they see? What is this fucking face?'

Yonah's open eye settled on the father, and widened. 'Maybe you see this too . . . you would be like them. Maybe you are already . . .'

The father wondered what he should do. He worried he might lose his voice before he could ask more questions. But what questions? And Yonah was delirious with pain and no longer making much sense. The father's mind was becoming a blank, wiped clean from shooting a man in both knees, and from killing a woman. But he believed some of what Yonah had said, just like he'd believed Murray Bowles and Rory Forrester. He got results in the same way these men had, because he'd used a language they understood. This made him feel absurdly better about the nurse and all of the blood swiping, smearing and staining the floor and rug of the living room.

He thought of the girlfriend with the sock tied tight inside her painted mouth. He needed to check on her. *Now!* But could not move his feet. If she had heard the names her lover had just confided to him . . . If she had, she would tell others, associates, or the police, whoever arrived here first, and it would be known why he had made a move tonight, and who he was prepared to become a bestial killer for: *a child*. Had she overheard the names, Oleg Chorny, Semyon Sabinovic? If she'd heard of the connection to this lawyer, this go-between, Oscar Hollow, then the other *man* who had paid for his daughter would also be warned. They would all know that the father was coming.

She was taken for so much money. *Why?*

The father clutched his cotton-skinned head to try and still the small explosions inside his skull. His mind offered problems aplenty but no solutions other than . . . what he couldn't face now. They all had to go. *Another woman. As well as Yonah*. Two more murders on top of the nurse. Another spree. The police would surely intervene. Both sides of the law would want rid of him.

You go in and you gotta be the only one who comes out alive. But he had not been told about the girlfriend, and the nurse shouldn't have been on duty. 'Oh Jesus Christ Almighty.'

The father moved around the room looking for weapons and cameras. The handgun he had removed from Yonah's jacket in the garage was already inside his rucksack. He had found a third handgun in the master bedroom in a bedside drawer and slipped it inside his bag. He was playing for time, delaying the inevitable.

Back inside the master bedroom he closed the door. The girlfriend had not moved. Her no longer so lovely eyes watched him. He put his fingers to her lips, listened hard. Through the closed door he could hear Yonah moaning, sometimes shouting. But his voice was muffled through the door. The father struggled to recall how loud their voices had been during the exchange about who had taken his daughter.

And, my God, he knew now. *He knew.* He had the names of the two men who took his daughter. Men apparently deceased. Men paid to snatch his daughter, but then murdered by their own boss. And the lawyer who brokered the deal, he had that name too. He had never been so close. No one had been so close. A loose word from Bowles, then Rory's sand-blasted face confessing at gunpoint, and now this fat criminal bound on the floor of a mansion. 'I am justified. I am justified,' he whispered to himself. 'Did you hear what was said?' he asked the girlfriend.

She didn't understand. He repeated the question twice, then embellished it with, 'What we discussed? Did you hear the names? You know of these people that were mentioned by your pig?'

She frowned, shook her head vigorously.

The lawyer. He had the lawyer's name: Oscar Hollow. Yonah had his details, idents, an address: the next move. The father rose from his knees, went back into the living room and removed the gun from the nurse's hand. She had small hands, silly hands, dead hands.

Yonah sat up and stared at the wet ruin that was the front of his trousers around the knees, the silk now sopping black. The father wiped his forearm across the man's wet eyes, but the second one was still closed, the first as red as fresh blood. 'You come here for your daughter, yes. I respect that. You are a man who has been wronged. *Oui, oui.* You will do anything for your family. It is all we really have, family. Am I not right? My father . . . Are you a man of honour? A man of your word? Your daughter, if she is . . . I can get her back. I make the call. I can do it now. Call the lawyer. He is your only hope. He knows where she was taken. We go straight through him and to the fuck who give us money to take a child. Had I known she was the child of such a man, I would not have let them take her. I have little to do with this snatch. I am just taking the money for the Georgian faggots. You think I can make these things happen? Just me here? I hear things. Know people. Nothing else.'

The father realized the bedroom door was open. He'd left it that way, was slipping now, couldn't coordinate so much inside his head. 'Shit.' If she hadn't heard Yonah before, then what had she just heard? Though Yonah had only just mentioned Oleg and a lawyer, he thought, but couldn't fully remember.

The father went and closed the door of the master bedroom without going back inside. Yonah's voice followed him. 'The lawyer. We call him now, yes? Yes. Come. We tell him the deal is off. I buy her back tonight. If she is alive, you will have your daughter in one day. What you say?'

'The number. The address.'

'I do it for you . . . In my office.' Yonah paused in his frantic monologue to wince and shudder white from the fresh onset of agony inside his devastated legs. 'My office . . .' The sweat-covered head nodded at the hallway before the front door. 'There is a safe.'

A ringtone trilled again from somewhere inside the house.

'Marie! Marie!' the old man called from his room.

Yonah's face screwed up. He wiped again at the cold sweat that pulsed from under his hair. 'No! I cannot move. My legs. Don't touch me. Please.'

Hands under the man's sopping armpits, the father dragged him quickly across the floor, out of the living room, and across the hall. 'Which room?'

Yonah was breathing heavily, his good eye had shut again. Drool had made an appearance at the sides of his mouth. The man was in hell. His legs had left draglines right through the house. 'This door,' he whispered.

'This one? This one!'

'*Non*. This . . .'

By the time the father backed him into the office Yonah had passed out. He knelt beside the man and slapped his cheeks. Pulled out a bottle of water that bumped against the weight of so many handguns inside the rucksack, and doused the man's head and face in water. Slapped him again. Yonah did not respond with anything but the vague movement of his bottom lip.

'Christ.' The father laid him on the ground. The lawyer, the lawyer's name was Oscar Hollow. It might be enough. His eyes flitted about the room looking for a safe, and saw the shrine. Squinting, he moved closer. Took it all in, then looked away.

On the wall of the office the screen pinged with an incoming call. Deeper inside the house another screen trilled. A third beeped from inside the kitchen. The house was being besieged by requests for contact, for signs of life, and at such an early hour of the morning. The sounds grew and swelled in urgency. The chirrups and bells pinpricked the father's sparking nerves. He needed to leave and fast. A two-mile walk to the car through the rain-doused darkness awaited.

From the distance the elderly man called for Marie again. In his mind the father saw the heavy-set nurse running sideways through the lounge, near-gibbering with fear, firing a gun wildly into the walls of the devil's palace. He imagined men rushing through the night too, coming to the house, holding black guns inside the unlit interiors of fast, expensive cars; all of them ready and able to smash vertebrae with hammers and electrocute testicles until they'd been cindered to olive pips, but only as a prelude to lopping through a neck with an oily machete.

The father stepped away from the unconscious figure on the floor. Withdrew his handgun from the side pocket of his trousers.

The closed eyelids made Yonah Abergil look dopey. Thick lips and a double chin gave him the appearance of being harmless and too ordinary for depravity.

He has to go.

The father squatted three feet clear and aimed the pistol at the man's faintly pulsing temple. Closed his eyes and squeezed the trigger.

EIGHTEEN

Back inside his shabby room at the guest house, the father stood upright and naked, his wet and soiled clothes strewn about his feet. In the age-speckled glass of the dresser mirror, he looked like a half-starved torture victim, superimposed onto an old page of history. But as he assessed the damage sustained in his retreat from Abergil's villa, he made sure not to look at his own face, the face of a killer that had its daughter's eyes.

After he'd dropped from the main gate of Yonah's villa, he'd seen distant white headlights shining across the black fields, no more than a mile away. If those had been reinforcements, he'd escaped with minutes to spare.

Nor would he ever learn how assistance had been summoned to Yonah's house: a panic button depressed by the nurse before he shot her, the failure to raise an answer from the incoming calls, an offsite detection through hidden cameras on the property? And as he staggered from the property the father had wondered whether those rushing into the breach after midnight were private security personnel or Kings. Home owners were permitted to use deadly force against intruders; it was close to the most popular policy introduced by the first emergency government, eight years earlier. A fear of which he'd carried on every move, churning like an unstable gas inside his shivery bowels.

Fleeing back to his car he'd been forced to go off-road, knocking and scraping his legs against tree branches, fences, fallen logs, and the bristling brackens engulfing the woods. Livid weals and scratches now flecked the angry bruises the length of his legs. A hot and insistent ache around a deep crack in his shoulder suggested the scaffolding of repaired tissue and sinew had come undone; the long pink knife wound in his hand transmitted the muscle-deep sensation of a fresh hole, as if Rory's blade had bloodlessly passed through his body that very evening. His lungs were peeled meat, depleted black wings cupping a near-expended heart. How many times could he go through this?

It had taken him two hours to find the car. The terrain on his retreat had been near-impenetrable, his feet hidden in darkness as he kept to narrow bands of woodland protecting crops from the road. Energy shortages forbade street lighting at night, but there had been few settlements or houses near Abergil's property. Dense, sopping clouds had covered the meagre iridescence of the heavens. Twice he'd stumbled in the wrong direction and crouched to catch his breath and re-orientate his retreat. But despite the discomfort of his wounds, and the fresh horror of killing two people, it was the lingering sense of being followed through the dark that now gave his hands a slight palsy.

Bedraggled and bleeding, rent and grazed, he had eventually returned to his lodgings. The grey-toothed and mute landlady had still been awake. Appearing crushed beneath some permanent weight of personal misery, which dimmed her eyes to a watery blue and sank the flesh at the sides of her mouth, she'd not said a word to him and only watched him stumble up the stairs to the room he'd now need to evacuate by morning. But all he'd mind for was the *thing* in the trees.

Deciding against his torch, which would have been seen for miles, unless absolutely necessary when he was caught on a spiny branch, or after he'd stumbled into a dead end, he'd hauled himself through the undergrowth at the side of the crop fields, and splashed through ditches already knee-deep with rain water, at the side of the roads that took him away from the criminal's home. And he'd become certain he'd been tracked all the way back to the car he'd parked earlier, tight to the hedgerow of a strawberry field. Only then did he stop casting fearful looks backwards, prepared to shoot whatever it was that seemed to be skittering through his disorderly wake.

Once the possibility of a pursuer had infiltrated his thoughts, he'd never stopped sensing it nearby. Every ten steps, he'd paused to peer about in a din of rainfall and heart thuds, ready to shoot at the closest crackle, snap, or the most immediate flurry of wet motion. But he'd seen nothing save the jagged outlines of black tree branches, the sway of leaf clusters buffeted by the wind, or the smudge of the stone walls bordering the road.

Onwards he'd pushed, more quickly each time, only slowing again when catching anew the rapid rushings of a thing scraped by twigs and flapped by wet leaves close behind him, or to one side. Twice he'd hissed a challenge and been answered only by heavy splashes of water funnelling above his head. But whatever was disturbing the branches and verdure behind him had consistently failed to reveal itself, as if *it* were invisible.

Over the last half-mile he'd blindly run into trees, scratched and speared himself, had his face repeatedly branch-whipped, his knuckles tugged at by brambles. He'd then continued with his face upturned, trying to catch a better sight of the suggestion of thin limbs that began launching from a tree branch to disappear into another silhouetted clump of cover; nearly seen swoops and winged flashes, beneath a black sky, or sudden bustles amidst the ocean sounds of the wind, shrieking through the tallest oaks and mountain ash, as if something large had periodically thrashed about, and directly above his head. Falling several times, and twisting onto his back, his gun hand wavering in the wet, inky atmosphere, he'd been convinced he'd become the quarry of something of the air.

Back in the room, hindsight assured him his flight had been marked by nothing more tangible than paranoia and the after-effects of traumas, the shock of ending lives with a handgun, from scaring a beautiful woman witless. All before seeing the collected *artworks* of Yonah Abergil in his office, as if that private viewing had been the apex of a terrible momentum, the final layer in a ritual he'd unwittingly attended.

The horrors of his actions travelled back through his limbs like vibrations. He felt again the ghostly imprint of Yonah's soft face against the top of one foot, heard the crack and crump, the glassy tinkle, after bringing down the whisky bottle against the back of the man's skull; tactile spectral imprints of the violence he'd inflicted.

Again, in his thoughts, the nurse's tunic punctured and filled red.

An old man called for Marie in the deepest fissures of his ears.

Ochre smears upon white marble.

The moist temple of Abergil's head, the quiver of the pulse.

And the bones he had seen upon the walls danced again in the father's mind. He covered his eyes as if that could shut such visions out. But once seen, the most terrible things remain inside forever. He knew that better than anyone.

Behind the polished glass protecting an alcove in the wall of Yonah's office, red candles had burned before a mess of photographs in a crude shrine: they depicted shots of waste ground, concrete walls, stained tarmac, darkened timbers and cement, even the sea's surface. The case had been stuffed with votive offerings of paper money, dimly glowing jewellery, a bottle of vintage champagne, an old wooden crucifix, a primitive-looking machete dull with age, and all arranged about the centrepiece: a human skull.

But amidst the sinister pictures, and arrayed like playing cards stood on end between the candles, he'd also looked upon photographs of people. Faces mostly, and captured in black and white: sullen with hunger, famished and empty-eyed, the scruffy-headed dead on pillows of their own black blood, faded uniforms on clay, greying fabric collapsing on papery bodies, antique crime photographs and holocaust panoramas, African genocides. Though which conflicts and atrocities they captured he couldn't guess. The pictures could have been taken from any number of crises over the last thirty years, and even intermingled with those from previous centuries.

The wall of the bar had also been dominated by a gaudy picture, transmitting a not-dissimilar message to that of the shrine. The painting was reminiscent of the art that illustrated garish religious pamphlets, dispersed by the innumerable varieties of evangelists. In the painting there had been a great figure with an open maw, empty eye sockets, its flesh blemished and withered by emaciation. The expression had been one of an unseemly joy, or a cruel excitement. The ragged thing was also crowned in wood, its form below the head comprised of dirty smoke as much as actual cloth and limbs.

Tinged a bruised apricot like a sulphurous dawn, the skies behind the head of the tattered central figure had broiled with opal cumulous, edged black as if charred. A sickly jaundice had glowed in the gaps between the clouds as if a heavy, nauseating, yellow light was struggling to come through from beyond. It had made the father think of water-borne diseases and cheap shrouds.

The cityscape the father didn't recognize, but it was haloed in a ruddy orange to suggest fire. The painting had a ribbon of scarlet painted along the bottom. The text was French: *L'Homme devant la mort*. The father didn't know any French.

He thought the painting medieval and European, yet primitively striking, while the shrine suggested the avant-garde with suggestions of the Americas. Another collision of decimating and colluding cultures, old and new, indigenous and foreign, densely coded and alien to his eyes. Ignorance, superstition and distant eras of darkness, seeping back as the seas rose and forests cindered. Of most concern was the incongruity of something so ugly, so malevolent, so brazenly despicable and yet perversely sophisticated, in a luxury villa occupied by a foreign criminal; a place from which he may have been followed. *But by what?*

He'd experienced a sense of an unaccountable awe too, after he'd knelt and executed the unconscious figure of Yonah Abergil; had even imagined himself making an offering, a sacrifice, to initiate his participation in an arena he could barely guess at. Strangely euphoric, after the savagery he'd indulged in, he'd been enveloped in a curious atmosphere and was momentarily reminded of the cathedral in Canterbury. He'd once attended a service there, to represent his company, around the time food aid stopped, when the great vaulted building had filled with people to beg God to intercede in the lives of further millions threatened through starvation. The study in Yonah Abergil's house had seemed to fill with the same hushed and fearful respect that accompanied a silent candlelit procession he'd watched in London years before too; one that had stretched for miles in support of Bangladesh, each flame representing the thousands of faces that had disappeared beneath the violent brown waters. The atmosphere distilled all that was inspired by the iconic picture of the two blonde orphans, the twins, shivering amidst the wreckage of their home in Florida, benumbed but painfully innocent, their dead mother in the foreground, whom they had covered with a duvet as if she were only asleep, following a hurricane in 2027.

Inside that room, he had fallen into a mute and stunned reverence that had seemed to elevate into a sudden, unbearable comprehension of something else, vast and ineffable, that had reached away beyond his mind and its vague notions of time and space. That was how it had seemed. A gripping fatalism for his species had finally chilled and clutched the room, then popped, as if a door had opened to release a mounting pressure, moments after he had squeezed the trigger. The epiphany couldn't have lasted for more than a few seconds.

He'd been left shaking, and wondering if the rumours about what these Kings of ruin believed had some merit.

Inside his dingy room at the guest house, the father slumped upon the bed and gulped at a bottle of rum. All about him were faded pink walls, orange curtains, china oddments rimmed with black dust that still managed to hang from the dross-furred wall brackets; an antique ghost-installation of bank holiday weekends for poor couples in decades long gone. And he tried to process the montage of bullet wounds, the faces inside Abergil's house, the faces of the shrine, the sound of a presence shadowing his rout through the wet, black trees that played on repeat behind his closed eyelids.

He drank more of the rum, and resumed his pacing of the dismal room as the storm slapped the side of the guest house. He knew . . . he *knew* now. If Yonah Abergil was to be believed, then two years ago, for two hundred thousand pounds, paid by an affluent individual who must have been intensely aware of the father and his family, his daughter had been stolen to order by two members of an organized multinational criminal gang: Oleg Chorny and Semyon Sabinovic. Those were the men who had driven the black car away from his home, up the street, to turn at the summit of the road, and to take *her* away.

Oleg Chorny. Semyon Sabinovic. Oscar Hollow.

He focused on the names. Scrabbled for his equipment. Activated the screen and inputted the details he'd tortured from Yonah Abergil's corpulent mouth.

My God, he'd executed a gang lieutenant in his own home. The enormity of the act, an assassination no less, suddenly became too large for his thoughts and he feared he'd begun to hyperventilate.

But he found nothing, not a trace of any of the three names he had been given. There was no listing for any lawyer in the British Isles called Oscar Hollow. He clawed at his hair and began to scream, wanted to go for a gun, but to do what? Then he stopped. Gene Hackman would know if they were on file, if they'd used an alias. All was not lost; Gene would know. The father had to find out, or he'd just murdered another two people for nothing.

Yonah hadn't been lying; the father trusted his instincts; they hadn't let him down so far. In fact, they'd led him this far . . . *and no further?*

What else had Yonah told him? The two kidnappers had addictions, were witches, shamans? Seers who had looked for, and seen, *something* unnatural. Men who were seekers. Seekers, but of what? That's what Yonah had communicated while in tremendous pain, fearing for his father's life, and using broken English on the blood-smeared floor of his villa. Yonah had confirmed that his daughter's abduction had been no opportunist snatch and grab of a passing sex offender. It truly had been a professional job.

But for who? Why would anyone go to such lengths,

and use such diabolical personnel, to steal his four-year-old girl?

'Oh God . . .' The father cramped and curled into himself upon the bed, while his entire consciousness seemed to slip, or collapse, through a sluice, at the arrival of the most unwelcome, but the most convincing, answer. Because such a price was paid only for a little girl that had looked a certain way and been a certain age. She was selected to satisfy the sadistic tastes of a deranged and pathological individual, who had probably amassed his wealth by utilizing those very same traits.

At the end, was there a terror so great that your heart burst? Were there agonies inside your small and perfect body that I have clutched to my own chest, so many times, to calm your distress? Did you encounter what no child ever should?

The father fell to his knees and scrabbled across the floor to his rucksack. He took out the four handguns, then stood up, gripping two of them, half-drunk and deranged; a witless, naked scarecrow in a speckled mirror who wanted to run outside, back through the storm to the house of Yonah, where he could shoot dead anyone he found, by simple association with Abergil, and of what his brokerage must have ultimately inflicted upon his daughter.

My love, my world.

Maybe he should dedicate his last few days alive to executing, without warning, any man that bore any connection to King Death, any affiliate, associate, prospect, or sympathizer. Perhaps a great levelling through bloodshed was needed to lance the corruption in the flesh of this beleaguered era.

And I could do it. Because if they hurt you, I could kill forever, and never feel a twitch of remorse.

And beloved is the virus that will streak so hot and shivering through their numbers. Precious is the tumult of water and debris that sweeps them away and holds their rat faces beneath the sewage and mud-thick swill. Sacred is the sun's fire that chars them back to carbon.

I will decimate them.

If you no longer exist, then they will no longer exist.

The father laid down his weapons and crawled to his bed, where he buried his face in the covers, and all but buried his daughter in an unknown grave, cold these two terrible years gone.

NINETEEN

What had followed him home from the murder scene billowed wide and black through his sleep.

He came awake from a dream in which he'd opened the door of a cupboard inside some grey place, only to find a collection of weathered bones amidst soiled clothes. Children's clothes buried within an earthen cavity, dug through the floor. *We can show you what we found.* His mother-in-law had said this. But when he'd turned, weightless with shock, he'd seen the body of Yonah's girlfriend, stood tall in her black lingerie and high heels as she packed handguns and his daughter's toys inside a leather suitcase. Her head was veiled, but he sensed that another woman's face smiled behind the black chiffon. The face of a woman he knew well when it pressed against the gauze. He'd shouted, *God, no!* But twisted within sleep, and quickly passed through other strange, at times seemingly familiar, scenarios. He found himself in a room, a black place with horrors painted upon the walls. A painted corpse twisted and danced in a distant corner, all the time grinning with satisfaction. The father then climbed and took his place within a shrine inside the room, amber-lit by candles in a cold darkness. Stepping over bodies turned to wood and paper and barely held together by their disintegrating clothes,

Yonah Abergil said, *And you, and you now*, directing his path at gunpoint, up through the famine's dead. Only for him to emerge in a concrete room, greened in the corners, with a cement floor stained dark and thickly. In there, he knelt beside his wife, the detective, and a woman hooded inside a sack.

You did this. You! Scarlett Johansson said through the bag over her face.

You did, Gene Hackman agreed, quietly, nodding.

His wife spoke while crying. *The moment you meddled with that bitch, you did this to us all.*

Out of a dark doorway behind them came a figure carrying a machete.

No matter how much he thrashed, shouted and struck his face within sleep, he'd not been able to break from the disorderly bed he found himself in next, in a badly decorated room. An object like a yacht's mainsail smoked and yet cracked like wet cloth, where a ceiling should have been, over his naked body. The thing glistened at its heart, and from its internal oiliness the vapours became as black and fine-haired as those of an insect under magnification.

Sleep's insistent torments would not release him. He next dreamed of himself and his wife standing in water, thigh-deep, black and cold. They held their daughter's little wrists as she sank into the void. Something was entwined around her legs and waist that they could not see. Only her head and arms broke through the surface. They had the feeble strength he so often encountered in persecution dreams; their arms were numb, near-lifeless, perhaps able to cling for a while, but not to raise a weight. In a voice of enforced calm, his wife had said, 'We need to say goodbye to her now.' The idea caused the father the pain of being impaled upon an icicle. He looked down and into the small and frightened face and knew he would never let her go: instead, he would go down to where she went, deep into the black.

At six he fell awake, fatigued and harrowed by the night's carousal. Dropped from the bed to go and douse his punished body in shallow, tepid bath water, meagrely drawn from what sputtered out of ancient pipes that made the floor of the communal bathroom shudder. Once his metered ration had dripped to an end, he dried his body and forced himself to swallow a dry bread roll and a cup of black coffee. He dressed in clean clothes that felt like a holy blessing around his punished skin, and packed away his belongings. He needed to move far away from where he had been an agent of murder.

The night's visions had left his nerves jangling, his thoughts at the edge of panic; it took hours before he felt better. He'd never been religious, and soon after his daughter's disappearance he'd lost all faith in the instinctive vestige of belief that there must be more than this world. He had no faith in justice or fairness, or any of the old values of the old world, but he didn't know what he believed in after the previous evening at Yonah Abergil's. King Death's notions of an inevitable and engulfing chaos, encroaching upon everything about him, even impressed him as the most realistic current option, informed by his experience. He truly felt as if he'd been touched by . . . he did not know what.

In a wind-maddened dawn, he drove through a sopping

world to the place Yonah said the kidnappers had kept a lair, an old church in Brixham; a place only a few miles away from where his daughter was taken.

While he waited for Gene Hackman to call and take his report, he planned to make certain that both kidnappers were dead. And the father understood that his motive for such an early start was mostly driven by the knowledge that he had finally brought himself to the attention of people who would not rest until his actions were avenged sevenfold.

TWENTY

'Where are you now?' Gene Hackman's call broke the father from a doze he'd been unaware of entering, and returned him to the noise of rain pelting the car. He'd parked on the outskirts of Brixham and the windscreen blurred the sea grey and spray-hazy. The police officer was using a new ident and no visual.

The father coughed sleep from his voice. 'Brixham. For good reason.'

'You alone?'

'Yes.'

'Distance from Somerset is no bad thing.' The man's voice had changed from the last time they had spoken, and verged on breathless. 'There's a shitstorm brewing. I wonder . . . if you should go to ground, for a while.' The father sensed the detective's serious misgivings over their association.

'Not possible. The men who took my daughter were down here. It was a local job.'

There was a loaded silence; the father prompted the detective. 'Gene, you sound different. Can you talk?'

'For a while. I've some bad news. Because of last night, your activities are already queue-jumping the murder squad's busy agenda. Rina Agnelli, Yonah Abergil's missus, has described your visit in great detail. And some clever prick over here has identified similarities in the recent slayings of at least two Kings, Rory and Yonah. There's a pretty good description of you from The Commodore, and Bowles's neighbour looked right at you too. Those two eye-witness accounts have been matched, and now linked to Abergil. Further forensic investigative measures are going to be pursued across all of the crime scenes. If that happens, we'll soon have your DNA because you puked in Bowles's house and dripped blood all over Rory's floor. Your records are in the national database. So it will just be a matter of time, my friend.

'Ballistics are also checking the slugs you left in Rory, and these will tie you to Murray Bowles and Nige Bannerman, but not Yonah. There's already some talk of how you chose your targets, and why. Some people are nervous. Like me.'

The father closed his eyes. 'The weather will hamper things.'

Gene disregarded his last comment as if it were wishful thinking that didn't warrant serious consideration. It was all the father had had to hold on to: the idea that everything else was far worse than what he was doing, and that what he had done didn't really matter. He'd also stopped believing this sometime during the previous night.

'Yonah Abergil has *friends* on the job. I knew that. I told you. Council too. So once you are in their frame, Yonah's little helpers on the force will track your movements, your vehicle by satellite, your financial transactions. Your car's legit, so back-dated movements and expenditure will give them the caseload. All of it puts you on the spot for all the shootings. Open and shut case. Because of your car, your whereabouts will be ascertained in no time. If you're lucky, it'll be us that come for you. If someone here makes a call and tells *them* where you are, the Kings will get there first. Count on it. It happens. So ditch that motor and fast.'

'I can't.'

'You will. Your motor has to go. It is your only chance to run for a bit longer. Your family hatchback needs to be driven a very long distance from where you are sitting, or you will not have the time to finish this. Leave it where I can find it. Message me the location at this ident. And I will scrap it. Don't buy anything unless it's with cash.'

The father swallowed. A cloud of unpleasant gas erupted from the floor of his stomach. He thought he was going to be sick into the footwell. 'I'm sorry.'

'You didn't finish up. I couldn't have made it any clearer about what was at stake if you went up against one of *them*.'

'I couldn't . . . her, the girl. She was, I don't know . . . just there, a girlfriend. She couldn't have heard anything.'

The officer's voice hardened. 'I gave you a new shooter. I told you. No witnesses.'

'She wasn't supposed to be there, or the fucking nurse!'

There was a long pause, both men breathing heavily as they bit back on trading the accusations they needed to let fly. The officer changed his tack. 'OK. OK. This shit always gets complicated. Let's cool our heels. Think.'

'I . . . I won't be apprehended. I can't be. I know that. Because of what would happen to me. But they'll never know about you. I promise.'

'You think?' The officer laughed unpleasantly. 'Upstairs is suspicious about the getaway in Torre, and there are some very good descriptions from Rory's little mates, who are all pointing the finger at a plain-clothes cop and vigilante collaboration.'

'I'm sorry.'

'It's a shit sandwich that we're spread on, any way you look at it.'

'The information you gave me, it was good. Abergil gave up the men who took my daughter. I know now. I know who they are, or were. And I'm pretty sure he wasn't lying. If you hadn't helped me, I wouldn't have this. It matters. What you did matters.'

'That's something. I'm pleased for you. I am, I mean it.' His voice trailed off and he sighed. 'You really worked him for it. Christ alive. You shot out his fucking knees. Blinded him in one eye. He'd never have got that eye back. Detached retina from blunt trauma. You royally messed him up.'

The father couldn't speak. The strength leaked from his body at this recital of his savagery.

The officer laughed. 'And he deserved everything he got. His end was the cause for some celebration, shall we say, for some on our side, and let's leave it there. I have no problem with what you did. But the girl, Rina, his missus, you'd have more time on your clock if she wasn't in the picture, shooting her mouth off like a tragedy queen in a three-grand dress, all because that sack of shit she was screwing got whacked.'

'She came home with him in the car.'

'It happens. At least for some. She's a bit of all right.'

'I separated them. Secured them. The nurse got free. She went for a gun. Jesus Christ, they had them stashed all over. The other woman, Rina, I restrained her. Twice. I watched her. I questioned Abergil in another room so she wouldn't hear. I don't think . . . I don't know . . . I couldn't do it. Not her. I tried to think of a reason. A way to—'

'Kings will know it wasn't a hit from a rival. Not business, or the old boy would have bought it too. They'll most likely guess that this was a private matter and that isn't good for your future either, my friend.'

'I'm going to assume that his associates—'

'A little annoyed? Burning up. That's what they are. They're all over us, or their proxies are. There's top brass in local government on their payroll. What some people will do for a pork chop, eh? But I mean *they* won't hesitate. You know that? Not with you. Or your wife. Or your girl, if she is . . . You know. It's not my lot who should be concerning you right now. But you've no way out even if we take you. They'll get your head off your shoulders with a sharpened spoon in the nick. This shit will come full circle. But *we'll* also know about you too, so then you've both sides, and where they meet in the middle, coming at you.'

The father blew out his breath. He clenched his fists, started to shout. 'I don't have much choice, do I? I never did. They take my little girl for money . . .' His voice broke, forcing him to choke the emotion back down. 'Money . . . from some sick bastard! But if there is any complaint from the parents, then out comes the machete. How . . . How did this happen? To us? To people? How? Why am I here?'

'I know. I know. I know.' The officer repeated himself distractedly, as if his mind had wandered. The father recognized the thin, vague tone. It came from men out of their depth, who only later considered the full repercussions of their actions; men who were never made for this work. 'What did Yonah give up?'

The father still fought for control of his voice. When his breathing had returned to normal and his pulse settled a little, he gave the detective the details and names from Yonah Abergil's forced confession.

'I'll check them. All new to me, but that doesn't mean much. Our knowledge of who's running with them down here is patchy. I'll see if anything turns up and call you back.'

'Thank you. I had to do it. Back there . . . I didn't have any choice.'

'Might still be bullshit from Yonah. Even with no knees and one eye gone south, we can't assume that a piece of shit like him would start playing fair, or go making any deathbed confessions. It's like they became a different kind of animal years ago. They're really different, you know? Like they know something we don't. But it is a small comfort to know that my interference might not have been in vain. Especially if you find . . . if you know what happened to her. I can guess what that will mean to you.'

It's like they became a different kind of animal years ago. The father thought of the shrines, the painting, the sense of being chased through the night to his car, his dreams. He wondered if he should mention this, but then didn't know how to express it. How was such a subject broached? 'You will call me when the police know . . . when they know it is me who did all of this?'

'Count on it. But I'm guessing that before our lot mount any kind of manhunt, because of all the shit that's going on with the new bug and the blustery weather, your details will be passed to the Kings. Anything to do with Kings always gets out. They've friends in higher places than we'll ever have access to. So if you haven't done so, I'd brief your wife, right away. She'll need to go somewhere a lot safer than her home address.'

'Jesus Christ.'

'You'll be calling on his dad too when the Kings fancy you for this. He wasn't top brass, but Yonah Abergil was blood. They've done scorched earth, root and branch clearances on whole clans for a lot less than this dust-up. I can't remember the last time they had such a personnel setback either. And when I shut my alarm system off for a few minutes, I am secretly bloody elated about that. But we are in the deepest shit. Make no mistake.'

The father began to shake. The atmosphere of the car seemed to thicken, the temperature rise. Unless he got a window down and got that wet, violent air onto his face and inside his body, he thought he'd have a seizure, a total shutdown. 'I'll . . . I'll never give you up. Know that.' He couldn't get anything else out of his mouth.

'Hey, what the hell, you think I didn't know how this would go if we tried it on? Maybe it doesn't matter any more. Have you seen the news? Who'd have thought a pandemic would have an upside for someone.'

The father wasn't sure who the officer was talking to.

TWENTY-ONE

After he abandoned the car in Newton Abbot, he took one of the few cabs still outside the train station back to Brixham, and called Miranda on the way down. She had never picked up at her new ident. Praying she'd heeded his request, he left a message, urging her again to run if she hadn't yet done so. He took a long moment and forced himself to imagine her safely ensconced in a warm cottage, hundreds of miles from her parents' house, or at least on the move out of the Midlands. Any other scenario he simply could not bear. In case their idents were being monitored, he decided against calling Miranda's parents.

Once the taxi had pulled away, the father walked on legs he could only marginally feel beneath him to the only pub in Brixham still open above the harbour. The other functioning businesses behind the seawall were closed in anticipation of what was building out at sea. He needed to eat something substantial and then investigate accommodation too, but the prospect of being in a small room with his thoughts, while he watched the world fall apart onscreen, had made the public house an attractive digression.

A locally brewed beer in hand, the father made his way to a window seat at the far side of the bar room, the furthest point he could retreat from the other customers, to wait for his handler to call again with information on the lawyer, and confirmation the abductors were dead. No time had been specified for further contact. Days might even pass until the detective called, to tell him where to go next to resume the cull – the lawyer, this facilitator, the go-between, the enigmatic Oscar Hollow, because the father would need an address for him. And once he had the lawyer in his hands, he would get the identity of the man who paid for his girl.

There was transport to consider too. *Ditch it.* He was stranded here now, and near-broke. The spectre of the search grinding to a halt was too appalling to consider, and it now mantled him like a black cloak. Next time they spoke, he'd beg Gene to get him a new vehicle.

There had been nothing on the news yet about his move in Taunton. At best, the crime would only make local news anyway. But before he abandoned the car, even the south-west channels on the vehicle's media had failed to mention the home invasion. Its omission made the father feel even weaker and more nauseous. When he took a sip of his beer, he immediately wanted to spit it out.

But he was closer. Despite everything else, he was closer to *the one*. And closer to the truth of what happened to *her*. A notion of Semyon Sabinovic and Oleg Chorny, these Kings of Death, appeared again in his mind and quietly burned there. Somewhere around here, behind a shuttered window and locked doors, perhaps the men had once planned their own move: to step upon his family's front lawn two years ago and take his little girl. He almost wanted at least one of them to be alive so that he could destroy him. He'd make sure they were deceased while he was in the neighbourhood.

Anger remained his only source of strength through exhaustion, and that alone must carry him across the finish line. Because if the abductors were dead, two other men remained: the one who had paid for her, and the lawyer that had brokered the kidnap with Yonah Abergil. Maybe three if the second car, which took his daughter to her destination, had a driver. They were the men who'd reduced him to a scruffy transient with blood on his hands. A spree killer, a vigilante. And, by God, he would deliver their fate, if his own fate delivered enough time. Two more, maybe three more killings and then he was done. It didn't seem possible, and nor did it seem real that he was making such calculations while drinking a pint.

The father became aware of a figure seating itself, to his left side, who he spied from the corner of an eye. An old man, bearded, mad-haired: another solitary figure, wet and crumpled from a scurry to this miserable cave that offered small comforts while the sea battered the town. He turned away from his new neighbour.

There was little chatter in the pub, no music. Mostly loners sat about the old tables and slumped in mismatching chairs; their sombre air was matched by the dim yellow lighting. All were watching one of two screens. Each broadcast different news channels quietly. Both had recently switched from India to show the fires in Australia. The great tinderbox had really gone off this time. Fire superstorms had surrounded Perth and Melbourne. Sydney and Adelaide had gone up days before. The bulletin said there were over twelve hundred separate fires surrounding and converging on Sydney. Crown fires in every city, flashing through the dry treetops faster than cars could accelerate, burning out the oxygen beneath. One hundred and twenty firefighters dead already, trapped between narrowing walls of smoke and flame. Heat and drought for years were the culprits yet again, but accompanied by fast winds this time, which would not abate even while the rain fell hopelessly onto the sea. Chronic water shortage, rationing: a too-familiar pattern. The father thought of the past summer and took a long drink of his beer.

'They've had six weeks of fifty-degree heat in the interior towns. Imagine that.' The old man next to him had just spoken; the back of his matted head still confronting him. It wasn't clear who the old man spoke to: the father, or the room. No one nearby seemed eager to engage with the shabby figure.

'We broke forty this summer, for a few days. But they've had forty-eight degrees seven times in the cities this year.' He half-turned to the father, speaking over his shoulder. 'Their agriculture has gone. They won't even try to keep what's left of the wheat farms after this.' The old man shook his head wearily, but knowingly, as if he had been waiting for this news after a long period of being ignored. 'Tasmania can't take any more from the mainland. New Zealand doesn't want any more. They already got more Chinese than the Canadians. This is the worst they've ever had it in Australia too. They have pyrocumulonimbus now. Thunderstorms made from smoke. Hundreds of miles outside these cities, the hail will be black.'

The screen showed a map; three-quarters of the east

coast of Australia was bright red. Cutaways showed what looked like a mountain range only it was black smoke, as wide as the camera could capture. A rim of tiny orange flames flashed near the foot of the black mountains. 'That smoke's going into the stratosphere. Could turn the place to winter. Block out the sun. Only a volcano or nuclear war would do the same.' The man spoke with an authority that was somewhat jaded and dry. He'd probably been in business once, something now defunct. The father recognized the old chummy tone, forceful and deceptively benign. 'Chinese and Indians will do the same thing very soon out of desperation, mark my words, with sulphur. They'll fire it from artillery to block the murdering sun. Treaties don't mean anything to them. Then we'll all be in trouble.' The man shook his grizzled head and finally looked at the father with a face leathered by weather hot and windy, his flesh deeply lined and black-spotted with melanoma, the stark contrast of pure white hair making him look slightly aboriginal. There was no drink on the shelf before him. That was what he wanted: a sap to buy an old rummy a round.

The father returned his gaze to the bleary window and looked at the froth rising, seeming to hover and then crash behind the seawall. In the far distance, he could see the thin, blurred outlines of two surviving wind turbines.

The old man followed his eyes, and his thoughts. 'An installation from a mad artist. That's what I always think when I see them on a clear day. The ones still standing. There were two hundred out there, twenty years ago. I watched them go up. A fitting sculpture upon the tomb of a species now. The ruins of a civilization already falling, don't you think? Red herrings, false hopes.' He sniggered. 'I piss upon their graves.' The man laughed louder. 'Wind farms, biofuels, zero point energy, carbon capture and sequestration. You old enough to remember all of that? I've seen it all come and go. But you're probably too young to remember the space mirror plans. Ha! Then it was cold fusion. Now it's geo-engineering with sulphur, to save us from the heat. Last roll of the dice, and it will be the last roll. Sulphur will drop the temperature and kill the only crops that are still growing. We've already crossed the line. Why make it even worse? Desperate people, desperate times, desperate solutions. All counter-productive. Just let it go to hell, that's what I'd do. It's what the planet wants, but we can't accept it.'

Despite his misgivings, the father found the man's monologue a welcome distraction from the infernal wait for Gene Hackman's call. He found himself smiling too, as if the vagrant's pessimism had discovered a comfortable chair inside his mind. 'Drink?'

'I can't get you one back. But if that's not a problem, I'll take a glass of that.' He nodded at the father's pint.

The father went to the bar. The landlord asked him if it was for the old man. 'I don't like that old bastard coming in here. It's your money, but that's his last drink before we shut. You got that?' The father nodded, ordered a second glass for himself and made his way back to the window. 'Make it last,' he said to the old man. 'You've already got me in trouble.'

The old man looked embarrassed and uncomfortable upon his stool, and the father's heart spiked with pity, briefly. 'Cheers.' He raised his first glass, still half-full, and nodded at the sea. 'You keep up with this, so what's next?'

The old man swallowed half the contents of his pint glass in three gulps, then gasped, grinning. 'Season of hurricanes this year. Worse than two years back. We'll be going up a notch on the graph. Wind's already coming in at sixty-four—'

'No. Out there. Further out. I've lost touch, with so much.'

'The sea? We're waiting. Still waiting. Nearly ice-free now. Gone for good in a few years, I think. They're still mourning the last of the cod round here, but they won't be coming back, they've gone the way of the pliosaurs. It's the hydrogen sulphide I'd be worried about. Under the ocean floor. If it bubbles up, that sea out there will look like jellied sewage. The stink alone would knock you out. I think our descendants will smell that within a hundred years.'

The father smiled. Ironic that it was no longer human emissions doing the most damage to the atmosphere; the earth's own expulsions had become far more deadly, and the planet now seemed to be pursuing a purpose of its own. Great fields of permafrost were releasing their terrible and long-withheld breath into the air, while the forests and oceans absorbed less carbon dioxide than ever. 'There's still a bigger picture,' he said to the old prophet. 'Everywhere. Here. Us.' There had been a time when nearly everyone spoke like this too. Such a discourse had since become socially unwelcome, once the climate was no longer an existential problem, part-denied and easily ignored. The father wondered if he was one of the few people remaining who could withstand what the old man predicted. But they had once held court everywhere, men like this, in bars, streets, public transport; platforms for their bits of science, an obsession with the news, their Armageddon scenarios. They became popular after local disasters, then just as quickly tiresome, often contradicting each other.

The old man's avuncular tone hardened. 'I can't tell you a thing that wasn't already known forty years ago. And that's the craziest thing. What did we think would happen? We deforested the land to cultivate livestock, we allowed our numbers to burgeon without limit. And we still burned the coal. We are still burning coal. Two hundred and fifty years, give or take a few, of intensively burning coal for this? What were we expecting? That's the only thing that astonishes me. We knew. We've known what was happening for close to a century. But we kept burning the black stuff. And now we have those feedbacks everywhere. This storm is because of the coal we burned twenty years ago.'

The father couldn't contradict the man. From the theories of the scientists down to their street apostles and evangelists, the most accurate guesses and realistic scenarios had been present, hinted at, suggested, even explained, for decades. As the father knew from his time in logistics, no matter how deep the slide into the appalling became, nothing had ever been allowed to disrupt an economy. Even now, in some places.

The old man wiped his beard. 'The planet's been more than patient. It was around for over four billion years before we set the first fires to clear the land. But it only took ten thousand years in this inter-glacial period for us to spread like a virus. We were the mad shepherds who didn't even finish a shift before we poisoned the farm and set fire to the barn. We've overheated the earth and dried it out. So it's time for us to leave, I think. Don't you? We are already deep into the sixth great extinction, right now, this very minute.' He nodded at the window. 'There's no whimper or bang, just a long series of catastrophes. Year after year, decade after decade, always worsening, always leaving things changed after each crisis. The past is unrecoverable. Extinction is incremental. There is no science fiction. Advanced physics, inter-galactic travel, gadgets? An epic fantasy, the lot of it. There is only horror ahead of us now.'

The father smiled. 'How long do we have?'

The scruffy figure took another long drink and smacked his lips, encouraged, his murky eyes possessing an inner light. 'In less than ten years half the species on this planet will be extinct. That's a fact and that should be the indicator for us. To live through that. Think of it. But this place isn't about us, not any more, if it ever was. We've already overheated by four degrees. Some places are already at five and rising. And there must be close to nine billion of us. The earth cannot carry us any longer, not in those numbers, and not even close to that figure. If I was a betting man, I'd guess that at least eight billion of us will die back, in order for our species to even continue for another couple of centuries. Eight billion over the next two hundred years, give or take a few decades. It's more than we can imagine. But I think we're beginning to get the gist of it.'

They sat with that thought between them, like an uninvited stranger at the table, and they watched the fire onscreen as the rain belted the windows close to their faces. *Where can we go?* the father wondered. *We are alone in space. There is nowhere to go.* The quick, cold realization never failed to produce an icy tension, the size of a snooker ball, behind his sternum. The very earth was getting smaller. To migrate north as a species and to go higher and higher as the heat rose, and to compete for fewer and fewer resources . . . The closing of borders. The end of food exports. The ever-emerging hostilities to seize fresh water and arable land . . . All of these things were part of the penultimate stage of mass collapse; the idea could still take his breath away.

One of the screens switched to an artillery barrage in Kashmir. The landlord pushed the volume up. A few more tousled heads in the bar turned to the news. The father couldn't hear clearly from where he sat.

Subtitles indicated that Pakistan was now demanding half of the water in the Sutlej, Ravi and Beas rivers, and for India to completely desist using water from the upper parts of the Jhelum and Chenab rivers . . . During the last twelve hours, the British and United States governments had urged all their citizens to leave both countries. Diplomatic staff were in the process of being evacuated.

The vagrant had finished his drink and was licking the tangled beard around his mouth. The father checked on the barman: he was watching the latest from India intently with two customers. Carefully, the father moved his second glass of beer towards the old man. Slid away the empty glass and hid it under the window counter. 'You're local?'

'Lived here for sixty years. I—'

The father cut him off. 'I'm looking for someone from near here. An addict.'

'You'll find plenty of those.'

'I don't want plenty, I only want one. From the east.

Russian. Georgian. He had a lot of gang tattoos and lived in an old church around here somewhere.'

'Church? They're everywhere now. And if you're looking for a free feed I recommend the Temple of the Last Days. They do a good soup, with a—'

'Where do the addicts collect, do you know?'

The old man gave him the names of three missions and the dispensary. 'Not my poison, I'm afraid. I don't even touch hard liquor. So I don't mix in those circles.' He said this with such sincerity the father wanted to roar with laughter. There was hierarchy everywhere.

'This man had connections. Organized crime. I don't think he'll be under the pier.'

The old man stroked his beard, sipped the drink, watched him in a curious role reversal, as if it was the father who might be unstable, or dangerous. 'Gangs with tattoos, I know who you mean. But I don't get involved. I steer clear, my friend. And around here, the organization you are probably referring to took all the big houses up in Dartmouth,' the old man said. 'They tend to operate out of there. I don't go over there any more. Can't say as I've heard much about them from out Brixham way, other than the usual.'

'Which is?'

'They're in everything. Came down with the trafficking and to get a stake in the camp constructions. Took over the drug crops on Dartmoor. Years ago.' The man rolled his yellowy eyes upwards. 'Even this place, or so they say. Girls upstairs. Or there used to be.'

The father nodded his thanks. 'Enjoy the drink.' He went to find somewhere still open that sold food.

TWENTY-TWO

Early in the morning, two days after the shooting of Yonah Abergil, Gene Hackman called. The father had moved to a room in a guest house, one mile east of Brixham; he wouldn't leave the area, but would move each day until he could leave for good.

Delivered in a voice thinned and tightened by nerves, the information came fast. 'Forensics went through Abergil's mansion on all fours. A very fast response to the death of a dirtbag. But as I said, his demise has jumped a big queue. And samples have now been harvested from the evidence that's not next to useless at two further sites yesterday, Bowles's house and The Commodore. Word came down the food chain requesting that forensics take another look at these illustrious residences. So you're as good as nailed for those two. Your DNA will have been pulled off the national. The fact that the investigation is being partly suppressed in-house makes me fear this has already been outsourced to Abergil's mates in the local Kings. It's probably their gig now, housekeeping.'

The father closed his eyes. 'What else?'

'When his body was found two years back, shot through the head with his hands and feet bound, it was news to us that Semyon Sabinovic was even in the country.

A hit from the Moroccans, the file says, and revenge upon them was swift. That might have been Abergil's cover story to take out one of his own? But how about this: Sabinovic was taken out one week after your girl vanished.'

Gene Hackman then confirmed that Sabinovic was Georgian, deported from three European countries for people trafficking, all charges occurring around the mid-thirties when the cross-border activity became hopeless to monitor. Oleg Chorny was Georgian too, but had operated under different aliases and with many passports, doing hard time in Belgium and Germany in the early thirties for trafficking, and his part in four sexual slavery rings. Chorny's original outfit had probably been recruited, or amalgamated, into the burgeoning Kings organization while he served time in Hamburg.

Gene also told him that both men had form farming female teens into prostitution on the continent. And that detail fell upon the father's heart like a steel axe with a frozen blade.

In addition, Oleg Chorny had been caught on surveillance cameras in Bristol, around the time of the Chantilly Road massacre and of numerous gangland hits in South Wales attributed to the Kings. That was the only reason why Gene had found an out-of-date dossier on him. Then the man had dropped out of the picture for three years, only to reappear in Torbay on the outer limits of Yonah Abergil's outfit in the late forties when the vast refugee camps were being extended at bewildering speeds across Devon.

But Gene Hackman could glean no further news of Chorny's whereabouts, or activities, after the spring of 2050.

The father's daughter had vanished in the summer of 2051, a year later. But the information, more or less, tied in with what Abergil had said, and it put Oleg Chorny in South Devon.

'It fits. They both fit.'

'Hundreds of them will do. But at least Yonah gave them up while you kneecapped him and put a gun to his dad's head. As motivation goes, you gave him a huge incentive to squeal. It's also all we have to go on, so, for your sake, I hope there is something solid in this.'

'You didn't say that Oleg Chorny was dead.'

'No, but that's not the same as saying he's alive either. People vanish without a trace all over.'

'But if he was alive, how would I find him down here, this Chorny prick? Is there someone I could speak to who knew him, who would confirm his death?'

'Hang on. I'm not done, and this is where it all gets intriguing. I've no pictures, no notes, no records of his last alias, but a colleague with his ear to the ground on the drugs that way, and what is moving in and out of Brixham, has told me something interesting, and this information was further embellished by a contact in a sheltered housing project for addicts across the Bays. There's every nationality shooting up or smoking along the sea front from Plymouth to Exmouth, but in amongst all of the colour in Brixham was an individual of eastern European extraction whose appearance once really stood out. We know the Kings entourage like a bit of ink, but this chap had his head done, meticulously illustrated with a King Death figure. It's no prison tattoo. Too recent, too vivid. Apparently it was quite eye-catching. He was what they call an *enlumineur*. You said Yonah Abergil fingered this Oleg Chorny for the same trade?'

'Yes. Do you have a name?'

'No, but this guy was something of a guru years back, and considered a prophet amongst smack heads. A nutter with a bit of apocalypse fever like the evangelists. Was very generous when helping others open their doors of perception, by all accounts. It was generally presumed that he'd died a while back. But my contact is sure that this individual has been seen this year, during the summer. Never been picked up or even questioned, but my source is sure he was seen around. Popped up, apparently, to score, and appeared to be at death's door. My contact only remembers this incident because his other *clients* had no idea how this illustrated guy was even still alive. This guy looked like a walking corpse, inked black and gold all over. The crowd my source had been treating for addiction were pretty freaked out, convinced that the dead had risen as predicted, et cetera. But I'm guessing that if this character is still around, and even if he is not Chorny, then he would have known of Chorny. Same profile: gangster with religion, an *enlumineur*, and once devoted to King Death, a junkie, and in the area.

'There's an old church, a Baptist pre-fab, used by the end-times Africans in the camps. Originally, it was a slaughter-house, an abattoir, before the camps were built. It's no more than some kind of old shed, at the edge of the oldest quarter of the camps, and that's where this guy was once known to reside. I'll send the location in a message from this ident. Didn't Abergil also say that Sabinovic and Chorny owned a church, somewhere near Brixham?'

'Yes. He said Chorny lived in an old church, and Chorny was found dead inside it. Or under it after an overdose because Semyon Sabinovic was killed. But maybe there was no overdose.'

'Then this guy is worth looking at, but I don't know how it can be him, if Yonah sent that pair on a suicide mission to seal the leaks about the snatch. But this is all I've got.'

'Thank you.'

'There's a caveat. Including the camps, you have a population close to two point four million on that stretch of coast, that we know of. It is a haystack and this tattooed guy is a needle. I've stuck my neck out and pushed my beak into two places, on your behalf, where it has no official business. If something very public happens to an illustrated man who looks like a corpse, it'll be a bit coincidental. You follow? Very costly for me if this guy has some King credentials. So your usual impromptu firework display is off the table.'

The father exhaled. 'So what do you recommend? Can you come down?'

'And supervise you? No chance. But this will be no snuff movie. No blood bath. I don't want to hear of some joker in a mask going on a binge with nerve gas and a shooter in a camp. It will pull even more of the world down upon your shoulders. And mine. You are already inside the machine. I'm getting the impression from early speculation that you're considered a vigilante by our side. One of many paedo-killers. More savage than usual, but without the religion or politics. But what is still hard to reconcile about all of this is why your girl would be snatched through pros, as you had no cash-rich enemies. So we can only assume that the snatch was ordered by a wealthy stranger, as yet unknown, for a high price, but extortion was never the aim. I'm guessing here.'

'I'll find out why. But I can't torment myself any more about his motives.'

'OK. Now, all eyes are on the weather and the new bug for a bit. Which, I might add, is looking to be something far worse than anyone expected. The Department of Disease Control is in a right lather. It's in the Midlands and south-east now. First point of infection they actually think was a Hong Kong Chinese tycoon, flown in to see the best immunologist in Oxford. He brought something very nasty along on a spot of health tourism. There'll be a right ruckus if that news travels, as we've one hundred thousand dead pensioners from the summer who'll still be going on the bonfire till Merry fucking Christmas, and this guy was fast-tracked to the best private care available. Happens all the time.

'But in the calm after the storm, the eyes of the law, and those above the law, will return to Abergil, that stalwart of the community and local economy, and the man in the mask who's been clipping kiddie fiddlers. So you need to start thinking of an exit strategy if . . . well, you know what I mean. If by some miracle Oleg Chorny is still alive, and he leads you to some pretty terrible news, to a resolution, then what are you going to do? I'd like some idea as I am balls-deep here.'

The father slumped into his seat. He would not lie. 'If my girl is not . . . then all the men involved who are still alive are going to die by my hand. Chorny, who drove her away, the man who bought her, and the man who brokered the deal, this lawyer. And anyone else I find out was involved. They'll all go. You know this. After I'm finished with them, I don't really care what happens to me. But if I was apprehended . . .' *if I lose my nerve when all is done and decided* '. . . I won't ever give you up. I promise you.'

The father swallowed the lump in his throat. He'd long been grief incarnate, vengeance and desolation made flesh. And he was acknowledging the *thing*, the eventuality, *the end* that he had considered for himself in his wildest, most rage-charred moments. When he had stood naked in the dismal rooms of barely functioning bed and breakfasts and clawed his hair out after drinking a bottle of cheap spirits; when he'd punched pillows and old mattresses until he collapsed sobbing and sweat-foamed; when he'd ground his teeth into tiny hard white shards that had felt too big beneath his tongue; when he'd shot Bowles like an animal run to ground, and executed Rory and Yonah Abergil in their homes, and tortured old men in their living-room chairs . . . He had known that all the vengeful fire of hell now burned too fiercely inside of him to ever be extinguished, and that he must accept a violent and bloody end for himself, an eventual dousing of the maelstrom. Because if there was to be a continuance in this life only without his little girl, then he would choose oblivion. He was still breathing, but he had never survived her loss.

'What if she is alive?'

The father took a moment to control his hope. 'If I ever bore witness to a miracle and my girl was alive, if she was recovered, then what could I do? I could write a statement omitting any details of Scarlet Johansson, and you too. I could think of something to explain how I found her, and why I have done what I have done to extract information. But I doubt any authority would believe that I acted alone. They will know I had help. And I would be sent down, then put down by the affiliates of King Death.' The father took a deep breath. 'I would lose her again. So if I find myself in a preposterous situation and discover that she is alive, then I would vanish . . . with her.'

The police officer sounded tired, perhaps relieved, but also saddened. 'Agreed. If there is a god, then you'll both have to disappear. You and your girl, and her mother, and for good.'

'Yes.'

'And Oleg Chorny. If he is alive and you find him, what is your plan? Maybe I should rephrase that, do you even have one?'

'If Chorny is alive, then he will either lead me to her . . . wherever she was taken . . . or he will live for as long as it takes him to tell me where he took her. Then he will disappear. The man who bought her will be next. The lawyer I will have to deal with later, when I have a name that I can trace. But I will do everything in my power to prevent anyone from finding them. Any of them. I will reduce them to ash.' The last sentence seemed to emerge from a recently discovered pit inside himself, and it was as if his conscious mind could not catch such utterances from this pit before they left his mouth.

Both men remained silent as if to digest the enormity of such events, of such practical barbarism.

The father steadied himself because he'd started to shake. 'This is what you would do if you were in my position. It's why you saved me in Torquay. It's why you are helping me now. What else can I do? You'd be mistaken in thinking I have a taste for this. Your own loss has been terrible and your grief will never end. I know this, and if my own heart wasn't so broken, then it would break for you and your boy's mother. But if there is even a slim chance that I could bring my daughter back from the dead, then I will do anything. We know this, you and I. This story will not change. No one even thinks of her now but her family. And the angels who have helped me.'

After a period of intense silence, the officer spoke. 'Easy with the angel shit. But if Chorny is in that chapel, and if he can take you to the next level, then he needs to be breathing to do it. You'll have to extract the truth from whatever planet he lives on now, because if this illustrated junkie is our man, then he doesn't appear to be on this one any more. Once his usefulness is exhausted, I agree, he will have *to go*. For both our sakes. The ways and means of his disappearance will need to be thought through. Very carefully. He cannot be found. But where will you go after?'

'I'll face that later. What about a car?'

'Let me see about replacement wheels. I'll send you the location of a pickup near Brixham. It'll be there later this afternoon. Best I can do, so don't go in before it's dark, because you may need to haul this guy's arse out of the area and for that you will need wheels. Oh, and use one of the new shooters and find a new mask, unless you want a big finish. Plenty will oblige on that score.'

TWENTY-THREE

Through the rain's drenching violence, a dark shape snapped out its length. Curled back upon itself, then unrolled wetly to smack hard, like a leather strap, upon the water-glazed bricks of a wall. The father flinched to a crouch, disbelief matching his fear at the sudden billowing, the raggedy slapping above his head, momentarily settling to a lapping upon a garden wall, like a thin, predatory tongue.

At the very moment he turned a street corner to climb the last rise to the church, from within a walled garden this *form* had lashed out, or even appeared to reach for him. Had there been an arm stretching from its wet folds, concealed in the rain-blurred dusk? A lowered head, a face? The possibility of such a presence within the air had immediately returned his thoughts to the woods and his flight from Yonah Abergil's villa, and to a fragment of a dream in which he lay helpless beneath a great black presence in motion. His most volatile instincts warned again of a pursuit from a thing unnatural.

But bent low to the wet paving, his sight found nothing more than an old sheet, blown from a washing line and caught upon a spiked fence; fabric seemingly invested with life in the turbulence. Begrimed by traffic and dust, but now restored to suppleness by a month's rain in twenty-four hours, the linen had recreated itself in his mind as a flapping shroud, released from disinterred remains.

The tension leaked from the father's muscles and left his limbs jittery. *There is nothing else*, only this wounded earth and us upon it.

Refuse swirled. Rain flooded over every doorstep, kerb and car tyre. Water sheeted down the hill, overran his boots, plumed clear from drain grates. Narrow lanes of terraced houses, their paint faded, their rendering pocked and worn, created channels for the black waters to hurtle down to the thrashing waves of the harbour.

Between the terraces he could walk in a straight line, but in this weather, no one else risked the streets. At intersections and on the wider streets, he'd stagger, head down, the wind trying to lift and roll him at the same time, as he watched for detached guttering and sheet iron blown loose. He'd heard the clangs and groans in the places beneath roofs where materials had broken free, and he had seen roof tiles skitter like giant woodlice across the road he'd come in through.

Dim candlelight chinked through curtains and around the storm shutters of the houses. The street lights were out; the power had been down since the previous night, another incentive to leave his room on the outskirts and to enter the roaring tumult of the dark. But towards the end of his journey, up through the harbour town, such was the force of the wind that the father was forced to pull himself from lamppost to doorway, storm porch to front garden wall, car by car. He'd struggled up through the streets from the harbour in similar fashion, his slicker shiny as eel skin, his front-strung rucksack a tatty water bladder blackened by rain. But on the higher ground, the weather now seemed cursedly worse and portent-heavy.

Near the summit of the hill he reared into the stone front of a small house, its sooty cement cold through his poncho, transmitting a chill into his bones. He peered up at a new form that flicked out between two chimneys, a ribbon or shred as long as a serpent, thin, darting to strike, black as jet.

But only a flag, its pole shuddering in the wind. This night, he knew his mind was going to be his greatest enemy.

Earlier that evening, the detective had sent him a message and the details of where he could find his getaway. *Good luck. I'll be in touch tomorrow.* The replacement vehicle waited one mile north of Brixham.

For a mile on foot, from Churston Ferres to Brixham, he'd been battered and blown sideways across the fields of crops he'd crossed, taking cover behind stone walls and earth works, where they existed, to avoid the thrashing trees and fall of branches in the woods set back from the coastal path. Then he'd advanced up and through the wind-flayed town from near the harbour. As he moved through the evening, lower sea-level sections of the headland and the harbour wall had entirely vanished, every few seconds, beneath the enraged surf.

From the end of Churston Ferrers and the town limits of Brixham, the great Moor Edge refugee camp now continued to the banks of Long Wood on the River Dart, engulfing Kingswear. Oleg Chorny's last known address, the chapel, was close to Raddicombe Wood, set back from the Kingswear Road. The father had another half a mile to walk, through the fringes of the vast temporary encampment, now larger than many British cities. Three miles wide and five miles from tip to tip, but still growing northwards to join the Riviera camp behind Paignton and Preston. And from that point unto North Devon, the largest drought-resistant grain-producing area in Britain – over two hundred square miles of wheat, soya, maize, millet fields, five nuclear power stations and the three new reactor sites that were hastily under construction.

Through the dusk and rainfall, pressed into the saturated earth beneath the coal-black sky, the father could see the silhouettes of the first great blocks of white prefabricated neighbourhoods that comprised the vast refugee settlement, the entire grid divided by wide lanes to prevent fires jumping. The pale, unchanging, cuboid mass of housing was silent, but tens of thousands of candle flames pinpricked the wet vista upon the hills.

Hundreds of thousands of Spaniards and Greeks lived alongside the southern Italians, the Portuguese, Bangladeshis, and half a million North, East and West Africans, in two-room buildings. Three- and four-storey apartment blocks, each living space as long as a chalet, had begun to supersede the bungalows on the eastern side of the camp.

Like watch towers about old Roman forts, the newer apartment blocks faced an older, alien world, from which the buildings' inhabitants had streamed, aboard anything that would get them across the Channel and sea.

The father eventually found the old Baptist chapel, trembling in the wind, fifty feet behind a shuttered healthcare centre and a large primary school for refugee children. He moved carefully, now close enough to the residential areas to be within reach of the security patrols, recruited from within the camps to deter smuggling, thieves and the direct-action nationalists that hounded the settlement.

Not good weather tonight for any nocturnal activity outdoors. The entire area appeared to have locked down as the storm swept across the south-west. If the winds broke eighty miles an hour, a great many of the prefabricated dwellings here would be uprooted and destroyed. If the hurricane season returned as it had done for the past six years, the cabins would soon have to be replaced by the sturdier towers.

At the edge of the chapel's front lawn, and a long untended pumpkin patch, a faded wooden sign had been bent and shaken by the wind and now lay flat upon the earth. GLORY TO GOD AND HOPE TO THE WORLD had been stencilled above a hand-drawn picture of an open bible. Like an old wound, a metal crucifix ran to rust down the painted cement blocks on the building's front. It was an agricultural building, from another time, with a galvanized roof, but converted from slaughtering livestock, or poultry, to human use or habitation. The doors to the old church were locked, the windows shuttered.

The father assumed the abattoir had been engulfed by the refugee settlement when the land was reclaimed by the emergency government, and later procured on the black market by Oleg Chorny and his lover. The National Land Registry still listed it as a private building, the purpose religious. Whatever new use the place had been put to, someone with money had once chosen to live amongst the dispossessed, on the edge of a vast camp, a new city with a population created solely from the stateless, the homeless. Perhaps a good place for a serpent to hide and to operate if he was part of the many organized criminal enterprises that now controlled most of the camps, in the same way they controlled the city ghettoes and prisons, and had allegedly captured half of the world's money within half a century.

The father flashed his torch around the perimeter. No alarms. No cameras. Weather-worn signage filled a frame beside the front entrance: *For we wrestle not against flesh and blood, but against principalities, against powers, against the rulers of the darkness of this world, against spiritual wickedness in high places. (Ephesians 6:12.)*

The father turned about in the darkness and flashed his torch across the ground and the neighbouring buildings, and over wet cement, silvery cascades of rain, white roofs, wires shaking like skipping ropes, treetops panicking, grass and flower beds blown flat. In the distance another of the many greenhouses imploded from the pressure of the fast wind. They'd been going off like light bulbs since he'd left Brixham.

The father circled the building. Three entrances. Double metal doors at the front. Two old wooden fire exits: one at the rear, the other at the side. No light shone within. It looked deserted. The father wiped his bare face. From out of the rucksack, he withdrew a handgun that he'd boosted from Yonah Abergil's house. He holstered the weapon in the front pocket of his trousers and slipped the nerve gas into the other trouser pocket at the front. Once inside, the handgun would be only a back-up for the stun charge and gas; he dared not hold the handgun in his business hand. The torch occupied his free hand.

He chose the emergency exit at the side. If this tattooed man was here, the father knew he would have to reach the target quickly before he could arm himself. And then he needed to immobilize him with the stun charge or spray, cuff and gag him, before extracting him through the storm to where the new vehicle was parked, less than a mile away. They would have to wait out the night inside the car, and that is where the interrogation would take place.

The father briefly steadied himself against the cinder-block wall. Closed his eyes and thought of his daughter's small face.

Tucking the handle of the torch under his arm, he brought out the small crowbar from his rucksack to lever open the door. The father forced the wedge between the handle and tin frame, and pulled on it, using his body's weight like an oarsman fighting the surf. The door snapped open, and the father stepped from night into something altogether darker.

TWENTY-FOUR

The building did not feel abandoned. By men, perhaps, though not by the presence suggested by the appalling things daubed upon a wall that his thin torchlight found a few seconds post-entry. And within the void, the beam of white struck a sickly yellow face first, its eyes red and vacuous, the mouth open. The face grew in the disc of illumination until the father realized it was attached to a hairless head, crudely crowned, but barely supported by a thin body, bound more than robed in red. The figure occupied a rust-coloured throne.

The corpse king's feet were fleshless and he sat beside a queen lacking in all of the grace, elegance and nobility expected to accompany a royal title. Her face was a bloodless oval, her head covered with grubby linen bindings. Small pink eyes peered with an imbecilic intensity into the black air about the regal seat. The female figure's raiment was plain, whitish, and resembled a nun's habit.

The couple stared blankly at what stood before their thrones: another emaciated human emblem of bone, naked save for a loin cloth, the parchment flesh lacerated from the sharp heels to the hairless scalp and weeping black tears. Before its stitched-up eyelids, it carried a box filled with small brown skulls, a gift to the abominable royalty that sat so straight-backed and listless before the messenger.

The father had shut out the roar of the storm by pulling the door shut behind his swift entrance into the building. But the dimming of the volume seemed to make the pictures even worse than they were, as if a reverential hush had descended about him in the rank darkness.

Unlit, the building would have been unnavigable without a torch because he could see that the windows and rendered walls had been covered in thick layers of black emulsion, before being further vandalized by the lurid paintings. Extending from the throne-room scene, the father's torch revealed that the same artist had covered all four walls with his ghastly mural.

Dumbfounded by the assault upon his eyes and senses, the father operated on instinct and immediately replaced his stun weapon with the heavier resin handgun. Some inner cry demanded a greater protection in this place, but even the unholstered weapon felt insufficient in the face of the horrors plastered upon the walls of the Baptist chapel. He feared they might move.

Disorientation further warped the dimensions of the room, suggesting that the blackness between the multitude of painted figures went on forever. It was as if he'd come into a space that was far larger than it had seemed from the outside. If any pews or chairs had once been present on the black cement floor, they'd been removed, presenting the ground as that of an empty warehouse, reaching into an infinity underlain by the vague taint of blood and dung: the very residues of where the livestock of the past had jostled before skull-splintering slaughters.

The air of the building also carried the smell of stale paint, dusty cement, the cold rain outside and the sharp kidney taint of human urine. The artist may have pissed where he worked. Flavours of an ecclesiastical history had remained in vestiges too, as if to hallow the desecrated room with a sense of the apocalyptic despair that must have once been conjured by the Baptists' shrill preaching. Instinctively, the father became momentarily convinced that something was still worshipped within the terrible room, even enshrined in the unpleasant visions on this broad canvas transforming the interior.

More of his dumbstruck glances revealed an artist's obsession with poorly drawn sarcophagi or crude caskets, stood upright, and filled with murky silhouettes. And bone-faced bishops, equipped with sceptres, soiled surplices and hoods, stood upon daises, their pointed hands more like surgeons' anatomy diagrams than those of the living. These skeletal church authorities drew his attention to the pallid shapes lying below their unshod, bone feet: a dead congregation that barely indented or impressed their insubstantial bodies upon twisted linen, or winding sheets open at the neck. Black-socketed, eyeless, open-mawed: many of the dead figures on the ground wore the caps of popes, the headdresses of sheiks, the crowns of kings; as if receiving last rites from an already dead and decayed clergy.

The father hesitated, to make certain these figures all around him were not actually moving. It may have been a trick of the torch's light that suggested motion, perhaps a vibration, even a distant squirming at the edge of his sight.

And elsewhere, on all four walls he could see a great violence, and the resulting slaughter; suggestions of battles on grand scales amongst the other miserable components of war: the stick-figure silhouettes hanged from rafters and leafless trees, the dead children and emaciated mothers. More of the black-eyed corpse kings sat here and there in the devastation, immobile, enthroned, surrounded by riches but lifeless.

Sometimes the figures in the mural were depicted on all fours, their faces a mixture of the mad and the animal; beggars and kings alike had degenerated with a peculiarly apelike quality. There was something of the chimpanzee or bonobo in the toothy grimaces, the bulbous whites of the eyes, idiotic in their rage, gleefully insane, committed to a bestial savagery everywhere, and into the far-reaching hell on earth, if indeed it was even the earth.

The paintings seemed to represent events that were about to happen or archetypes of what had always occurred. The same thing. The eternal tragedy. A monstrous fantasy that made the viewer envy the pale, still cadavers, now mercifully excused from the energy of the great dieback.

Across other swathes of the walls, the bones of the departed were stacked in numbers beyond the confines of any charnel house. About sickly ruins and the ragged, forsaken humanity, starved insensible and queuing into a meaningless distance, a robed thing often stalked, either sat upon a cadaverous mare, or bent from the weight of its scythe. Death. The Reaper. King Death.

The father averted his eyes from its skeletal prancing, but between the figures the black chasm, the empty space, gaped. The chapel's devotion to human horror was total and unflinching. It continued inside his mind and shortened his breath. Nothing yet seen on any screen had made him so aware of the world's deterioration, a course set in motion that could only gain a greater momentum.

But the building's true purpose still eluded the father. This could not be a grim depiction of the times alone. He believed it had to mean more, was perhaps a physical embodiment of a faith, something revered. The father then feared this shrine imparted knowledge; that this was an oracle for the profoundly disturbed to ask their questions. He forced himself to suppress a new and unwelcome suspicion that his presence might make possible the awakening of a deity within the unlit space.

Leading from the large room, two wooden doors offered a retreat from the disfigurements of the chapel. The father guessed the doors must open into what had once been a vestry or the church offices. He moved to them, but stopped when his torch flicked across what he took to be an upright figure. He panicked, brought his weapon about and made ready to fire until the clip was empty.

Rising from the lightless floor, before the backdrop of a black wall, he saw what he'd thought was a cowled figure, the head bowed. And then realized that it was static, solid, and not a figure at all, but a pillar. Whatever the object was, it had been built over the place where an altar or pulpit should have stood, or maybe the black installation had consumed and superseded the holier feature.

The father moved closer to the pillar. Perhaps it had been intended to represent a long head, oval and tapering to an apex, like some primitive ancestor facing the sea on a Polynesian island, where civilization was long-collapsed and gone to dust. To pass to the rooms at the rear he would need to encircle this column that had seemed to suddenly manifest, between the desecrated walls, as if to prevent him going any deeper inside the building.

He washed the structure with the white beam of his torch. And it didn't take the father long to realize that the subject matter embedded upon the column was similar to what he had seen inside Yonah Abergil's office, though that specimen was a fraction of this one's size. But this was another shrine, and about this shrine must stand a temple.

Materials used in the construction of the dolmen would have been illumined by the plethora of red candles in glass holders, had they been lit, though the father found his torchlight was more than sufficient and he illumined more than he wanted to see. The creation had more of the primary school craft room about its design and crude manufacture than the antique sophistication of the feature in Yonah Abergil's study; as a result, this effigy created a more grotesque impression.

Perhaps the Baptist congregation had left behind a quantity of their hymn or prayer books too, which formed a dark mortar and stucco, plastering the original frame, or actual altar, which had been extended and built upwards, with thousands of pages and pamphlets carrying sacred words and evangelist messages. The plaster stank. In places the pale sheets of paper had dark red smears across them, and the father suspected the paste was manufactured from blood.

Over the defiled pages, scores of photographs had been pasted as if the papier-mâché dolmen had been collecting the images as trophies or mementos: bone fields in Cambodia, the skeletal remains of Iranian towns hit by Israeli nuclear weapons, a recent genocide in one of the Congos, a Nigerian civil war, a Chinese famine, the cannibalism of Pyongyang, the Californian dust bowl of the thirties, the ghost towns of Texas, long-exhausted and near-forgotten pandemics in Asia, the repeated failures of the Indian monsoon . . .

Other things were represented here too, higher up, at eye level, people he did not recognize: individuals, strangers, random victims? Their expressions were unmistakably those of distress, shock and fear, or had been captured during their final, gasping respite from life.

A message had been carefully written near the base of the mound, in an antique-looking scroll or ribbon, similar to the paintings and graffiti he'd happened across on his moves. *Nemo deum vidit*. Latin again, and again he had no idea what it meant.

The father wondered if the artist had been the executioner, or gaoler, of the subjects in the photographs. These higher images seemed personal. They were amateur pictures, not culled from a news service, and had been printed on precious photographic paper. They were presented cleanly and not smeared with the reeking glue.

Around the totem he walked, compelled but unsteady on his feet, his ears attuned to the darkness about him, the torch beam illuminating the tiered column. He would occasionally pause in front of a photograph before moving to the next: the tear-stained face of a woman, looking up through what might have been a manhole cover, or a trapdoor in a metal container; the bruised face of a Middle Eastern man, whose vacant eyes confronted oblivion; polythene stretched over a distorted face, the throat roped; a kneeling figure wearing a cape of black blood, its severed head resting beside its knees; the heavily tattooed back of a man lying face down, the colourful sigils of the skin riveted with black bullet holes; a river bank; the grey chop of the sea with no sight of land, and several patches of disturbed soil in settings that appeared quiet and yet more sinister because of the stillness.

Psychopaths must have once exiled themselves here, amongst imagery of climate catastrophes and their myriad consequences, to reflect upon their trophies. *Chorny and Semyon Sabinovic?* The witches. The shrine was a mortuary roll that depicted nothing but disaster, death and decay: chaos, the great passage from civilization to barbarism. In this place, the father suspected that *someone* had grasped some deep, personal connection with the wider diaspora and depopulation. The whole edifice suggested the morbidly spiritual, which further convinced him that there was meaning behind the selection of this place too, as if this room ended another journey, or a hideously idiosyncratic pilgrimage. It was an installation of the King Death group for sure, but a shrine for a seer, priest, or whatever kind of witch doctor or shaman the group's nihilistic mysticism and superstition generated. Some Damascene moment had called true believers here. The father was sure of this. An awakening had occurred inside sadistic minds, leading to a fuller connection with *something* the father had but glimpsed. Here *it* was celebrated, and that *something* was perceived as the black-miraculous. A thing closer to this world than it had ever been before. *Afterdeath?*

Everywhere he searched for his daughter, he found this morbid sickness, continuing and expanding, signs encircling him. And had he not dreamed of this place too, and recently? He suddenly felt trapped, funnelled further into a hellish gullet he could not anticipate the end of, but did not understand.

The father had seen enough and made to turn away and to find the fiend that had built this tribute in defiance of decency, erected beneath the sagging roof of civilization, but paused, and returned his torch to a spot three-quarters up the column, level with his own eyes. He took one step forward with his breath trapped painfully at the top of his lungs, as if everything inside his torso had just surged upwards to press on the bottom of his throat. The picture had been taken from the front path of his family's old house.

Upon the middle tier of the garden, amongst the sprouting leaves and white flowers of the potatoes that they had grown to fill the pantry, stood a little girl, *his daughter*. Keenly alert and curious and staring at whoever was taking her picture, she wore an expression that was half-amused, verging on a smile, eager to engage an adult's attention.

A slither of pain slipped through her father's heart. He suffered a sudden and terrible sense of the broken world he'd walked for two years and of the broken people he had murdered. All through that time her little image had been here, surrounded by horrors too sickening to view at more than a glance. And her image had been here in the reeking darkness without him, *her daddy*.

Dizzy, the father staggered sideways. Recovered his feet. A whimper and then another escaped his mouth. His scalp and the nape of his neck prickled. Nausea lapped the edges of his stomach. His head flooded and swam with too many thoughts.

She was the only child featured on the papery skin of the effigy. With shaking hands, he reached out and tugged the picture free. Noticed what she was wearing: blue shorts, a navy t-shirt, and the red hooded top patched with cats. Not the clothes she'd worn on the day she was abducted. So this photo had been taken some time before the afternoon she was taken: the men, Oleg Chorny and Semyon Sabinovic, had crossed the line and entered their property to take a photo before they stole her. The revelation made him prickle cold.

The father stumbled around the pillar on numb feet, shining his light again at each photograph, desperate to see more of her, but also praying that he would not. He came back to where he'd started and through a tear-blurred vision, his eyes implored the three images of disrupted soil not to be telling him some unspeakable truth. Those pictures could have been taken anywhere, maybe in the vast crop plantations of Dartmoor; places he'd long had to discipline himself not to think about. If there were no witnesses, abduction and murder were easy crimes to commit.

Spiking from a renewal of the red energy that made him career like a drunkard, the father went for the doors behind the altar. He desperately wanted to find someone at home. Should he blast through joints, shoulders, elbows, knees and hips, or just shoot away the genitals?

He'll bleed to death.

No, if there was a custodian or chaplain, then he must be taken alive. And he would impart all of the secrets of his vocation, and its sacrifices, before the father took apart the man slowly and unto a madness wherein the only cogent desire would be death. He would know *why* his daughter's image was here before the sun rose again upon the broken earth.

Flashing past the father's face, as he moved to the doors, came again the crimson skeletal witnesses of the walls, holding childlike machetes or badly drawn, out-of-perspective firearms, their faces weirdly beatific, white eyes gazing upwards to the black heavens. The father looked down to avoid seeing more, but beside the doors the white-robed dead knelt and prayed before a lion with an ape's bestial face. On the other side of the frame parodies of saints raised bone-thin arms from the ground towards their grinning executioners.

She had been taken by the criminally insane. The father bit down on the scream that wanted to shatter the rafters. Looking up within the black nave, he unintentionally glimpsed what billowed upon the ceiling.

Transfixed, stumbling to regain balance in the darkness, he moved his light around the great central figure, perhaps winged, that had been painted upon the plasterboard ceiling. The thing was similar to what he had seen on the walls in Torre and Paignton, as if those sightings had never been accidents. In this depiction the deity was faceless and its front was littered with redundant paps. The preposterous accident of life, the giving, as well as untimely death, the taking, appeared to have been depicted as a female preserve.

As if prompted by a sudden opening inside this depth of the missing face, a carousal of horror swept through him, and he suffered a sense of rising out of himself and up to the rafters, towards the very absence, arms wide, eyes wide, mouth muttering in sublimation, in hapless obeisance to what swayed up there, surveying the ruin it administered.

The terrible passage.

The father supported himself against a wall. Gripped his head to ease the eruption. Few minds were designed to withstand such a place. But it wouldn't stop, wouldn't cease, and the visions came all at once now, stacking, superimposing, reeling . . . the black air of the temple had filled him up as if the trance of a ritual had been evoked. The dead were piled against a fence in Bangladesh . . . an American town, with not one telegraph pole standing . . . El Niño's scythe on a satellite picture . . . the sacking of Cairo by the Islamic militias . . . the last great crucifixion of the Christians along Salah Salem . . . the little silver dragons of the Israeli air force against a blue sky . . . a mountain range of black smoke.

The world is ending.

He kept his eyes shuttered and clenched his jaws. It was only paint, drawings, torn pages, candles, ghastly photographs, grotesque juvenilia: the creation of men, of the men who had abducted his daughter. Seeing her here had unhinged him, and he must focus and find where she had been taken. That is what he had come here for. He opened his eyes and saw himself upon the wall he had fallen against.

As if he had been dreamed above the door of the room that he was now desperate to flee, there was an impressionist's deranged sketch of a masked man, the face bone-white, death-white, skull-white. The tired but committed form was caped in black and crowned with a scarecrow's hat. *His* hat, the detail of the camouflaged band was crude but unmistakably his own. The man possessed one outsized hand, carrying a handgun. The similarity was no coincidence and it portrayed him dressed to invade, torture and kill, only this figure wore a halo, painted red.

The father's mind scrabbled for the reasons why he had been scrawled upon the wall. Someone, perhaps Chorny, must have known of the pursuit, the coming avenger. Had he been told? The image was dust-specked and glazed dry, yet it must have been added to the wall within the last three months, when he'd been active, because only then had he been attired this way.

How do you know me?

The father moved and placed his ear an inch from the surface of the vestry doors. Heard nothing but the drumming of the rain upon the metal roof, the buffeting and distant roar of wind between the surrounding buildings. He replaced the handgun with the stun weapon.

The doors were unlocked.

The father let himself inside.

And noisily disturbed a cluster of empty paint tins.

The skeletal figure lying upon the mattress didn't stir.

The room was tainted by vomit, blood-ironed, excrement-infused, and so powerfully it made the father wince.

He feared he had come here too late, and that the man partially wrapped in a soiled sheet, and so motionless upon the stained mattress, was dead. He quelled the errant notion that the figure had been laid out in a ghastly preparation, ready for his arrival.

The figure's head and throat were completely inked by tattoos. Only the face was left clean. *Enlumineur*.

A further moment of confusion and disorientation brought the father to a standstill. Yonah Abergil had said Oleg Chorny was found dead of an overdose and a broken heart underneath this place, two years before. Could history repeat itself so vividly, or was this coincidence and just another human junkie ruin that had crawled in here to expire? Chorny would be bones now; this thing was still coated in flesh.

Closer, crouching, the rain still dripping from the tail of his poncho, the father thought he heard the corpse breathing, faintly, the incoming air tinged by a rasp. Yet he couldn't be sure, and how could anything so thin, so skull-contoured about the hairless, hollow-cheeked head, still be living? Surely no organ could still murmur within the skeletal remains of the misery artist. He was tempted to check for a pulse.

The father shone the torch onto the vials and the coke-blackened glass tubes, the aluminium inhalers, plastic injectors, baggies scattered beside the disorderly bedding: an addict's detritus, the messy artefacts of a haste to depart the world. The illustrated man had been loading up by a variety of means. Sachets and plastic jars of powders, blister packs, canisters of paste, gas burners, a pestle and mortar inside an old wooden box upon a table indicated the man had been a keen amateur chemist too, manufacturing his own catalysts and accelerants into the deeper fathoms of consciousness.

Around the father's feet, piles of strangled, twisted clothes, sticky kitchen utensils, food packages and empty plastic bottles covered the floor like flotsam on the surface of a fetid canal. Pages from the Baptists' books rested amongst the mounds of refuse. Stiff brushes, rollers, paint trays and encrusted palettes had been dropped and now stuck to what they touched. The air itself seemed thickened and warmed by the thermals of the miasmas rising from the bedding and a blocked toilet.

A bathroom adjoined the ramshackle living quarters. The father peered inside. A good fire would be required to purify it. He looked about the yellowing ceiling, the scuffed walls, and wondered at the dreamtime vistas, the surreal landscapes and communions with hellish delusions through which this man's subconscious had eagerly soared.

Within his bafflement, flickers of his own image on the pitch-black walls, and of his daughter in the photograph, made his breath seize and the father stiffened with a self-generated cold that made his hands shake. He imagined he had stepped inside a place of old magic, of unnatural laws. Faint cries from the edge of his consciousness seemed to issue warnings, and what seemed like an acknowledgement that what he'd thought impossible was possible.

The father forced himself to return his attention to the bed and he asked himself again if this could truly be Oleg Chorny: the child taker and the man found dead two years before, according to Yonah Abergil, and laid beneath what must have been this very building?

Abergil had lied then. Chorny, the King's celebrated *enlumineur*, must have been allowed to live. No two men, *enlumineurs* and junkies both, could be found in the same place by their would-be assassins. He would not believe that. So the man before the father must be his daughter's abductor. Incredible. This man had taken her from her home and sold her, but was just lying here, like this, laid out, as if *waiting* to be found.

His hands were in plain sight; no weapons were visible. If he so much as twitched, the father would discharge the immobilizer, though that would surely stop the heart of this figure who'd deliberately removed himself to the edge of life, perhaps to madly depict what he saw at that border.

The father trained his weapon at the birdy chest, and peeled back the sheet. The *enlumineur* of the King Death creed had truly displayed his skilful wares upon his own flesh. To his throat he was patterned gold and azure with sigils, signs, runes and inscriptions of black deeds mercifully coded, but borne proudly to represent a devil's status. Was his daughter's name on that unwashed flesh? If it was, this father would cut it out.

Could the thing even walk? The wrists were so thin they resembled lengths of doweling. The hands at the end were cartoonish claws. They were crossed over the bony chest, to suggest repose, as if the figure was ready to be lowered into the ground or placed upon a pyre. The angular jaw sloped to a wattled neck, ribbed with cartilage over the throat. It had no teeth, just greyish stubs behind a lipless maw, through which air marginally wheezed to activate a distant rattle. The skull beneath the skin. The very face of death. A painted corpse. *Aping what you serve?*

Bloodied tissues were caught up in the folds of the sheet.

Consumptive. Tubercular. Maybe one of the antibiotic-resistant strains. Seemingly the creature had moments to live. Would it even survive the journey back to the car, let alone endure questioning? The father would have to carry it across his shoulders like a bundle of sticks with a lolling, oversized head.

He hovered above the figure, unsure of himself, confused by what he had seen in this place of tribute and divination. But he failed to identify the full power of his murderous hatred for Oleg Chorny. It was mostly pity and revulsion that he felt now.

TWENTY-FIVE

At seven a.m. the captive came round from a stupor that had lasted most of the night, only interrupted by two seizures, and suffered another fit inside the car. Arching his back off the rear seat, he salivated, exposing a throat ringed with grime. His legs kicked out and struck the door.

The father quickly alighted from the car and stood beside it, looking through the rain-blurred windows at the figure inside, thrashing despite two sets of cuffs locked tight at the ankle and wrist. This was the man's third seizure since his capture, the worst yet. Eventually, he rolled off the rear seat and into the footwell.

Through the entire journey from the chapel to the car, and then through the remainder of the night and into the dawn, the captive had remained unconscious, repeatedly coughing and making incoherent sounds, without waking fully. During the extraction through the storm, an ordeal that had near-wasted the last of the father's strength, his prisoner had spoken once, but briefly. In a thin, feminine voice, he had muttered into the father's ear. It had been hard to pick out the words against the sound of the wind, until the man's lips had flopped against his skin and he had heard, 'He leans over us at birth. Stands behind us in life. Sits beside us at the end.' The sound of the sibilant hiss, as much as the contents of the utterance, had forced the father to drop the bound figure onto the wet, wind-flayed grass, to withdraw a weapon and point it at the bony face. But the eyes had not opened; the man had only spoken from within a drugged slumber.

The father was additionally surprised that anyone could survive the powerful seizures the man was suffering. A hospital was out of the question. He knew little about first aid, but if necessary he would lever the man's tongue out of his throat, with a stick or gloved fingers, because that mouth had some use. Twice he'd attempted to awaken the man, but had been unsuccessful. If his captive died, the father would have to bury him, and his secrets, out here amongst the drenched crops.

He'd brought the drug stash from the chapel too, along with an army holdall he'd found beneath loose floorboards. A sudden withdrawal from the concoctions the addict mainlined could be catastrophic, he knew that much; he would have to give him something to keep him alive, for a while. The creature's chronic addiction might even be useful during the interrogation; he might awake eager for a fix. Most strains of recreational drugs were powerful enough to prevent any possibility of getting clean.

The father mulled over his options to force a confession. But how long would this creature linger under the duress he knew himself capable of inflicting? If his rage erupted he could not trust himself.

Chorny's canvas bag contained guns and enough ready cash to keep the father going until the following summer, if he lived that long. How had it not been stolen? Though the idea that the thieves in the camps were averse to entering the chapel was not implausible. There were more drugs in the bag too, some tools and emergency rations: clear preparations for a getaway, and maybe one that had been anticipated, if the father's image upon the walls was an indication of what the man knew was coming for him.

There were more pressing matters to attend to now that it was light, like checking in with his wife again and driving as far from South Devon as he could manage in the stolen vehicle during the storm. He'd hoped that he would have known, by now, where to drive to: the very place his daughter had been taken two years before. But that information remained inside a comatose mind.

A call came in.

Standing in the rain, shivering inside his poncho, he scrabbled through his pockets. As he fished out his screen, a pair of unnaturally bright eyes opened on the dirty floor of the vehicle, and began to explore the interior. The father stepped away from the glass, as if suddenly shy before an introduction to who was probably his daughter's kidnapper.

An unrecognized number. It had to be the police detective, Gene Hackman.

He'd driven the new vehicle a short distance from where the detective had left it, and parked at the foot of a small valley, as anywhere more exposed was still being hit by horizontal rain and winds strong enough to knock a child over. The depression in the earth was one of the few places that attracted only agricultural traffic, and he doubted that would make an appearance today.

The father accessed the voice-only call. 'Hello?'

'What have you done? What the fuck have you done?' The reception was terrible, but the speaker was immediately recognizable as Scarlett Johansson.

'Scarlett?'

'They know about you. I'm being followed. I was interviewed yesterday by my line commander. An inspector! Here!'

'I don't understand. How would they—'

'A man was killed in Somerset. Yonah Abergil. You hear me? Ring any bells? A trafficker with links to lowlife in Torbay and Rory Forrester, who's now been linked to Murray Bowles and Nigel Bannerman. They're trying to tie this on me.' She paused to get her breath. 'Where are you now?'

The father swallowed, and scratched through his thoughts. 'They mentioned me? What did they—'

'Of course they bloody mentioned you. That's why I am calling you! If you'd stood down, it wouldn't have bloody mattered. Those sites weren't going to be investigated by forensics. Not for dead sex offenders. I told you! But you went for a King, a bloody King! You were told to stay away . . . They're bringing more people in now. I saw them as I left the station. People on our side, *friends*. We're all being questioned. Someone has given us up. All of us here.' The woman was becoming shrill. 'Where are you?'

He had to swallow to ease the constriction in his throat. 'Devon.'

'I told you to stay away. Where are you in Devon?'

The father wanted to tell her but held back. He looked at the sky as an instinctive suspicion made him tense. He had a new handler now, Gene, and the idea of his old car being tracked had been terrifying. Inner circles and need-to-know arrangements in Scarlett's enigmatic world must have recently been ransacked like burgled rooms, and he was weak with fear all over again, but perturbed at how a link between him and Scarlett could have been made. Only her partners involved in the same illegal trafficking of information to vigilantes would have known she was handling him. His thoughts leapt into thin air, into vast open white spaces devoid of answers. He wanted to kill the connection. 'I can't. Not safe.'

'Safe? We're way past safe. You've put us all in danger. Jeopardized everything!'

'I . . . I couldn't stop. I was close.'

'I could be killed.' She said this quietly and without emotion as if she were talking to herself. 'You know that? For helping you? Because of what you have done. The inspector was scared. More than me. Do you know what *they* do to people, even the police?'

'But how have we been connected? How does anyone know we ever spoke? This set is unregistered. I change them all the time. The accounts are all unregistered. You gave them to me. You said they would never be traced. They were completely secure.'

'They've put me in the middle of this because they now have all of the accounts that I have been using for you. Every bloody one of them.' Her voice was shaken to the point of breaking. 'Calls, times, places, they've traced the activity of all the identities attached to the accounts.'

'Identities? These identities . . .'

'All deceased. I've been using the accounts of the deceased. It's what we use, their identities. They were the only connections between me and you, the dead. The accounts you used were traced to my idents and to wherever you were when I called you. And that's even more evidence to link us to every hit. Christ, it doesn't even matter about the accounts, they have your DNA at two sites, and they have eye witnesses.'

The father knelt down in the wet grass and gripped his skull. 'Someone on your side gave you up because I killed a King? Someone in your circle? Once they had you, they checked all your comms? But how . . .'

Scarlett sniffed, her voice quivering. 'They've tracked your car, the vehicle registered to you.'

'Jesus Christ.'

'It gets worse.' Scarlett took a deep breath. The father heard her swallow. 'The man you know, who took you on, the police detective. He's dead.' Scarlett Johansson broke down. 'His head . . .'

Unguided by the vague, useless thoughts that follow shock, his voice came out as a whisper. 'Dead?'

'They wanted *you*. And *he* . . . they caught up with him, and killed him. They put him . . . his head, inside the car. A message for you.'

'God, God, no.'

'The investigation is pinning this on him. On me, and him, and you: a vigilante and police conspiracy to murder. You have torn years and years of planning to pieces.' He heard her swallow again to regain control of her voice. 'He swapped vehicles for you?'

'This account that I am using is one of his. He gave it to me. If you have it . . . You shouldn't have called!'

'Fuck you! This isn't only about you and your fucking

daughter . . .' The woman stopped and sniffed. After a pause she said, 'It's over.'

A terrible shadow fell across the father's thoughts. 'Oh, sweet Jesus. I know . . . I know how they got you. *He* gave you up. He knew you. He knew me. Gene . . . The detective. He was the only link between us. He knew my idents . . . Because he had no choice. They made him tell who'd handled me before, which comms she used. He knew about your idents?'

'Yes.'

'When they caught him, before they killed him, they must have . . . They must have threatened his wife . . . or something. Torture . . . and he gave you all up . . .' The cold air and wet soil sank through to the father's marrow.

'Leave. Run. Wherever you are now, go. Get out, move. Christ.'

The father's dirty fingers were in his wet hair, tugging. 'Jesus Christ, I've got to call my wife. I've got to go. We both have to move. This call, if it's being traced, will put me here. Jesus, Jesus, Jesus . . . Would they know about the car I have now? Would he have told them?'

Scarlett's voice changed, became urgent, but frail, as if she were about to start crying again. 'I could come to you. It'll be safer. Better if there are two of us. Tell me where *here* is.'

The father looked at the screen, then at the figure inside the car that had propped itself upright to study its metal bonds. 'I'm sorry. They might be listening.'

Her tone suddenly changed, became frantic again, but the fear was gone. 'Tell me you're close to her now.'

And the father felt sick, wondering if *someone* was listening. 'Closer than I have ever been.'

'God bless yo—' The call was abruptly cancelled from her end.

The father threw away the device, as far from himself as he could, and ran back to the car. Ignoring his captive's unblinking eyes, he tried to contact his wife's new ident from the service inside the car. He couldn't get through.

TWENTY-SIX

As the father began the drive to Birmingham, the wind was so strong the vehicle locked itself to thirty miles an hour on the motorway. He parked not far past the exit for Taunton and made three more attempts to contact his wife from a public comms post, taking the total to a dozen calls since he'd crawled away from Brixham. After the final unsuccessful effort he was close to tears.

When he returned to the car, the prone figure on the back seat sat up so quickly the father gasped. He swivelled around in the front seat and the two men stared at each other, one grinning, the other tense and already fingering the handgun clamped between his thighs.

When the father's shock ebbed, the bony head instilled nothing inside him but odium, and desperate hope. A gangly wreck, clothed by a blanket and coloured ink, with eyes more serpent than human, too large for the face and yellowy with inner toxins from sustained substance abuse, smiled at him, as if pleased to make his acquaintance. Men like this had so recently murdered a police officer, his friend and his guardian angel. Revulsion alone granted him a reprieve from his terrors for Miranda, and for Scarlett's impending fate.

But he still had a problem believing that his daughter's

abductor sat within the vehicle. The move had been too easy, fraught with a psychic worrying, but bloodless. It seemed preposterous, after all this time and after all that he had done to get here, that the kidnapper would have just been *there*, and now here in a car with him.

And the location of the snatch, the chapel; festooned with the most worrying resonances of what he had either failed to process, or refused to engage with since he'd seen the graffiti in Paignton, escalated his fear of being engulfed by something, perhaps predestined, that was far greater than himself. Bewilderment and fear ran his parliament today.

'You knew I was coming,' the father said.

The figure's smile broadened. More of the grey stubs were exposed in purpling gums that shone with too much saliva. When it came, the voice was more a rasp than actual words. 'You have water?'

He'd given the man nothing all day; his prisoner must have leaked a litre of sweat. Uncannily, the criminal's eyes near-twinkled, were too bright and alert for someone who'd seemed to be coughing out his last breath through the hours until dawn, and then most of the morning too, asleep or semi-conscious. But somehow this creature was still alive and exhibiting no sign of fear at its captivity. Not a trace of anxiety was evident. The man was confident, even complacent, in his new circumstances. The attitude was as alarming as it was disarming.

The father would need a smog respirator to muzzle the criminal. He'd always queued for his jabs, but the new TB strains could be resistant to drugs and he was run down, weakened, susceptible. He also wondered if the man had concealed drugs and administered a tonic to himself. With bound hands and ankles, the father couldn't see how, and he'd searched the man's body at the chapel as soon as his limbs were secure. The sticklike form had been all bone and parchment between the father's rubber-gloved fingers. Searching him had been akin to sorting through the disinterred contents of an old grave.

The father handed a bottle of water to the man, and watched the long neck quivering as it gulped the bottle empty. 'And now,' he said, smiling broadly after a gasp of satisfaction. 'I need to take a shit. You have clean underwear for me?'

The father climbed out and opened the rear door, watching the man's large hands carefully. Oleg's dirty fingers were entwined as if in prayer. 'It might be your last shit, so make the most of it. And make it quick.' He removed Oleg from the car and laid him on the grass verge at the side of the rain-raked road, then pushed him down and into the sopping drainage ditch, using one foot. The figure slid into the watery trench, then studied its new surroundings with a modicum of pleasure. Smarting eyes, unused to light, blinked at the grey sky.

The father glanced back at the village they were near. Rain and wind had been keeping people indoors and off the roads, but there was no guarantee that would continue. It had gone noon and the storm was moving further north.

The father pointed the gun at Oleg's face as if he were about to execute him at the roadside, surrounded by drought-resistant soya plants that bustled like a vast green crowd. Oleg merely smiled. 'Today, I knew a grim face would look upon me. *L'Homme devant la mort.* Is this the hour of my death? This I do not know.'

'That depends on you. You don't seem too concerned. You doubt me?'

'To come so far just to see me? No, I don't doubt you. I am pleased it will be you. But this is also a pity that we close a door so soon, one that has opened for each of us.'

'Your name is Oleg Chorny.'

The figure in the ditch grinned. 'One of many, but still my favourite.'

'That was me on that wall, back there in the church. Who told you I was coming?'

Oleg laughed as if a child had asked him a silly but sincere question. 'Signs are my guides. There is meaning in the void, in the deeps, but not in words.'

'What the fuck does that mean? I'm not one of your junkie disciples. How did you know I was coming?'

Oleg's grin broadened. 'Because of the confinement between the signs. For me and for you. You should have some vision now. But please, if you are not going to finish our meeting prematurely, may I?' He pointed at his lap.

The father stepped away, so that he could only see the man from the shoulders upwards, keeping the gun trained on the thin head.

'You have towel, paper? Underwear?'

He would have to provide a pair of his own, and toilet paper. The act of kindness made his guts writhe. And the man was trying to confuse him with psychobabble, with bullshit. He'd need to rein it in by setting a swift and brutal example, and one that wouldn't be forgotten. Yet as Oleg squatted the father was again reminded that the man might be too fragile for violence. But the father would risk the evil shit. That got results. From there, he would move on to the man's limbs and joints, later, and somewhere remote, once he'd contacted his wife. The encroaching notion of what he might find in Birmingham made him feel faint and desperate to lie down.

There was no time for delay. Not now. People were looking for him, in earnest and by the most uncompromising means. They might know of this car. If Gene Hackman had given up Scarlett, her colleagues, the idents, then what else had he told his executioners? *Under duress. They* might be closing on him right now. A last stand might be hours away, or less. The idea of being killed beside a stolen vehicle, as Chorny looked on, grinning with his grey stubs, was too much to tolerate.

The father's heart beat sickeningly. He became short of breath and found it difficult to think clearly, to know what to do. But he did know that he wanted to get to work on the painted devil, to finally know what had been done to his daughter. After all that had happened, after coming so far, that must come first.

Oleg spat. Stood up and gathered the towel, underwear and paper that the father had placed at the rim of the ditch. He cleaned himself by passing his hands between his thighs, tottering for balance in cuffed ankles, then inspected the underwear with disappointment. Like most of the father's clothes, the pants were faded from repeated washing in hotel sinks, sagging and near threadbare at the seat.

From the pocket of his jacket, the father fished out the photograph he had taken from Oleg's shrine. Presented it to the skull-face that blinked in the rain. 'Tell me where she is.'

Oleg looked at it for a few seconds, intensely, and finally nodded. 'That one.' He nodded some more, appearing wistful, as if acknowledging a long-held but unconfirmed suspicion. 'There were so many in those days. But I can see now that it was her that brought you to me. The father. A Red Father, yes. That would explain the rage, the grief, and the guilt.' He looked away, his face a committed grimace. 'The death wish of mankind is the strangest urge, but the strongest, just as death is greater than life and love. It is a path you and I have both followed, and so we are together now. But we have some way still to go, Red Father, to finish this.'

'What did you call me?'

Towelling the rain from his scrawny torso, Oleg didn't answer but said, 'It is raining. Soon I will be wet again. Please.' He pointed at his ankles then held up the underwear.

'You can die in the rain with a bare arse. You can lie in your own shit for all I care.'

Oleg looked at the gun pointed at his face. Jagged contours and thin skin refashioned themselves into a wistful sadness. 'Before we begin, you must understand something: we are *nihil*. You and I. We are *nemo*.'

The father thought of the painting on the wall of a dead ogre's cavern. 'What?'

'We are nothing. We are nobody. Only in death do we transcend. And it is better to know where it is that we will go. To the terrible passage. I have known this for a very long time. And I am ready. 'Tis a good time for me. I am in contact with a patron, over there. But you? I don't think so. You kill me and you are closer than you have ever been to the hour of your death too. Without me, I think the part that you have played will end for you unsatisfactorily. Alas, and you are so close.'

'Part? You think this is some fucking game?' The father nearly squeezed the trigger.

Oleg saw the subtle tightening of the sinews in his gloved hand and smiled. 'The distance from life to death is narrow, and I do not fear death. Your threats are no good. As I say, I expect as much from you, until your eyes are fully opened. But know this: I only came back for you, from the place where I was waiting, a border. I came back for whoever was coming to me with an answer.'

'You want me to think that you're mad, is that the angle?'

Oleg smiled, humouring him. 'From time to time I returned, to see who could help me, to see who else was confined inside *something* that was started many years ago. A ritual. A great ritual. And it has not always been easy to go from *there* to here.' He gazed at his naked, ruined body, as if at soiled clothing. 'The distance between life and after-death is . . . monumental. The journey is tiring.'

'Shut up. Where did you take the girl? Who paid for her?'

Oleg raised his thinly papered skull to stare at the sky. He looked like a corpse arisen from a grave on Judgement Day, but one that had been lied to and still remained a ruin. 'Red Father, I will try and make it simple for you because we do not have much time, and because you hate me more than you have ever hated anything. Hate is good, but only when properly directed.' He sighed, as if impatient before the great task of instruction ahead of him. 'What do you hear, Red Father? All around us.'

'Don't you call me that!'

Oleg ignored him. 'I hear the silence of centuries, of millennia. There is nothing left behind us. But afterdeath is a cacophony. And that is ahead of us. In there the past has gone. The past and all we seek and love is swallowed. The world is being devoured. As every moment passes, we are all one moment closer to afterdeath. Nothing here matters.' Oleg then grimaced as if he recalled some episodes in this other place, this afterdeath, of which he spoke. 'There is no more future. We do not need to record any more history. No one has any use for it. Signs and marks alone have power. In chaos they shine. I have made so many signs, as have you. Make another now if you wish. I have been ready for a long time to finally let go. Why delay what is inevitable? Why care so much?'

The father wanted to discharge his weapon and keep on firing until the mad thing in the ditch was broken apart like the crockery in a dead king's barrow. He couldn't decide whether this show of suicidal insanity was authentic, or an act to prolong a meagre existence.

Oleg turned his head quickly, cutting the father's thoughts in half. 'Do it. Here. If you lack the strength to go further, if you have lost the will to know, then go make another of your signs. Your marks. They are incandescent. They make such light in darkness. I have seen your lights coming closer and closer. I wish I could have seen you light those tapers too, but at least make this death between us a terrible art and sever our bondage in this ritual. Death is poetry, the highest sensation. You know this. So make me part of your ecstasy, and one of your signs, if you cannot carry on. If you cannot bear to know what it is you have found while you sought something else . . .' Oleg finished with a cryptic smile.

The father lowered the gun before the desire to use it became overwhelming. Even though it was him holding the gun, he was far more uncomfortable than he wished to be. He didn't understand the man's riddles, not literally, but there was meaning, a sinister subtext, that struck strange chimes at the back of his mind, and he resented the awful notion that this man in rags was trying to be a tutor, an educator in something he was now in danger of believing.

There might be another inference in the exchange too: a confession about his daughter's fate, or whereabouts, would only come slowly; information would be only dribbled out in prophetic-sounding gibberish, as if his captive sought a way into his mind, and out of captivity. If so, it was time for him to impart a lesson of his own, and to destroy the equivalency between them that this man was trying to create.

Oleg looked past the father again and into the distance as if he addressed that. 'In this world we are smudges, brief traces, smoke rings, small vanishing vapours. And when our smoke vanishes' – Oleg clicked two dirty fingers – 'we will see better in the darkness of afterdeath.'

The father stepped into the ditch and engulfed Oleg's head with a cloud of nerve gas.

Oleg whimpered, fell forward, clutching at his face, then writhed and kicked like a dying spider at the side of the ditch.

After a minute the father hauled him out of the turf by his upper arms and dragged him to the car. He sprung the boot latch. Raised and dumped the coughing man inside, pushing his thin legs down as if they were kindling being packed into a fireplace. He covered the twitching figure with an oil-stained blanket, then made to slam closed the lid.

'That was not necessary,' Oleg said, snivelling. 'I am here to guide you.'

'Fuck you.'

Oleg cleared his sinuses and mouth. 'You can if you wish. It has been a while for me, but you waste our time, so let us go back to the sea. Let us get closer to what you seek, Red Father. I suggest Portsmouth.' He grinned knowingly through the tears and mucus that had formed a glistening coating across his red skull.

Confused, but also stricken, the father hesitated. This was either a clue regarding his daughter, or a ruse leading to a trap. He withdrew the nerve gas and let Oleg's horrible, swollen and solitary open eye see it. 'This is nothing compared to what will happen to you, if you do not tell me where you took my daughter. A lawyer was involved. A go-between. I want his real name. And the location of the place you took her to, two years ago. I will either break this information from you, or your last moments on this earth can be painless. I'll even let you overdose. How's that?'

'Such consideration I never expected from you, whose rage I have watched like a star in another place that has no light, and whose very fire I brought into this world . . . and into that other place too.' Oleg tittered, like a camp puppet. 'But who can afford unacceptable delays in such pressing times? We are going north? If you seek what you have lost, you will not find it in that direction. And I can only hope that in your efforts to find me you did not meddle with King Death. By the look in your eyes, am I to assume that you did? Well, if they catch us, my old friends will not hesitate, and they will be enthusiastic in their work. They have no soul, most of these Kings, only a banal purpose. But you have such fire, and it should be allowed to grow brighter before I leave you.'

The father closed the boot and returned the man to darkness. As he walked away, his prisoner embarked upon a coughing fit.

He sat in the car and thought his way through a tangle of options pickled by indecision. He thought of Birmingham and he tried calling his wife again. If the person you loved was in danger and did not answer your calls, then you would return to the place you last saw them. There you would start looking. But he considered who might now be waiting for him in Birmingham if he continued north.

The father instructed the car to take him to Portsmouth.

TWENTY-SEVEN

On arrival in Portsmouth, the father checked on Chorny. Inside the car boot that stank of wet carpet and urine, the man now shivered and whimpered from withdrawal. The father dropped a bottle of water inside the boot and slammed the lid.

Outside an old municipal car park he found a public comms post on the street and tried to connect to his wife. He tried four times and gave up, held the post with both hands and dipped his head. When the spike of his dread passed, he used the terminal to access the last accounts that Gene Hackman and Scarlett had used to make contact with him. If the Kings wanted to communicate with him, to send a message, they might use his old idents that they were now familiar with. But if they had the means to identify the places in which he accessed those accounts, then they'd also know which city he was in. But they would not be able to follow a handset in transit, as he no longer had one, or the car if he only used public comms on the street.

If Gene Hackman had given this vehicle up, his end could come any time and his quest would be over. But why had they not come already, today? *They* were everywhere and into everything, but they had not found him. Not yet, and he could not abandon the car even if they knew of its existence and easily traceable registration. All further movement towards the truth of his daughter's abduction depended upon the use of a private vehicle. He lacked the skills to steal another, and couldn't waste time trying to buy one. A rental would be registered to him and would quickly give up his location. He'd been careful on the journey to Portsmouth on the available roads, looking behind constantly, two loaded handguns ready at all times, and was sure he had not been followed. His sole hope was the possibility that Gene Hackman had omitted this one crucial detail, in a confession tortured from him prior to execution. Or perhaps the vehicle's traceable identity had even been erased? Criminals did it to their own transport. And the father *had* to believe the stolen car was safe.

There were two messages waiting for the father at the account he'd used for communicating with Gene Hackman. Each communication had visuals. He also checked the last account Scarlett had used, which hadn't been discontinued either, and that revealed the same two messages as the pair in the Hackman account. They had been recorded during the previous evening when he was snatching Oleg Chorny. Gene Hackman may have recorded the messages before he was murdered. Perhaps a frantic warning awaited him here, even pertinent advice for his continued survival.

The father opened the first message, and gasped when a black cloth bag was whipped from a head onscreen, revealing the face of a kneeling figure: his friend, Gene Hackman. Briefly losing his balance, the father gripped the media post. Rain slapped the canopy. He looked about himself, at the wet street, the mostly unlit windows of the commercial buildings. Nothing, no one.

We are nothing. We are nobody.

He returned his attention to the naked figure onscreen: a purple, black, red visage, with closed-up eyes, that had once been the face of a man. The police detective began speaking. 'It's over . . . our time.' The figure then shuddered as it was pushed or kicked from one side. Someone spoke a prompt, their voice muffled. Gene repeated what they had said to him. 'They know who you are. They know everything about you. All is being settled.'

The screen jumped to a scene a few minutes later. The officer's head was bowed and he wept. The recording returned to him speaking the same message as before. The loop was repeated. The father prepared to close the communication, but suddenly found himself looking at a new scene, but in the same place – what looked like a grove in a dismal, wet wood. A gloved hand gripped the wet hair of the police officer's scalp, pushed his head further down so that he was facing his navel. And before the father could make the screen go blank, to remove the sight of the pale but blood-smeared shoulders, and the tangled, damp chest hair, a voice, off-screen, said, '*L'Homme devant la mort.* Yonah Abergil.'

The partial shot showed a hand gloved in black that held a machete. A rustle of cloth, a swish and a fleshy thump: the officer's head dropped from his shoulders. A red-white stump slid to one side and fell from view. The scene's crude edit kicked into repeat.

The father closed the message and bent over to vomit at the base of the post. He clawed the metal with weak and quivering fingers as if he were tethered to a stake.

Finding his feet after the worst of the nausea passed, he turned about and scanned the street again, raked the area with his juddering and leaping vision for a face directed at him, for vehicles with watching occupants at the kerbs. There was nothing, no one.

We are nothing. We are nobody.

The Kings would now know where he had activated the message, but they could not have known that he would come to Portsmouth before the communication was opened. Even so, he could not stay here for long or the monstrousness that decapitated a serving detective would be upon him, and that would be him upon his knees, waiting for the steel to scythe down, from behind, from beyond his blind, panting anticipation and terror.

He needed to get out of here. There was no one to help any more, no more sympathy or assistance to call upon from allies. Friends and guardians had been sacrificed for him. For his cause, they had been abducted and killed. The idea was too great for his mind to withstand. He wanted to get back to the car.

Miranda.

'God, please . . .' Thoughts of his wife intermingled with images of the detective's gored shoulders. The father retched again onto the pavement.

Second message. There was a second message. This one had also been sent from the police officer's account. One hour after the first film was posted; so both would have been sent from *those* who were now hunting him. Perhaps the second message was a further taunt, or more to horrify, sicken and weaken him with terror. He briefly imagined watching a desecration of the policeman's remains as he stood speechless in the wet street. His whole body tensed as if a scream was close to emerging from his throat; he wanted to fold in on himself and close down.

Find a place to end this, to end all of this.

At the comms post, he opened the second message. Decided to look at it quickly, and then run. *Run where?* Until Chorny gave him somewhere specific to go, a location, a name, he had no destination to pursue. That information would have to be extracted from the man, and fast, as soon as he returned to the car. No more clues or riddles. Chorny spoke or he died within the hour.

A road appeared onscreen, lit dim amber at night, flanked by brick apartment buildings. The father didn't recognize it. The scene had been filmed from street level, from inside a car. Two men came out of one of the buildings and approached the car. They wore black Balaclavas, like guerrillas, with a suggestion of lighter colours about their eyes. As he studied the men, more figures left an entrance to the apartment building in the background. Three other people had emerged. Their arms were linked, until they began walking in single file. The gait of the figure in the middle was distinctly feminine, her coat long, her face lowered. But it was not his wife because this woman wasn't tall enough.

The scene jumped and here was another plain room: cement walls, narrow, low-ceilinged, white. A new scene in the same room was dropped into the montage. This act featured a cast of one: a thin, naked woman, narrow-faced, her breasts small and covered by her arms, her hair tied back; someone he had never seen before. Make-up ran down her cheeks from wet eyes. Her mouth opened. 'Every door is closing.'

She lowered her gaze and looked at something to the left of the camera, at whoever was sat there. The woman swallowed. 'You knew me as Scarlett. My real name is Amy. I also have a child. I am a mother and I love my son very much. My son and I are in danger because of what you and I have done.'

'No. No.' The father spoke to no one but himself in the windblown street. He slapped the side of his head as if to knock these images out before they settled. So they already had Scarlett when she called him that morning? They were listening then, and had made her call him to get a fix on his location. What choice did she have? She was a mother.

'All of this must stop, now. My son and I will be reunited. We will be safe.' She tried to smile, but her face dropped before she finished the sentence she clearly did not believe a word of. 'Use this account to arrange a meeting. It's very important that you make contact. This is about your daughter and your wife. Information you need is waiting for you.'

The father wanted to terminate the message, but knew he was now incapable of doing that because his little girl and his wife had been mentioned. *They* knew he would listen, and while he did so his skin shrank at the idea that a vehicle was on its way right now, to finish this carnage he had brought into so many lives. The longer the messages lasted, the more time the Kings would have to reach him.

His legs started to twitch, as did his hands, his face, his thoughts.

They're coming.

Scarlett spoke again. 'Your daughter is alive. She is a happy and healthy girl. She is six years old. There have been reasons why she could not be with you and your wife. Your wife understands now. Everything has been explained to her. She will be in touch with you too. Soon.'

'God. God.' The father spoke to the rain and wet cement, to the rattling of a security shutter. An alarm screamed in the distance. Only seagulls answered it with sounds that seemed to swallow the father's mind.

'There is no way you will find your little girl. There never was. But she can be brought to you, both your daughter and your wife, if you cooperate. You don't have a choice because this matter is closing. The man they wanted was the police detective. Not me, not you, not your wife. Not my son. We played no part in the murder of Yonah Abergil. Please let us know where you are. Where we can all meet, safely, in public. No one will be harmed. This can all end soon, and we can all be reunited with those we love. *Please.*'

The woman swallowed and her eyes welled up. She struggled to compose herself, to straighten her face. 'They understand you. Understand what you have done out of desperation, out of a desire to see your daughter. And you will see her . . . soon. But you must . . . you must get in touch from this account, or this will not end and the consequences of your actions will be addressed in full. For all of us, please. Please . . .'

The screen jumped and the message restarted.

For all of us, please. Please . . .

The father killed the connection and staggered away from the post.

TWENTY-EIGHT

The vehicle's navigation found another car park two miles away. On arrival, he couldn't recall the journey, either through the streets or up inside the concrete levels to the sixth storey. Too many thoughts were clambering into his head and getting stuck in a limited space. Images from the communications appeared red and vivid in nauseating bursts; fragments he would recall for as long as he lived.

He near-fell from the car and pressed his face into the cold metal of the roof.

His wife had been mentioned. The Kings had his wife? It was why Miranda wasn't answering. She was unavailable. *And will be forever now. They* had moved so swiftly, so decisively, once his identity had been established. *They* had killed a police officer. Surely another one by now, the woman he knew as Scarlett. Maybe her son too. *God, no. Please God, no.* They would kill his wife. A cull: this was their message. If he opened another mail at the account Scarlett had given him, he might see his wife on her bare knees and he would hear her pleading . . . 'Oh Jesus Christ, Christ, Christ, Christ.' He buried his face in his hands and groaned. He sounded monstrous, bovine.

They said his daughter was alive. The enormity and impact of that thought was too sudden for him to process.

Instead, he went limp to the soles of his feet. If they weren't lying and they knew where she was, where she had been taken two years ago, they could also go and collect her. They could . . . The beheading: their signature. 'Bastards!' He struck the roof of the car. 'Bastards!'

Inside the boot, Oleg Chorny coughed and made the noise of a dog. The skeletal figure began to bump about.

Did they even have his wife? *A ruse. Maybe.* They could be lying about everything. There had been no film of his wife. But why didn't she answer his calls?

Everyone you know, they cease to exist. In one week they all in hell.

Root and branch.

No more sleep, no more resting for the scarecrow. No more disinformation from an addled consciousness. Chorny confessed now or he died. The father yanked open the boot. Seized Chorny by his ankles and hauled his legs out of the car. Grabbed his shoulders and positioned him on the cement. The figure was dazed and the light smarted against those big yellowy eyes. He covered his skull-face with his long, bloodless, crab-leg fingers.

The father carried him like a roll of carpet to the side of the car park and to the waist-high wall. Understanding the intention, Chorny pushed back, weakly, into the father's side.

'Time . . . You're going over. You're done. You shite. This ends!'

Oleg's face mooned with terror. 'No! Your daughter, think. Think. I am helping you. Together we do this. We get her back.'

'Liar. You're all liars.' The father pressed his face into

the veiny skull as he held the man's hollow cage of a torso, gritted his teeth and whispered. 'I've just heard from your old friends. They removed the head of someone who helped me. They filmed it and showed me. They're onto me and they are coming. No more delays. You love death. You all love death.' *But maybe not this one*. 'This is the hour of your death. I'll see you on the other side. And I will come for you there too.'

'You don't listen. Please . . . this, no.'

The father manoeuvred the man to the cement wall and pushed his head over and into the rain-specked air beyond. 'Down there. You'll break apart on the street . . . I'm done. I'm done with you all!' The father gripped Oleg's body in a bear hug around the top of his thighs, and raised him up as if to bundle him over.

Oleg attempted to fold himself in half, his pale face discovering a new shade beyond white, his spindly arms grasping for the wall. Spittle flecked his mouth, his nostrils flared horribly. And as his bony head hung in empty space his eyes became even vaster, expanding as he looked at the sky. He then glanced over his shoulder at the immensity of air below that a man could plummet through like a brick.

'Time to go to your afterdeath.' As if placing a sacrifice onto a plinth to await a god, the father rested Oleg's pointy hips upon the ledge. Witless before the drop, the man's mouth fell open, but he appeared too frightened to speak. Two-thirds of his near-fleshless bones were draped over the ledge, the sky above, death below. The father didn't like heights either, but had never before seen fear so vividly erase everything but itself upon a human face. Today, they were all traders in fear. Merchants who negotiated inside the deepest aquifers of each other's nightmares: a stolen child, the prospect of a beheaded spouse, the terrible thinness of the air and the cool breeze preceding a fall to one's death on concrete. The father had drilled deep into the only thing that mattered to all of them who bargained in such places as this: life and death, how you and those you loved died. There was nothing else, not really, not any more. Every man, woman and child would know this too, in time. Destiny. Maybe this afterdeath was nothing more than acceptance.

The father pushed the jabbering skull another inch into the void, then turned it over so the big-eyed face could fully see the smashing floor below. *Whoosh, scream, cement.* He wanted to let the figure go and knew he could do it. If Oleg did not speak now and reveal where his daughter had been taken, the father would let the body drop.

The figure found its last breath, its final cry, and . . . began to laugh, and the mad laughter ascended the scale into something raucous, queenish. His entire body shook with mirth as if another drug-deprived seizure was imminent. 'Death is larger than life!' He reached his bound arms into the air as if preparing for a high dive. 'Always it has been this way. So let me return to the terrible passage, Red Father. You disappoint me, but at least the fire of your rage will give me a fitting re-entry.'

A gun pointed into his face, the withdrawal of narcotics: nothing had made Chorny do anything but act out, lie, resist. Here was more evidence. This man was truly unafraid of death. His recalcitrance and doublespeak had merely prolonged his time. This lover of death had played him. It was as if he was privy to greater opportunities that not even death could spoil.

The father felt his body heave towards a sob of frustration at the utter futility of the tasks he had been set. Despair soon encased him like lead. His wife, Scarlett, Gene, had died for nothing and he was just wasting time in a public car park with a junkie. 'You have no idea! No idea . . . what you did to us!' The father screamed to rouse himself from torpor, from shock, from the dread that this man would never tell him what he wanted, what he needed. 'She was everything! She was ours. We loved her. You have no idea what you did . . . to me . . . to her mother . . . You don't know . . . You don't know what you did . . . What you all do . . .' He sobbed and let the man's thighs loosen under his arm. He clenched his jaw, swallowed. 'I wished . . . I wished I'd had the chance to kill your lover too. You bitch! But I'll finish what that fat prick Yonah started. He got to your lover first, but I'll finish all of you who touched her, who paid for her—'

Oleg turned his head to fix his serpent eyes upon the father. His legs tensed and he hooked his calves behind the father's waist. The mad eyes narrowed, confused but searching at this mention of his old boss. 'Yonah? Yonah Abergil?' The man paled again, but from not from a threat of death this time. The features withered under a sudden and terrible comprehension. The mad intensity in his eyes went out. 'Simmy. He . . . Abergil had him killed?' The man's shock was not fake, but then the father had been certain that his terror was no act either. 'Tell me!' Oleg shrieked so loudly that the father nearly let go of the bundle of cuffed bones. He finally had the man's full attention; had accidentally learned how to hurt him, and deeply.

The father spat and began to laugh. 'You didn't know! Your messages from the other side didn't tell you? Yes, Yonah murdered your lover. He had him killed. Your own boss had your lover killed, you skinny fuck. My daughter was his last job. And you didn't know. The devil that paid for her paid for your deaths. It was part of the contract. You can't even trust each other. There are no words. No words for people like you. There is no death to fit your crimes.'

'Simmy,' the skull whispered again, his body now entirely limp and hanging upside down, a hanged man, crucified by the remembrance of his own loss.

'Yonah lied. He said you were dead. But you've limped on for two years. For two years that made me wish that I was dead!'

Oleg placed his hands over his wet face.

'You're not going to tell me about my girl. And there is no one who you love that I can kill. There's only you to punish.'

Oleg dropped his hands and looked at the father, transfixing him with a gaze of near-inhuman rage. The collection of bones within the father's arms seemed to expand with a strength that pushed him backwards. Even with his ankles cuffed, Oleg curled his lower legs around the father's waist as one tight vice, near-crushing the breath from his body as they pulled the father against the waist-high wall. His body became an anchor. Oleg then seemed to twist his upper body around and sit up in mid-air solely using the strength in his stomach muscles. Using his bound legs behind the father's back as one belt of bone, he pulled himself forward and out of the wet, grey abyss. Long, sinewy arms whipped the air and knocked the father away from the wall, the metal cuffs splitting his lips.

As the father's vision settled, he found himself staring at the concrete ceiling. A yellow light flickered as if trying to revive his blunted consciousness. A tone hummed deep inside his ears. Dripping from the bottom lip, he tried to speak, but only gargled. He needed to convince himself that what now sat before him, with its back against the wall, was even human. He had never been struck so hard before. And Oleg Chorny had managed to swivel his thighs between the father's arms, wrap his lower legs around the father's waist, and pull himself back to the wall that he'd been draped over. He'd struck the father, before dropping to a crouch in one quick, fluid motion. A man who had seemed close to death had done this as if he were some acrobat or escapologist; a man reported dead two years gone, and a man whose ankles and wrists were still secured with steel cuffs.

The father made to stand, fumbling for the handgun in his pocket. Oleg stood too, poised like a perfectly balanced corpse-dancer, and looked out, distractedly, into the town. 'We go to Yonah. Enough of this bullshit. We go to Yonah, or you never see your daughter again.'

'Yonah is dead.'

Oleg's attention returned to him. The red eyes narrowed.

'I killed him.'

'You?' This was said with contemptuous disbelief.

The father nodded. 'After he gave me you, I killed him.'

'He gave you . . . Yonah would not speak, unless . . .'

'I shot him. His knee caps. But I believe it was my threat to kill his father that broke him.'

Oleg's long fingers traced the contours of his inked skull. 'The mad old bastard? He is still alive? Maybe that would have done it. Not the knees.' He raised his chin and blinked at the tears filming his big eyes. 'Yonah, Yonah, Yonah. It was you?'

'You knew I was coming for you. You knew that I was killing to find you. You painted me onto that bloody wall. You say I have made . . . these signs. But you did not know that you, and your partner, were betrayed by your own boss? You're not much of a seer.'

Oleg's thoughts drifted for a while and his eyes became near-vacant. 'I looked for Simmy. I went to hellmouth. You can't imagine . . . But the pit has no specific answers. It's not like that. And who could ever take Simmy down on their own? Such a man you have never known.' Oleg slapped his own head. 'I once considered Yonah as the culprit, but I decided this is not possible for Yonah. Simmy would have been warned first, by friends. He had more friends than Yonah ever did.'

The father dabbed his numb mouth with his sleeve. 'You want me to believe that you have some special relationship . . . with some *thing,* this afterdeath, just like all the nut-job evangelists and prophets? You think you're special? You bore me rigid. A demon, was it, that made you abduct a child? So you tell me now. You tell me everything right now, or you die. I swear that you will die here.'

Oleg shrugged. 'You confuse what I have told you about with . . . with an intelligence you would recognize.

There is no negotiation with afterdeath. No favours. I have spent many years looking to find this out. There are only visions in the great chaos that are similar to what is upon my walls. Pictures of what has gone and will come. But eventually it is possible to find a patron out *there*.'

'Bullshit.'

Oleg ignored him as if he were tired of the father. 'Simmy looked for this place first, afterdeath. He was the artist who tutored me. He was the seer. He knew there were guides for us, patrons over *there*, that we could . . . follow. He knew that we could always be together, and over *there* too, after this life. And something he found . . . that *we* found, we offered to and it came closer to us. It came to us as we made more and more of our own chaos. It found us through our signs, the ones we made in the ritual. You would not understand . . .' Oleg shrugged. 'How could you? Only we, and those seers before us, will ever know about what is so near and what can be beckoned closer. You think *this* is something that can speak, or be understood, or controlled by something as pitiful as us? We are dust. Dust that seeped through a crack, dust that soon gets swept back to what we all came out of.'

'Enough, enough of the bullshit. I'm warning you! My daughter . . .'

'Her? You ask me for only a tiny piece of the great truth, because you have no interest in the whole picture. You lack the mind, even now. You can't understand that what gave life to us, here, that tears itself into blood and flesh, only waits, impatient, for us to return to the terrible passage. We are of it. We are small parts of something that spread into a multitude, here. There is no time over there, no space. And we are all nobody here. Here, is nothing.' Oleg seemed to believe his own delusions. And, as was customary when faced with insanity, the father felt uncomfortable, tired, and strangely solemn.

Chorny was not reading his signals and was again ignoring the gun pointed at his face. 'We made our patterns in blood, can you not see, Simmy and me? We made our signs in a ritual that could truly be seen in another place, bright enough to be seen by a patron. It was all part of Simmy's bait, the ritual. And between the signs we became stuck. Every time we slept, we saw how badly. We saw his end. Yes, and we tried to alter it. But what was seen was inevitable once it all began. I saw my own nemesis in the dark too, *you*. All I knew was that my final hour was tied to Simmy, and to something we had done to someone. To your daughter, it now seems.'

Oleg leaned forward, his eyes bulging, the most excited the father had ever seen him. 'And when you have acquired the vision, of what came before and what comes after, you see the other things in afterdeath, traces . . . bloodless shadows, those already over there, the long-returned. *Patrons*. Who knows their origins? They are so old. But they see and they can leak between the right signs if they are made in the right sequence. We glimpsed them many times, and we learned that death is the only thing that gives life meaning. This!' He looked up and around himself as if to encompass the entire world. 'This life will soon be only a culture of death, all that we can expect or will ever see again. Soon. Our reign is brief and we must go back to what we came out of.

'For the next part, for the return to afterdeath, we

decided it was best to be aware over there, to frequent the court of a patron, and to remain together, while all others find blindness and oblivion.'

'There is nothing else but this world. And you were the cause of this world, and the consequence.'

Oleg shrugged. 'You have no idea, father. If only you could see. *La mort*, the finality, the endless distance. This world is one spark in darkness forever. It has only ever been this way. But we found something . . . in this dark. Truly. Something too great for us to know, to understand. Something that does not care for us, for anyone, but it felt our vibrations, our antics, at the mouth of the terrible passage that we looked inside. Simmy lured *it* from the darkest pit.' Oleg paused to spit, nodding at the father. 'And *you*, you stepped between the signs, our signs. The hole that we could see through, the one that we made. And the one that I have used again and again to look for Simmy over *there*. We pulled you in because you . . . You would be a part of our deaths. His, then mine. But we did not know who you were, or how you were connected to our destruction, or from what deed of ours you came to be linked to us.' Oleg dropped his head, as if his task was futile. In a quieter voice he said, 'Don't you see, ours was the experiment the scientist loses control of, and there were consequences. I can't explain it to you in another way. I always prefer to paint it.'

'Bullshit.'

'I am contagious, Red Father. There is an *awareness* of me, over *there*. I wanted this observer to be Simmy. It was not. But it is *the one*, I am sure, with whom Simmy keeps company now. A patron. If this is so, my love is not lost to me yet.' His sincerity was more unnerving than the preposterous claims the father mostly failed to grasp.

The father spat more blood from his mouth. 'This? This is what drives you to kill, and to take a child? This black magic bullshit?'

Insensitive to insult, Oleg turned his hairless head to stare blankly at the lightless office building opposite the car park. He spoke wearily, and more to himself than to the disappointing presence of another unbeliever. 'After-death is eternal. It is terror sublime forever. Maybe death itself. We don't know. Part of a god? Or just the absent dreams of something else, from another place. And it is none of these things. No one can see a face that is not there. *Nemo deum vidit*: nobody has seen God. It is . . . ineffable. Unlike anything. But close to here. So big, everywhere, just outside this . . . Closer, and closer now comes the great dark flow.' Oleg looked at the father as if he were looking at a child. 'People always sense this presence and call it lots of things. Devil. God. Instinct. Imagination. Maybe you do too. But the true source is closer than it has ever been, because never has so much been ready to travel through the terrible passage.

'This place brushes our minds, but comes no further. When it is close, ordinary things start to have meanings they did not have before.' Oleg's reedy voice slowed, as if in some final, hopeless confessionary moment. 'Dreams, they scrape it. Dreams that make you terrified of falling. The dreams when you sink and cannot move. You scream, you panic, but still you sink. Terror in sleep is the opening of the terrible passage. Hellmouth.

'It is why we came to the chapel, the abattoir. People

prayed to what they could not understand. Their minds were too small and already too full. But they had faith. People had prayed and begged for mercy in there, where so many animals were killed. Thousands. All of them together. Crowded, frightened, for years. They lived in fear, like we do. Their heads were smashed, their throats cut. Chaos was there, the great unreason, the beginning of the opening, and the place was made special. The walls were worn thinner in a place of such horrid light. Thin enough for Simmy's magic. Thin walls between places, between here and *there*, the other place that is coming closer, to swallow us.'

Oleg grinned, as if recounting some great accomplishment. 'We evoked a glimpse, with our intensity, the force in us. We made such magic, you cannot know, you cannot believe it. We made such drugs to unbind us. We made sacrifices and we prepared ourselves. We went far, me and my Simmy, deep. Little holes we made for our dreams to fall through. Dreams that were eyes. And only in them did I see you burn your way towards me with a message, because of something we had done. Something me and Simmy had done in our fury. The great mistake, we called it, which meant we had to go before we wished to, before we were ready. In our time, we have been responsible for so much' – he paused to smile – 'suffering. So I only came back from time to time. Awoke, now and again, because I could not find him out there. I still cannot find him . . . but maybe you, the Red Father, could tell me why he had to go, so soon. Could tell me who initiated the hour of his death. And when he is avenged, maybe he will come close to me again. Maybe he will see the fire of my vengeance. This is how the confinement of a ritual works.'

Oleg turned his head so quickly, the father flinched. Chorny's yellowing eyes widened, and his head slid from side to side as if it were mounted upon the trunk of a serpent. 'So I waited to speak with you, and it was all because of a girl. The little girl! After all that we did, that is the reason that a great seer was lost . . .' He shrugged as if astounded that such a trifle should have been his undoing. 'But I have come to know that I am dealing with a man who is burned by such rage, strangled by such guilt, that he makes powerful signs between our own signs. You, the hour of my death, I have seen you coming towards me for two years, and so has *another* . . . You have joined the ritual.'

The father stiffened, reminded of the expressionist image of himself on the black wall outside the vestry, and of what had billowed upon the ceiling: the possibility of its existence took his breath away. 'You were dead. Yonah's men found you. You were dead. Under that church. They wouldn't have made a mistake.'

Oleg nodded. 'Without my eyes I saw a dead man die. After his death he was not dead. Still he lives and yet he is dead. All this after death I see.'

'You want me to believe that you were dead?'

'There are places between here and there that do not observe such distinctions. Has this not always been so? I am a simple reader of the dark, Red Father.'

'Shut up!' The man was an illusionist who'd somehow faked his own death. Faith healers, prophets, evangelists, the world was strewn with tricksters, now that hope was dying. 'Your junkie disciples put you underneath that place, and you played dead.'

'The office of the dead. I asked to be laid down, for sure, facing east, beneath the altar. I told those who were around me that I wanted no lamentation. If I sank away, I would lie upon the ground like a beast, like a pauper. I was untouchable, as it should be. At the end we are all the same, we are *nihil*, we are *nemo*. I asked those who followed me for one last act of devotion, that they wrap me in a shroud and leave me in the crypt. These preparations always achieved results. Is the grave not closer to hell? And under that place I have journeyed far to find Simmy, that is all.' Oleg paused to wince. 'I saw things you cannot imagine. But what little I could remember when I returned, I painted . . . including the patron, our guide, who has followed the trail of our signs. My signs and Simmy's, and yours too, Red Father. Your offerings were delicious to it, and you have become its servant also, blind though you are. And so, here we are.'

'You're full of shit.'

Oleg humoured him with a smile. 'You too, I think? Mmm, you've seen the things that wait for us, what we stirred up. Maybe you have glimpsed *it* too. Bad dreams, Red Father? It clings because you have been noticed, through me. Our journeys are visible in another place. Do not fool yourself about this a moment longer, Red Father. And your daughter's sign burned so brightly. Simmy knew the energy around her would be strong if we took her. It dragged you in, and you are so close to her now.'

The father was on his feet. Yonah Abergil's handgun was in his fist. The sights wavered over the skull before him.

'I am very sorry to get you mixed up in this, Red

Father, but at least you can get your daughter back, for a while, I think, if it means so much to you . . . but only if you don't squeeze the trigger.'

The father thought he said 'What?' but wasn't sure he had even spoken.

'You want to know who has your daughter? I will tell you. A woman has her. A woman paid Yonah to take her. And Yonah paid Simmy to make the snatch. Simmy asked me to drive. We did everything together.'

For a few seconds the father did not understand what the man had just said, could not interpret it, but then the final part echoed between his ears. He comprehended that there had been the words: *A woman has her.* 'Who?' He had to swallow to repeat the question. 'Who is she?'

'Through the fat larva that was Abergil, it seems the same bitch who has your girl had my Simmy killed too. This is of great concern to me.'

The father became frantic. 'What woman?' He moved towards Oleg.

'She had no children. And she wanted yours. She wanted a child, but she wanted to make you suffer too. You and your wife. Oh, she was bitter. In this work there was revenge, and madness. I think maybe that also made the ritual so much more than we could control.' Again, the nonchalant shrug. 'I will tell you her name, and then you will give me my drugs. I am not feeling well. To go between *there* and here so much, it takes a toll. And the boot? There will be no more of that.'

'Tell me.' The father could barely speak. 'You know where she was taken. Tell me where she was taken.'

Oleg nodded, and smiled wistfully as if recalling good times.

'Tell me!'

Oleg raised his claws and spread his talons to appeal for calm. 'In a place by Swindon, there was a car waiting for us and our little *passenger*. We tagged her clothes.'

'The girl, she was put in a second car?'

The skull nodded, its lungs rasped. The father turned away to escape the spray teeming with bacteria that erupted from the grey-stubbed mouth.

'The second car. Where did it go?'

Oleg recovered. 'We use our navigation and we followed the next car until it stopped for a security check in . . . some place . . . in, in Wroughton, yes, Wroughton. By the forest, the New Forest. The car was not searched. The security waved it through. So we knew this car belonged to *someone*. Someone important.'

The figure swallowed, wheezed and took in more air. He spat blood onto the cement. 'This car finally stops and we have the location, so we went in on foot, through all of the lovely trees. And we found a most magnificent house, big. Then we found out who lived there. This was a woman's house. A very rich woman, so Simmy thought we might visit her again one day.'

It made sense, horrible sense, like everything else these dreadful creatures did. They would steal a child to order, but they would want to know where the captive was taken; they would want to know everything about a person with whom they did their foul business, like a woman who had enough money to pay for the abduction of a child; the child of a nobody. Because such a paymaster could also pay them more at a later date, or she could be beheaded and shuffled deep beneath the cold earth.

The father barely heard himself speak above the pressure pulsing between his ears, behind his eyes, and bass-thumping his chest. The anticipation of the final details was near-erotic. 'Her name. Who? Who is she? What is her name?'

'My drugs first.' Oleg snapped two long fingers in the air. 'I want them now.'

The father moved, but felt as if he was wading through water to retrieve the man's stash.

'And the bitch you seek belongs to me. I will kill this woman. Those are my terms.' The bony wreckage spoke matter-of-factly, smiling all the while, as if the grief he had experienced on learning of his lover's betrayers had vanished.

The father stuffed the bag of paraphernalia into Oleg's clawing fingers. 'Her name? The name!'

'You give me your word first that I can kill the bitch who paid for Simmy to die?'

'I give you my word.' For this last piece of information, he knew he would do whatever was necessary, to anyone, anywhere. He'd make a pact with any devil. And according to this criminal, his daughter was alive. If a woman had paid for his daughter, then his daughter may not have been taken for human horrors from which there could be no recovery. His little girl may not have been abducted for the worst act a human being could commit: the rape and murder of a child. A concept forbidden from the father's thoughts, which appeared only in the nightmares that had always made him want to die.

If Oleg Chorny was telling the truth, then she might well have been stolen from her parents to live another life. He and his wife had once prayed together that this was so. For many months after his daughter had been taken, he would imagine this very scenario so that he could fall asleep with tears of joy in his eyes. To know that she was alive somewhere, and not hurt, had been the greatest mercy imaginable for the last two years.

Oleg closed his eyes. 'The woman's name is Karen Perucchi.'

Disbelief was followed by sickening jolts of acceptance, and the father sagged to his knees.

TWENTY-NINE

Oleg slumped upon the back seat, his head back and eyelids trembling, mouth agape and his ridged throat exposed. The father stared through the windscreen, without seeing much. Just as preoccupied as the intoxicated figure in the rear, he swept his memory backwards, and into a minor episode of his past; a regrettable experience that had suddenly, and traumatically, devoured the present.

When the father first met Karen Perucchi, a few years after the final collapse of global food exports, she had been the CEO of the Open Arms charity. And long before then, there were water-cooler rumours about her organization.

They discovered each other at a conference held during a lengthy period of looping discussions about agricultural capacity in the United Kingdom. Talks in which it was impossible to discuss the matter of food self-sufficiency without finally acknowledging the end of food aid to Africa, Asia and the Middle East; a common dilemma in a Europe swelling with refugees.

Word on the logistics vine implicated Open Arms in embezzling billions of euros in food aid. As the prices in international food markets last-gasped at stratospheric highs, Perucchi's Open Arms was one of many organizations suspected of an enterprising repackaging and selling of foodstuffs, and medicines, at inflated prices, to countries fatally stricken by drought and famine.

Even on a transparent legal basis, no more than a fraction of her organization's revenue had ever reached the starving. Plenty of NGOs and charities were caught with their snouts in a diminishing trough, as public sympathy peaked during successive Chinese, African and Central American famines. But what little had been reaching the needy had clearly been too much for Perucchi and her corporate peers. As had been the case with many of the crisis enterprises, as soon as large sums of money became involved in addressing the catastrophic effects of runaway climate change twinned with overpopulation that had followed centuries of environmental vandalism, the unscrupulous in the higher latitudes initiated one last freeboot, before the world they knew vanished forever.

As shortages became critical in territories stricken by drought, and governments collapsed, black markets empowered organized criminal franchises, armed militias, and even legitimate armed forces, who took control of all aid and relief operations, from warehousing to distribution. Eventually, as most financial donations and every case of food aid were seized by criminals or political rebels, first-world contributions to the beleaguered masses carpeting the planet were consigned to the past. A dismal end to global interaction.

During their affair, he'd learned that she'd also siphoned off a cut of her organization's considerable funds into an eye-watering salary for Open Arms's senior executives. And had done so for years. So high had she soared into the troposphere of the highest earners across successive years that she had, in effect, become untouchable in the eyes of the law. In his lifetime, the father had never met anyone else as privately wealthy as Karen Perucchi.

Even though his association with her was relatively brief, he'd quickly identified an equivalence in the fear and sycophancy that she inspired in those around her; the two key human responses that orbit affluence. After five months of inconsistent and difficult relations, he'd wanted Karen to leave him alone forever, going to great lengths to extract any trace of himself from her determined radar.

But despite repressing Karen Perucchi in his memory, he now had to accept the incredible: this former lover had subsequently ruined the lives of his family.

Way back then, his abstinence, self-control and caution had always been compromised when he was on the road, and when he first caught Karen's lacquered eye at the conference, he'd held her fixed, unsmiling stare, and transmitted that near-imperceptible flicker of desire back to her, then looked away. And that was *the* moment, the very first moment that had delivered him here: a ruined man, a killer, sat in a stolen car with a rucksack full of guns, while a drug addict and kidnapper shot up in the rear seats.

An old girlfriend. *Her.* Impossibly, it was *her*.

In the conference hall, his eyes had returned to Karen's face a few seconds later and she had noticed him too. The *come hither* exchange in the auditorium had not been planned. When her attention fell upon the third row of the conference hall, in which he sat, all of his instincts had screamed for him to lower his face. But unsuitability charged with danger had often made women attractive to him, until he met his wife. He'd eventually figured out that a reciprocation of risky sensual possibilities was a kind of mirror that served to confirm his own desirability to women. It had not taken a therapist to make him acknowledge this. An insatiate narcissism had trapped him as an adolescent gazer into reflections, following him out of youth, and had demanded that he test himself with a giantess of the business world that day; a woman elevated by an intimidating reputation far beyond his own rung of the career ladder.

At the time he was a single and recklessly promiscuous man; in one of his phases, usually followed by a retreat into monogamy. But during his predatory periods, his desire to seduce, to encounter novelty, to perpetually rediscover anticipation and satisfaction, would consume him after a few drinks. The same compulsion had driven him through his twenties. Back then, he'd been popular, but commitment cautious; a bad bet, but illogically irresistible to some women, and often the naive or damaged. He'd been frightened by the need of several women to possess him entirely, but unable to change his habits. When half cut, he hummed with an erotic electricity before he was fully aware of what he was doing.

Through the long working hours and the miles travelled, he'd even seduced colleagues, at least five, including an ill-advised digression with his last boss, Diane Brown. An entanglement that Diane had possessed the sense to kill quickly. Sleeping with her a few times, whilst knowing that passion might flare between them in the future, had been sufficient. Ideal, in fact. That was how he'd rolled.

He had met his wife just over a year after Karen: ending an anxious time that seemed to cure him of his incautious fixations. Coming together and then settling down with Miranda had been motivated, in part, by the shock of Ms Perucchi. He'd never denied it, and he had subsequently buried the memory of Karen.

Back at the conference, he'd spoken well in his keynote speech and Karen's attentions had grown by the second day. She appeared to circle him, incrementally drawing nearer, and he'd toyed with what he assumed was her yearning for flattery. On the final day of the conference, he arranged to be near where she would be talking to the Swiss trade consulate. Nothing more had been required of him: exchanged glances and a physical placement beside her. She'd taken it from there.

The suddenness of her vast presence all about him had led to a vertigo that was both unpleasant and perversely narcotic. And he'd engaged in something he wasn't sure about, with someone despicable, and even more so than himself, though in a different way. He'd still pursued ideas of social justice, fairness, of egalitarian systems, during the greatest perils ever visited upon civilization. He'd opposed the final disastrous stages of economic inequality and the tax arrangements of the wealthy, though to no end. Karen more or less stood for everything he hated and blamed for worsening the crisis, so he'd known all along that he was seducing a devil. But there was no place for reason in his love life, and his curiosity about Karen was never going to be anything but self-destructive; he'd even recognized this at the time, but had never fathomed just how devastating the consequences of his compulsion would be, until now, and she'd comprehensively destroyed his world.

Making Karen laugh had been too easy, and he'd not

been able to restrain himself as they'd flirted. Nor could he cap his brazen and superficial charm. His superficial charisma had resonated and gleamed brighter than ever before. He'd felt guided. Messages were sent within the hotel, mostly from her to him. Blinded by the attention, the possible professional advantages from the connection, and the sudden dysfunctional urge to bed a powerful woman, he'd accepted an invitation to drinks after her final engagements, during the dying hours of the conference.

The size of her hotel room could have matched the ground floor of a town house, one furnished with a luxury he suspected only a tyrant could demand. And once inside her private suite, there had been something about her too-smooth face, her tactical décolleté, the broad compactness of her thighs and bottom that had drawn the libidinous fool out of him, making him writhe with a reckless, hot desire that had felt toxic as it smelted his bowels.

When her security closed the door and left them alone, the father had felt himself adrift in warm, deep waters, too far from familiar shores, but even that had been exciting. A sobering awareness of his own dissolute nature began changing positions with sudden, irrational lusts that had left him dizzy.

After the sex, he'd known in a heartbeat that he'd made a grave mistake and placed himself somewhere unfortunate. As he left her rooms that evening, he'd been light-headed, and slightly nauseous with anxiety. Excitement had shortened his breath when he'd entered the same suite hours earlier.

Over dinner, she'd been eager to impress him and contributed the major share of conversation, choosing the subjects, mostly connected to herself, or her idea of herself: her achievements, the seemingly effortless affluence, a version of a past he didn't believe, and who she knew, with an emphasis on world leaders. Tantalizing suggestions of his potential in her world were also thrown out nonchalantly. And he'd liked her less as every minute passed, sensing a deep, unquenchable anger inside the woman, manifesting in a readiness to judge and castigate rivals, reformers, or opponents to her interests. Other patterns formed the more she drank. She loathed younger women and he suspected she made them suffer in her professional life. She exhibited signs of jealousy at the merest details of his past relationships. His too-familiar connection with his boss, Diane, she'd circled, like a shark smelling blood in the water. He'd been inclined to lie, feeling an instinctive need to protect his boss.

And the more Karen drank the more she talked, and the more distant from the situation the father had felt; excluded and lessening as a true object of her curiosity. She knew all she wanted to know. His role had been assigned quickly and he'd assumed he was to be a hollow vessel with an irrelevant past that she would fill with her own judgements and aspirations. His dislike quickly became an aversion, but his distaste mingled with animal desire, making his lust ugly, volatile, urgent, even vengeful. He had gone to her bed engulfed by all of the wrong feelings.

His repulsion manifested in a cruel appraisal, once they were in her bedroom and undressing under dimmed lights. That plasticized mask of haughty indifference, the vast hair, a coiffured, pedicured, manicured illusion, her heavy body silkily folded away inside expensive tailored suits, all suddenly combined to temper his ardour. The final revealing, the very unwrapping of her flesh, had seemed like the unveiling of a stark white madness in a penthouse-turned-interrogation cell. And she'd watched his eyes carefully for even a flicker of disappointment. So he'd focused on the stockings, the fine details of the lingerie, the cold eyes, and let that all swirl through his own drunkenness to revive his excitement.

In bed, she'd opened to him quickly. Was hungry, not at all bashful, but the father suspected a world-weary resignation was incompletely hidden. She went into a performance that he'd thought contrived, even vulgar. She became aggressive, fierce, more than he liked. She bared her teeth, pulled his hair until his eyes watered. *Look, I am a great lover, terrible in my passion*: another boast amongst the many he had already weathered that evening, as her self-aggrandizing had grown monstrous after the second bottle of wine was uncorked. The unstable tyrant had engulfed him, and the father had smelled the danger growing like a gas ring left on in a small kitchen. Yet still he'd unbuckled when the call came.

Her surrender into near-debasement, as his lust removed the last inhibitions that alcohol failed to erase, had been equally as enthusiastic as his own, and alarming enough to tarnish his enjoyment. The whole carnal episode became wrong: doggish, combustible, clumsy, competitive, near-spiteful on both sides, and his loathing of himself peaked as his climax subsided.

Resistance would have caused friction. A trap had been sprung and he was suddenly in her debt, as if an unspoken agreement had been reached without him reading the small print. And as the last tawdry rags of his ardour for the adventure unravelled, his paranoid mind suspected that he'd become a component in a strategy, beginning the moment they established eye contact at the conference.

That first time, the con artist inside him began to speak the moment the sex was over: *why can't a man and a woman just enjoy intimacy and affection without any hang-ups or complications?* The same routine had always been received by his lovers with coldness and contempt. Karen was no exception. Such an attitude to commitment should have been shared before sex, not after. But out it had flowed from his mouth, propelled by fear and clownishly insincere. He'd felt especially thin, meek and white as he'd hauled his trousers back on, but he dressed too quickly for her not to notice his haste.

The incremental retraction of his enthusiasm that evening had already made her tense and angry. She may have sensed the beginnings of his perturbation and rushed into the sex to give him no way out.

The terrible causality of actions and their consequences near-choked him now. Inside his mind, as he bowed before the cold tonnage of concrete dread in a near-derelict car park, he could see her again and more clearly, and he attributed much more to the experience than he ever had done at the time. Once again, he found his toes edging over a precipice on the floor of human depravity. This was more evidence of the kind of behaviour he'd mistakenly thought incapable of ever surprising him again. But *a woman*, an actual woman, and one of considerable professional status, had paid criminals to steal his daughter because he had rejected her years ago.

He clutched his head between his hands as he struggled to comprehend the ugly affair as a motivation for child abduction.

In the car, the father spent hours searching Karen Perucchi online. Though not a single posting about her existed in the two years following her stepping down as CEO of Open Arms: no functions, no interviews, no endorsements, chairs or boards, no gossip or retrospectives, and not a single image. The woman had no current public profile.

Through the car's computer, he'd used the best search services on both nets, the regulated and the dark, as far as Scarlett Johansson's former tuition could enable him. But all traces of Perucchi's existence had been removed from each channel. Not uncommon for the powerful and rich to delete bad press; the practice was decades old. But to erase yourself entirely from publically available electronic data on the unregulated networks was a feat only feasible for those who had the most advanced take-down and hacking expertise at their disposal, or those with friends in regulation. The super-wealthy or the most powerful criminals commanded such measures, and he guessed he was now dealing with a combination of the two.

He abandoned the search and let the news play so he could keep up with weather reports. Roads were closed all over the south-west and south-east. Only one route could take him to the gated community that Oleg had tracked his girl to, two years gone. The rest of the news carried only one story on every channel.

Pakistani and Indian troops increase their presence on the international border of Kashmir . . .

. . . As part of Operation Spharaka, the Indian military has now amassed eight hundred thousand troops, and six armoured divisions, on the line of control in the Punjab.

. . . Indian troop increases described as a response to the movement of midrange ballistic missiles by Pakistan.

. . . The Pakistan military currently maintains four hundred thousand troops and four armoured divisions in the disputed region.

The father racked slender recollections for more details about Karen Perucchi; his memories of evading her were clearer than those of them together. When you were forced to, you could remember most things.

After their first dinner date, and the first time he'd slept with her, he'd tried to cut short his association by going to ground. After two weeks of his silence, she notified him of an emotional crisis that he'd triggered and needed to repair. Only to become her old self again in other calls, or the inflated persona she'd adopted when they'd first met.

In time, other personae appeared too, and he cared even less for those. One was more sage-like, as if Karen was a deliverer of important information about their 'connection'. Astral and mystical links between them were suggested. Destiny was cited. And fate. Their whole coming together was practically foretold, at least to her. She'd known the moment he'd looked at her in the conference auditorium that he was *the one*.

Mystical gibberish. He'd simply been intrigued, drunk, libidinous, reckless and bored. But to placate what he felt was a growing and unstable rage in the woman, and to assuage his own destructive passions, he'd met her again, and again.

He remembered one time clearly, in an exclusive hotel bar that he'd never have got inside without her invitation, where he'd tried to appear relaxed to cover the smell of his own discomfort and fear. He'd attempted to charm and fool his way back into a world of maturity and reason, of calmer hearts and more feasible expectations between two professional people. It had only made Karen want him more. When he began crying off the invitation to the sleepover at her flat, citing an early start at work, he'd soon found himself backing away from her physically in the atrium of the hotel, feeling absurd. Her bodyguard had looked uncomfortable too. The man must have seen similar before.

The father had watched Karen's expression alter from a bloodless rage to sorrow, and then to a faraway look as she rambled about her contempt for those 'who feared responsibility' . . . Something like that, but he couldn't remember what she'd said with any precision, though it had that tone. Spite followed and burned into anger. They were soon in *a scene* amongst the tropical plants of the mezzanine. He'd not been able to see the end of her capacity for drama, but he'd known he was in trouble. He couldn't have guessed how much. He'd broken away, to move past her scowling bodyguard, scrabbled into a cab on the forecourt, and left. Only to have her turn up at his apartment an hour later. She left the following morning. They'd both seemed intent on tormenting each other and themselves. Mutually assured destruction.

Over the following months, her will to secure what she wanted the way she wanted it, to make the dream come alive again, made things difficult for him. At work, Karen began to pester him. His own manager, the ex-lover Diane, had made a cryptic comment in a lift going down to a reception. By that time, stiffness had replaced his ease of movement, and his boss had noticed the lack of focus in his usually quick eyes. She'd said, 'You really should be careful where you *stick it*. She's dangerous. You're playing with the big girls now. But I don't want her calling me again. I don't want her near here.'

That had snapped him out of his stupor, and he'd just stared at his boss, wordless and frozen with regret. Karen reaching into his working life should have been an indicator of what she might also do.

Afraid of professional damage, he'd continued to meet Karen in order to play a new hand. He had tried to make himself appear pitiful, weak-willed, untrustworthy, a really bad bet. It had come easily and she hadn't disagreed with him, but had seen through his strategy and considered it even more of an appalling rejection.

But there was no row the last time he saw her, when he finally and decisively ended the connection. She had sneered at him; had seemed transformed into a bird of prey, a masked goddess that demanded blood sacrifice, and an angry little girl that wanted to punish all of the other little girls, who came to her party and had the audacity to talk amongst themselves.

After that, he'd physically hidden from her for months, while missives sent under pseudonyms arrived infrequently in the early hours of the morning, when she was loaded and accessing the worst parts of herself. She haunted a few events she had no business being at. Co-opted herself into groups close to his work. Appeared bemused to see him across at least two rooms that she'd ingeniously guessed would contain his presence. The messages, demands, occasional gifts, threats, and the coincidental appearances, eventually abated. When Karen finally fell silent, about five months after they first met, the release was similar to a stream of cool air in stifling and claustrophobic humidity.

He'd vowed to never repeat the experience with the powerful, the unstable, or the powerfully unstable, and eventually he stopped flinching when his screens chimed. In time, and after other quick affairs, culminating in the courtship of his future wife, he mostly forgot about the unfortunate interlude. Within his wife's deep-seated gentleness and grace he'd sensed a merciful release from himself. His secret suspicion that he was condemned to forever repeat his compulsive, inebriated seductions, seemed to pass. He married and had one child, believing his marriage and daughter had saved him.

But he'd fooled himself, and knew he'd begun to feel the destructive, libidinous demon revive inside him, around the time his daughter turned four. *It* had wanted to come out of retirement. And he'd slipped, but only once; the affair was never consummated, but he'd been preparing the ground the afternoon his daughter was abducted. Those messages alone had been enough for him to lose everything. They had distracted him, and his daughter had been stolen.

He no longer knew who was most to blame for her abduction: Oleg Chorny, Karen Perucchi, or himself. He didn't know who should be shot between the legs and left to bleed out in a ditch.

The breaking news intruded into his thoughts. He stared at the screen vacuously.

Washington, Moscow, Beijing and the UN have all appealed to Islamabad and New Delhi to exercise restraint and prevent further escalation in Kashmir.

A voice from the back seat. 'You still watch this? Why?'

The father grimaced. 'You're not interested in the opportunities it presents to you? The shortages your kind can exploit, the destitute that you can run as slaves or whores?'

'I am retired. I have learned to pursue less worldly matters.'

'Your visions? Graffiti daubed on walls?'

'I think you are being facetious. I do not respond well to the facetious.'

The father ignored his captive and sank again into his wretched and morbid reverie. Karen had clearly not been able to forget him, and she must have studied his life from afar before she made her own move. Tracked him, perhaps, his fortunes, movements, his marriage to a younger woman, and all from a safe distance. And in the intervening gap, the world had become a different one; the people different. Rules and boundaries were always changing. Ways of enforcing the older rules were decaying. Everything was on fast-forward now.

He wondered whether memories of the distant affair, and the woman's psychosis, should have mattered more to him after his daughter was taken. Had the spectre of Karen Perucchi appeared in the long interrogation of his soul, when his guesses about why his daughter was abducted veered from the ludicrous to the unbearable? Once or twice, he seemed to recall, but Karen had never been a true suspect because Karen had not been the first. He'd been through similar bad scenes with at least four other women before her. Borderline stalkings, and one fist fight that he'd lost to a man who punished him on behalf of a very disappointed woman in France. And the father had simply been unable to suspect a woman of such a crime. He knew of no precedents.

But his rejection had been sufficient cause for Karen to abduct his child. Karen's fury at his choice of a younger woman, and at his wife's subsequent fertility, must have been incandescent. And neither could Karen have expected that anyone would suspect her. She'd even paid Yonah Abergil to kill the abductors, and she'd nearly got away with it. Only a painted, drug-addled corpse had somehow survived the purge, by playing dead under a hideous chapel. And Oleg's presence troubled him more than he wanted to admit.

His captive smiled at him now, the azure- and gold-inked shoulders spiking out of the blanket on the rear seat, the reptilian mouth seeming to recognize the father's acknowledgement of such terrible truths.

The father sought an escape from the yellow eyes within his preoccupations, and they were many. Why had Karen waited for so long, until his daughter was four? She'd waited years to avenge herself. *So long?* There must have been a continuing slippage into a bitterness and resentment so vast and black, and endured amongst the worst kind of company, a criminal fraternity, until she'd decided to steal a former lover's only child. He had no other theory.

Without any help from the weather, the father felt colder than he had ever done in his life. Had he truly been a victim of a long, patient campaign driven by a scarred woman's vengeance? Maybe Karen was infertile? But the desire to wound and disable others on this scale, because of a trivial romantic disappointment, struck him as grotesque, ludicrous, spiteful, and hateful beyond belief. The motivation seemed too monstrous, too fantastical, to unreal for credence. But when he, in turn, considered the dying world, and how his species turned upon itself daily, and what he had done in the private homes of those he suspected of wronging him, then he had to accept that what Oleg Chorny had told him was possible.

Ultimately, his intuition failed. A sudden crime of passion was one thing, but to actually wait years to steal a man's child was *inhuman*, and he didn't know who, or what, he was dealing with. Or what such a maniac might have done to his daughter subsequently. Had she . . . would she have killed . . . or had his daughter killed?

Killed. Sold. Transported.

Those seemed the most likely options.

Or would she have kept her? To gloat and prolong her revenge by plunging him and his wife into abject despair and desolation, since they had both wronged her by defying her? Satanic. Is that where society was now? A place where the most affluent, using their affiliates in organized gangs, abducted the children of private citizens over slights, while the authorities would no longer properly investigate their crimes?

Inside the car, the father bent double and spat sour saliva from a drying mouth. Straightening up, he caught

Oleg's idiotic, beatific grin as the drug continued to course through the man's veins. The insolent levity had gone from his eyes, as if he were now losing patience with the father. This powerless man, cuffed at wrist and ankle, who had done so much damage, had the temerity to mock him.

As if walls of bronze inside his mind were suddenly beaten by red tongues of fire, and reflective depths flickered with the deep blood of a voracious sun, the father was consumed by rage, charred by a loathing for himself. He produced the handgun, turned sharply, and reached into the rear of the car. He forced the weapon inside his captive's mouth. Not pulling the trigger might have been the hardest thing he had achieved in his life. It had come down to the gun going inside Oleg's mouth or his own.

There has been a continuation of fierce artillery and mortar exchanges. Within the last twelve hours the British and United States governments have urged all remaining citizens to leave India and Pakistan immediately. Diplomatic and aid agency personnel have been evacuated.

The father withdrew the weapon from the King's mouth. Oleg spat blood onto his blanket, then grinned anew, and the father recognized that Oleg knew a great deal more about the situation than he had shared.

The father unlocked his door and made ready to get out, to make the call he dreaded with every vibrating atom of his being, and had postponed for hours: to the old accounts that Scarlett Johansson and the police detective had given him. He needed to face up to what had been done to Miranda. Oleg seemed to read his intentions, even before he had them. 'Maybe your wife is already dead.

Why confirm it now? But the girl, your daughter, I think we can save.'

The father never opened the car door. Instead, the blood leaked from his heart to leave him cold and unable to move. The very air seemed to darken around his head.

Oleg spoke quietly, reassuringly, as if to a child. 'As you suspect, they are confident that they will catch you. There will be a message from your wife too, but I do not think you should look at it. They wish to destroy you, even before they kill you. This is how King Death works. This is how terror works.' Oleg nodded at the screen and the news from India. It was now being cut again with rival stories about the pandemic. 'We waste time. Soon there will be greater shocks that will make the world stand still, and even the Kings will take their eyes from you. Here is a pause that you must take advantage of. Soon, even this war will be insignificant. Something worse is already here. *Again.*'

The father stared at Oleg, dumbfounded, and only half-registering the coloured skull's prophetic assurances. 'All that will happen next I have seen in other forms, in another place. Many are going to afterdeath. So many, you can't believe. You suspect this. You feel it build. If we know this now, then we are the kings in this life today.'

'Cut the mystical crap.'

'Quarantines and closed roads will not favour a man who flees with a child he has stolen.'

'Let's keep our communication right around there.' What other news there was originated from outside hospitals within various parts of the UK. Patients and medical staff were dying in increasing numbers, but only a few hundred so far, in the south-east, London, the Home Counties, Oxfordshire, as well as the Midlands. But a pattern of red dots was growing across the map of a country still reeling from the devastation of the summer heatwave.

Oleg would not be curbed. 'There is no last judgement, but there is resurrection in a new form, amongst horrors and in chaos. Simmy and I learned this. We prepared for this. And now I am almost ready to call upon our patron again, one final time, and to embrace the mad court. I believe Simmy dances there, while waiting for me. But there is something I must do first, and you have told me what it is.'

'What are you fucking talking about? Save the horseshit. I need to think.'

'I tell you this because you need to hear it. There is a *witness* to my final trajectory, and yours too . . .'

'What? You think I'll buy this crap about a . . . this bullshit. A patron?'

'*Nemo deum vidit.* Nobody has seen God. I already tell you I don't know what it is. I am too small to know. But death is not *terminus*, it is *transitus*. And the cosmos is full of great beasts. I have passed by dragons. I get too close and they fill my dreams with hell. You have seen this on my walls and in your sleep. And *they* are drawn to our hell. We who are confined by signs see it first. What you see on my walls is coming. We are both trapped inside Simmy's ritual. Unless I make a final sign, you may never be released.'

'There are no signs. No patrons. There are only despicable and revolting people, like you and the bastard you loved, and Karen Perucchi, who stole a child and ruined lives.'

'Ha! It is always easier to deny than accept. But see it another way. Greed and arrogant power made us snatch your girl. That was the first sign in Simmy's ritual. Jealousy and revenge made a woman steal her. Pain and terror released my name from a devil's lips and it fell upon your ears. Your rage and your guilt made you a killer. Am I right? These were the greater parts of us. Our power. They were the brightest lights in the window that Simmy had opened to find a patron. His ritual created the chain of reaction, and this has lit so many lights in the other place, where he is. When you crossed my path, your rage opened you to me, joined you to *it*, the patron that is so close, and it brought us to this, here. It was all inevitable. You came within the confinement, and now we are bound to each other. How else did I see you coming?'

'You want to die. You are ready to die. You said so. And you know I am happy to oblige you, so why would you help me, if that's even what you are suggesting?'

'We are pushed together, closer, the remaining players. Two of them must work together to finish this ritual, what Simmy began. *Us*. We each have business in the same place. You seek the lost object of your desire, but you are in the crypt. I am only offering you the stairs to lead you out. I only want the head of Medusa. The one who paid the devil, Abergil, to kill Simmy. I believe he and I can find each other again if we make this final sign. There are . . . connections that you cannot understand. But you must be my mirror, Red Father. It is all I have lingered for, you, the messenger. You have delivered your message, so now I tell you where we go, so that we can close this circle and sever ourselves from this woman that binds us together. The one who has destroyed us. We are both guided on this journey, make no mistake. And we too will be severed from each other, broken from our connections, when we make a great light together. Simmy wants me to finish this way, with blood, so that he can find me. I can sense this. Her death will be like a star to him, and will draw to me the company that he now keeps.'

'Jesus wept. If you say one more word about this bloody—'

'So, Red Father, listen to me carefully and I will tell you where to go. To the place where you will find your daughter.'

THIRTY

As the sodden and blustery afternoon turned to dusk, the father found a place in the trees, just outside the security fence, offering a partial view of Karen Perucchi's house. And judging by how long it had taken him to find the fence, only to then be confronted by the size of the property, he knew he wasn't supposed to see this. No one was. An essential part of maintaining an affluent lifestyle was now dependent upon concealing it. The survival of the rich was becoming contingent on their ability to hide wealth and remove themselves from public life. Years of riots and home invasions had given rise to permission for affluent communities to defend themselves too; conflicts had left hundreds of looters and trespassers dead. The suspected summary executions of thieves had failed to reach a court in years. The country was way beyond all of that now. Knowledge that made the father feel sicker and weaker as he lay in the wet soil like a tired animal.

Through the rain-blurred air, the father caught faraway glimpses of hardwood floors, suggestions of elegant furnishings, luxury and comfort. How deep the building reached he couldn't tell from his position. A vast disc of a covered swimming pool, ringed by a white stone patio, was the most visible feature on the other side of the fence. The pool area led to a long, pavilion-style building, shaped in a crescent; a new design, one storey high, with floor-to-roof windows and sliding doors at the centre, to catch the sunlight. Lights now blazed inside the large communal area at the heart of the building. Around the glass more white stone glimmered, and a cedar-panelled façade on either wing blended into the wooded backdrop.

This was a well-insulated property, and probably built to order, with rain-water recycling, a solar-energy receptive roof, all energy self-sufficient and off the grid; no doubt storing its own power and fitted with a ground source heat pump.

The perimeter wire was electrified, as signs indicated. Wire panels, taut between concrete pillars, reached twelve feet high, with an outward overhang of black razor wire on the last three feet. Placed twenty feet apart, and topping each fence post, was a small camera, directed towards the house. Outdoor floodlights to startle and light up intruders were positioned close to the cameras and would be motion-activated.

Several acres of immaculate lawn stretched from the house to the fence. Growing up to the property's border, a dense wood of pine, oak and beech acted as a further layer of concealment and protection. With the exception of the drive leading to the closed gate, there were no roads near the house.

Serpentine in manner, the father had spent three hours pushing through a sodden, unmanaged and occasionally wind-lashed forest floor, until he'd come upon a thin track. He'd eventually followed it across another mile, the path slippery with gelatinous mud, and through near-impenetrable woodland until he reached the fence. Even wearing his poncho and hat, by the time he'd reached the perimeter he was bemired to his elbows and hips, and his underwear clung to his skin.

With the exception of out-of-date satellite maps, there was no public information available about the address, and little about the gated community in which the building sheltered. Two years had passed since the abduction, so Karen may have moved, or be abroad in another lavish residence. He vaguely recalled her bragging about her overseas property portfolio years before. The only course of action to verify current occupancy was the direct approach, a trespass and break-in while armed.

But if Karen Perucchi no longer lived here and he went in armed, there was a chance that he might engage in a lethal conflict and die fighting his way into the wrong house. The mere thought of crossing the floodlit bowling green beyond the wire made him feel sick.

And the tools he had available were no use in the face of the insurmountable fence. Automatic locking might ultimately seal off the entire house, once the security lights on the boundary fence startled anything living that had strayed onto the lawns. Shatter- and bullet-proof glass might have been fitted into the doors and windows of the house. Prolific home invasions over the last twenty years, as well as the unflagging abduction threats, had meant the wealthy left little to chance. This New Forest community employed its own security patrols; this entire area was listed as private property.

At the border of the easterly section of the forest, the father had been forced to turn the car around when the navigation system issued a warning preceding immobilization of the vehicle. He'd spotted distant camera masts on the secondary road, and they allowed him to drive no closer than five miles from the first house in the community. With no way of getting any closer by road, he'd parked and continued on foot, and he'd needed the navigation function of the military binoculars he'd found amongst Oleg Chorny's weapons to get this far.

Looking at the glowing windows from his distant position within the dank weeds, and while the ceiling of trees crashed above him as the winds built for the night, his teeth came close to snapping as he ground his jaws together. *She got away with it.* Karen Perucchi had stolen his daughter. She'd pocketed a little girl in the way she'd pocketed charitable donations intended for the starving, and she got to live here. He could only think of one punishment worthy of such crimes.

Closing his eyes tight and taking deep breaths, he reminded himself that choking indignation was the bedfellow of murderous rage, and could derail his ability to think clearly and rationally. Back in the car, Oleg had warned him of this. The journey to the fence had also consumed three hours. A journey he would now have to repeat to return to the car. And he would have to come back here, along the same route, the following morning, but with *something* to get him through this fence, and then he would have to make his move while exhausted.

The hurricane had blasted north, but the tail of the storm still raged, so at least the weather offered some natural cover. The flooding in Dorset and Wiltshire, power outages, numerous closed roads and treacherous driving conditions in a forested area might hamper the arrival of any assistance once he'd tripped the alarms and lights. How quickly private security details could respond to calls, and how substantial the patrols were, was pure conjecture.

The weather was his only ally, but that would not help him cut through the wire, then traverse the grounds quickly and get inside the house. There might also be onsite security: a permanent bodyguard, particularly if the residents had children, was standard for the wealthy in the cities and towns.

There were the Kings to consider too. How long might it be before they ran him down out here? The Kings knew who he was, and who he was searching for, but how many of them knew his little girl had been taken for Karen Perucchi? Yonah Abergil was dead, as was Semyon Sabinovic. Besides Oleg, he didn't know who else had been in the loop about his daughter's abduction. But if even a minor figure like Rory had known something, then others would too. Abergil had admitted he'd confided in associates. The Kings might appear soon, or already be in place, waiting for him. He was pretty sure now they weren't tracking his car, or he'd already be dead. *God bless you, Gene Hackman.*

The father opened his eyes as if to release his skittish thoughts before they panicked into a rout, and brought the binoculars to his eyes. Old DEV-13s that would still provide good magnified recordings of anything he could see, footage equipped with directional sound, and he could study this more closely in the car.

Through keyholes in the ground scrub and treeline, he sighted the fence, cameras, the position of the visible security lights, then the other parts of the building and grounds that he could make out.

Bright orange wall lights, a long white leather sofa, an expanse of wooden floor, a dark rug before a broad fireplace made from steel; all appeared in his magnified vision as the building's windows revealed a portion of the interior. The rear wall of the central area was constructed from long sheets of glass and sliding doors, facing another patio on the other side.

As the building curved, one side of the room was lost to sight, but beyond the fireplace he could see a large open bar. A person could just walk out to the pool from the bar, or right through the middle of the house to the rear patio and gardens. There would be access to other rooms too, in either wing, from the large communal space that had been designed for entertaining.

While the father assessed the very real possibility of being killed before he made it across the broad, open grounds, there was movement in the living space. Sudden, quick movement behind the glass. A figure moving from left to right, then disappearing through a door, on the right of the building.

He didn't twitch, and let the wet earth, the cold and rain, engulf his stationary form as he waited for the little figure to reappear. As he lay barely breathing and unwilling to blink, the few minutes stretched into fifteen, then twenty. The child did not re-emerge.

Heartbeat thumping from the sudden infusion of adrenaline, the father replayed the footage. Dressed in a blue tracksuit, her raven hair tied in bunches, her small, eager face in profile, a young girl appeared and ran across the living area on the tiny screen of the binoculars. She'd run from left to the right, from one wing of the spacious building to the other.

'Baby,' he whispered into the wet air. He felt concussed, even paralysed, before disbelief seeped through him like damp.

He watched the recording again. And again, and again, all the time refusing to acknowledge this was his daughter, while unable to recognize that it was not.

Pausing the footage on the child's face, at the moment he could see a fraction more in profile, he enlarged the frame until he was staring hard at a snub nose, the slim angles of the cheeks and forehead, and a partially open mouth. He played it again. The child was tall, but the vaguest suggestion of a residual infantile plumpness about her cheeks and posture, the short gait and speedy flit, rather than a mature running technique, made it possible for the girl to be around six years old. The hair was the right colour too. If he could see her face fully, he would know her; he was sure that he would know *his own child*.

His thoughts were routed. Brief notions of his daughter erupted. Memories flooded in, even those he had not known to still exist. Her image was suddenly brighter; his sense of her more distinct, less imaginary. His heart seized, but the pain of recall was less acute. Briefly, he wrestled with a mad desire to throw himself up the fence and into the razor wire.

The father did not know for how long he lay in the mud thereafter, sobbing into his wet, dirty hands. And as he cried, he said his wife's name.

Eventually and slowly, his limbs stiff with cold and

damp, he packed away his sodden equipment and slid carefully backwards, through the mud and into the trees. And so shaken was he, with what might have been hope, even euphoria, the discomforts of his passage out never registered.

There had never been a real choice about him breaking into the house. When and how were the only questions he entertained now.

THIRTY-ONE

'Who knew? Besides you and Sabinovic, who else would know that Karen Perucchi took my daughter?'

On the back seat, the thin head studied him in the dim light. The big eyes were hooded but still shining. 'How did you find me, mmm?'

'I'm asking the questions.'

'And I have given you the answer. That fat rat fuck, Yonah, gave you me and Simmy. But who gave you Yonah the pig?'

The detective, but only after a tipoff from Rory that King Death were involved. *Rory.* From a conversation in a pub, Rory knew it was the Kings. If that degenerate knew his organization had carried out the snatch then others in his world knew even more. 'Your old friends, the Kings, would have asked the lawyer where my daughter was taken. This go-between. This Oscar Hollow. The Kings, they will be here?'

'I would think so. Soon, they may even do our work with the bitch for us. They are thorough when they cover their tracks. Kings are always in the service of death. But that would not be so good for what I have in mind.' Oleg smiled pleasantly when he noted the father's renewed attention, and his growing dependence upon him as a source of information, even guidance.

'What do you mean?' the father asked.

'This woman. You have to ask yourself, is it more trouble to make her and what she covets disappear? Or is it easier to kill you?'

'I'm the path of least resistance.'

'Mmm, I would think so. But she will have to pay two prices then, maybe three.'

'Prices? What prices?'

'You. Your wife. The two pigs. All will carry a price as Kings do the bitch a big favour by removing problems and erasing history. After sales. We always made big money this way. And what has been uncovered can just as quickly be buried. You see? But no one will look for you when you are gone.'

The father ground his teeth until his jaw lit up with pain. 'Pigs? Don't you call them that! And don't ever mention my wife again, or I will shoot you dead where you sit!'

The man fell silent, but still grinned.

The father's thoughts returned to the film of Scarlet Johansson, her face, the terror in the eyes. A recording of his wife was surely waiting for him too. The father sank his face into his hands. There was no question of him travelling back to the Midlands. He'd made his decision.

Gradually, his thoughts returned to the twelve-foot fences, the razor wire, the lights and cameras, the probability of private security with exceptional military expertise, and the comrades of the addict who had stolen his little girl two years before, all biding their time within the cedar-panelled walls of a fortress. All of these things he would have to confront in a few hours.

To be so close, and yet . . .

The impossibility of the venture impaled him. He was a chunk of lava that had cooled to a small, black, porous rock. Discarded, burned to carbon by the cruelty and tragedy of having been given this life. And even that was a life much better than most would ever know.

He thought of the little girl running through the house in the forest, this palace of the undeserving, the malicious and cruel, protected by an electrified stockade. Had there been a hint of a smile in the girl's eye? When he thought of her mother again, the father cried. And he could not stop. The noises he made were the deep cries of an animal reaching the last of itself.

He'd never been religious but the father prayed for this to end, and perhaps he now spoke only to a memory of warmth and light that had managed to remain inside his degraded heart.

Night pinched out the last of dusk.

In the mornings, when you were a baby, we would go downstairs together while your mother got ready for the day that she would spend with you. The morning was our time together before I went to work. You used to lie on me and hold my finger. Sometimes I can still feel your weight and your softness. I can smell your hair . . . You would wrap your hand around my finger. You always held what made you feel safe . . . Your father's finger. And I am your father.

*

The father finished recording his story on the car's media, and set the recording to play live on the website devoted to information regarding his daughter's disappearance: who had taken her, for whom, each name, a timeline, every shred of information he'd gathered in his time as the Red Father. He set the timer for his recording to go live in two days; by then he would have her or he would be dead.

He made other preparations for the recording to be sent to the police liaison officer, whom his wife still dealt with, the two sympathetic journalists who had periodically tried to revive interest in the case, and his family's legal representative.

If he died in the morning, then at least his story would be with those able to investigate Karen Perucchi. The public would know that he was a killer too, but he didn't care about that.

THIRTY-TWO

At four thirty in the morning, the father roused himself from a brief sleep, joints cracking, the painful stiffness slowly passing from his neck and joints.

Chewing on an energy bar without any pleasure, he checked his existing tools again. On the passenger seat beside him, his equipment was laid out: four handguns, the nerve agent, binoculars, mask, water, torch, gloves, the metal cuffs he had taken from Oleg's limbs and replaced with wire ties. The sight of the steel upon the cloth gave him a brief leap of confidence. But the bag of tricks that had enabled him to invade other homes, and to destroy criminals, soon appeared insubstantial and primitive. A drive to Southampton was unavoidable, to better equip. He'd need an open store that sold wire or bolt cutters.

In the rear-view mirror his eyes were grim, the surrounding flesh unnaturally pale and wrinkled like wet cotton. Dreams had left him shaken. Omens, portents, the gibberish of a shattered mind; he didn't know. But above all, for the first time since he began the search, he'd awoken afraid that he was a man too ruined to ever be a father again.

Oleg must have stayed awake, and probably since the father had taken him outside at one in the morning to empty his bowels in the undergrowth, then given him the sugary drink he had asked for.

'How will you do this?' The voice that rose from the darkness of the rear seat was clear of sleep, but tight, near sibilant. The eyes were large discs, too bright, too still. The father could only hope the man would die from withdrawal to save him another execution. He ignored Oleg.

'I can help.'

The father packed a pair of small rucksacks. He chose his original handgun, for familiarity's sake, and the one he had taken from a bedside cabinet in Abergil's house. When he returned to the car the previous evening, he'd made himself familiar with that weapon, by firing it into a fallen tree trunk in the forest. The handgun had barely kicked or made a sound, but had broken apart the dead wood. The gun must have contained high-impact ammunition that would shatter bones around the entry wound. Whoever was inside the house might have them too. The idea seemed to drain his dim resource of strength through his feet.

Oleg's bag had also contained a small automatic rifle. The father wasn't sure how to fit the magazine or unlock the trigger mechanism. He couldn't face asking Oleg for assistance, so would leave that behind. He could only risk using a weapon at close range, aimed at a clearly identifiable target. There could be no stray shots if his daughter was inside the building.

'How you get in, mmm?' The questions continued from the back of the car, as if talking was easing the acute symptoms of the man's abstinence. Oleg had folded in on himself as stomach cramps overwhelmed his frail, shivering body.

'You going to kill me before you go, mmm? Though maybe the overdose you are considering is best. I will even tell you how to do it. But you kill me and we are both leaving this life today. And maybe today your daughter asks this Karen a question, this bitch who she thinks is her mummy. The little girl will ask who the man is, the one caught on the fence. She will never know that it was her own father that was shot on the wire. And at that moment, Karen will know that she has won. All her tracks are covered and the girl is hers forever.'

The man was trying to manipulate him in return for a fix. 'Shut up.'

'Is this the plan for today, mmm?'

'I'll shoot you before I go in. For the last two years, I have wanted to make you suffer slowly. Make you feel something, know something . . . experience something that now you can only imagine. Make you feel what you inflicted upon us, me and my family. But I don't have time. I will drag you into the undergrowth out there. I know the spot. I marked it out yesterday. And I am going to shoot you in the face while you look at the father of the girl that you stole.'

Oleg grinned. 'Good. 'Tis good. You solve a problem. Two problems. Mine cus I feel bad now.' The figure was near-rearing off the seat in his discomfort, straining bony ankles and wrists against its ties with such vigour the car began to shake, the prelude to a seizure. 'And before noon you die too. The storm will take away your screams. They will bury you in the trees, close to what you came here for.

Your daughter will never know her own father again. She will never know that he is buried close to her. In time she even forget what she—'

The father turned in his seat and punched the barrel of his Beretta against Oleg's wet forehead. The man winced from the sudden shock of the blow, then slowly returned his skull to the end of the barrel. 'Please. Yes? We do this now. It doesn't matter. You, me, our thoughts, are nothing. Our lives are nothing. Nothing matters any more. Best to have no thoughts, no memories of this place. And no one dies easy of this pestilence.' Oleg nodded at the silent, flashing media screen that had reported mostly the spread of the Asian virus since they'd arrived in the New Forest, occasionally interspersed with the great battle lines drawn up in Kashmir.

'*Usque ad mortem.* Soon so many will be sick unto death . . .'

'Go to hell.'

'I just thought you wanted to save your daughter, mmm? I am going nowhere, and you need help, so why can't we help each other? That is all I am suggesting.'

'Shut it!' The father nearly squeezed the trigger.

Oleg opened his near-lipless mouth and took the barrel inside. He tried to say please, but with a gun inside his mouth it sounded like 'Pliss.'

The father climbed out of the car and made his way to the boot. He hadn't expended any time at all thinking of how he would dispose of Oleg, but the sooner the better. He considered it strange, but ever since he had taken the man captive, his intense loathing and hatred for the figure had not so much subsided, as been replaced by new involvements, possibilities, second guesses, and terrors. And all set to the soundtrack of the man's esoteric and mystical nonsense.

Instead of taking revenge against Oleg, he was now being made to think of who had been killed because of him, of who he had killed, and who he would have to kill next. His daughter being alive had changed everything, swiftly introducing so many new considerations, memories, regrets, doubts and emotions into the existing maelstrom that was wearing him to sand. The father could not contain all of this. There was no part of him left over to consider the fall of man, and this world, that had accelerated around him across the last few years. He wondered why men were so poorly built to withstand suffering when its possibility had always been so assured.

His mind was moving too fast. He needed to find some space to think through his move. He would have to silence Oleg first. An overdose, as the man suggested, was low key. The father climbed inside the car, the bag of drugs gripped in one hand. Oleg shivered with delight at the sight of the nylon sack.

'How much?'

'May I?' The figure's entire body shook, but his hands remained still enough to take the applicator. 'You have to find the vein for me. And then you must decide if we part company now, or later.'

'Where do you take it?'

'Foot. Left foot.'

'Jesus.'

'Between the toes. Give me all of it if you want me to

go now. Or only give me half. But if I don't wake up . . . that would be bad for you.'

The father pulled the applicator out of Oleg's fingers. 'Bad for me? How can you help me? Why would I trust you?'

The man swallowed and widened his feral eyes. 'There is still a fence at this house, mmm?'

He had the father's attention.

'Maybe you hate me a little less while I help you with this, or you will have no chance. Your anger, it—'

'Why? Why would I trust you?'

'You think I have grown a soul?' He laughed. 'At last I see the error of my ways and I am a better man now, mmm? No, I don't believe in atonement, but like I said, I want the bitch. We have history and she is the beacon I want to light up, in another place.' He nodded at the drugs stash. 'And for this I do anything too. My will is not my own. I am a vessel.' He grinned his grey-toothed, slippery grin. The man then rolled onto his side and spat into the footwell. 'These fences . . . You can't dig under and can't climb. They'll see you on camera. Your weight will set off the alarms. Was that how you planned to get inside, to climb?'

'Cut my way through.'

'I see. So you think you can cut through this fence, then move to the house, then break in? This is your plan. But the steel will be too strong for the cutters you can buy. Maybe even the army bolt cutters will struggle. But if not, it will take too long. A good torch might do it, eventually, but they would see the flame from the house. You have no torch either. You can get one, but that means delays and my old friends can smell you here. So maybe you could cut down a tree. A big one. Let it fall on the fence. But where will you get this saw? And they will hear it anyway from the house. You have no plan.'

'Piss off.'

Oleg held up one long dirty finger. 'They will hear the alarms when you are on the grass. Motion cameras will set them off. I remember there will be lots of grass for you to run across too. The bitch has a nice place, mmm? The doors and windows will lock when the alarm trips. And there is no way through that glass anyway. I know this. I have some experience. Their houses are fortresses.'

One by one, the man carefully outlined every fault in the strategies the father had tried to make convincing during the night.

'How? How do people like *you* do this?'

'We wait. Watch. You snatch when people are moving, like in a car, or in the street.'

Their eyes met. Oleg stopped smirking.

'How long did you watch my house?'

'How will this help you?'

'Tell me!'

'Not long,' he said quietly.

A silence thickened the stale air of the car. The father could not think straight on account of a compressed but expanding rage, could not speak. He did nothing but tense and tremble.

'The devil has your girl and she wants to keep her. But thinking of what was done back then will not help you with what must be done now. Another way is you take this bitch hostage, and when she takes you home—'

'No! I don't have the time. They won't leave that place until the storm is over. That could take days. Your shithead friends will get here, if they aren't already.'

'True. I know this. But I am not finished.'

'Get the fuck on with it!'

'Listen, you think of all ways in and how they don't work, until you find the way that *might* work. So, if you will allow me to finish.'

The father gritted his teeth.

'Now, I would like half of what you have in that applicator. When I have it in me . . .' The man paused to shudder as if with the expectation of ecstasy. 'Then I will tell you how you get inside this house.'

The father spat, but handed the applicator to Oleg, who immediately became busy with his left foot. With some reluctance, the father helped him locate a usable vein.

When Oleg's head flopped back, his trembling subsided, and the brittle, sticklike form seemed to melt into the seat. 'Thank you.' The man's speech slurred as the narcotic tried to take him away.

'How do I get in?'

Oleg smiled. 'Best way through such a fence is explosives. You blow in the fence. The alarms go off for sure. The house will lock down too. Everyone is awake inside and panics. They go for weapons, make calls. All that bullshit. No problem. You just get to a door, a big window, whatever. You put another explosive on the glass. And that house will open in three seconds.'

The father swallowed. 'Explosives! Where do I get bloody explosives, you stupid junkie fuck? I suppose you'll take me to some of your mates, who'll kit me out? Is that it?'

Oleg watched the father, his face near-expressionless. But the eyes narrowed and gleamed with a profound cold and the father knew he was looking into a mind that had long dispensed with anything approximating mercy or sympathy; here was nothing but a vital, calculating self-interest. But he'd let the man into his circle, and now sat in the rain discussing the emancipation of his daughter with the same chronic addict and murderous criminal that had taken her from him and his wife. Not for the first time in his recent life was he stunned by a situation he could barely fathom.

'You kill like us. You have learned that much. But you don't think like us. You could be a rich man already, and maybe have your daughter too, today. But your anger will kill you this morning.' Oleg moved his head towards the nearest window. 'If you let it. You need to clear your mind. And listen. You have to listen. To me.' The man's voice dropped to a softer tone, was hushed like a whisper, and slithered its terrible range inside the father's mind. 'Now, when you take me, mmm, from my place, you brought my shit along too, with the drugs, yes? Inside my army bag there are guns?'

The father nodded.

'Good. Very soon men without guns will have no chance here, or anywhere. Now you have plenty. Inside this bag, there are also six blocks of protein. In with my tools, you see the survival food, yes?'

The father had seen the military cartons, amongst the

weapons and spare clips of ammunition, a field medic's kit and the binoculars he had taken. 'Yes.'

'This is not food. This is gel explosives.' The man's thin face split into a huge grin. 'With these you will get inside.'

The father got out of the car and moved again to the rear of the vehicle, collected Oleg's tools from the boot, brought them inside. The thin head on the snaky neck watched him through the glass the entire time. Oleg even chuckled as the father opened the bag and gently took out one of the soya protein packets.

'The soldiers that get inside buildings by going through walls to kill the terrorists, this is what they use. Very effective too. We get ours from the same supplier. And this will get you inside, through the fence and then into the house. Let me know when you want me to teach you . . .' The man shrugged, smiled, and lay down on the seat, closing his eyes.

THIRTY-THREE

Face pressed into the leaf mulch, fingers in his ears, he heard the charge detonate. Powerful reverberations thumped beneath his prostrate body. A great length of fence shuddered between the concrete posts on each side of the blast. A hail of metal zipped away, the shards like the bullets of Torbay that had chased him from The Commodore and into the hills. And he was up.

The father's feet slid on the wet ground. Unsteady legs made him list. A sudden riot of nerves and adrenaline flooded his skin. He seemed to be looking down on himself, his mind strangely detached, but he ran.

As Oleg predicted, the wire mesh had ripped vertically around a rent. The edges of the hole were blackened and smoked in the grey light. Batting the swinging sheet of steaming wire away from his face with his gloved hands, the father stepped through the aperture.

At the same time his front foot touched the lawn, the floodlights brought premature daylight to the grounds, casting an elongated shadow of his tatty shape.

Knees knocking together, his heartbeat in his throat, he skittered across the grass on feet he still couldn't fully feel. After ten yards, he righted his lurch and rediscovered a proper command of his legs, breaking into a run towards the wall of glass in the centre of the great curved building, which grew vaster during his frantic approach.

Lights glowed in the left wing. For the first time he saw the full great curving length of the pavilion and the sheer size of the swimming pool.

An outbuilding clad in the same cedar panelling stood at ninety degrees to the main house. A long red gravel drive disappeared behind him. There was a double garage with three vehicles parked outside the red doors. *So many?*

The glass wall in the centre of the house flickered bluish from within.

Blood thumped and rushed behind his eyes, interfering with his vision. His feet soon left grass and slapped the white paving slabs of the pool area, his breath a wind about his masked face. Running the last few feet to the windows, he caught sight of his own reflection running towards him upon the face of the floor-to-ceiling glass panels. His face was a Halloween pattern of white cloth and smears of soil.

From out of the mess of the shadowy confusion, screened upon the patio doors, came another movement from inside the flickering interior. A swift motion that slowed and padded up to the glass he stood inches away from. And despite his chest-heaves and noisy exhalations, his sight settled upon the face of a little girl, standing behind the glass.

Somewhere in the distant reaches of the large room, beyond the glass and the white leather sofas, a jumble of holographic images from a cartoon capered. They threw a blue-white glow into the remainder of the room. When the perimeter lights exploded upon the patio, she must have been drawn to the glass doors.

The girl wore pink patterned pyjamas. Her mussed hair was still tied in black bunches, sagging at the back of her head. And in the precious few seconds before she screamed and ran, the father looked into startled, wide blue eyes that were unmistakably his. Behind the shocked features of the girl's face, behind the ghost of his wife's freckles and snub nose, an approximation of his own bone structure had already formed, spliced with his wife's narrow forehead. It was a recognition so powerful, the father believed his heart stopped beating. It was her. *Her. Her.*

She's alive.

Penny.

The girl fled, bunches swinging behind her, small white feet speeding across the tiled floor, away and past the flash of the hologram, until the small pink shape vanished through the wide aperture at the side of the room.

'No! It's all right!' he shouted, but the glass was thickly glazed, no doubt soundproof. 'Wait! Peeps, wait! Penny!'

Inside his cloth mask, clinging about a face dampened by the wet world and the sweat of his terror, his voice became confined, trapped and hopeless. He banged both hands against the glass. She had not even seen his face because it was concealed by the horrid, dirt-smeared, nightmare mask. It was the closest he had been to the girl that half of his heart had sworn was dead for two years, and yet he had only succeeded in terrifying her.

He tugged the mask from his face, banged the glass again. Then moved the second charge towards the window, only to pause, stricken by the idea of blowing out the glass with a child – *his* child – somewhere on the other side; a child transfixed by the monster on the patio. *What to do?*

His pause became hesitation. He panted, he wheezed, he did nothing.

Distracted by the scuff of a shoe's sole behind him, he straightened and began to turn. Then heard more footsteps skimming the wet grass behind his head, and in the reflective glass surface of the patio doors, he saw a masked figure, wearing a black leather jacket, walking towards him. The father came about, clawing at the pocket that bulged heavily with the weight of the handgun he had taken from Yonah. The very moment he spotted the second man, standing by the edge of the pool, he saw a darting flash.

The father's vision exploded white.

His feet rose up behind him and whipped over his head. Muscles bulged and split along his bones. His joints separated. Before his thoughts disintegrated, a pain so vast made him certain that his entire body had come apart, and had smashed into the glass wall between him and his daughter.

After the black, he looked at the world sideways from hard, white stone, but didn't know who or where he was. When the world stopped slanting and flickering and settled grey and wet and cold upon his mind, his body parts winched themselves back, on painful metal cables, into his traumatized trunk.

He was too winded to move, even when the booted feet stood before his face. Disembodied hands moved his agonized, still-crackling meat about the paving slabs. Tugged and emptied his clothing. A black sack was yanked over his head.

Coherent thoughts slotted together post-trauma, but the world and a dying sense of some distant hope went out with the light.

THIRTY-FOUR

Stiffening the cloth over his face were stains made by the desperate, the inside of the hood long-soured with traces of its previous occupants. Outside the hood, pulled so tight about his throat with a drawstring, no one spoke.

On the paving slabs he had been sure he was dying. It now seemed death would have been a mercy. Around the time feeling began seeping once more into his limbs, a man with hands as rough as untreated wood was painfully securing his wrists behind his back with a plastic tie. The father's ankles had already been secured to the legs of a chair, after his feet had been kicked into position on what sounded like cement.

Shivers goosed his flesh because he was naked save his underwear. They had pulled his clothes off his limbs and torso and then quickly slashed the fabric from his body with what he presumed were knives. The entire process was swift and casually effortless, because they had done this before with their cruel fingers, gripping men like fish hoisted upon cold slabs.

The shock of the powerful electrical charge had gradually subsided as they carried him from the patio. But everything from his buttocks to his shoulders seemed bruised. His body would have ached terribly in the coming days that he would never see.

Once he was secured, footsteps retreated. A door closed.

Trying to move his hands and feet caused him pain. The sensation in one foot was dying, so tight was the binding.

This wasn't the work of private security. *They* had him, the Kings. The black hood and his stripped body were the giveaways. Some of the parked cars he'd glimpsed must belong to them. They must have been waiting for his amateurish attempts at entry. He knew what came next and he thought of Gene with what little of his wits he still possessed, and the father saw again the bloodied shoulders, the familiar face toppling, falling away. 'Oh, dear God,' he whispered to himself and to the empty, cold space he sensed outside of his stinking blindness.

From one black into another. That's all. That's all it will be now. There is no afterdeath.

Then he thought of Penny and the father cried from sheer frustration. Tried to choke out despair both cold and relentless, which weighed down his heart as if it was filled with wet sand. She was alive and still living with her captor and he had failed to rescue her; had failed to take back his own flesh and blood.

To increase his torment, he recalled Oleg's mocking words as the wretch clamoured for his fix. He'd said something about her never knowing her own father, and had talked about him dying on the wire. But he had made it through the wire and up to the door, only that was his lot and his allotted time in her presence: dirty, monstrous and masked for a moment, and now *they* had won.

To have been so close to her. A thin pane of glass had been the only thing between them, a barrier cruelly transparent. He saw her little shocked face again. And in his memory he watched her scurry away, a thin figure in pink, with messy hair, fleeing her own father, who had walked through a hell vile and absolute for two years that had felt like a century to save her. That had been the last time she would see her father. He wanted to die before having to endure the realization for much longer.

It may have been a groan or even a baying that rumbled from the pit of his bowels and scorched his throat. It could have been the lowing of a beast before its end in an abattoir. But within the sound, which surprised his own ears, was a noise from the deepest fathom of desolation; one that required no words to communicate its message. Now that all had been decided, that's all man was, all he amounted to: a beast, weakened by terror and awaiting extinction, while enduring the horror of this very recognition. Billions had already acknowledged this. Billions more would too. These were his thoughts.

There were no reckonings for evil. There was no justice for the wronged. But there was meaning. Oleg was incorrect because life, increasingly, was the triumphant preserve of the unscrupulous, the selfish, the criminally rapacious, and the murderous. They had already laid claim to what was worth having in his world, and in *the* world. Their will had become the only meaning.

THIRTY-FIVE

After he'd lost the sensation of one entire foot below the ring of pain on his lower leg, a door handle turned. Beyond the hot darkness of the hood he heard a pair of feet slowly and cautiously enter the room. The single set of steps calmly approached his position.

The father flinched as the feet paused before his chair. He clenched his jaw in anticipation of a blow, but the hood was loosened. A scent of rubber invaded the fetid cloth about his face. The stinking rag was removed and the father blinked in the bright yellow electric light of a garage. The dry white hands that appeared before his face stank of anti-bacterial rubber, and quickly fitted a surgical face mask over his mouth and nose.

The father peered up at the head of a small man whose face was also covered to the eyes by a mask, and further encased by glasses to protect his tear ducts. Around these barriers on the stranger's head, he detected short, dark hair and brown eyes, with a suggestion of plump, chummy features distending the mask. And those were the sort of eyes that appeared permanently set in an expression of detached amusement, as if restraining mirth at whatever pitched up before them. There were still enough clues to suggest that the figure's normal state was one of careful grooming and a neat presentation. Despite the dressing gown, pyjamas and uncombed hair, the night clothes were expensive, the ends of the tousled hair perfectly cut. Inside the transparent gloves the nails on the pale hand that had softly but contemptuously raised his chin were manicured.

'Incredible,' the man finally said.

The presumptuous fingers left the father's chin. The stranger stepped away from the chair and withdrew some distance. He produced a vial of antiseptic from a deep, lined pocket and sprayed the already gloved hands with an aerosol. The expression in the eyes of the small man altered and became wary and calculating, with a slight stiffening of distaste too, as if the father exhibited the signs of some contagion.

The father said, 'My daughter . . .' He had nothing else to contribute.

The man raised an eyebrow. 'I didn't come in here to get involved in complicated discussions about ownership. She came here before my time, but rest assured, the girl you knew as Penny is well loved, by both of us. Very happy and in the best of health. She's a lucky girl. Though what is ironic is that her true origins have only recently been revealed to me. In fact, I've only known for a matter of days. I've always known her as Yasmin, and Yasmin she will remain.'

The father suspected that the masked man was smiling.

'Quite a lot to take in. You and I have that in common. That is assuming you have only recently discovered where she was, and that she was even alive. Though I doubt you wasted much time getting here once you knew.'

The man drew a garden chair out from the side of the

garage and made himself comfortable. 'Although I haven't had much time to let it all sink in myself, what Karen actually did two years ago, and who you actually are, hasn't changed my feelings towards my fiancée or my adopted daughter. Not at all. I'm encouraged by that.' The man smiled again, pleased with himself, pleased with his advantage, pleased that it wasn't him bound to an antique wrought-iron garden chair, with one foot either purple or completely white; the father was too scared to look down that far.

Engulfed by his desperate frustration, when so near his goal, the glowing coals within his belly seemed to flare, and he thrust against his bonds, only to suck in his breath and become still again. His eyes streamed with tears at the renewed pain circling both ankles.

'There is a vague resemblance too,' the man in the mask said. 'But my incredulity has been monopolized by you being here. Here! That is truly incredible. Last night, I heard a précis of how you managed to arrive at our little home. You see, our other guests arrived ahead of you and briefed us. And I must say I admire your grit. The sheer determination. Jesus, I mean, you were never a killer before, were you?'

The father stayed quiet.

'They said that you took out a lieutenant.' The man grinned. 'Some sex offenders too, which we are not, incidentally, so let's get that out the way first. I'd imagine that assurance, at the very least, would be some comfort to you. Though Penny-stroke-Yasmin even being alive would trump that.'

The man stood and began to walk around the father.

'I'm told that you even went into one of their strongholds, some fetid hive down the coast, and blasted your way out.' He came back into sight, grinning anew, and maintained his jovial, gently mocking tone. This man was amused, but the father was too tired and uncomfortable to waste his time guessing why, and his captor was no King either. He'd said he was Karen Perucchi's fiancé.

'But I think you'll agree that the clean-up they have performed in your wake has been extensive. Though the washing of their spears has had some unfortunate . . .' The man's face changed. 'You won't believe me, but for what it is worth, I am deeply sorry about your wife. We played no part in that.'

The father swallowed. A sob burst from him. He clenched his entire body to prevent the scalding grief he would never be able to stopper once it broke his insides apart. He had refused to check messages or watch any more films, but here was confirmation of what he would have found had he done so.

The man's voice dropped to a conspiratorial whisper. 'I think my fiancée more than sated herself two years ago on that account, exacting her retribution. So your wife's blood will not be on our hands. But they have her here.'

The father stiffened upon his chair. 'Miranda is alive?'

'Yes. They brought her with them, last night, either asleep or drugged. She still hasn't roused, but she is alive. And I have made a request that they let you see her when she finally comes around. It's the least they can do, considering the circumstances.' He chuckled. 'For the sake of your daughter, you'll be pleased and relieved to know that Karen is a very different person these days too. I certainly am. Your daughter changed her. Both of us, to be honest. I believe that child changed everything here when she came to live with Karen. She's a very special girl.'

The father's temporary relief that his wife was still alive was tempered by the inevitability of her not being so for much longer, and he was dumbfounded again by this man's avuncular tone, as if he were discussing some distant sporting event seen from the stands.

The man placed one rubbery finger next to his lips and frowned. 'Karen was sure that no one would ever connect her to the abduction. She paid handsomely to make certain there would be no loose ends. But here you are, so there is a missing link. And I'm really curious. Karen has assumed that this Yonah Abergil, whom we were told about last-night, and whom she never met, by the way, gave us up. Or maybe his old father did when you paid them a visit? I'm told they shared everything but hated each other. Strange people, eh? We know the kidnappers bugged your daughter's clothes and followed the car containing your daughter here. So we must assume that they told this Abergil chap about Karen?

'Or, was it someone else who let it slip? Someone we don't know about, yet? The problem with criminals of all stripes is that they like to brag, and Karen was never quite sure how discreet the firm she hired through a go-between would be. It's what you get when you go off-piste, I suppose. Double-dealing, betrayal. So is that how you found out about Karen, from Abergil? And if so, did he get the information from the two men who carried out the grim work of kidnap, before he had them *retired*? These are my concerns.'

The father blinked the sweat and fog out of his eyes. If this man was telling the truth then he didn't know Oleg was alive, and he and Karen were in the dark over how he'd learned that his daughter was here. 'Go and fuck yourself.'

The little man's face stiffened while the grin remained fixed. 'Well, you can tell me, or you can tell *them* later.' He nodded over his shoulder at the door. 'I know which I'd prefer, and if you are candid with me it may help your case. It's your call. But we can only assume, until we are better informed, that the two kidnappers told Abergil about Karen, prior to their final exit from the stage.'

The father imagined a beheading was not going to be sufficient today. Torture had a part to play. He swallowed the lump that had swelled inside his throat. *They* would want to know about *others* who may have offered his crusade assistance, any other guardian angels beyond those already slaughtered. A fresh onset of a comprehensive weakening, in limb and neck, at the thought of his coming travails at the hands of the Kings, tempered the rage that smouldered at the sight of this portly peacock, mocking him inside the garage belonging to the woman who had ruined his life. But if neither his interrogator, this prissy fiancé, nor the Kings knew about Oleg's involvement, that would mean Rina, Yonah Abergil's girlfriend, hadn't overheard the confession he'd extracted from Yonah at his villa, when Oleg's name was mentioned. And if Yonah had never known Karen's identity, then what Semyon Sabinovic and Oleg had discovered after bugging his daughter's clothes was never shared with Yonah Abergil either. This also meant that Oleg's faked death by overdose beneath the chapel had been convincing to whomever went to kill him. And it must have been good too, because no man could return from the dead, no matter what that man believed about ritual magic and his 'patron'.

The father remoistened his mouth with saliva. 'You shacked up with that psychopath . . . You condone what she did. You're now an accessory to kidnap, to murder. But it doesn't trouble you. What kind of animal are you?'

Widening his eyes with excitement, the man raised his hands and spread them wide to encompass a vastness beyond the bricks and mortar of the room. 'The animal that will survive this little challenge, as well as the almighty setback that is on its way. That's the kind of animal that stands before you this morning, one who intends to continue into the new year with health and portfolio intact.'

The man read confusion in the father's eyes, and he seemed pleased with the opportunity to elaborate on his cryptic suggestions. 'You should be grateful that the girl you fathered, a long, long time ago, *our* daughter for argument's sake, will have parents, a family, in the immediate future. A future that is, quite honestly, unbearable to even think about at this point in time. Plenty of children are already without parents in this world, and many more will also lose their own, and soon. That is, if the young even survive at all. It's really not looking good for . . . well, anyone really. Besides those of us who are prepared.'

The man saw something come into the father's eyes and he stepped further away from the chair. He pointed at his own face. 'You'll have to excuse the mask. It has nothing to do with my identity. That's hardly relevant now, I'd say. But you have been running wild out there, and this morning you compromised our little quarantine here, which we've observed since the first infections in Oxfordshire.'

The father almost laughed. 'You're hiding inside here because of a bug.'

'I'm afraid this is a bit more than just any *bug*. It's actually the tediously inevitable NBO. The *next big one*. An idea that's been knocked back and forth between microbiologists for the last fifty years. Sure you've heard of it. It's what we've all been, ultimately, waiting for. God knows there are enough distractions competing with the pandemics to occupy our minds these days. No sooner does an outbreak reach a dead end and most people forget about them. I honestly doubt we have the mental capacity to do much else. There's just too much going on these days, don't you think?

'But there have been a great number of people with expertise, privately funded, who have continued to fastidiously measure, test and assess risks, on behalf of those with their eyes on a much longer strategy. People like *us*. And there are a great many people that have a chance of . . . how shall I say it, *continuing*.' The man chuckled. 'Ask me and I'd say that when I knew that this virus was probably *the one*, the news brought some relief. You believe that? Hallelujah, the future is finally here!

'Thank God some of us had the foresight to prepare for it. And here's another thing, Karen really did do you a favour.' The man raised a proprietorial finger. 'Hold on! Bear with me. Before you go off, you really should thank Karen for taking Yasmin. I mean it. For taking on that responsibility. Because any alternative for the girl doesn't bear thinking about, does it? Not now. Not out there?' The man mock-shuddered. 'When you think of what is coming . . . well, what is already here and extremely infectious.' He paused and squinted, appearing to peer into the distance of his thoughts. 'It's happening right now.'

The father spat to clear his mouth of what now tasted like someone else's faeces. 'You shitting little cowards. Another pandemic begins and into the keep you go scurrying. Over and over again. Like you do every time. Out here in your little castles. Extending your longevity with gene culture, but the one thing you can't entirely own is your health. But fuck the rest of us, yeah? You fucked us all a long time ago. You weakened and divided and destroyed everything around your walls. But when everything finally breaks down, I will be gone, and I will take a secret delight in the likelihood of you all being torn apart. You have no idea of the rage that awaits you, out there.'

The man pretended to yawn. He checked his heavy wristwatch. 'The significant minority that you so despise will have expanded proportionally, when this bug has run its course. Because the much-thinned-out dissatisfied majority, and it's a simple matter of mathematics now, will consist of but a shadow of their previous numbers. I'm afraid you'll have to forgive my rather dry summary of something impossible for any of us to really grasp, and I'm talking about the consequences of what will probably now be the biggest sudden depopulation since the Black Death. Yes, that's right, so hold that thought. And here's another for you to consider: how else do those of us with influence and primacy even address such a monumental and inevitable change? So it has come down to hard choices about survival, continuing the species and a *version* of civilization. And that can only occur if there are far fewer than nine billion of us still around.'

The discomfort in his leg was now bringing the father to the breathless condition just prior to passing out. He found it difficult to focus on much besides the idea that his foot had finally separated from his leg. Stupefied with pain, confusion and the choppy sea of rage, he just stared at the man. He even began to wonder if the figure before him was mad, or just privileged, isolated, and paranoid.

'We're all at fault, or maybe we never were and this is an old and indifferent planet's doing. But we don't all need to go. Nor do we need to allow an arbitrary cull. There's far more at stake now than who has what, who is rich and who is poor, and whose fault anything was. Some of us have moved on from that debate. Those of you who cannot accept that, well . . .' The man offered the palms of his hands to indicate the precariousness of the father's circumstances should that need any confirmation. 'The short of it, the burgeoning Asian pandemic must be seen as a necessary evil. An opportunity.'

The father kept his eyes and teeth clamped shut until a wave of pain and nausea relented. 'So you came in here to make me feel better about what your bitch did . . . to ease your conscience about what you are complicit in, by telling yourself that you are securing my daughter's future. Is that it, the new script? During the latest viral dead end that's got you all shitting bricks in your woodland retreats, these are the new positions of the goalposts . . . You want me to ratify this, or sign something, before you have me murdered?'

'Murder? We're not murderers. Oh no. Your fate lies with others who are eager to get started on what they came here for. Please see my fiancée and I as merely providing a facility for an unpleasant necessity that your own actions created. But Karen believes that you should, at least, be offered an explanation of how things are going to pan out for the girl. For *Penny*.'

'At least?'

'Yes. She's actually furious with you, for bringing another necessary evil at one time, I am now told, out of the woodwork. But you,' the man pointed a stubby finger at the father's face, 'you brought them back within her orbit, where they arc not welcome. One's exposure to such things, I think you will agree, should be limited. So this is a very nervous time for her, and for all of us here. I don't even have to be here with you. I'd rather not be. But she thought you were owed something before . . .'

The man was doing him no favours. Even in such pain the father could differentiate between gloating and an attempt at relief for the condemned. 'Soon enough our considerations of the past will be altered beyond recognition, because the past won't really matter. Who has done what to whom. None of that will matter. A terrifying thought. But also an incredible opportunity if you're smart. It's what we do in the next couple of years that will count for everything.'

The more he spoke, the more the man reminded the father of those distant, wine-fuelled executives from food distribution who held forth at parties, their baritones rising to the ceilings of the rooms they quickly came to dominate; people who had drifted into the executive level of agriculture, construction, nuclear power, the emergency government, water management and resettlement planning, after their opportunities in finance diminished as the world's markets began to collapse; men who considered anyone unlike themselves as without worth. The father felt his face contort into a sneer that he had no control over. This was a man the father would feel pleasure in destroying. He now wished that he had started destroying people much earlier in his life. He blinked his blurred eyes clear. 'Have you any idea what that woman has done? To me. My wife. Her parents. To so many . . . because she stole our child?'

The man resumed his seat beyond the range of a sneeze. He seemed intent on more justification. 'The bigger picture, if you please. Let's put your natural outrage to one side, for one moment. You look at the same world as we do, and you've seen where this is all going. The country is a powder keg. The resentment, divisions, sectarian violence. My God, who can keep up with it? Between the Islamists, between the nationalists and the Islamists, between the nationalists and the refugees, the bloody socialists, the underclass and anyone near them who has more than they do, which isn't hard. The nationalists have even recruited from the camps, as have the Islamists. The rival criminal clans are directing most of it. Our friends out there.' The man nodded at the door. 'They're even in government now.' Dismissively, he wafted a small, feminine hand in the air. 'Drone strikes, curfews, riot control, it doesn't work. And with so many without work, don't you think it's all really come home? I mean, the children still living with their parents beyond their forties? Do you know how many deaths have resulted from sibling rivalry this year alone? How is any of this going to improve? Anarchy is unavoidable, inevitable. We've seen it getting closer for years. We're only about two years behind the States and you saw what happened out there when the south ran out of water. Jesus Christ. We've all that coming, right here. This isn't bloody Norway. So we'll continue to destroy ourselves from the inside, with the ethnic divisions, the class war, the sheer territorial rage of cornered, hopeless animals, while the climate reduces us, storm by storm and drought by drought.'

The man took a deep breath and slapped his hands against his thighs. 'There is far too little for far too many, even here on the lifeboat called Great Britain. We're considered the lucky ones, with the Kiwis, of course. You believe that? But look at the influenza alone that we've seen in Europe. Not to mention the diseases that have killed millions across thirty years globally. Mere warnings. Labs have always managed to produce vaccines, eventually, but this is quite different. This is the *one*. And the world it has entered is very different to the world that cured AIDS and cancer. This world is no longer even remotely cohesive.

'And . . .' He paused as if from the gravity of what he was about to announce. 'Nature, King Death no less, is inhabiting SARS CoV11 and about to take its course, here as elsewhere. And it will have to run and run, or soon everything will be lost to chaos. This isn't about you, me, Karen, it's about . . . well, it's about your daughter. She is the future. She and others in her privileged position can make it, and make it comfortably. We'll make sure of that. She wouldn't have a chance otherwise. Not a hope in hell.

Because when that "bug" came in through Oxford, the gates of hell truly began to creak open in Britain. You see, your daughter has already been inoculated. All of Karen's family members and staff have been too.'

The father raised his face.

The man tapped the side of his nose. 'The Gabon River Fever is relatively harmless compared to the Asian bug. Ha! And mostly used as justification for the Italians, French and Portuguese to sink the refugee boats, and for the northern hemisphere to close its borders. Still, you wouldn't want to catch that and it is around, but Gabon River Fever never spreads far enough. We've had outbreaks in Europe twenty-one times, but it's always a dead end. We took our eyes off that one years ago. But the new SARS? Oh, boy. The Chinese have lied, like they always do. And so have their neighbours in case we shut them out for good.

'This is an archetypal zoonosis, from the animal to the human animal. Fucking rats again. Isn't that the rub? A country struggling to breathe and grow food began to eat the entirety of the animal kingdom at its disposal. They were breeding rats in China for food. They farmed bamboo rats and guinea pigs very successfully, but the problem was storage and distribution. They sold them in wet markets in appalling, overcrowded conditions, and we subsequently became the amplifier host. But the bug is changing again as it passes through us, and has become even more lethal. Bats were the reservoir host, rats the cultivating host, and we're the dead end, literally.

'Time has finally been called. Because this strain is spread by exhalation. Exhalation! By breathing. This strain has been observed living in seawater for six months. It isn't going away. We've got years of it ahead, wave after wave.'

The father swallowed. 'She . . . there is a vaccine?'

'Yes, and I'm afraid this strain of SARS has proven itself ninety per cent fatal so far. A respiratory cluster-fuck, like an extreme form of pneumonia. But some very clever people got the antibodies from the right bats. And the first vaccine has been ninety-seven per cent successful against SARS 9 and 10, in some rather hastily conducted trials, and ninety-three per cent successful against 11, so we're still taking some precautions against exposure.'

The father's captor moved his head from side to side, casually pondering his advantages. 'But the drug will never come close to wide availability. Production couldn't even begin to match demand this time around. It is scarce and very, very expensive right now, like everything else that people need that is a matter of life and death. Nothing unusual there. Family members of those with access to it, I'm afraid. Then key workers. All a bit vague now, but we can assume that those with the expertise to keep the power stations running are in. Same with the farmers, and the experts that will be needed across all the primary fields. You must have known how it would go down if we ever reached this point. A vaccine couldn't be distributed fairly. So what's the alternative, a lottery?' He laughed. 'This is not something that will be thrown off the back of a truck any time soon. The isolation wards, the barrier nursing, and quarantine in a population of this size? Impossible. The dieback is just going to be off the scale. Some people are talking seven billion or more worldwide, though others claim that forty per cent is a more reasonable figure. Only a third of Europe died from bubonic plague, and medieval Europe was more primitive than our world, just about.' He lowered his voice and whispered. 'Close to *four billion*. Can you fucking imagine that? The wretched living conditions of most of our fellow creatures, and their close proximity to each other, is going to be key, and it'll take four or five years, but . . . Wow! The dieback in historical terms is going to be . . . epochal.'

The man recomposed himself, wiped his fringe back from his forehead. 'So, a collective in business at the highest level, well above that sham we call government, had to make the difficult decisions. I'd say people in certain positions are much better at doing that now, because all the rules changed, quite literally, some time ago. I'm sure you of all people noticed. And now the clock is ticking far faster than anyone thought. Most Centres for Disease Control in the first world don't even know about the vaccine. They suspect some of us have something, but they don't know what. Most of the current emergency government doesn't know either, though they will soon enough. But private industry looks after its own first. We discovered it, so it's only fair. And do you think the emergency government will distribute it fairly when they receive their limited supply? It's not like you can expect government to sort anything out, anyway. This all goes way above government, way above the media, you know that. These levels of corporate organization stopped even trying to avoid being seen as a conspiracy about four decades ago.

'But the antibodies have been cultivated from a tiny bat that was pissing onto the rats in a wet market. Discovered by one of many private enterprises with field operations in

Asia, in which Karen has a sizeable interest. So the vaccine has been passing between a select few, for months now. In the nick of time, I'd say.'

'You bastards.'

'Pragmatic bastards. Those feedbacks this year, with the plant stress? Jesus Christ. They're producing carbon dioxide. Collapse has been on the cards for a long, long time. We'd face starvation eventually in the UK, later than most, but it's on our dance card. Soil fertility is already becoming an issue, as are crop losses from the droughts; even with the water management in Europe, yields are worryingly down again, and far worse than they are claiming in the news. Our recent fecundity is a blip and actually very fragile. But with your background, you probably assumed as much. There are seasonal variations from one year to the next, but it's all getting worse over the long haul.

'So the bigger picture, who can feed themselves now? The British and French, Canadians, Scandinavians, Polish, Russians, Japanese and Koreans. But what still remains in Mexico, Central America, the Caribbean, every single country but France that borders the Med, India, Pakistan and the Middle East, are all on their way to final collapse because of water, or a distinct lack of it.

'We can only surmise that our own summers and winters are now standard too. But we'll fall apart from within, even before we have a major food or water crisis here. The population is at least one hundred and twenty million now. We don't even know exactly how many people are here, with more and more coming in every day, but it stopped being ninety million a long time ago. And the people won't stop coming. Most of Central Africa and North Africa, southern Europe, is still on the move. Asia too . . . where are they going to go? Look at India and Pakistan. We're already going the way of America, as well as much of Europe unlucky enough to not be Scandinavia or an island. You're an intelligent man. You must have seen this coming from way back when.

'So try and imagine the numbers . . . every man, woman and child on the move across the next four or five decades in Africa, Asia and the Middle East. Can any more be taken in, and absorbed in the bits and pieces that will still be functioning? Nine billion. Nine billion of us at the last count, and nearly all in the areas that will fail to support human life beyond a bit of hunter-gathering and cannibalism. You do know what happened on Easter Island, to the Mayans, and to the Vikings in Greenland? Well multiply that, Daddio, into the billions until only tens of millions would be left standing. Inconceivable.

'And it would all be in full swing by the end of this century. Your daughter might still be around then. Her children will be for sure. You ever figured out what's coming to our children and grandchildren? We have. And it cannot happen. *Our* child cannot go out like that. Yasmin cannot see *that*: total collapse.

'A few more years like this, maybe a decade. Then a decade of it being worse. Then another decade of it being even worse than that. Cumulative collapse. Can technology keep pace with such disruption? Afraid not. Never has done. Not really. You must have known all of that *vision of the future* stuff they piped out was bullshit. We're maxed out. We can't even cope with our own public health requirements in a heatwave. The statistics are false. At least one million people died this summer across Europe. We'll never generate enough juice to air-condition every home, only some, and we know how much resentment that causes. The speed of climate change has taken us all by surprise. It just has this momentum, you know?'

He grinned. 'And you really can't believe anything you hear any more, out there. We all educate ourselves with online rumours from the indie journos. But here's another rumour: everything is actually far worse than you think and have been told. Much worse. There are going to be very few winners. The needs of the many cannot be met, blah, blah, blah. That is what it has come down to, but the needs of the few can be met. Something drastic is required that doesn't involve the nuclear option, before the nuclear option is standard practice. How many years away is that? Or is it weeks these days? India and Pakistan? Jesus Christ, they'll kill us all. The Chinese are already taking what they want from what's left around them in Asia. Can you see the US standing in the way when Japan and Taiwan finally get rolled? Who knows?

'But a pandemic is a solution, an accidental lifeline for the species. If you like, the final solution. Think about it. Fucking brutal. Cold, but . . . Refugee problem: numbers reduced and better managed. Food shortages: solved. Land and housing shortages: solved. Water crisis: managed. And globally. It is going to be horrible, and you're best off out of it, but our girl will be all right. You have *our* word on that.

'Now, I think I'd like my breakfast. Karen has requested a few minutes with you, before . . . well, we all live in a time of inevitability. And for what it is worth, I did try and put in a good word for you, considering your grievances, and on behalf of this charming old-fashioned model of justice and fairness that you still hold dear, and have carried like one almighty cross for years. But, my pleas for clemency fell upon deaf ears. Sorry. But look at it this way, soon the pain stops.' The man rose from his garden chair and walked to the door.

The father scratched through his near-numb mind for something to say. 'They'll kill you all! And Penny.'

The man paused, still smiling. 'Why ever would they do that?'

'The man who gave Karen up, he is one of them. He told me how this would go down, today. How *they* close the book when things go bad. How they cauterize loose ends. Your head will be separated from your shoulders this morning. Many people, good people, will soon know where my daughter is, and who took her. You think I'd come here without insurance? You think I care about what happens to me? The police know. The good ones. There are still good men and women out there who helped me. So you'd better hope the bug kicks things up a gear real quick, because if you somehow survive this morning, you're both going to prison. Try covering your mouth then, cocksucker, when you're in a cell with the swine.'

It was hard to read the man's face as he departed the room. He seemed embarrassed for the father, as if he had behaved in an undignified manner in a public place. But there was also a new preoccupation in what little the father could see of the man's eyes: *doubt*.

THIRTY-SIX

'You frightened her.' Karen Perucchi closed the door and came further inside the room. 'Have you any idea how much?'

Amidst the smell of rubber, stale electric engines, cement and his own sweat, her perfume wafted across to the father, reinforcing the sense that all the ghosts from his past were assembling in his final hour. And Karen had changed a great deal since he'd seen her last. A lot of work had been done to her face to reshape her eyes and lips, and she was thinner too. Too thin, as if she'd withered every ounce of fat from her frame. But she didn't walk easily in the heeled mules, as if unaccustomed to the elevation, and her newly sculpted face seemed marginally askew atop the bony shoulders. The temptation to bite one side of her mouth in testing situations still pinched her inflated lips, and just below the unnaturally smooth planes of her refashioned features, there still lurked a hardness, and a suggestion of innate hostility.

She came to him determined and on the attack. 'You look terrible. Did you even consider what her reaction would be? But from what I remember, you always were incapable of thinking about anyone apart from yourself. I mean, what were you going to do, use an explosive on the doors with a child inside the house?' She shook her head, closing her eyes to add emphasis to her outrage.

'She is not your child!'

Karen flinched, then instinctively bit the inside of her cheek.

'You stole her! You took a child from her parents! For revenge! Because you were disappointed? Because you couldn't handle rejection? Because you are fucking crazy, you abducted a child! I knew you were damaged, but this . . .'

Karen's mouth tried to smile, but became a rictus. Her eyes did not even come close to supporting the intended expression. Nostrils thinning, she inhaled deeply. 'None of that matters any more, the whys and wherefores.' She shook a thin arm in the air as if to dismiss these trifles for which she was now being held to account. 'And do you know something? When I look at her now, I don't even think about you.'

Dumbfounded, the father gaped. 'Are you . . . insane? It's not about you. This is not about how you ever felt. You took a child. Her mother . . . her *real* mother and her father are going to be murdered in your home. *Murdered* because of you!'

Karen closed her eyes and spread her twitchy fingers in the air, in line with her hips, as if engaged in some calming technique. 'I doubt we will ever agree on who is to blame for that, for anything. I mean, how could we?' She then laughed loudly, as if at his idiocy. 'But did you know that I lost a child? Your child, our child? Mmm? I miscarried, and I couldn't even share it with you, couldn't turn to you when I needed your support. Because you'd run away.'

The father swallowed, even now still able to be concussed by these revelations of the life, all of the life, that he had been unaware of.

'But I am not going to revisit that, revisit how much you hurt me. All that matters now is what is best for Yasmin. Have you understood nothing of what my partner explained to you? Yasmin's best interests are never going to be served by you. My God, have you taken stock of yourself lately? How far your life is off track? Even here, the moment I stepped through that door I could see how murky, how discoloured, how all wrong, you were.

'And what would she think of you, if she knew what you have done? Do you honestly think you are fit to be a father? That you are capable of caring for a child? Yet you still intrude here, after all this time, to endanger her life, so that you can stake some claim to a privilege that you forfeited a long time ago?'

The father pulled with all of his strength against the chair, which shifted slightly upon the cement floor. 'She is mine! Mine . . .' He roared into the cool air and drowned out the distant, incessant hushing of the wind. The skin on the underside of one wrist slit open. A fresh shock of agony circling his ankles turned down the amplification of his rage, quickly, and left him panting with pain upon his chair. His body shuddered as if a large cloud of bubbles were rising through his blood; when they reached his head his vision nearly whited-out.

Through the soiled wrappings of his indignity and despair, he was also aware that Karen was taking a moment to revel. An opportunity she had probably secretly craved since he'd walked out on her. And there was nothing he could do about it.

'You and your wife, that boneless bitch . . . The best kind of family? A family for that special little girl? For Yasmin?'

The father received the sense that she was pointing angrily at the closed door to the room, but he could no longer bear the sight of the woman before him and he kept his eyes on the cement floor. Yet her voice still came to him just like the voices of all those who had become empowered in the endless crisis, twisting the truth and adverse circumstances, remodelling perspective to suit their own interests. 'The myth of this primacy of natural parenting that you cling to will soon quite literally be that, a myth. My partner and I are all that girl will ever need. And I will give her what you could never provide. You still have no idea, no idea how lucky she is to be here, with us.'

Her confidence rose with the volume of her voice as she reassured herself that she was right and justified in her actions, as she always had done, and always would do. 'You think I am going to let the mistakes you made have any bearing on my daughter's future?' Karen's voice became a distant cry beyond the narrowing red walls of his mind, and the father wished for profound deafness, for a stroke, for death.

'Yes, my daughter! My daughter will want for nothing. Know that. She will have a better life than you can imagine. The past doesn't even figure here. Not any more. What's best for my child is my only concern now. And you must know that what's best for her is not *you*. Or what's left of you.' Seemingly relieved that, at last, he must surely be getting close to an understanding, Karen lowered her voice and the father sensed that a smile of satisfaction had relaxed her bitter face. 'And this . . . this scourge is no accident either. It is a blessing. A gift from out of the chaos. It will be terrible, but there will be resurrection. A controlled rebuilding. Yasmin won't suffer. She will survive and live a long life, healthy and protected. Always. With us. My girl will survive. My family will survive. And I will let nothing endanger my family.'

If he had been looking he knew he would have seen Karen widen her eyes, challengingly and characteristically, at the conclusion to the words that he presumed had been prepared ahead of their confrontation. He guessed that she had prepared her outfit and appearance too, after he had woken the household and been taken down. She had spent hours preparing herself so that she would look her best during their final conflict. He guessed she'd been near-trembling with excitement at the prospect of facing him to tell him that she had won, that he had been wrong, and that she was better; it was all that really mattered to her. Competitive to the last, she hadn't changed in any meaningful way. And though he deeply regretted killing a woman, the father knew that he could do it again.

His eyes rose again, but could only look at her in the way a wounded, cornered child would look at an adult deranged by fantasies and rage. He spat at the floor. 'Penny is not yours. She never will be. She is not your daughter.' He shook his heavy, so tired head. 'And I will die knowing that, as will you. As will you, devil.'

The door opened and the masked face of her fiancé

appeared. 'They want to come in now, Karen.' He spoke like a PA delivering an instruction to his employer.

Distaste stiffening Karen's plumped mouth, a nervous blinking followed this reminder of who else was on her property, and of what was about to be done in her home. A quick anxious tapping of one hand with an index finger, and then she turned her head towards the door and nodded. 'I'm nearly done.'

The door closed.

Karen looked at the father for the last time. 'You could have been someone. But my daughter will be.' Fond of dramatic exclamations, she turned and swished to the door. 'Better to be a devil than a dim, sentimental fool.' The door closed and he was alone again.

The father wondered why she'd let him live two years ago. Maybe because a double murder and a kidnap would have drawn more attention; she'd have thought through every angle for sure. But he understood that there had been another motive: she had wanted him to suffer, to hurt with the worst kind of agony: the loss of a child. Her sense of herself was godlike, as were her ideas of punishment for those who dared to wrong her, or to simply defy her. There was no great revelation to be sifted from the situation either; he was just another soul, lost within a herd of animals stampeding away from the forest fires, whinnying before flood water, or sinking knock-kneed and bone-thin to the dusty ground from hunger. People were murdered every day, left to starve, enslaved, drowned, crushed, killed randomly by pandemics, even by viruses imparted from the mouths of their loved ones whom they nursed. Only the cruel and ruthless, the conscienceless, appeared to triumph in what was left. And, for his species, that was perhaps the most terrible tragedy of all.

His thoughts seem to derail, then become too active, as his mind accepted the end. But he spared a thought for the monarch that was coming, King Death in its rags, with the black seeds that fell from its bony fingers, and he thought it tremendous in its scything indifference. And the father prayed that King Death would be thorough with all those who had crowned themselves upon this terrible earth.

And maybe none were worthy of inflicting life upon a child. Perhaps oblivion was for the best. The world had cored him, desiccated his flesh, salted and hung him up to wither. He'd had a good run and was amazed at how far he'd come, to within inches of his daughter. And she was alive. At least there was that.

A tired, old voice spoke aloud inside his jumbled thoughts. *It's over.* Shaking with cold, he acknowledged that death was the only mercy for him now.

The door opened and the men came in. Their faces were concealed with Balaclavas. Without speaking they laid out a plastic sheet, unfurled the body bags and unzipped them. They set up a small camera on a tripod. From a black case an object inside a dirty cloth was retrieved and unwrapped. A machete was unsheathed. Old steel glimmered.

One man left the room and returned with Miranda. Her head was concealed by a black hood, and her long body was limp and held beneath the arms as she was dragged into the makeshift abattoir.

At this moment of their death, the father prayed that she would never wake again, and he released a sob and its sound shocked him. He prayed that his wife, the mother who had brought Penny into this life, would never know how close she had been to her little girl at the end.

When they cut his ankles from the chair and pushed him off the seat, onto his knees and upon the plastic, the father knelt beside his inert wife and tried to reach her with his bound hands. She was too far away, just like she'd been for most of the last two years. He thought of his daughter instead. And he recalled a memory of holding her hand as they walked along the red sand of a distant, wind-swept beach, looking for shells, so many years gone.

Inside the room the lights flickered.

'Daddy loves you,' the father said to the image of the girl who had never stopped smiling inside him. She was nearby, but she had never been further away than she was now.

And then he closed his eyes on the whole damned world.

THIRTY-SEVEN

The ceiling lights went out.

Each passing moment seemed to expand from the centre of his mind, humming as if it carried volts through a cable, and still he waited for a cold incision through his neck. He kept his head down, and his eyes clenched as tightly shut as his jaw, for fear he might soon look back upon his kneeling body from where his head bounced and then settled upon the floor.

The father attempted to stop the rotations of his final thoughts, because the sole image he would die cherishing would keep him buoyant until the very end. The last of him would be *her*.

Behind him a heavily accented voice said, '*L'Homme devant la mort*. Yonah Abergil.'

The door opened again, and the smell of wet air and the rushing of the wind came into the garage.

One set of footsteps retreated across the cement floor.

Two shots struck the air, followed by a sudden bang against wood. A heavy thump completed the interlude.

A rustle of clothing behind him suggested hurried movements, complemented by a hissing exhalation.

A short snap of rapid shots slapped again, from the

direction of the first salvo, producing a faint echo off the cement walls.

From behind issued the sound of a man surprised, close to his ear. That noise was followed by a deep grunt. Someone rustled and then smacked, fleshily, against the floor behind where the father crouched.

Some words in a foreign language were muttered quietly.

Silence.

Eventually the father moved. Turned his head and looked behind himself. One of the Kings, the one wearing a leather jacket, was sprawled upon the grey floor. The father raised his head to better see through the semi-darkness, the space only lit by the grey light that fell through the door and solitary window set in the gable above it. Salt on his face cracked as the father noticed the second man propped against a wall near the door; his masked face glistened blackly and appeared to smoke. They had both been shot dead: his captors, his executioners.

'You could not do this on your own. I told you this.' Already deep inside the room, Oleg Chorny leaned against a wall on the father's left side, a pale, thin silhouette that grinned horribly. He cradled the assault rifle the father had seen in the tool bag. 'I took care of the bitch's bodyguard too, outside, then these two.' Oleg spat in the direction of one corpse. 'The bitch and her boyfriend didn't want to watch you die, so they scattered like little birds into their house. I think I will leave one of them for you. The fool. But the bitch, I am very sorry to say, is mine. On this there is no negotiation. She paid for Simmy to be killed, and she will be my final sign. Your girl is alive and you will get her back today, so I think my argument wins.'

The father swallowed and looked again at the dead man behind him. 'Why?'

A quick grimace of pain stiffened the skull mask in the shadows. It looked at the ceiling and seemed to spit this time to expel pain. 'You think I do not know loss? Maybe Simmy and I were not as free of who we once were as we had hoped. It is not unusual to be used and killed in this life. We knew this.' He turned to the father as he came away from the wall. 'But are lovers to be denied revenge? Is this the sole right of fathers? You came for the purpose of your vengeance, but you came to deliver mine also. Think on this, neither of us could have done this alone. What walks beside us, in the confinement of our signs, brought us together. Did we both not offer everything for our revenge? Are we not the same, you and I? Do we not forsake ourselves for the ones we love but have lost? We have crawled around hellmouth for two years. Powerful magic, my Red Father. In another place, we have been incandescent.'

For a while the father stayed silent, too shocked, relieved, and bewildered to speak. The true question that emerged was no longer who stood before him, but what? He could not allow himself to believe Oleg. His theory was delusional and impossible, as was the idea that this man, who had just saved his life, could retire from life, and yet return at will; rising from the dead for the purpose of his own vengeance. But nor could he explain how Oleg had known about him and foreseen his arrival at that hellish chapel. What Oleg had said about the patrons of afterdeath he would not allow himself to believe.

A cooling of his flesh accompanied a new revelation:

Oleg could kill him now, and his wife. Once his revenge on Karen had been sated, what then? Oleg could close this old account completely, and kill him, his wife, and his daughter. Isn't that what they did, murder indiscriminately to cover their tracks? It was in their very nature. The man was also deranged, and he'd never met any living thing as dangerous as Oleg Chorny. In fact, Oleg might have killed him at any time during his captivity, as he'd freed himself to get here. When writhing for a fix, if he'd the means to remove his bonds all along, then Oleg's self-restraint must have been enormous. 'You got free.'

Oleg tittered. 'Do you think I would ever sleep without a tool in my arse? Prison taught me many things. But I wonder, do I have to kill you now, or can we put our disagreement aside until this ritual is finished and our alignment is washed away in blood? I'm afraid our little ritual will require a final sign, if I am to be embraced within that terrible passage. And I think you would rather I make my offering with the blood of the bitch, and her fool, than with yours . . . and your wife's.'

The father looked at the machete in the dead man's hand, the fingers blackened by the tattoo ink of a mortuary roll. 'Agreed.'

'Good. And you have seen the girl?'

The father nodded.

'Then we will collect her after we have concluded our business here, together. Today we end the confinement that binds us.' Oleg smiled. 'We sever it.'

An elation to still be breathing, and so close to his daughter, tried to rise from the father's heart, but Chorny's use of the word 'sever' seemed to now echo within his skull, as did this talk of blood and sacrifice. He had no choice other than to follow the man's lead, and to play along with his mystical delusions.

Penny.

The dark room and his long-in-shadow mind filled with an unstable light, and such was the inconceivability of his daughter ever being found, he understood his journey to this place had only ever been navigated by hatred's molten core. He was truly confined, but not in the way Oleg espoused; he was trapped by his own murderous madness, from which he'd long stopped believing that any escape was possible. Vengeance had inadequately prepared him for what came next.

What to do?

Doubts bustled, thoughts became insects in smoke, frantic, then sluggish. Where hatred and rage and misery had combusted for so long, he now weakened at the idea that his own daughter would no longer recognize him, and he could barely remember who he had been two years before either. And despite the timeless malevolence of Karen Perucchi, and the casual cunning of her partner, what they had said about the virus now stirred his greatest unease. If what they claimed was true, and they would have commanded a far better insight into a pandemic than anyone watching the news, then how could he protect his daughter from the chaos that was coming?

There was no way he could care for his daughter. She had spent two years with imposters who had treated her to a cosseted existence of plenty and luxury, as the rich did with their own. She had been vaccinated. He had not. If he and Miranda became sick, Penny would be lost again, but lost out *there* as things fell apart, amongst . . . Without him she would be taken by other strangers. He could not bear to imagine that. So cruel was the world that for his daughter to have any chance of survival, it would have been better for him to have died in this empty room, to have been bundled headless inside a rubber bag and buried in the woods.

A little money, a stolen car and a bag of guns, but no home to feel safe within if they were to be pursued by the killers of the King Death organization, and the Kings would kill them as soon as they found them. They would probably kill his little girl too, or do something even worse. And he was a murderer, wanted by the police. As bad a father as could be imagined, though he had done everything for love.

Her mother was broken and had been for two years. Could even the reappearance of Penny put her back together?

'Dear God.' He bent over until his face was a few inches from the top of his naked thighs. And what slowed the blood in his veins, until it appeared to stop moving altogether, was the inexorable acknowledgement that Penny probably considered Karen Perucchi to be her mother.

'For now we will put your wife in one of their cars.' Oleg knelt down, felt Miranda's throat for a pulse, and nodded. 'They gave her something strong. But you can rouse her later when our work is finished. I think that will be for the best, don't you? I think it better she never sees the Red Father at his work.' Oleg smiled. 'I will cut your bonds and give you a weapon. But I think you will walk in front of me, mmm?'

As Oleg sawed his tortured, half-numb limbs free, the father raised his tear-stained face to confront his rescuer, the man who first turned this wheel and set everything in motion two years before. 'There is a virus. A pandemic.'

'For sure. And I have seen its reign foretold. It will be as it is depicted upon my walls. Did you not tarry a while in my gallery? I heard them talking to you this morning too. And the fool did not lie to you. But they only understand this in one way. Virus, pandemic . . .' Oleg smiled, shrugging. 'There are other meanings in another place, which you resist. An unfortunate scepticism. To see the world in another way is to lose your fear.' His voice dropped to a whisper. 'I cannot waste any more time trying to convince you of what you cannot deny, but there is *another* here with me. Close to me. Close to you. Today. The one who has watched me since I first trespassed into that terrible passage with Simmy. The one that is between the signs with us, the signs that brought us together. And our energy here has been irresistible to the patron, so it is now very close.' Oleg nodded at the dead gang member. 'I have already made a start on those things that shine so brightly, over *there*.'

The father ignored Oleg Chorny's rambling. 'My daughter . . . they said there is a drug. They said she was vaccinated. She has a good chance . . . I can't . . .'

The man angled his head to one side, inquisitive, surprised even. 'You doubt yourself?' Oleg then looked upon the father with pity. 'Interesting. But I think they will have this drug here, somewhere. For you and your wife we will find it. We will *make* them give it to us. Now, move.'

The father tried to stand. The foot that felt strange and

hot did not support his weight and he fell onto his side. The cold of the concrete against his bare skin sobered him enough to curse.

Oleg nodded at the body behind the father. 'Maybe this piece of shit is your size. Put his clothes on.'

The father rose to one elbow and eyed the corpse with horror.

'You go to your girl in pissed pants? Better to wear the clothes of a dead man. Get up. You waste time.'

The father scavenged the clothes from the still-warm but cooling body. They stank of his would-be executioner's sweat. He limped about, both feet shod in drying blood, one foot tingling but mostly disembodied, the second foot only aching, and he yanked on the jeans, the hooded top and leather jacket. Then he slumped beside Miranda and felt the faint warmth of her cheeks, her hands, and kissed her forehead. 'I'm bringing her back, soon,' he whispered.

Oleg let his rifle hang on its sling while he emptied the pockets of the other corpse's jacket. 'Turkish. Bastard.'

After the father had mangled his feet into his own boots, Oleg said, 'We go and put your wife in the car.'

'What then?'

As if happily making a simple choice from a menu, Oleg rolled his eyes, smiling. 'I have already told you. *They* have to go now. Two candles must be lit in the window. Put your mind to that task first, and no other.'

The father thought of the well-heeled, self-satisfied couple and how they had so recently gloated. *Yasmin. Our daughter.* He clenched his jaw. Karen Perucchi was about to lose everything, and lose far more than she had taken from him. He nodded his assent. 'Karen is yours.' And he swore to himself that Karen's fiancé would be the last person he ever killed.

'No,' Oleg said, grinning, as if the father had spoken out loud. 'There will be other fights, Red Father. This is only a beginning of your awakening. Getting your girl back was the easy part. In a time of warlords and chaos, hell awaits you all, and soon. But at least you are prepared now. Never hesitate.'

Stunned, still wondering if he were so broken that he could not tell which of them was the least stable, the father said, 'My daughter . . . She cannot see . . . what we are about to do. She will think *they* are . . . her parents.' He spat on the floor as if the words were caustic.

Oleg's hateful face grinned. 'What do you think I am?'

'You're so fucked up I have no idea who you are, or what you will do.'

Oleg Chorny found this amusing. 'Now you understand me better. But I tell you this, I took a kid from a person for money, for sure.' He shrugged. 'From strangers. A long time ago. And for this my lover died. For this I was to die also. You think I have not paid some price too? You think I matter, or that you do? Does anyone matter? You, me, your girl? Have we not all learned this the hard way? How many lessons do you need, Red Father? We must stop feeling in the world that is coming. Life, love, whatever, all of these things must go. I have seen inside the machine, the body, of what walks beside us. And this body is black and cold and terrible. It cares not for us, Red Father. Afterdeath was there before existence, and it breathes heavily upon life once more, waiting for our return.' With the end of his gun, Oleg prodded the father towards his wife. 'Come. We carry her out. Then we go to the false mother.'

'My gun.'

'Patience.'

THIRTY-EIGHT

Outside in the rain, out of sight of the windows of the main house, Oleg surprised the father again by returning the two handguns he had carried to the house. 'These I know you can use.'

Hands trembling, the father took them.

'We go to them now. Already they will be thinking that maybe this morning is going wrong for them. Soon they will call their local security. Maybe as they shit their pants they have already made the call, who knows? And there are patrols, maybe more than usual because of the storm and Kashmir. We don't want to shoot our way out.'

The father swallowed, checked his weapons. The handguns had become dead weights. 'Wait. The vaccine, we have to make sure, before . . . They were all inoculated here. My daughter won't stand a chance out there unless me and her mother have it too . . . otherwise, I can't . . . how could I take her into that?'

'To get this far and not take her? But if it is here, they will give it up for sure. Relax.'

The father scrutinized Oleg's face for a flicker of deceit. He could feel one of his eyelids twitching from the nervousness and fear that made him want to throw up. 'Let's say they do have it, what then? What will you do, after?'

'I shoot up with something nice myself too. And then we part ways.' The man smiled, sadly, and he swept his gaze across the building and the pool. 'I like this place. Once, I would have waited here for things to settle, out there.' He nodded at the fence. 'These people had a good plan. And I would listen and I would know what would be required next. Only then would I open the gate.' He touched a wall as if surveying its size and said to himself, 'But my work is almost done.'

Mystified, the father continued to stare at the man, and infuriatingly he still awaited a straight answer. But Oleg merely pulled one of the dead Kings' Balaclavas over his head, and indicated that the father should do the same with the second mask. 'Crown yourself, Red Father. They see us come to the house on camera and they will think we are Kings. Come. You first.'

Still wearing his surgical mask and gloves, Karen's fiancé waited in the vast living room. Fully dressed now, he quickly rose from the white leather sofa and nodded gravely, as if he too had performed terrible and dark deeds in a garage that morning. 'Coffee? Or something stronger?' he said in the chummy tone, but one barely bolstered by a superficial confidence. 'We've—'

Oleg never gave the man time to finish the sentence, cutting him off by pushing the end of the assault rifle under his soft jaw. 'We go get the vaccine for the bug. This you can share.'

The man's eyes widened with fear and the flesh around the surgical mask became bloodless. 'I don't . . . Of course. We agreed . . .' And then he realized he was not speaking to either of the two men who had arrived at his home the night before, with an unconscious woman in tow.

Oleg ripped away the man's surgical mask and glasses. Kissed his mouth hard, using his tongue, then turned him around quickly. 'Your bitch, Karen, soon you will call her out here. But you will call her like normal, or I will fuck you in the arse with my gun and shoot out your lungs, mmm? But first you show us the drugs. Then we make a call to Karen, but not for the little girl. She best stay in her room. All very simple. You understand me, mmm?'

Karen's fiancé spluttered, his legs as unsteady as those of an old man on ice. He wet himself too as his legs gave way. 'Please . . .' His voice was nothing more than a whispery squeal. Oleg pulled him from the floor, effortlessly, and removed a small handgun from the man's jacket and tucked it inside his own trouser pocket. Through the eyehole of his Balaclava he winked at the father.

The father looked around the room, holding a handgun at his side, his throat closed, his heart now walloping with relief that the vaccine was onsite, while the prospect of seeing his daughter made him giddy. And then his skin chilled as he again tried to guess Oleg's real intentions. The man was insane, but functioning, and at a speed and level that he could not keep pace with. And yet his deepest and most profound instincts suggested that trying to shoot Oleg would be his and his family's final mistake. The painted man danced through his imagination. Unwelcome recollections of his dreams, and of the chapel, made the father quiver, while the persistent suspicion that Oleg Chorny was no longer entirely human would not abate.

Oleg began to whisper encouragement to Karen's

fiancé. The man said his name was Richard, but Richard could barely walk as they led him from the entertaining area. When he eventually recovered his voice, the father could hear the man's piteous attempts at negotiation. Offers of money were made, good sums too, offers of vaccines for their families, their friends, 'anyone really', and claims of his innocence in the matter of the kidnap.

The father saw excitement in Oleg's devil eyes, which rolled white and insolent in the holes of the mask, and he could not look at them for long. Oleg continued to cluck and coo horribly, a camp skeleton, encouraging the man to talk, while obviously delighting at the prospect of the coming slaughter.

They passed many elegant rooms in the concourse of the wing closest to the garage. His daughter had run in the opposite direction so the bedrooms would probably be on the other side of the building. And in their beautiful home, Richard and Karen must have thought they were about to inherit the world after the 'dieback', after the 'sudden depopulation', and whatever other strategic terms Richard used to encompass the coming and incalculable horrors awaiting the condemned. The couple had thought they would wait it all out, in here, with someone else's child. Yet this was no longer a home, but a long scaffold.

One room in the utility and recreation wing featured a white baby grand piano. Another was filled with many colourful toys, an indoor slide, and a vast hammock that his daughter must have swung upon. The father looked through a window and into the rear of the grounds, and saw an adventure playground out there, the size of a small house, that resembled a fort, all made from hardwoods.

There were two guest rooms with en-suite bathrooms that put to shame those in the best hotels he'd visited many years before. A library with real books had been installed, a vintage cinema, and a stainless-steel kitchen the size of the entire floor of his old family home, equipped with a walk-in freezer. The air throughout was filtered and kept constant by the house's computer, which provided information via discreet screens, placed at intervals along the corridor. All of this had come from intercepting money allocated to the starving.

When they reached the end of the curved wing, Richard unlocked a door using a keypad: a storeroom. And the father was soon staring at enough packaged food to sustain three people for years. He had never seen so much wine stored in one place either.

'The drug.' Oleg pushed the gun into the back of their prisoner's perfectly cut hair. Richard turned and looked at the father. 'I, I, I didn't take her. Please . . . You know this.'

Oleg finished the fifth injection in the father's abdomen, his long bony fingers working gently, expertly, feather-light, upon the skin. Nearby, Richard sobbed as he packed bales of cash into two leather bags. Oleg had made him open the safe. In the father's pocket nestled the address of Karen's barrister, and the address of his chambers; and perhaps the final link to the abduction.

'You must "do" this one,' Oleg whispered to the father as he removed the applicator and dabbed cotton wool upon the puncture. 'The terrible passage yawns for such a fool.' The remark made the father suffer another chilling suspicion they were about to perform a sacrifice, so that something beyond his comprehension could open, or at least be accessed in a bewildering but terrifying manner. The very idea was incredible enough to both frighten him and make him feel ridiculous. But he nodded his agreement.

Oleg grinned. 'He's getting on my nerves. He's no more use to us. And you don't need reminding how it works in this fucking world. Never hesitate, Red Father.'

'How do we know this is the right drug?'

Oleg glanced at Richard, so busy upon the floor giving away his hoard. 'He's too scared to be clever. Trust me.'

The father eyed the two leather bags at his feet, containing more money than he could earn in two lifetimes. He watched the money because he could not bear to see Richard call Karen on the intercom. 'Darling, in a few minutes would you be so kind as to come to the living room. We're all . . . good. Come alone please.'

The father overheard Karen's voice as she spoke to his daughter in a distant room. 'Mummy's popping out to see Richard. Can you be a good girl and stay here?'

His daughter's voice was audible, though not her exact words. She sounded happy, upbeat, slightly distracted. The floor of the father's stomach dropped away.

The world outside was blurred by the rain upon the long windows. The father dropped to a crouch and tried to swallow. The smell of the dead man's clothes filled his mouth and nose and throat. Richard edged closer to the father to whisper, 'You can take her. What belongs to you. I promise you, I swear on my life, that no one will come after you. Please. I had nothing to do with your daughter or your wife. Nothing. Please tell me that you understand?'

Oleg placed his hand on Richard's shoulder and nodded

towards the corridor that led to the living room. 'Maybe you need a drink, my friend. Come, come, relax.' Glancing over Richard's head, Oleg nodded at the father. The hard unequivocal expression in his eyes alone served to awaken the father's fragile purpose.

Back in the vast living area, the father took over the shepherding of Richard, and in a breathless voice asked him to stop beside the vast bar. He then moved to stand behind him. 'Penny's mother . . . She never came to terms with our daughter going missing. It broke her.'

'I'm sorry.'

'Don't look at me. I don't want to see your face.'

'Please!'

The father gripped the man's shoulder and made him look forward. 'What Karen first brought into our lives two years ago has come back. And those men were going to behead my wife, Penny's mother, in your home with your blessing. She would have died without knowing that her only child was alive. And even if they'd told her Penny was here, it would only have been to make her suffering worse.'

'What could I do? Please. Please.'

On the far side of the vast lounge, Karen clattered into the room in her high-heeled mules. The father heard her gasp.

The gun went off in the father's hand.

Richard slid down the bar and his head smacked upon the marble floor. Melon thump. Rivulets of blood, tributaries of matter. The father did not look away soon enough. The bullet had taken away the roof of the man's skull, and that flapped like a clod of turf.

Karen screamed and tried to run from the living room.

Oleg didn't need to chase her. She fell over unassisted between two vast leather sofas. 'You . . . you can have the vaccine too!' she cried out from the floor. 'There's enough . . .' She turned her attention to the father, still standing beside the bar, and near-screamed, 'You can have it! You! You! I'll get it for you!'

Oleg crouched beside Karen and commenced stroking her hair. He muttered to her for a long time while she sobbed and, strangely, clutched his tattooed arm. With his other hand, he began cutting or stroking the air above his head, as if drawing invisible signs. Upon the wall behind him, the shadows cast by his thin limbs weaved and circled. The father looked away, and found a bottle of vintage rum, all the time keeping his back to the room and the people that were in it.

'God no, God no, God no,' Karen suddenly said aloud.

'Come, come,' Oleg murmured, and in the mirror between the optics the father saw a silvery suggestion of the man holding Karen by her arm. He pulled her weak and flopping body into a kneeling position. From his rucksack Oleg withdrew the machete that had been brought here to behead the father and the mother of a stolen child.

The father watched the skeletal figure's reflection as it straightened to what appeared to be an unnatural and freakish height in the mirror – a hairless, tattooed bone man, unnervingly straight-backed and agile, who looked no fitter or firmer than a corpse, but transformed here as if by hidden energies evoked by blood. And for a moment he believed in the nonsense of the addict, about the signs, the confinement between them, the patron . . . For the father, all was becoming too vivid within the space about them, too bright, supernormal.

Upon the false mother this emissary of King Death turned, this thing in rags, who held a scythe above a dethroned queen, perversely suggesting the final act of a ritual: the throttling circle a vengeful father had been drawn into, baptized by his grief, by rage, which was now closing. In the silence, the only movement came from Oleg's arm and the shadow signs upon the great white wall. And for a moment, the father could believe that a great worm had finally swallowed its tail and that all had come full circle.

How could he reconcile his own dreams, the coincidences, the mosaics of surreal torments that he had witnessed, with reason? And right there and then he feared he truly had been touched, or infected, by a patron from out of Oleg Chorny's afterdeath, a presence ineffable, imminent, and not seen beyond dreams. Maybe the distance to another place, one beyond the world, had lessened again, as the addict had claimed. He didn't know, nor would he ever, but such a thing suddenly seemed possible.

The father twisted the cap off the rum bottle.

He heard Oleg speak softly, near-musically: '*L'Homme devant la mort*,' followed by a man's name. 'Semyon Sabinovic.'

There followed a sound of a spade thrust deep into wet soil.

THIRTY-NINE

The father's thoughts moved rapidly, then seemingly not at all. Around his head the stark, chic interior of the living room reflected what might have been his own nervy trauma, before amplifying it. Oleg's voice drifted in and out of his mind. '. . . some sheets on this mess . . . these two go outside. Old times, Red Father, old times for you and I.'

The father stared at the open door leading to the wing that housed his daughter's room. Shouldn't he be running down there to seize her, to hold her? But when Oleg dragged Richard's motionless form away from his feet and out to the rear patio, he could only close his eyes and hold his own body upright by placing two hands upon the bar.

'Go now,' Oleg said from outside, 'before she comes in here. Better if she never sees me. As wonderful as our friendship is, let's not risk a squabble.'

The father only half-heard the instructions, but enough to feel confident he understood. Such had been the shock and dreadful anticipation of his impending execution, he'd been left emotionally concussed, unable to identify a shred of satisfaction during the subsequent cull. One atrocity had bled into another. But he would feel something later. And there would be a *later* because Oleg had saved him and his wife, helped him recover Penny, and now seemed to be releasing him from a pact he'd never agreed to and didn't even understand. A man he had wanted to kill so desperately for two years was dismissing him. And yet, in all that now impacted and blocked his struggle for comprehension, the father was becoming even surer that he was no longer in the presence of an actual man.

He left the living area and walked down a corridor, half-lit by natural light and the dim glow of the blue panels beside the doors. Three-quarters of the way down, he came across a door covered in stickers. A sign in the middle of the wood, at a child's eye level, indicated 'Yasmin's Room!'

Removing his mask, he crouched as the strength deserted his legs. Covered his face with his hands and thought all the way back to their grief and shock that first afternoon when Penny was taken. He filled his mouth with the Balaclava's salty fabric to stifle a sob and screwed his eyes shut. The revelation came harder and colder; they had both nearly died mere feet away from their daughter, and it seemed they had just evaded the cruellest of all the injustices. If he let out a cry, others would follow. He could not even begin to grieve for Scarlett and Gene, his guardian angels. This wretched life moved too quickly and forbade it.

Attempting to gather his wits, and readying himself to look upon his daughter's face, he realized he had never truly believed that he would stand outside any door with his daughter on the other side, save one inside a police station or a hospital morgue. But slowly, his sense of being bludgeoned by futility began to ease. The pressure weighing upon his heart, a pig-iron cage fitted too tightly, loosened. Hopelessness and loathing were slipping away.

He wasn't sure whether it was elation, shock, or even terror that inhabited the new space.

Glancing down the corridor, he also considered what he and his daughter's kidnapper had just done. So what would he tell his daughter about *those people*? How did he stop being the Red Father and become again the father she had once loved? 'Oh Jesus, oh Jesus.' The father's hands trembled upon the wood.

Beyond the closed door, small feet bumped rapidly towards where he knelt. 'Who's there? Richard?' the little girl called out with delight. And before he had time to stand, the bedroom door was pulled open.

FORTY

He retained his retreat from the house only in fragments, punch-drunken memories. Later on, these moments appeared too vividly, yet out of sequence, pulling him back to another time and place: back to the terrible sweat that coated his entire body beneath someone else's clothes, his heavy legs heaving through air thick and slowing, the wet sandbags of his lungs, the eternity of mowed lawn he laboured across to the car, pulling a child behind him, holding leather cases of money in the other hand.

She didn't remember him. His appearance had changed a great deal, and she had just turned four when she last saw him. Two years had been a third of her life, her permanent memory only beginning some time just before she was lost. Karen would have done everything possible to make her forget what she knew of her parents, and her other life.

Other details from his escape from the house in the New Forest could appear at any time too, and often words he had thought forgotten.

Where's Mummy?

We need to go now, quickly.

Where's Mummy? The voice warbling with impending tears.

Penny's smooth face had whited in panic, crumpled. She

had started crying when he pulled her from the house, and the pieces of his long-broken heart had split further apart. He'd realized he was abducting his own child from what she knew as home, two years after she had been taken from him. He suspected that her old terrors from an afternoon on a distant front lawn in Torquay may have awoken right then.

We have to leave for a while. It's not safe for us to be here. Can you carry this bag? We have to go to the car.

As they had turned, ungainly, him panting and her whimpering, into the living area, he remembered trying to block her view of the room with his body. She had looked down and seen sheets there and the girl had clearly but wordlessly wondered why so much bed linen was spread and crumpled over the floor of the place where she had played, so safe and warm, for two years. And then the father had seen Oleg.

Before he had left the room to find his daughter, Oleg had been walking backwards, slowly, talking to himself, or at the sky, while dragging a body by its feet into the rear grounds. When the father returned with Penny, and tried to pass through the expansive white crescent of the living area, to reach the glass doors – by then clutching more than holding the girl's hand and shepherding her before him, this small stranger who held the little bag into which they had shoved a few articles of clothing – Oleg was sitting down.

Upright, his eyes wide and bright, he had selected one of the large white chairs beside the media centre. The man had been grinning, though it had taken the father a while to realize that Oleg could not see them. An exhausted applicator had lain unclutched in one upturned claw.

The father had found the long silhouette of the man's thin shape especially unappealing as it sat propped up like a cadaver unearthed in a tomb. But once he'd understood what unnerved him about that actual corner of the room, he'd stopped looking at it and begged the frightened girl to go outside with haste.

Don't look back. This way. This way. To the car.

At any time later that night, and for many nights afterwards, yet more could feature upon the screens of his mind at any time, including those memories he could not trust.

Cloud cover had only allowed sparse light into the open-plan centre of the building, so the cause of the motion around Oleg's death seat could have been nothing more than the reflected arrangements of rain-black clouds in the sky outside. But beyond the lounge windows, as they staggered onto the patio circling the covered pool, the father suspected that day had already surrendered and that night had fallen. That was not possible as it was still not even noon.

Another backward glance into the darkening room revealed in the far corner, upon one wall, a seemingly impossible unfurling of lightlessness, momentarily convincing the father that shadows were moving like water, except upwards from the floor, and perhaps surging too like a visible gas.

The dark flow.

He'd told himself this effect was caused by the storm, because further up the white walls he could see the great shadows of the tree limbs from outside. It was unfortunate, because they too appeared to his frenzied mind as long arms, or even wings. Wind that had been inaudible inside the house was now gusting through the trees along the fence, and the movement of their branches was, of course, cast upon the walls behind Oleg's chair. Shock and trauma were the only reasons the darkness had suggested facets of that loping king in rags, the one he had seen depicted in other places. The maelstrom of emotion that interfered with his breathing, and his very heartbeat, was worsening the effects of the wind-stirred tree shadows, and it was nothing more than that, or so he told himself for hours afterwards. But then the shadows and even the gloaming air had also seemed to expand on those interior walls and move not unlike a large octopus in inky water, before the shape flitted as fast as a black spider, disturbed from behind wet wood in a garden; up and across the ceiling it seemed to go and then away.

To the car, the car, the car.

The walls of the main building and garage became a cover he had then longed desperately for, as if he and the girl were small creatures, like mice, electric with panic, scampering beneath something vast enough to alter the air pressure, the very density of the atmosphere. And as this sensation spread out above them, it also suggested that they were cast under a dreadful scrutiny.

A swoop of vertigo had discouraged him from looking up. He'd been convinced they could fall upwards, together, into the black sky, and just keep on going, gathering speed, until they were unable to breathe . . . until they came apart from each other and from themselves. He'd thought himself dreaming while awake.

Mummy. My mummy.

I can't tell you now . . . I'll explain . . . do you remember your old house, before you were here? The house on the hill.

Mummy. Her crying, her crying and then him crying because she did not know him.

You lived with your mummy and daddy in another house, a long time ago, by the sea. There was a garden. A big garden . . . There was Nan and Poppo. Cloth Cat . . . Cloth Cat . . . Oh God, Cloth Cat. Your name is Penny. Not Yasmin. Your name is Penny.

When the girl saw the car, she had tried to sit down on the lawn. As her whole body convulsed with misery and fear she had looked back at the house. Her father had dropped to his knees beside her. Released one of the bags of money, a lifetime's riches that would remain on the grass. He could not carry both bags one step further, and knew he would need to carry the girl and the other bag of money the entire distance to where Penny's real mother lay unconscious inside a car. When he thought he heard what might have been a copter in the distance, he surged up and onto his feet and swung the girl into the air, holding her under the arms. It was the first time he had embraced her for two years, this clutch, this clasping to his chest that was, that day, crisscrossed with the straps attached to a bag full of guns and explosives.

And he'd run to the black car, ungainly, his sweat-lathered face whipping from side to side, his eyes not seeming to register anything, a crying child slung over his shoulder.

And into the place where fugitives have always sought refuge they vanished, driving deep into the trees: a man, an unconscious woman, and a frightened child.

FORTY-ONE

As he drove, and as his leaden, bruised body began to warm inside the car, the father asked Penny repeatedly about what she remembered, asked her about the first thing she could remember, and he told her over and over again that she was taken from him and her real mother. He told her that her real mother was asleep and lying on the seat next to her. But Penny didn't understand, or was too frightened to even acknowledge his questions.

He'd abandoned the car he'd driven out of the grounds, and carried Penny and Miranda to the stolen vehicle that Gene Hackman had procured for him in Devon. There was enough of a charge in the vehicle to get them to Wales, and he knew it must surely be safe from the scrutiny of King Death.

Miranda began to rouse near Salisbury, her jaw slack; her eyelids remained heavy and what could be seen of her eyes was red. She didn't know where she was for several seconds and panicked. When she sat up, she began to be sick, so the father pulled over and helped her out of the car, and into a cold wind with spiny teeth that carried a light, fast-moving rain.

The sky was a flat, cloudless grey, like a low ceiling that had trapped a violent and relentless maelstrom of air between the ground and the heavens. At the side of the road, the pines lurched and screamed, funnelling the tail of the storm down and across the tarmac. Through the noise, he tried to speak but the wind chill made him stutter. He had to hold Miranda upright while she was ill. There was no way of knowing what they had given her, in order to transport her from one place to another, but the powerful tranquillizer had not worn its way out of her legs. Once she knew who he was, she said in a thirst-croaked voice that she couldn't feel her feet, or her hands. Disoriented, confused, her judgement so impaired, she twice asked him, 'Where's Mummy?'

Eventually the father managed to make his wife look at him, and to stop talking. He gave her water, and she drained an entire bottle in one draught. Then he made her swallow most of an energy drink. Beside the car, leaning against him in the layby, Miranda began to shake violently with the cold and he realized just how thin her clothes were, and how inactive she had been, and probably for more than twelve hours.

As she revived, she began to remember the details of her abduction and clawed at him. The father held her tightly and told her repeatedly, 'They are gone. The men are gone. They're not here. You're safe. Safe now.' He kept saying this, though didn't believe it. He feared the arrival of the police, or far worse that may also be nearby, at any time. Vehicles passed, but the drivers merely glanced at them and continued. The drivers seemed especially committed; he suspected they knew things that he did not.

'I'm so cold,' Miranda said, and pushed towards the

car. He still hadn't told her about Penny. The situation was becoming absurd.

'She's here . . . here. I found her. I have her. That's why they took you, because I was so close to her. I have Penny.'

'Who?' his wife asked, and blinked and pulled at her face with numb fingers as if to revive the muscles around her jaw.

'Penny. I found her. She's in the car.'

His wife squinted at him, confused; he could see bewilderment filling her murky eyes. Then she must have imagined that she was dreaming, or that he was mad, because she said, 'No. Stop now.' And as he strained to hold her long body upright, she looked past him and must have seen the small figure on the rear seat of the car.

Miranda tried to scream, but the noise was so weak and frail that it sounded like the wail of a woman who had just lost her only child, rather than one who had just seen her own child, and one given up for dead, for two years. There must, the father thought, be an equivalency to those kinds of shock.

'Miranda! Listen, Miranda! Miranda . . . It is her. Penny! She's alive. She's well. But we can't stand here any longer. You're frozen. And I need you to come back to me, to . . . to be with her, while I get us away from here. It's not safe. We're too close to the place I took her from. Do you understand? We have to move now.'

'Penny?' she whispered.

'Yes, but she doesn't know me. Nor will she recognize you. It's going to take time.'

'Where? Can't be . . . It's not true. Where was she?'

'Later. There isn't time now. We have to move, and I

need you to be with her. Please. Be her mother again. Please.'

And then Miranda was crying and so was the father.

Just past Salisbury, Penny became hysterical. The father pulled over again and had to restrain her flailing arms. But the girl didn't strike out for long, and went limp moments after he embraced her. Miranda had been talking to Penny in a voice so low and quiet that he couldn't pick up what she was saying. In between moments of shock that made her weep, Miranda had done her best to revive herself, though her hands were still leaden and unresponsive, and her speech was slow and slurred.

Intermittently, Penny cried softly, until they reached Bath, where she had finally allowed Miranda to, at least, hold her. Not until they were skirting Bristol did she speak and only then to ask for 'Mummy' and 'Richard' through her tears.

Who? Miranda mouthed at him as he leaned over to the back seat, but the father shook his head to deflect the inquiry, saying nothing more than, 'The people who had her.'

Miranda gave Penny drinks and two of the energy bars she found in the father's rucksack, sucking in her breath when she saw the handguns, and the money in the bag that he had taken from Oleg's vestry and Richard's safe.

'I'll tell you later. Now is not the time.'

Penny always said, 'Thank you,' when she was given things, and her instinctive good manners, twinned with the depth of her fear and shock at being in the car with two unfamiliar adults, left the father's eyes moist for hours. Her innocence, compared to what he had done that very morning, made him feel desolate.

The wet, grey stirrings of the crops and copses and hedgerows flashed past the car, mile after mile. Occasionally and fleetingly, so as not to be distracted from his traumatized daughter, he scanned a few channels for weather and traffic reports and learned the hurricane had mostly passed. There was flooding behind him, and across the north-east, but little along his prospective route into North Wales. But information about nearly everything else was scant because of the escalation around Kashmir.

The father kept the service mute, but just from the visuals and subtitles he could see the evidence of mass strikes from the air, reaching beyond Kashmir, far inside both India and Pakistan.

The Punjab was on fire and the two countries were deep into drone war. They'd smashed as many of the other's satellites out of orbit as they could manage. Walls of long-range artillery produced monumental cement and dust clouds in all of the major cities close to the borders. Events seemed to have escalated during the early hours of that morning as the father had fought his own desperate battle. India was continuing to exercise the long-threatened Water Option policy, and had increased the diversion of the head waters of the rivers the two countries shared.

Almost as a footnote, there was an increase in the amount of information about virus outbreaks in British hospitals. Hundreds more staff and patients were being reported dead in several parts of the country. CDC precautions were now being announced publically and regularly in the affected areas. People in several counties were being asked, amongst other things, to isolate those they suspected of infection. Outbreaks seemed far worse in Central Europe and the eastern seaboard of the United States. The ministry for health in the United Kingdom believed the virus was being passed by touch, sneeze, and coughs. The father believed he knew better. As soon as they arrived at their destination, he would need to inoculate Miranda.

Abandoning the news, he found children's channels and left one on for hours on all of the vehicle's screens. His daughter stared at the shows as if the screens were blank. When they reached Gloucester she started to shake.

Approaching Worcester, the roads became clearer, even unnaturally so. The rain remained incessant.

The roadside services in Shropshire, where he'd stopped to use the toilet, and hoped to buy supplies from, were closed though it wasn't yet five p.m. A twenty-four-hour service was advertised from the motorway. Few cars were parked at the facility. Most of the freight was immobile, lights off. The motorway had been near-deserted for the previous forty miles too. What traffic he had seen was mostly emergency vehicles. Private cars had been travelling far too fast in the wet conditions, their automatic functions overridden by manual operation to achieve greater, unsafe speeds in terrible driving conditions. For his family's own safety, the father had kept the vehicle locked into automatic and let the computer transport them, albeit far more slowly than he would have liked.

Food he bought from a vending machine he left with his wife on the rear seats. His daughter had fallen into an exhausted sleep by then, her nose and eyes red from crying, her head at rest upon Miranda's lap. Even that small contact and suggestion of trust and familiarity filled him with a hope that made him dizzy. And watching her sleep engulfed him with memories of doing so when she was a baby.

Before the final leg of the journey, he leaned his weight against the car. He gripped his scalp as if to contain the riot of his memories, and to calm his shock over the girl who was his again, at least in body, as was her mother, the real one. Attempting to process all he had done within the past few days, and all he had seen and experienced, was futile.

He climbed back inside the vehicle and they set off again.

As they drove, he began to tell Miranda in hurried whispers about how he had found Penny. She never interrupted, but stared at him in horror.

At dusk, he suspected night was falling earlier and faster than usual. He left two new messages for the owners of a cottage in Snowdonia for which they were headed, giving them his expected time of arrival. Promising to pay in cash, he had booked the place in the car that morning, just after they had cleared the trees of the New Forest. Four cottages were still rented out in an old slate quarry as holiday lets. Two were available. As a family they had once stayed there when Penny was eighteen months old. It had been their last family holiday, and was the remotest location the father knew of that he knew how to get to. Besides three new nuclear power facilities and some chemical plants, the mountainous region had not become overcrowded, nor entirely divided by gated communities, though there were more of those now than ever before.

He cancelled the transmission of the message that he had made in the car before his assault on Karen Perucchi's compound, and also checked the news regularly in the front screen so no one in the rear could see it, still fearing reports of a home invasion with multiple casualties in the New Forest, and the sight of his face on national news services. He kept the sound on mute and read the subtitles. If he was apprehended, and that was a very real possibility that he refused to imagine in detail, suppressing the idea with a struggle, he would need time to form a cogent explanation, and to think of a way of ensuring his safety in custody. But instead of news of a national manhunt for him, he instead saw and read that there had been a massive exchange of nuclear weapons on the Indian sub-continent, within the last three hours, as children's cartoons had flashed and jumped inside their car.

They arrived at the old slate works' cottages in Graig Wen after nine. Mighty Cadair Idris and the surrounding mountains had been swallowed by low cloud and nightfall. Few lights shone in the valleys. Paranoia that the region had suffered a power failure had chased his thoughts right through Wales. He feared that the madness and destruction in Asia had already reached here too, and thrown the mountains and sea into a blight of darkness and silence.

As soon as he alighted from the car, the sharp, thin, cold air, the starless sky, seemed to get inside his mind and his chest, like an absence of gravity that briefly suggested again that he could be swept from his feet to plummet upwards. Here, they were three grains of sand lost in a lake of ink.

He had to carry his daughter out of the car and up to the door of the cottage he had secured for one month, while his wife hobbled behind him, the numbness of her feet and hands persisting, but at least fading. The key to the cottage was in the place the brief, terse message from the owners had notified him of. Perhaps they thought it inappropriate for someone to go on holiday the same day in which tens of millions must have been burned alive on another part of the planet.

Inside, the father had hurriedly closed all of the blinds and then returned to the car to collect what little luggage they had, the money and his weapons. Miranda settled Penny on the sofa, and wrapped her in three blankets she ferreted out of the airing cupboard. The father double-locked the doors.

As he returned from checking the rooms upstairs, his daughter had woken up, and began to meekly unwrap and nibble at the food he had left on the coffee table. Miranda couldn't get the packets open, but hunger had driven Penny to take what had been offered. She soon lay down again, under the blankets, and Miranda tucked them beneath her thin body.

In all the time he had been searching for her, he had never once looked into how to tend a traumatized child, and knew nothing about when or how details and information from a stolen past should be introduced to a young mind. Had he ever truly believed that he would find her alive?

He placed a screen on the small table before the sofa.

Without speaking, Miranda accessed the files and played a collection of family pictures on rotation. Pictures of Penny as a baby, a toddler, of them together as a family and at the very same cottage they were slumped inside now. He inserted three of his favourite home movies into the montage, including the last film recorded in Berry Pomeroy Castle, five days before she was abducted. Lying absolutely still, Penny watched the flickering screen with an expressionless face. Miranda whispered a narration to accompany the pictures, while stroking her daughter's hair. Before the father withdrew from the room, he placed Cloth Cat beside the screen.

The father went into the kitchen area. Opened a bottle of rum and supped from the neck. Resting his back against a wall, he thought his muscles could have been dishcloths wrung out around his bones. One hand and his shoulder throbbed with aches. About his ankles, the broken skin silently screamed beneath circles of dried blood.

You are here, with her.

For how long?

He checked the news broadcasts with the sound muted. It was all India and Pakistan.

'Jesus Christ. Oh, Jesus Christ,' he said to himself, as he looked at the earliest pictures of the devastation. He was thankful that his family was in the other room.

FORTY-TWO

He lay on the bed beside his wife, but on top of the bedclothes, with their daughter between them. The lights in the room were switched off, but he'd left the hall one on and the bedroom door open as he and Miranda had always done when Penny was small. Downstairs, their daughter had eventually fallen into a deep and silent sleep on the sofa, but still hadn't said much. He and Miranda had carried her upstairs to the largest room.

Inside the little bag that Penny had carried from the house on her back, there were only two changes of clothes. The only toys were the few items he had brought down from his last trip to Birmingham, and she'd not seen those since she was four.

The past for all of them was severed, at least physically. He doubted they could ever go back to Birmingham, or even the south-west. Like for the rest of the planet, the north now called even more loudly. His wife's parents had driven to Scotland an hour before Miranda was abducted; she had told him in the car. They would break the news to them about Penny the following morning. But such things, like their next move, where they could go, who they could tell about Penny, and when, he would have to think about at another time, on another day. For now, they just had to exist together, in the same space, and the girl had to *know* them again. Until that happened, they weren't moving from the cottage. King Death's most loyal supporters would not know where they were.

In the half-dark, the father stared at the side of Penny's head for hours. Most of her face was concealed by her raven hair. He listened to her sleep. Not long after she fell asleep, Miranda had drifted away too, squashed, as if for dear life, against her recovered daughter.

The night before I lost you, I did what I always did, I stood outside the door of your little room and I listened to you sleeping. Peering into darkness, I would hear you turn under your bedclothes, I would hear the odd puff of air, silence, a sigh, a word, and then the deep, steady breaths. From the day you came into my world, I did this every night I was home. I never wanted to miss a day of you.

Eventually the father extended one arm out and over the waists of his daughter and his wife, and carefully placed his chest against Penny's back. The smell of her hair engulfed him and their three hearts beat together. The blood of the parents warmed the little one in the middle.

He made a vow. Unto death he'd never let them go, and if death were to divide him from them, he'd go first. But before he left, he would find a place for them to be safe, and he would fill their hearts with so much love, it would glow within them long after the last reactor died.

Tears made his cheeks slippery. Into the hair that tickled his nose he whispered, 'Daddy loves you.'

A profound silence seemed to fill and then become a pressure in the darkness. He was afraid to fall asleep in case he woke up and found himself alone again. But gradually, the exhaustion he had held back for those days that had seemed like years thickened within his aching body and swaddled his conscious mind, leading his thoughts deeper and into strange places.

ACKNOWLEDGEMENTS

For informing and inspiring the state of the world in this story, as well as many of my own suspicions about what awaits us in this interconnected world's future, I owe much to the ideas and books of James Lovelock (*The Revenge of Gaia* and *The Vanishing Face of Gaia*), Mark Lynam's *Six Degrees*, Jared Diamond's *Collapse*, Gwynn Dyer's *Climate Wars*, David Quammen's *Spillover*, *The Spirit Level* by Richard Wilkinson and Kate Pickett and *McMafia* by Misha Glenny. Writing this story made me imagine other things, and it was near-unbearable to do so, like the worst kind of treatment of children, and I don't think I could have imagined that side of the father's story as vividly without recourse to the work of Harry Keeble, Kris Hollington and Kate McCann. *Master of Death* by Michael Camille provided Oleg Chorny's verses on pages 271 and 312 and augmented his 'afterdeath' philosophy, and *The Black Death* by Philip Ziegler completed about fifteen months of reading that became as horrifying, grim, ghastly and terrifying as our own (near) future as a species might be.

Thanks to my readers, Anne and Clive Nevill and Hugh Simmons. For bringing my horrors into existence, thanks again to my literary agent, John Jarrold, Julie and team at

Gotham, Julie Crisp and colleagues at Pan Macmillan, Susan Opie for her eagle-eyed copy-edit, Michael, Loren, and the crew at St Martins, and Stefan at Bragelonne.

Heartfelt appreciation goes out once again to (many of) the reviewers who've taken time to read my books and write about them. Special thanks to Jim McCleod of Gingernuts of Horror, Anthony Watson, Delia of Postcards from Asia, Alex Cluness, The Reading Passport, Jo Playford, Alan Kelly, Wayne Simmons, James Everington, Pam Norfolk, Theresa Derwin, Marie O'Regan, Gemma Files, Mathew Fryer, *SFX*, *Sci Fi Now*, The British Fantasy Society, Tim Lebbon, Mark Morris, Paul and Tracey Melloy, Hugh and Del Simmons, Gary McMahon, Gary Fry, Lisa Tuttle, Mathew Riley, David Willbanks, Simon Strantzas, Ramsey Campbell, Justin Steele of Arkham Asylum, Sean Kitching and the Quietus, Jeff Vandemeer, Johnny Mains, Stephen Volk, Gary Power, Jonathan Wood, John Roome, Zahar Znaev, Diala Atat, Rosil Barrantes, Ruba Naseraldeen, Emma Beckett, Lucy Twitty Halls, Jonathan Maberry, Scott Smith, Michael Marshall, Michael Koryta, and the many appreciative friends that I'm lucky to have in social media. Special thanks goes out to those booksellers who've championed my novels, particularly Forbidden Planet in Belfast, Patty Dohle of Waterstones, Witney, and Ellie Wixon of Blackwells, Edinburgh.

As ever, my final thanks go to my readers: without you, my books would be another endangered species.